The Hor

Acclaim for Susan Lewis:

'Spellbinding! . . . you just keep turning the pages, with the atmosphere growing more and more intense as the story leads to its dramatic climax'
Daily Mail

'Erotic and exciting' *Sunday Times*

'Mystery and romance *par excellence' Sun*

'Susan Lewis strikes gold again . . . gripping'
Options

'Will keep you guessing till the last page' *19*

'It's a sizzler. The tale of conspiracy and steamy passion will keep you intrigued until the final page'
Bella

'A tense heartbreak of a read' *Good Book Guide*

THE HORNBEAM TREE

Susan Lewis

arrow books

Published by Arrow Books in 2005

1 3 5 7 9 10 8 6 4 2

Copyright © Susan Lewis 2004

Susan Lewis has asserted her right under the Copyright, Designs and
Patents Act, 1988 to be identified as the author of this work

First published in the United Kingdom in 2004 by William Heinemann

Arrow Books
Random House Group Limited
20 Vauxhall Bridge Road, London, SW1V 2SA

Random House Australia (Pty) Limited
20 Alfred Street, Milsons Point, Sydney, New South Wales 2061, Australia

Random House New Zealand Limited
18 Poland Road, Glenfield
Auckland 10, New Zealand

Random House (Pty) Limited
Endulini, 5a Jubilee Road, Parktown, 2193, South Africa

Random House Group Limited Reg. No. 954009

www.randomhouse.co.uk

A CIP catalogue record for this book is available from the British Library

Papers used by Random House are natural, recyclable products
made from wood grown in sustainable forests. The manufacturing
processes conform to the environmental regulations
of the country of origin.

ISBN 0 09 945327 4

Typeset by SX Composing DTP, Rayleigh, Essex
Printed and bound in Great Britain by
Bookmarque Ltd, Croydon, Surrey

For my cousin, Karen,
with love and thanks

Acknowledgements

A very big thank you to District Nurse Sarah Moore for taking the time to guide me through Katie's illness and for answering my endless questions. I'd also like to thank Chris Floyd and Michael Evans for their help with the political story. Another big thank you to Hilary Andrews for the 'tour' of Washington. And to Mort Rosenblum for additional help with Washington. Much love and thanks to my dear friend Fanny Blackburne for showing me Pietrasanta. And more thanks to Ellie Gleave for letting me use her lovely home in Burgundy as a 'hideout'.

An especially big thank you and lots of love to my beautiful goddaughter, Alexandra Hastie, for all her help with Molly. I couldn't have done it without you, Alex.

Chapter 1

Strangely, the sky hadn't fallen. Nor had the ground split apart. Houses were still standing, trees remained rooted, people were walking on their feet. No, nothing had changed from the way it had been an hour ago, before she'd entered the building, yet now it all felt so different that she could be stepping back into another world entirely.

The automatic doors swish-closed behind her. She waited for a car to pass, then crossed towards a small patch of green. She could see Judy waiting and wanted to run towards her, but she carried on walking, zigzagging through the car park until she was close enough to make out the concern on her friend's plump, normally cheery face.

'Do you know what today is?' Katie demanded, looking at her over the roof of the car.

Judy eyed her, not sure how to respond.

'It's Day One of the rest of my life,' Katie informed her.

Judy looked surprised, then laughed as Katie

gazed around, seeming to absorb a whole new world.

'Did you already know?' she asked, her eyes coming back to Judy.

Judy nodded.

Katie felt as though she was seeing her friend differently to the way she had a minute ago, then, shrugging it off, she smiled and got into the passenger seat.

'Would you have preferred me to tell you?' Judy asked, sliding in next to her.

'Would you have wanted to?' Katie countered, not without irony.

'No.'

Katie laughed at the frankness that was her own stock-in-trade.

'So what would you like to do now?' Judy asked, turning on the engine. 'On Day One of the rest of your life.'

Katie's gaze was fixed ahead. Her face was gaunt, seeming to cling to the bones, the shadows beneath her hazel eyes were grey and blue, the texture of her skin was like ash, powdery and pale. There wasn't much sign now of the full rosy cheeks or wickedly humorous eyes that for several years had graced the small photo over her newspaper column. Nor was she the heavy-set, energetic woman who'd worked so hard to win the villagers over when she'd first moved down from London. She'd changed a lot in the past year, and now she was going to change again.

'What about a coffee while we decide?' Judy offered. 'We can go somewhere here, in Bath . . .'

'You know, I think I'd just like to go home,' Katie responded.

Disappointed, though not altogether surprised, Judy slipped the car into gear and headed for the exit.

'Blast,' Katie said, as they turned left out of the car park towards Penn Hill. 'I keep thinking of things I should have asked.'

'There'll be plenty of time,' Judy assured her. 'Did you speak to Simon himself?'

Katie nodded. 'Not the kind of task he could delegate,' she responded, 'though I'm sure he'd have preferred to. You know, a funny thing happened,' she went on, feeling faintly light-headed as the memory popped up, 'when he told me, you know . . . When he said it was all over I suddenly fancied him in a way I never have before. It didn't last. It was gone in a moment, but it was pretty intense while it was there. To tell you the truth, I wouldn't have minded running with it a while, because the next thing I knew I was right back in reality, and that's no place to be at a time like this.' She sighed, then chuckled and let her gaze slide over a rank of shops as they passed by. 'He's a nice man. I'm going to miss him,' she said.

Judy looked at her, and because everything felt so dislocated and absurd, from the weather to the words, they started to laugh.

'I didn't think I'd ever say that,' Katie remarked, as they headed up over Lansdown Lane into the countryside. 'It's true though, I will.' Before Judy could comment she ran on with her next peculiar thought. 'I could become one of those irritatingly inspirational women who write best-selling books about their miraculous recoveries,' she declared. 'You know. The ones who manage to digest enough spiritual guff to vaporize tumours the size of footballs, or start up empires after their husbands have royally dumped them. What do you think?'

'If anyone can do it, you can.'

'They're annoying though, aren't they, those women?'

Judy laughed. 'Some, yes,' she agreed. 'But Heather isn't.'

'No, Heather's an angel who managed to get it together without writing a book and crowing from the hilltops,' Katie conceded, picturing her radiantly blonde spiritual counsellor in a fetching celestial get-up. She'd never have imagined finding anyone like Heather buried alive in a concrete jungle just outside Chippenham. What a find. These last months would have been a total nightmare without her, even with her they'd been hell.

Her attention moved out over the sparkling green valley where sheep grazed and horses stood like paintings in the afternoon sun. Suddenly, a huge wave of panic rolled in from nowhere. *I don't want this to be happening. It has to stop. Now! Please make it stop!* She took a breath, and, like Canute, summoned her will to send the tide back to where it had come from. She wouldn't let it engulf her now. There was too much to do, to think about and put right. Her thoughts suddenly began hovering around the real danger area, Molly, but she quickly marshalled them back to the innocuous patchwork of passing fields and woodlands, and wondered how the tree she sponsored was faring. It was around here somewhere, she just couldn't quite remember where.

'Yes, we can do that,' Judy told her.

Katie frowned. Had she said something? Asked a question without even hearing it? Then quite suddenly she recognized the spot. 'Can we stop?' she asked. 'Over there. I think that's the right place.'

Surprised, Judy glanced at her, but flicking on the indicator she pulled into the lay-by and brought the car to a halt.

Katie gazed along the narrow track that led into the woodland. With all the misty bands of sunlight and glossy leaves it seemed as enticing as a fairy tale, and pushing open the door she stepped out on to the dusty patch of earth. The sun slipped behind a cloud and she frowned. A moment later it was back, like a child playing peek-a-boo and she walked into the copse, breathing in the woody scent of the air, absorbing the many shades of green, enjoying the playful sparkles of light that shone down through the leaves. She'd never been informed of which actual tree she sponsored, only of the woodland it was in, so on reaching a small clearing she looked around and decided to take her pick. It wasn't long before she settled on the towering old beech that was set slightly back from the glade, because, to her mind at least, there seemed something permanent and irresistible about it. She moved towards it, aware of the ground underfoot feeling soft and sponge-like, and the birdsong sounding more melodious and inviting.

Not until she reached the tree did she realize

from the smooth grey bark and sharply serrated leaves that it wasn't a beech at all – it was a hornbeam. She blinked in surprise. Such serendipity. Such a dizzying coincidence, for hornbeam was used to help ease the feelings of exhaustion at the mere thought of facing an ordeal. It was exactly how she was feeling now, exhausted by the thought of what lay ahead. She gazed up at the tree's magnificent canopy of tooth-edged leaves, so green and soft, and delicately pointed at the tips; the three-lobed cups of its fruit sprouting in thick clu___ of paler green, the unwieldy tangle of branches that for some reason made her think of a mother's arms.

What had made her come here today? What unknown hand had guided her? She rested the palm of one hand on the trunk, then her cheek. The bark was warm and fluting with age. It smelt of earth and damp and was prettily patched by moss. It would live for another hundred years or more, this tree of hers, never moving from this spot, watching the seasons come and go, releasing its leaves and fruit, and producing new in spring. She put her arms around it, and after a while was certain she could feel the gentle force of its energy flowing into her.

She'd never done anything like this before. Tree-hugging. Usually she left it to the New Agers who were into this sort of thing, while she scoffed from the sidelines, but her eyes and mind had been opened to many things this past year, and now here was another revelation. This sense of permanence and safety, of being in the right place at the right time, and of being so much smaller than nature yet as intrinsically a part of it as this tree, was what she needed to feel here, at this hour, on this day.

Judy was waiting beside the car when she returned, the expression on her round face with its large, velvety brown eyes and quirky mouth showing affection and understanding, even though she couldn't know about the tree or the strangeness of that brief encounter. How could she, when Katie barely understood it herself? But it mattered, Katie was certain of that, fruitcakish as it was. She was glad they'd stopped. She might even come again.

As they drove on towards home she was grateful for Judy's silence, because she felt the need to be quiet now. Shock worked its way through the senses in a randomly confusing fashion, she was finding, alighting on one, then another, then several together. It was bizarre, because a part of her had been expecting this. Well, dreading it, actually, but it had been there for a while, stalking her personal horizon like a shy lover, or, more accurately, a countdown clock. Now suddenly it was galloping towards her like a terrifying knight in dull, black armour, intent on carrying her off to a place she didn't want to go. She turned her head, as though to avoid the collision.

It was gone. Everything was normal. She was in the car with Judy, signalling to turn right on to the road that would take them home. For a fleeting moment she seemed to boil with rage, then a sick, pleading desperation flooded her heart. She managed to suppress both. She had now to work out how she was going to handle it all. With dignity, was the first thought that came to mind, and grace and calm. No hysterics, no pleading or ranting, or bitterness or self-pity. No clinging to the impossible, or trying to make deals with God. Just acceptance and strength, and endless understanding and support for Molly. *Oh dear God, Molly.*

Focusing again on her surroundings, she realized they were on the main Bristol to Chippenham road, speeding past Marshfield, a centuries-old village that was fast turning into an urban sprawl, then The Shoe that was cleared in a blink, then Ford that had a good restaurant in its pub. Not long now and they'd be home. Fortunately Membury Hempton, where both she and Judy lived, wasn't one of West Wiltshire's outstanding villages, so they weren't too bothered by tourists, even though most of the cottages, and some of the larger houses, dated from the seventeenth and eighteenth centuries, and the church went back to ancient times. It just didn't have the olde worlde charm of its neighbours such as Castle Combe, Biddestone and Lacock.

Now they were carving it up down the high street, two forty-something bombshells in a Fiat Panda, past the nursery school on the right, and the doctor's surgery and post office-cum-village store on the left. A few of their neighbours were gathered around the small war memorial on the grassy central island, gossiping and enjoying the fine weather. Recognizing Judy's car they waved and smiled. It had been a struggle for Katie, a Londoner born and bred, to make them all accept her when she'd arrived last year, but things were finally starting to improve now, largely thanks to Judy, who'd encouraged her to involve herself in the community. She had much to be thankful to Judy for, and wasn't in any doubt that it was going to stack a lot higher in the coming days and weeks. Where would she and Molly be without Judy, the district nurse, who'd fast turned into the best friend they'd ever had? She couldn't even begin to think, so stopped trying.

'Would you like me to come in?' Judy offered, as they passed the pub and turned into Sheep Lane. Katie's cottage was at the end, opposite the secluded, half-moon duck pond that was home to a noisy assortment of coot, mallards and moorhens.

'It's OK,' Katie answered. 'I'm sure you've got a lot to be going on with.'

'My time is yours today. Maybe I can answer some of your questions.'

Katie smiled. 'Actually, if you don't mind . . .'

'You'd like to be alone,' Judy finished in a Garbo voice. 'That's fine, just promise me you'll call if you need anything. You know where I am.'

'Of course,' Katie responded.

After they pulled up next to the white picket fence that hemmed in her small garden, Katie sat gazing at the quaint, grey stone cottage that had been home to her and Molly since they'd been forced to downsize, and felt as though she was seeing a photograph, or a painting, something that wasn't quite real. Roses bloomed either side of the front door they rarely used, a Virginia creeper framed the sitting-room and kitchen windows and the orange, weather-roughened roof tiles glinted like amber in the sun. The only other cottages down this lane were Mr and Mrs Preddy's, attached to the back of Katie's, and Dick Bradley's, which was the other side of the pond, next to the cowfield and overhung by the gnarled limbs of a very old sycamore.

'What are you going to do now?' Judy asked.

'Write a letter, I suppose,' Katie answered. 'I'd been hoping I wouldn't have to, but I don't have a choice now, so I might as well get it over with.'

'It'll work out,' Judy told her gently. 'You'll get the answer you want.'

Katie nodded, and after climbing out of the car she stood just inside the gate watching and waving as Judy reversed round the duck pond and drove back up the lane. Once the sound of the engine died away the place seemed eerily quiet, with just the odd squawk from a duck, a smattering of birdsong and the lumber of a tractor engine somewhere far away. The sun felt very intense. She thought the apples on the tree next to the shed seemed redder than they had this morning, while the potted plants around the well were starting to wilt. She walked along the front of the cottage and around the side to where the hose was curled up on the wall next to the back door. Trotty, their fluffy little mixed-breed, had obviously heard her, because she was scratching the door to get out.

'Hello, you daft old thing,' Katie smiled, scooping her up for a spot of fussing. 'Did you miss me? Eh? Is that what all this is about?'

Trotty's answer was to lick with more feeling, before scurrying off to find her ball.

Katie watered the flowers, threw the ball and felt the sun beating down on her head. How long before Molly was due to come home? Another hour? Maybe two or three if she decided to go to her friend's. Molly didn't always communicate her

10

plans these days, she was either too busy to remember, or too angry to share. It wasn't always like that though, because there were still plenty of days when Katie was the best mum in all the world, as opposed to she-who-must-be-disobeyed-and-never-seen-out-with.

The kitchen was cool and shady, thanks to the thick stone walls. It was surprisingly large for a small cottage, with two overhead beams, a big china sink, terracotta floor and a staircase in one corner that led up to the three bedrooms above. The pantry was beneath the stairs, the door to the sitting room was next to it, and a deep sill window looked out over the pond, lane and cowfield. At the centre was a table with four chairs, which was where, once she'd made a cup of tea, she was going to sit down to write to Michelle.

As she put the kettle on she wondered what she was going to say. It was a letter she'd tried not to think about over the past few months, but it was here now, needing to be written. Considering the rift that had grown up between them, the petty jealousies, which in truth were mainly hers, and the pride that made it hard for her to ask for anything, particularly from her beautiful and gifted younger sister, nothing about this letter would be easy.

'Dear Michelle, God and I are having a difference of opinion over my lifespan and currently he's winning, so please can you come back to England to take care of Molly?'

She guessed she'd have to be a little more tactful, and detailed, than that. After all, it could prove quite a blow to Michelle to learn that her only sibling wasn't going to be around for much longer.

She liked to think Michelle would care, though she wouldn't blame her if she didn't. She'd explain that the hysterectomy, chemotherapy and radiotherapy hadn't zapped all those dreaded diseased cells sufficiently to prevent more popping up in the liver, which had also had a good blast, but somehow the message wasn't getting through. They were marvellously comfortable where they were, thank you very much, and no way was anyone or anything going to budge them. Which all added up to Dr Simon being very, very sorry but there was no more they could do.

'Dear Michelle, I'm sorry I haven't been in touch for a while, but I hope you're well. Your last letter was from Pakistan, so I'm presuming that's where you still are, as you normally let us know when you move on. I hope your work in the Afghan refugee camps isn't too harrowing, though I'm sure it must be. You're very brave, the way you take on other people's troubles and try to help them, so I wonder if you could take mine on now. I wish I could say it will only be until I detach from this mortal coil, which shouldn't be too long, though they won't give me an exact time, but I'm afraid Molly is going to be in need of someone to take care of her after, and as you're her only relative . . .'

She wouldn't write that either, but she imagined it would be something along those lines, polite, to the point, and careful not to revisit any past resentments or fall into any kind of emotional blackmail. She wondered where Michelle was right now, this minute, and what she was doing. She'd have no idea that her world was about to be rocked too, and from a quarter she probably least expected. Was she going to mind? That was a patently stupid question, because of course she'd mind. Michelle was extremely dedicated to her way of life.

There was a time, she was thinking, when Michelle would have done almost anything for them to be as close as when they were growing up, but though Katie had loved Michelle, as they'd become adults and begun finding their own ways in the world, Katie, to her shame, had rarely dealt well with how charmed Michelle's life had seemed in comparison to hers. Not that she, Katie, hadn't done well, because she had, she'd just never quite been able to overcome a feeling of resentment towards Michelle that was, in truth, much more rooted in admiration than in envy. She'd never let Michelle know that, though – she didn't even admit it to herself if she could help it. Better not to think about Michelle, and just get on with her own life.

She was still sitting at the table, tea gone cold and surrounded by pages of scrunched-up paper, when she heard Molly's voice outside, calling to Trotty. Quickly she scooped everything into a drawer and went to busy herself with the few dishes in the sink. Everything must seem normal. Life was tootling along happily, nothing was about to change – except the major treatments had stopped, making a difference to where Molly went after school, because now she could come home instead of going to Judy's or wherever else she'd been taking herself off to lately.

'I've got about a hundred hours of bloody homework,' Molly grumbled as she bumped in through the door with Trotty in one arm and her

13

school bag over the other. 'And if you start getting on at me about anything now I'm going to go ballistic, because I've had like a really bad day and I hate that bloody school. It stinks. Everyone in it's a moron and no way am I staying on to do sixth form there. What have we got to eat?'

'Yes, I'm fine thank you, darling,' Katie replied cheerily. 'How nice of you to ask. Would you like a sandwich? I can stuff it with your attitude and see how *you'd* like to swallow it.' It wasn't what she wanted to say, but it was how they spoke to each other these days, and right now she wanted everything to stay the same.

Molly's green eyes flashed with hostility. 'You are just like, sooo not funny,' she told her.

Katie grinned. She knew there was a chance Molly might too, because her mood could swing from stroppy to sunny in the blink of an eye. Alas, it seemed today the pendulum was stuck, because she fired off one of her filthier looks, put down Trotty and tugged open the fridge door.

Katie watched her, feeling too many emotions to deal with at once, so she opted for love, then immediately dropped it, because it came all cluttered up with a need to embrace and gush. Molly would think she'd lost the plot completely if she suddenly clasped her to her bosom now and began spouting Mummy-talk as though Molly were four rather than fourteen. So she settled for a more normal maternal scrutiny of Molly's appearance, which was far too grown-up for Katie's liking, with all her make-up and unfastened buttons. It would be hard to reveal much more of the ample young breasts that were being hoisted

14

together by a couple of sturdy underwires without popping them out altogether, she reflected. The skirt was shockingly short too, and Katie would lay money she only had a thong underneath. Katie had to admit, though, had she ever been blessed with buttocks and legs like Molly's her mother would never have been able to get her hemlines down either. They were Michelle's buttocks and legs. She had Michelle's eyes too, moss green, slanted at the corners and utterly bewitching. Katie hoped Molly was nowhere near realizing yet how devastating they were. The rest of her was much more like Katie, or how Katie used to be, a full, peachy mouth, creamy skin with permanently reddened cheeks, delicately carved jawline and spiky raven hair. Actually, the hair colour was her father's, but that was about all she'd inherited from him, though she'd probably be able to tot up a few hefty debts and several embarrassments when he finally decided to depart this particular dimension.

'I thought you weren't allowed to wear eyeliner at school,' she said.

'That was my last school,' Molly reminded her. 'At this one you can wear what you like. Did you get the new *Heat* magazine?'

'No, I don't believe I did.'

Molly rolled her eyes and crunched noisily into an apple. 'I asked you to,' she said. 'Oh my God, I've got to do this essay on communism,' she suddenly gasped. 'You've got to help me. It's like, really boring, and so not anything to do with real life . . . Mum, are you listening?'

Katie blinked in surprise. 'Do I look as though I'm not?' she asked, having heard every word.

'No, but you know what you're like. You drift off and then I've got to say things all over again.'

'You have to do an essay on communism,' Katie told her. 'Would you like to make a start now, or shall we . . .'

'No way. I've got to go up and check my emails and get changed before I go out.'

'Where are you going?'

'Over to Kylie's to do some homework. And please don't start. I'm like, so not in the mood.'

Katie listened to her stomping up the stairs, and having no energy to protest she turned back to the table and sank down on to a chair. This distance that had crept between them wasn't unusual, she knew that, most mothers experienced it with girls Molly's age, but she could feel Molly's loneliness as acutely as she could her own and knew that deep down inside Molly was as scared as she was. If only they could talk about what was happening, but during her treatment Katie simply hadn't had the strength to, and since it had ended they'd both been in a fool's paradise hoping it had all gone away now.

Letting go of a long, shaky sigh, she sat back down to continue her letter, knowing she had to make herself do it today. It would probably take a couple of weeks to get there, and though she didn't imagine she was leaving home feet first just yet, time wasn't exactly her friend now. She looked at her watch to check the date. September 7th, so the earliest Michelle might get here was the middle of the month. That was presuming, of course, she was willing to come, and after the coldness Katie had treated her to over the years,

Katie would hardly be able to blame her if she weren't.

Michelle's lovely green eyes were sparkling with affection as she watched the arcane piece of theatre that was being staged for her benefit outside the mud-brick house she called home. It was at the junction of a dried up well, a food store and the Medecins Sans Frontiers clinic, where several patients were hanging out of glassless windows to watch and laugh and shout at the overenthusiastic performers. Next door to her was a row of doctors' huts, and across the piazza, as they had grandiosely named this dusty patch of land with its puddles and weeds, was one of the camp's eight precious bakeries.

Laughing as three skinny young children dressed in Tesco T-shirts and pyjama pants began singing a song that was making the others howl, she admired the two female performers who were swaying willow-like in the background, while Nazar, a roguishly handsome Hazaran who'd arrived six months ago with his wife and five sons, provided the music with an assortment of instruments he'd carved and strung himself. His wife was dead now, as were two of his sons, taken by dehydration during the cruel heat of the summer months. Nazar had mourned them, but now it was time to find a new wife. Michelle was hoping he'd choose Maryam, one of the dancers, who'd created this curious entertainment with him. Maryam was nineteen and had lost all three of her children, her husband and father during their escape from Afghanistan, and now devoted her

17

time to taking care of the many orphans who were struggling to survive here in the camp of Shamshatu.

Having only a small grasp of Dari, the language they were using for the play, Michelle was mostly unable to understand what all the shouting and strange noises were about, but it hardly mattered. It was enough that a small crowd had wandered up from the endless sprawl of delapidated mud-brick houses and makeshift tents, and that for these few minutes at least, their world was one of merriment and laughter.

'Will you be helping at the clinic tonight?' a voice beside her asked. 'Or will you be wishing to spend time with Tahira?' It was one of the doctors, herself a refugee, who'd come to sit beside Michelle in the sand.

Michelle drew back the folds of her blue shawl to look at the sad-faced young medic, but she didn't answer, merely let her eyes drift back to the lively group in front of her and on down through the main thoroughfare where oxen, camels, donkeys and goats mingled with proud, angry men in loosely tied lungees and shalwar kameez. Some brazenly carried rifles strapped to their shoulders, others touted carpets woven by children, while still others sat cross-legged on rush mats holding council and teaching young boys to pray.

Michelle had been here since the start of the bombing in Afghanistan. Though she carried out many tasks, her chief role was to drum up as much publicity as she could for the camp, generally by bringing in the world's press so they could write about what was happening here. Plenty came, it was always debatable how many listened or cared.

Nazar began to play his *sarinda*. Michelle watched his elegant fingers and felt the beauty of the music stirring a place deep in her heart. He'd been teaching Tom to play the instrument during Tom's frequent visits to the camp, and the memory of the two of them sitting together, both dressed in turbans and appearing as ethnic as each other, made her feel strangely sad today.

As though reading her thoughts Qadira, the young doctor, said, 'Did you manage to reach Tom? Does he know you are leaving?'

Michelle nodded. 'He's in Lahore. I'll go there before I fly to London.'

Qadira was resigned to partings, but it was plain she wouldn't find this one easy. 'I am very sorry about your sister,' she said softly. 'May Allah be gracious . . . Oh my, what is happening now?'

The sound of gunshots ringing out over the camp brought everyone to a stop. Angry voices could be heard coming from the direction of the mosque, then someone running and shouting Qadira's name.

'You stay,' she told Michelle as she got up. 'Tahira is here. She will be very sad to see you go.'

Not as sad as I will, Michelle was thinking, as she held out her arms to the scrawny, motherless girl whom she'd allowed herself to become far too attached to. She was probably thirteen, but small enough to be nine, and bright enough to learn considerably more English than Michelle had Dari. She helped in the clinic, made tea and ricecakes for the visitors Michelle brought in and secretly taught a handful of younger girls how to read and write.

Her ambition was to go to a university in America and become a journalist like Tom. She loved Tom above anyone else, possibly even Michelle.

As she sank into Michelle's embrace Michelle smiled and kissed her forehead. If it was possible to be more beautiful than this child, both in face and spirit, she was at a loss to know how.

'*Khwandi. Khurdza.*' Tahira said. 'Sister. Niece.'

'That's right,' Michelle told her, tracing the folds of her shawl around her face.

'*Dzem?* Go?'

Michelle nodded. 'Tomorrow. *Sabaa,*' she said.

Tahira gazed at her with wide, melancholy eyes. 'I come?' she said.

'I wish you could,' Michelle whispered.

'Emails?'

'Yes, we'll send emails,' Michelle assured her. 'And you.'

'We all send,' Tahira said, meaning all the children she taught in a small room at the back of the clinic. 'Dr Qadari and Mr Henri help. Tom go?'

Michelle swallowed and looked out towards the distant mountains, barely visible now in the dwindling light. 'No, Tom's staying here,' she said.

Tahira broke rapidly into her own language, using a dialect Michelle didn't understand, though she knew, because they'd had this conversation before, that Tahira was telling her she would take care of Tom, and maybe one day become his wife. Since many of the girls here were married to men thirty, forty even fifty years older than they were, Tahira's suggestion, at least in her world, wasn't quite so outlandish, though the fact that Tom was

American would certainly make it unacceptable in the eyes of her elders.

A few hours later, after the fun was over and most had lain down to sleep, Michelle sat on a rush mat outside her single-room dwelling, listening to the many different sounds of the camp, inhaling the malodorous stench of heat and raw sewage that she often forgot to notice now, and tried to imagine how she was going to adapt to being back in England after being away so long. Eleven years in total, though not all had been spent here, for she'd been in Sarajevo for two years which was where she'd first met Tom; then they gone to Rio where they'd worked in the *favelas* and plotted to expose a government backed death squad. It was after that terrifying ordeal, which had culminated in her son, Robbie, being kidnapped, that Robbie had gone to live with his father in LA. Not a day went by that she didn't ache for him, never a week passed without them speaking at least once on the phone.

Now she and Tom were in Pakistan, a country they both loved and feared. As Westerners it was far too dangerous for them to be here, but somehow time had gone on and they were still alive and it had never seemed quite the right time to go.

She'd be with Tom tomorrow night, at a friend's house in Lahore, where she kept most of her belongings and where she would stay before flying on to London. There had been no suggestion of him coming with her, nor would there be, for England, America, the whole pampered West, was of no interest to him. His heart was here, unclaimed by a woman, wholly dominated by a land.

'Katie,' she murmured softly, as her thoughts

21

turned to her sister and her eyes rose to the black, starry sky, 'I know you think I'll let you down, but you're wrong. I will come, but it doesn't mean I won't find it hard to leave here, because I will.'

'You're Molly Kiernan, aren't you?'

Molly looked up at the pretty, freckle-faced girl who'd come to intrude upon her private space at the edge of the woods.

'Your mum's Katie Kiernan, who writes in the paper,' the girl continued. 'My mum reads her all the time.'

Molly was perched on a stile, her school bag dangling off one post, her mobile in her hand with a half-composed message to her mum saying she was still at Kylie's. She'd never been inside Kylie Green's house, didn't even know where she lived, nor did she want to, because she was just a slapper who Molly totally couldn't stand.

'I've seen you sitting here lots of times,' the girl told her. 'I live over there.' She turned and pointed to the lumbering old farmhouse whose roof and bedroom windows were visible over the hedgerows at the far end of the next field. 'My name's Allison,' she added, turning back.

Molly already knew that, because she'd seen her a couple of times before, around the village, or in Chippenham with her friends from the private school. Molly used to go to private school too, in London, but when they'd moved here her mum couldn't afford to send her to one again, so she was at the comprehensive in Chippenham now. She hated it, because everyone hated her. They called her a stuck-up bitch who thought she was better than everyone just because she talked posh, had a mother who was like, so not famous, and had gone to some snooty school before getting dumped on them there.

Allison released her long red hair from a scrunchy, then tied it back again. 'Why do you come and sit here all on your own?' she asked.

Molly shrugged and looked down at the stream that was flowing beneath the bridge Allison was standing on. No way was she going to tell her, because it was no-one else's business, and anyway, it was embarrassing.

'I mean, like, it's a really cool place,' Allison said. 'You know, like pretty and that . . . Don't you have any friends?'

Molly's face tightened, her eyes stayed on the water.

'I could be your friend,' Allison offered. 'I can introduce you to Cecily and Donna too. They go to my school, and they're like, really cool, and we've got this like, amazing thing we do . . . It's kind of secret, so I can't tell you about it, unless you're part of our group.'

Molly's eyes wandered along the banks to where the stream rounded a bend.

'You don't say much, do you?' Allison remarked. 'I didn't think you'd be shy.'

'I'm not,' Molly told her. 'I was just thinking, that's all.'

Allison shrugged and checked the belt on her really low-cut jeans, that were the same as the ones Molly had, but better. She even had a ring in her belly button and loads of make-up, and a totally cool crop top.

'My mum doesn't write in the paper any more,' Molly said.

Allison's eyes widened. 'Why not?'

'She just doesn't. Actually, there are a lot of things she doesn't do any more. She's been like, sick and that, and . . .' Her eyes went down again.

'Is she better now?' Allison asked.

Molly nodded shortly.

'So what other kinds of things doesn't she do?' Allison wanted to know.

Molly didn't answer, because no way was she going to make herself look stupid by telling Allison how her mum didn't come and walk in the woods with her any more and think up things to put in their dream box. It was all just stupid stuff anyway, because no way was she, Molly, ever going to be a famous singer, or a supermodel, or go out with Justin Timberlake. Nor was her mum ever going to be a pole dancer, or go tiger-spotting in India, or do some dumb waltz in Vienna.

'I can't stand my mother,' Allison confided. 'She's like, so embarrassing. Even my dad doesn't want to be with her, so he stays in London most of the time. She's always drunk, like all day, and makes herself look really stupid with my brother's friends. Oh my God, you should see her . . . Toby, that's my brother, he hates bringing anyone home because of what she might say or do. He goes to a boarding school in Devon, but he comes home sometimes at weekends, and in the week if they've just got like, study groups and things. He'll be eighteen in November, the same week as I'm fifteen. How old are you?'

'I'll be fifteen in January.'

'You look older.'

Molly liked the compliment.

'Cecily and Donna can't stand their mothers either,' Allison prattled on. 'Cecily's ran off and left them a couple of years ago, and hardly ever comes back to visit, and Donna's prefers her older sister so just completely ignores Donna. That's like, what our group's about really. We've found someone better than our mothers. Someone really cool and like, totally out there.'

Molly's interest was piqued.

'Trouble is, you can't really join unless you hate your mother,' Allison told her. 'She's got to like, really get on your nerves, or have done something terrible, like mine and Cecily's . . . What's your mother like?'

Molly's expression closed down again. She wasn't going to say she hated her, because she didn't, but she didn't always like her very much, and she'd really like to be in Allison's group, because she was loads more sophisticated than the other girls round here, and anyway, it was boring and horrible not having any friends.

'Toby's home at the moment,' Allison said as they started across the field together. 'Cecily's like, really mad about him. They've snogged and stuff. She says they've gone even further than that, but I don't know if that's true. She makes things up sometimes, but she's like, so amazing. She's got this really wicked imagination . . . She's the one who came up with the idea for our group. She's quite brainy, and knows all kinds of weird stuff. I think you'll like her. She's coming over later, with Donna. Have you got a boyfriend?'

Molly thought of Rusty Phillips, the ginger-haired, goofy-faced brainbox in her class who was always hanging around her, and was so rank she wanted to gag. 'No,' she answered. 'Have you?'

'Kind of. His name's Miles. He's one of Toby's friends, at school. We've snogged a few times and I let him touch me up top once. It was a bit of a dare really, with Cecily. We kind of go in for that in our group, which is like, amazing. Oh God, I really hope they let you join, because I know you're going to love it. Have you ever snogged anyone?'

'Yeah,' Molly lied.

'Did you do anything else?'

'A couple of things, you know.'

Allison nodded as though she did.

As they approached the gap in the hedge that opened on to the Fortescue-Bonds' driveway, Molly was starting to feel quite excited. It was really cool to have someone she could talk to, so if she had to hate her mum to join the group, she could probably do it, because sometimes it really felt as though she did.

'Who's that?' she asked, wishing she didn't have her school uniform on as she spotted a group of boys over by what looked like the stables.

'Oh that's Tobes with his mates,' Allison answered. 'They're motorbike mad, all of them. Tobes has just got a new one, so I suppose they're all checking it out. Oh my God!' she suddenly cried. 'Martin's here. I'll have to text Donna. She'll totally freak out, because she's got this like, major crush on him.' As she spoke she was pressing a message into her mobile. 'I sent it to Cecily too,' she said, when she'd finished, 'so they'll be over here in like, two minutes flat.'

It was about half an hour later that Cecily and Donna actually turned up, flushed and bright-eyed as they joined Allison and Molly on the grass in front of the house. The boys were about twenty yards away, apparently too engrossed in Toby's mega new machine to notice they were being watched.

'This is Molly Kiernan,' Allison said, as Cecily plonked down with an ecstatic gaze in Toby's direction.

'Oh, your mum's the one in the paper, isn't she?' Cecily asked, flicking back her mane of glossy dark curls. 'Oh my God, Allison, your brother is like, *soooo* fit,' she gushed. 'He looks really cool on that bike.'

Cecily was so beautiful Molly was finding it hard not to stare.

'Has Martin said anything about me?' Donna wanted to know, her flaxen hair glinting in the sunlight, her flawless pale skin stained pink with hope.

'He told Toby he thought you were cool,' Allison answered. 'And he hasn't got a girlfriend, apparently.'

'Oh my God!' Donna gasped, clasping her hands to her chest. 'He is definitely like, going to be the one I choose when we, you know . . .'

Allison's eyes shot to Molly, but before she could explain the sound of another motorbike arriving cut her off. 'Oh my God, it's Brad Jenkins,' she gasped as she watched it go past. 'Molly, you wait till you see him. He is like, sooo fit. I mean, like he's

27

a god. I'm telling you, he's even better than Justin Timberlake.'

Molly was watching Brad as he pulled up alongside the others. In all his leathers and helmet it was hard to see what he was like, but then he took the helmet off and Molly's heart skipped a beat. He was totally drop-dead gorgeous with his long blond hair, jet black eyebrows and tanned face. She would just die to have a boyfriend like that, and wanted to die anyway that she was stuck here in her bloody school uniform. How embarrassing was that? But he'd never be interested in her. She was too young, and he was bound to have a girlfriend anyway.

Next to her Cecily was grinning. 'Bet you'd love to snog him,' she whispered.

Molly smiled and blushed.

'Imagine his lips and his tongue, and his hands going all over you . . .'

'Cecily!' Allison shrieked, laughing as she slapped her.

'Yes she would, look at her,' Cecily cried. 'She's panting for him already. Shall we tell him?'

'No!' Molly gasped.

'Just kidding,' Cecily assured her, and turning to Allison she said, 'Have you told her anything about us?'

'Only a bit,' Allison answered, 'but she's got like, a real problem with her mum, in that she can't stand her, haven't you?' she said to Molly, staring at her in a way to prompt the right response.

Molly nodded.

'So I reckon that qualifies her right off,' Allison declared.

Cecily and Donna turned to look at Molly. 'Have you ever heard of Lilith?' Donna asked after some frank assessment.

Molly frowned. 'What, you mean like a group, or something?' she said.

Cecily sniggered. 'No, try again.'

Molly shrugged. 'The only other Lilith I've heard of is like something to do with Eve, as in the first woman,' she said.

Cecily clapped her hands together in delight. 'Go to the top of the class,' she praised. 'Come on, let's go inside so we can show you the stuff we've downloaded, and if you want to join you'll have to go through the same initiation we all did. It's OK, it's nothing dangerous, but you can't become one of the Daughters if you don't.'

As they all got up, Donna was watching Martin while saying, 'Has anyone heard from the pop-video guy?'

'Yeah, I have,' Allison answered. 'You can read the email. It's totally outrageous.'

'Do you think he's genuine?'

'Who knows?'

As they chattered on they crossed the forecourt to go around the side of the house, passing quite close to the boys. Molly kept her head down, too shy to look, but then she stole a quick glance in their direction, and to her amazement found herself eye to eye with Brad Jenkins. A flood of colour immediately rushed to her cheeks, and when he winked she thought she was going to faint.

'Oh my God, oh my God!' she gasped, pushing past the others to get inside the house. 'Did you see that? He just looked at me. Oh my God. *Brad Jenkins* just winked at me.'

'I saw, I saw,' Allison cried. 'Oh my God, that is like, so wicked. You've got to choose him. You have to.'

'Definitely,' Cecily agreed.

'Choose him for what?' Molly demanded.

'We'll explain in a minute,' Donna told her. 'It's like a mission, and you have to do it, or you can't be one of the Daughters.'

'She'll do it,' Allison declared, leading them along a back hall and up a narrow staircase. 'Definitely. I know she will.'

Intrigued and excited, Molly followed them into Allison's totally amazing bedroom. It was plastered in posters, had two sofas as well as a bed, a DVD and CD player, a computer, TV, the biggest collection of CDs and videos she'd ever seen, and its own private bathroom.

'You've got to give us your email address and phone number,' Allison was saying as she sat down at the computer. 'And we'll give you ours.'

Molly was taking out her mobile ready to put in the new numbers when it bleeped to tell her she had a text. Guessing it was probably from her mum she toyed with the idea of ignoring it, but then decided she'd better find out what she wanted.

```
Stuck in
Guantanamo Bay.
Pls arrange
early release.
Getting hungry.
Mumx
```

Molly stifled a laugh, not wanting the others to know she found her mum amusing, because then they wouldn't believe she hated her. It was just her dumb way of calling their shed Guantanamo Bay, and telling Molly it was time to come home that . . . Well, it got on her nerves, but it made her laugh too. Then seeing there was more she flicked down to read it.

```
Michelle escaped
camp. In Lahore.
Bet she doesn't
come. Who cares?
```

Molly's spirits immediately sank, because she really, really didn't want Michelle to come, but she just knew she would. It made her feel all weird and angry even to think about it, because it was like, so dumb Michelle coming now, when everything was starting to go right again. It would have made more sense for her to come during the chemo and stuff, when they could have done with some help. And anyway, her mum didn't even really like Michelle, and didn't want her to come either, so why had she gone and asked her?

'What's wrong? Who is it?' Cecily asked, coming to look over her shoulder.

'No-one,' Molly answered, clicking off and hiding the phone.

'No. No. Secrets aren't allowed,' Cecily cried, trying to grab the phone. 'You have to tell us everything if you want to become one of the Daughters of Lilith.'

Molly's grip tightened as she struggled to push

Cecily off. 'My aunt's supposed to be coming here,' she said.

'So what's wrong with that? What's she like?'

'I don't know. I haven't seen her since I was twelve. I just don't want her to come, that's all.'

'Why?'

'I just don't. Anyway, forget her. Tell me about Lilith and everything,' and pocketing her mobile she went to sit on one of the window seats, where she could steal the occasional look outside at Brad and ~~the~~ part of her new friends' group, and not have to think about Michelle or her mum or anything else.

Chapter Two

Michelle was sitting with Tom Chambers in the café at Lahore airport. Usually they had much to talk about, but today they seemed to have few words left, as they contemplated the split in their worlds, the very different lives they would be leading now that she was giving all this up and returning to England.

Tom was dressed as a local, in kurta pyjamas, with a white turban wrapped around his head, and a two-day beard disguising the hard cut of his jaw. His eyes were grey, and sharp, his nose long and slightly crooked, his mouth stern until he smiled, when he became almost handsome. His height often set him apart from the crowd, but not always, for there were others as tall, though generally not quite so broad. He could boast many friends in this city, but Michelle knew there were few he trusted, for as a journalist he was viewed with much suspicion, as an American he was more often an object of hate than respect.

The noise around them was deafening. Sajid,

Tom's fixer, was beside him, talking incessantly. Though Tom was listening she could tell he was distracted, allowing his thoughts to take him out of this crowded airport café. Maybe he was thinking of the sweltering, dusty streets they'd just driven through, or perhaps mentally travelling beyond the borders of this deadly country, where life could be as cheap as the price of the next meal.

Catching her watching him he held her eyes, and seemed to query her thoughts, though he said nothing, just continued to regard her in a way that seemed either challenging or curious, she couldn't quite tell which. She would have liked to know how he really felt about her leaving, if he was experiencing any of the wrenching sadness that was inside her, or if he was thinking about something else entirely. They'd been the closest of friends almost since they'd first met, had always relied on each other in times of need, and had rarely been very far apart. In the past months, however, she'd spent much more time at the Shamshuta refugee camp than in Lahore, or Peshawar or Karachi, where he was more often to be found.

One airport announcement blended with the next. It would soon be time for her to go through. She wouldn't ask when she'd see him again, because it was a pointless question. There was so much else she wanted to say, but knew she wouldn't, because she'd left it too late, though once or twice, after they'd eaten dinner with friends last night, and strolled out on to the terrace to talk about her new life in England, she'd come close. Unless she'd imagined it, he'd seemed on the verge of telling her something too, and she thought he seemed that way now. Knowing him as well as she did, though, she suspected it was to do with a story, a detail that was niggling him, or a contact who was supposed to call.

She looked down at his hands, cupped around the small plastic beaker of coffee, large and rough, deeply sun-tanned and ringless. Her own were inches away, slender and female, smooth in comparison to his, but aged by the sun and marked by her work in the camps. It would be the most natural thing in the world to reach out and touch him now, for they often held hands, or embraced, but today, for some reason, they were both keeping a distance.

When she looked up again his expression was quizzical.

'What are you going to do?' he asked.

Surprised by the question, for they'd spent most of last evening discussing the reason for her return to England, she said, 'You mean when I get there?'

Amusement came into his eyes. 'Your flight's been delayed,' he told her. 'Didn't you hear?'

Frowning, she looked around. 'For how long?' she asked, unsure whether she was pleased or worried, only knowing that Katie was expecting her, and it might be easier to get this parting over with now.

'I'll go and find out,' Sajid offered, rising to his feet.

'I have to get back,' Michelle said, looking at Tom. 'I told Katie I'd be there today. I can't let her down.'

'It's probably only half an hour or so,' he assured her.

She nodded, and pushed a hand through her short dark hair that until a week ago had been shoulder-length and blonde. In the camps, and in town, she generally covered it with a scarf or shawl, but here at the airport the rules were more lax, though she still wore a voluminous dress that effectively disguised the litheness of her figure. 'You don't have to wait with me,' she told him. 'I know you, so I'm sure you've got a thousand people to see, or a hundred different places to go.'

His eyebrows arched. 'Why did you cut your hair?' he asked.

She shrugged, not wanting to tell him that she suspected Katie had lost hers, so it was a probably silly attempt at solidarity. 'A whim, I guess,' she answered. 'I didn't realize it would change colour.'

'I like it. It makes you look younger.'

She smiled. 'What would you say if I told you I'm forty today?' she asked, a playful light appearing in her eyes.

'Are you serious?'

She nodded, not surprised he'd forgotten, but a little disappointed.

His expression turned suspicious. 'You're kidding me, right?' he said.

'Now you're just being gentlemanly,' she accused.

He shook his head, as though in wonderment. 'Forty's a good age for a woman,' he told her.

'And why is that?'

'I don't know. I just heard someone say it once.'

She laughed and looked up as Sajid came back. 'They say plane no go until half past nine tonight,' he told her.

Her smile fled. 'But that's the next flight,' she protested. 'What happened to the eleven o'clock?'

'Is cancelled. They give you seat on next one,' he answered. 'You make change at Karachi and arrive in London at one forty-five tomorrow.'

'Oh no!' she cried.

'Katie'll understand,' Tom said. 'And what's one more day when she wrote the letter two weeks ago?'

'You don't know Katie. She'll think I've done it on purpose.'

'She didn't seem that unreasonable to me when we met,' he responded.

'Because you're not me. She's all right with everyone else, it's just me she has the problem with.'

'Well, flights get delayed, especially in this part of the world, so she's probably expecting it.'

'I'll have to call her. What time is it there?' She looked at her watch, and groaned. 'Four o'clock in the morning.'

He got to his feet. 'Let's go find out exactly what the story is here,' he said, 'and if it's really going to be that delayed, you should come back to my place. You can use the phone there.'

Half an hour later they were in a taxi bumping back along the main road into Lahore, swerving to avoid cyclists and ox carts, faces covered to protect them from the dust that was rushing in through the open windows. It was either that, or suffocate in the insufferable heat. Sajid was in the front, yabbering away with the driver, while Tom spoke to someone on his mobile in a torturous form of Punjabi.

Michelle gazed out at the passing tenements

where washing hung limply over balconies, and skinny children hawked stolen bangles and sweets on the roadside. She tried to imagine what life was going to be like back in England, but her thoughts kept returning to Tom, and how they might spend these extra few hours they'd been given. His schedule would probably be full of meetings he couldn't miss, and she almost hoped it was, for there could hardly be a worse time than now to be considering breaking their agreement never to spoil a beautiful friendship by confessing how she really felt.

'So, forty, eh?' he said, clicking off his phone.

She laughed. 'You're making me feel old,' she accused, 'and I believe you've got a three-year advance on me.'

He drew his breath in sharply. 'Two,' he corrected.

Her eyes narrowed. 'I think it's three.'

'OK, you win, but I think we should celebrate. God knows where we get any champagne in this town, but I'm going to trust Sajid to find some.'

She was about to respond when a car sped out of a side street, forcing their driver to slam on the brakes. She shot forward, hitting the back of Sajid's seat hard, and as the car slewed to one side, the door next to her flew open. If Tom hadn't grabbed her she'd have been thrown out on to the street. There was a howling cry as a cyclist hit the door and soared up over the top of it to land sprawling in the dust beyond.

'Are you OK?' Tom barked, already jumping out of the car.

'Yes, I'm fine,' she answered, wincing at all the

shouting and gesticulating that had erupted in the front as she got out too.

After checking the cyclist was only bruised, which was more than could be said for either his bike or the car door, they climbed back in to continue their journey, with Tom hanging on to the door to keep it closed.

'It won't be like this in England,' he warned, as they approached the gate that would take them into the citadel.

She had to laugh, and let her head fall back against the seat as they began battling a route towards the Shahi Mohalla bazaar.

'Sajid, we need champagne,' Tom declared, suddenly remembering.

Sajid immediately turned round. 'No problem, Mr Tom,' he responded. 'We take you to your home, then I go to find champagne. Fifty dollar.'

Tom's tone was dry as he said, 'That's what I love about you, my friend. You never miss a trick.'

When they'd gone as far as they could by car, Michelle stepped out into the seething chaos of the bazaar, ducking to avoid a dangling brace of dead feathered birds, and managing to skid on a pile of rotting veg. Tom tossed Sajid and the driver some money, then came round to join her. The air was stifling, the noise a booming cacophony of music, voices, animal cries, car horns and bicycle bells. Thousands of people in colourful saris, drab shawls, lavishly embroidered waistcoats, head-scarves, karakul caps, shalwar kameez and various forms of Western garb were pressing to and from the narrow alleyways, leaving no space between them. The only way not to become separated was for her to hold on tightly to Tom's hand and hope it caused no offence to the religious adherents amongst the crowd.

As they reached the first alley he suddenly stopped. 'Birthdays need jewels,' he declared, and began steering her towards a tiny stall where a tragically deformed young girl was holding out handfuls of silver jewellery studded with glittering stones of every colour and shape. Within seconds they were surrounded by so m ny sellers and their jewels it was as though the en e bazaar was a sea of glittering topaz and turqu ise, with swathes of rubies, emeralds and amber bobbing wildly around it.

'I must get some for Katie and Molly,' Michelle cried, admiring one piece after another, after another. 'Oh God, there's so much to choose from.'

'It's all my treat,' Tom told her as he selected bracelets, necklaces, ankle chains and earrings.

Laughing, Michelle somehow made her choices too, beautiful aquamarine earrings and choker for Katie, silver bracelets and shiny red and blue bangles for Molly. 'I should take them some shawls and slippers too,' she declared, wishing she'd thought of it before. 'And kites,' she cried, looking up at the azure sky where hundreds of colourful triangles swooped and soared like birds, while kids wove in and out of the rooftops, hanging on to the strings and somehow defying death.

Many dollars and rupees changed hands before they plunged on into the heart of the bazaar, twisting and turning through the network of ornate stone passageways and overloaded stalls until they reached Afshar's dupatta shop. Spotting Tom, the old man jumped up and called out.

'Mr Tom. I have package for you. It come by messenger.'

'You're a good man, Afshar,' Tom told him, taking the flat brown envelope and sticking it under his arm, as he fished for some rupees to thank Afshar for his trouble.

Unable to resist Afshar's exquisite shawls, Michelle bought two, then followed Tom up the dark, creaking staircase next to the shop, to a decrepit wooden landing where a broken window opened on to a maze of rooftops, and the pungent aroma of spices seemed to seep from the peeling walls.

'I'd forgotten how to spend money,' she laughed, as he unlocked a scratched wooden door.

'It'll all come back,' he assured her, standing aside for her to go in ahead of him.

'Heavens, is this where you were the last time I came?' she asked, stopping in the middle of the shadowy, red-painted room. His unmade bed was pushed up in a corner, lavish, hand-woven rugs covered the floorboards and one wall, and an old desk with his laptop, telephone and a lamp sat in front of the huge arched window.

'No. I was three streets away before,' he answered, closing the door and going to dump his packages on the bed. 'This place is normally home to Laila, who dances in one of the clubs, here in the Tarts' Quarter, but she's gone to visit her family for a couple of months, letting me take care of the place for her.'

'Laila the Tart,' she laughed, shaking her head.

41

'So you,' and dropping her parcels on the desk she pulled aside a beaded curtain to peer in. 'A bathroom with a real bath,' she declared.

'And real water,' he added drolly, going to the small kitchenette next to the window and taking a battered saucepan from a single electric ring. 'I can make some tea,' he offered.

'No, I think I'll wait for the champagne,' she decided, and turned to the window as the haunting cry of the muezzin began warbling from the minarets that soared like candles into the kite-filled sky.

Coming to stand beside her, he slipped an arm round her shoulders and rested his head on hers. During the craziness of the last half an hour, they'd forgotten she was about to leave, and now, as the prospect returned, they became quiet again.

'I'm going to miss you,' he told her after a while.

'I'm going to miss you too,' she whispered.

He kissed the top of her head and drew her in closer. 'I'm really sorry about Katie,' he said, after a long time just watching the kites, and holding her next to him.

She sighed softly and felt her heart stirring with the fear of how bad Katie might already be. 'I should call her,' she said, glancing at her watch. 'Or maybe I should wait another hour.'

'I could make the call for you,' he offered. 'I'd like to speak to her.'

Touched by his fondness for Katie, whom he'd felt an instant rapport with on the only occasion they'd actually met, Michelle wondered if it might be a good idea for him to call instead of her, when he could tell Katie she was actually on her way, rather than still in Pakistan and delayed.

'It won't have been easy for her to ask me to come,' she said, thinking of how mixed and turbulent Katie's emotions must be right now. 'She's got a lot of pride, and our relationship, as you know, hasn't always been smooth.'

'She obviously trusts you to take care of her daughter.'

Michelle's smile was wry. 'I don't know about trust, there just isn't anyone else, and considering what a great mother I've been to my own son . . .'

'Hey,' he said, gently cutting her off. 'You did what was best for Robbie at the time, and he knows you'd be there for him in an instant if he needed you.'

It was true, she would, and the important thing was that he was happy with his father and stepmother, so she said no more, only wished that her life didn't seem so full of painful partings. Thinking of how hard this next one was going to be, she rested her head on Tom's shoulder, and tightened her arm around his waist.

'I was thinking,' he said, still gazing out at the rooftops and sky, 'now you're giving all this up to become respectable, and English . . .'

'Go on,' she prompted with a smile, when he stopped.

'Well, I was wondering would this be a good time to tell you that my feelings for you have ventured a bit beyond the platonic? Actually, kind of a long way beyond.'

'I would say now was a lousy time to tell me,' she replied, as everything in her responded to the words.

43

'That's what I figured.'

Several seconds ticked by, then, without a word, he turned her to him and gazed deeply into her eyes. For a long time they merely looked at each other, as though drinking in every last detail of each other's faces, until finally his mouth came to hers and so much longing and emotion seared through her that she almost couldn't bear it.

'I've wanted to do that for a very long time,' he told her, running his fingers over her neck and up into her hair.

'So why didn't you?' she asked shakily.

'I guess because we made some damned-fool pact way back when, no relationship, no complications.'

'Does that mean you're going to start a complicated relationship with me *now*, when I'm leaving?' she teased.

He didn't smile, only searched her eyes again, and this time, when he kissed her, his tongue found hers, so that she clung to him more tightly and felt the strength of his desire building as unrelentingly as her own.

'Come,' he murmured, and turning her away from the window, he stood her in the middle of the room and unfastened the loose, black robes that covered her long-sleeved shirt and jeans. 'I bought you jewels,' he whispered against her mouth. 'Now I want to see you wear them.'

She stayed where she was, heart pounding, anticipation rising as she watched him unwrap a beautiful necklace of multiple peridot and crystal strands. As he placed it against her neck, he kissed her softly on the lips, then walked behind her to fasten it. When he came back he arranged it inside the V of her shirt and stood aside to admire it.

'It matches your eyes,' he told her, running his fingertips over the stones.

Her breath was shallow and brief as she looked up into his face. His eyes found hers, and he kissed her lingeringly, deeply, before going to take a pair of gaudy fake sapphire earrings from their parcel. He clipped them to her ears, and let the sparkling drops slide through his fingers. He touched her lips, and seemed to drink in their fullness, before he covered them with his own.

Next he selected a jangling collection of gold and silver bangles studded with emeralds and garnets and slipped them over her hands on to her wrists. Then dropping to his knees he removed her sandals, rolled up the hems of her jeans, and fastened an assortment of glittering chains and charms around her ankles.

When he stood up again she was smiling, her head cocked to one side, as she waited for what was to come next. Inside, desire was pulsing through her with such a force it was as though every part of her was alight with it. She felt if he didn't touch her soon she might beg. He lifted a hand and stroked the necklace again, running his fingers over it, watching his own movements, as though nothing existed beyond them. Then he raised his other hand and began to unfasten the buttons of her shirt.

She stood very still, watching his face as he pulled the shirt open and gazed down at her small, naked breasts and big, erect nipples. He touched them, as gently as he had the beads. The sensations darting through her were so acute they were almost painful. Her eyes closed, and she hardly dared breathe as he rolled and pulled and watched the changing expression of her face.

'You're beautiful,' he murmured, and pushing his hands under the shirt on to her shoulders, he slid it down her arms, over the bangles and let it drop to the floor. Her waist was narrow, her navel bare, and she moaned softly as he smoothed his coarse hands over her, to the zip of her jeans.

When she was naked he stood back to look at her, his eyes moving from the pearl-studded chains at her feet, all the way up her long, slender legs, to the jewels at her wrists, then to those at her neck and ears. The eroticism of his intent was lacing through her, her nipples and labia felt ready to burst. He touched the necklace again, his fingers descending over the strands all the way to her breasts, where he drew circles and other shapes, teasing her with his thumb, while with his other hand he began to undress himself.

'Let me,' she murmured.

His hands fell to his sides, allowing her to unfasten the hooks of his tunic, and push it over his shoulders to reveal the hard expanse of his chest. Then she pulled the cord to loosen the waist of his pants. They fell to his ankles, leaving him naked. She wanted him badly and immediately, but merely pushed him back on to the chair, dropped to her knees, and took off his boots, her bracelets jangling, her breath turning ragged. His erection was as hard as the precious stones in her jewels, jutting and eager for her touch. She drew her fingers gently over it, feeling its beauty and magnificence, before standing to begin unwinding his turban. His mouth sought her nipples, while his hands circled her waist and pulled her closer to him.

With the turban unravelled, she ran her fingers into his short, greying hair, then tilting his face up, she pushed her tongue deep into his mouth.

As they kissed she moved to him, and descended over the full length of him, until he was buried all the way inside her. Her bangles and bracelets clattered and jingled as she wrapped her arms and legs around him. Her head fell back and she moaned softly at the feel of his hands moving over her again.

Holding her tightly to him he stood and pressed her up against the wall.

'Does this feel good?' he asked, moving slowly in and out of her.

'Yes, oh yes,' she murmured.

'Do you want more?'

'Oh God, yes.'

He moved harder and faster, going all the way in, and making her shudder with pleasure. His mouth found hers, and as he kissed her, she knew she wanted this to go on for ever.

He took her sharply and rapidly, slowly and excruciatingly deeply. He found the most sensitive part of her, toyed with it and made her cry out. He kissed her again and again, until finally she could feel him starting to come. Then his arms seemed to crush her as the rush came dangerously close. She was almost there herself, for the feel of him, the strength of him, was pushing her fast to the edge, but then he was carrying her to the bed, lying her down and using a motion she'd never known before to take her soaring through the barriers to an erotically shuddering release.

'Let it go, let it go,' he urged, as she clung to him, gasping and clenching him with muscles that were out of control. 'Oh God, yes,' he seethed as he finally let his own climax erupt. His mouth sought hers and he claimed it, kissing her harshly as the clashing surges of sensation continued to shake their bodies.

It was only minutes later, as they lay, still fighting for breath and holding each other close, that a knock came on the door and Sajid shouted.

'Mr Tom. Have champagne. I am leaving outside door.'

Tom's eyes closed as he laughed. 'Good man, Sajid,' he shouted back.

As Sajid's footsteps receded down the stairs Michelle started to laugh too. 'Do you think he knows?' she said.

Wrapping her tightly in his arms, he said, 'Probably, but who cares? His timing's impeccable, because right now I reckon we have something to celebrate.'

She smiled impishly into his eyes, and felt her heart swell as he kissed her mouth, then her breasts, before getting up to go and retrieve the champagne.

She lay where she was, watching him walk back across the room to take two tumblers from a cupboard in the corner kitchenette. This was how she'd always wanted to see him, relaxed in his nudity, and sharing this kind of intimacy with her. It was a dream coming true, if only she didn't have to wake up.

'Don't you find it strange,' he said, pulling the

cork from the bottle, 'how we wait till the last to do things we should have done at first?'

'Are you talking about the champagne, or us?' she asked.

He laughed. 'Us.'

She stood up and came to put her arms around him.

'Which damned fool of us made up that ludicrous pact?' he demanded, putting the bottle down, and pulling her against him.

'You know, I don't remember,' she answered.

He brushed his nose against hers. 'I don't want you to go,' he told her. 'I guess I know you have to, but I want to keep you here like this, and just love you.'

It was what she wanted too, more than anything, but she knew it wasn't possible, so she had to keep it light. 'Wearing nothing but jewels while my master goes out to fight for a crust?' she teased.

He smiled and kissed her.

'You know I'd stay if I could,' she told him, emotion starting to lock her throat. 'Oh hell,' she laughed as tears welled up in her eyes. 'It was never going to be easy, and now this is going to make it so much harder.'

His mouth came tenderly to hers, and as his embrace tightened the need of their bodies began to build again. 'Champagne,' he whispered, when finally he let her go.

She watched him fill the tumblers, took hers and met his eyes as he said, 'To the most beautiful woman I know, dressed only in jewels.'

She smiled and touched her glass to his. 'I won't wear them again until the next time we meet,' she said, and not wanting to ask when that might be, or even if it would happen, she lifted her glass and drank deeply.

For the moment, the package that had come by messenger remained unopened.

Almost as soon as she'd put the phone down to Tom, who'd called to tell her Michelle's flight had been delayed, but she was on her way now, Katie had felt tears welling up. It was annoying, because in spite of how difficult life seemed to be with Molly lately, and the terrible fear that was a constant presence in her heart, she hadn't cried at all since they'd told her there was no more they could do. However, just those few gentle words from Tom were making her want to howl. She was still fighting it, trying not to feel sorry for herself, or frustrated, or helpless, but it was apparently unstoppable now, and it wasn't Tom she had to thank for it, it was Michelle, because wasn't it just like her to be late? And wasn't it just like her to have someone wonderful like Tom in her life too?

Though she hated the way she was thinking, she could no more stop the flow now than the tears that were carrying it along. Wrapping her head in her arms, she buried her face in the stack of papers she'd been reading before Tom's call. This shouldn't be happening. She wasn't this person. She was Katie Kiernan, the ambitious young investigative reporter who'd put it all aside when she'd become a mother. She was witty and lively, rose eagerly to life's challenges, and never failed to overcome them.

She'd always loved her column, though watching world events from the wings had often been hard when she'd so longed to be out there. Molly had to come first, however, so she'd used her column to comment on political madness and highlight social injustice, which was her way of remaining in the fray. One day she would go back to it, and even during this last horrible year she'd managed to persuade herself that the dream wasn't over. She'd kept up with it all, reading the papers, writing letters to editors, watching the news, listening to the radio, and she still did, but she was starting to wonder now why she was bothering, because who cared if she knew what was going on in the world? Why did *she* even care, when it was all death and destruction, and God knew she had enough of it going on here. Molly, her precious girl, the only human being in her life who really mattered, was doing everything in her power to reject her, and she just couldn't seem to find a way to reach her. What a useless mother she was, what a total waste of time she was turning into.

'Oh God,' she choked, trying hard to stem all the pent-up fears and emotions, but they just kept on coming, and if her heart wasn't breaking then it was because it was already in a thousand pieces. Why was this happening to her? Why couldn't she at least have had a husband who loved her, instead of some loser who was too busy in the gambling dens of Vegas and Reno to be there for Molly now? He hadn't even answered her letter, when she'd first told him she was ill. Just one cringing phone call, claiming not to have enough money for the fare to come back. He hadn't even asked Katie how she was.

It was thanks to him and his miserable addiction that she and Molly were living where they were, because the proceeds of their London house had mostly gone on covering his debts. Wasn't that just her luck that the bastard had come crawling back years after their divorce, not to tell her what a huge and regrettable mistake he'd made, but to make her sell the house and cough up his share or some Mafia lowlife was going to stick him. If it weren't for Molly she'd have happily stuck him herself, but as their prized Kensington home was in his name – even though she'd been paying the mortgage for years – she'd had no choice but to sell up and bank what little was left after saving his miserable skin. Just thank God this little cottage had been wholly in her name, or he'd have taken that too, and then where would she and Molly have gone? On her salary they'd probably have found somewhere, but then the cheery hand of the Lord had swept in with a message from her ovaries telling her there was a serious problem. So, hey ho, off they came to West Wiltshire, the Bath Royal United and a local comprehensive.

How quickly life had changed, how fast the downhill slide in comparison to the uphill struggle. So there was no point contacting Barry Kiernan to help out now, even if she knew where he was, for he was hardly the kind of father Molly needed with all his drinking, gambling and Godfather connections – in fact, she had a job now to remember why she'd ever married him. Perhaps because he'd been quite charming back then, attentive, witty, and a rising star in their journalists' world. How blinkered love could be, because the drinking and gambling had been a passion with him even then, she'd just refused to see it. And it hadn't even been that that had finally made her kick him out, it was his confession that he'd always secretly been mad about Michelle.

'Stop it! Just stop,' she told herself angrily, as her sobbing grew harder. This much self-pity was disgusting in anyone, and being ill didn't excuse it. It just made her as loathsome as she felt, for she should be putting Molly above everything, and Molly did come first, she always would, but it still didn't change the fact that Katie was going to die never having really been loved by a man, not even Molly's father, who'd only married her because she was pregnant, he'd claimed.

'OK. Just go and empty the washing machine *now*,' she scolded herself furiously. It was a lovely sunny day, so the sheets would be dry by tonight, and maybe she could light the barbecue later, invite Molly's new friends round, even allow them to drink some wine as long as they didn't get drunk.

'A barbecue! Here! I don't think so.' She could hear Molly saying it now, which was why she wouldn't make the suggestion. She didn't want to deal with the rejection, or fall into another of the terrible rows they seemed to be having lately.

The phone was still in front of her, making her think of Tom again, and how lonely she was. She took it back to the base, tugged a handful of tissues from the box on the window sill, cleaned herself up and started to rework her shopping list. She'd been planning to go to Sainsbury's, but now Michelle wasn't going to be here she'd just stroll round to the village shop and pick up a few essentials there. In truth she was happy not to go far, because it was hot again today, and when she was at home she didn't need to wear her wig. That was another thing she'd have to brace herself for, Michelle's shining blonde hair, while all she had now was half an inch of stubble that was more grey than the mousy brown it had been before. Molly hated it if she walked round the house with it uncovered – it was too harsh a reminder of the truth, Katie supposed.

Tears started welling up again, making her wonder if she was ever going to stop, or how sorry it was possible to feel for herself in the space of fifteen minutes. She could be trying for some kind of record.

'Oh my, what's going on here?' a voice demanded from the doorway.

'Judy,' Katie said, turning round as Judy, in her nurse's uniform, pushed open the bottom half of the door and came into the kitchen. 'Should I be expecting you?'

'No. I was just passing so I thought I'd drop in. Seems it was good timing on my part, because you're obviously in need of a bit of tea and sympathy.'

'Oh no, don't encourage me, please,' Katie protested, tugging out another tissue to blow her nose.

Smiling and shaking her head, Judy went to plug in the kettle. 'How are you on the physical front?' she asked. 'Is the pain under control?'

Katie nodded. 'Completely,' she said truthfully.

'What about the constipation?'

'I think it's getting better. The senna's helping and I'm taking more fibre.'

'Good.' She picked up the teapot and started to rinse it out. 'And Molly? Have you managed to discuss anything with her yet?'

'Chance would be a fine thing. She's hardly ever here.'

Judy glanced back over her shoulder.

'To tell the truth,' Katie said, 'I think she knows anyway, or at least senses it, and that's why she's avoiding me.'

'It's very possible,' Judy responded. 'Do you know where she goes?'

'She's getting quite tight with Allison Fortescue-Bond, which doesn't exactly please me. It's a world we've left behind now, and I'm afraid being around people who have all the privileges she's lost . . .' She sighed, and looked down at her hands. 'Or maybe it's a good thing,' she continued after a moment. 'At least she has a friend now, though it just leads me to wondering which I should be discussing first, boys, birth control and STDs, or my own situation.'

'You've already done the birds and the bees,' Judy reminded her.

'Yes, but I need to keep on top of it all. Should I put her on the pill, just in case, or get her some condoms? Or coax her into some kind of celibacy club?'

Coming to the table, Judy said, 'Are you sure you don't want me to have a chat with her about you? It might be easier to hear it from someone else.'

Katie shook her head. 'It should come from me,' she said, her breath catching on a latent sob, 'but to be honest, I'm not sure about making her face it yet. We don't know how long it's going to be, and maybe it would be kinder to let her feel some security with Michelle before she has to deal with losing me.'

Judy wasn't too sure about that, so passing over it, she said, 'Where is Michelle? Isn't she supposed to be here today?'

'Tomorrow,' Katie answered. 'Her flight was delayed.'

'Oh, I see. So is that why you're upset?'

Katie sighed again. 'Yes. No! Oh, I don't know. I'm feeling so confused about everything at the moment, and the heat doesn't seem to be helping. Who'd believe it was almost the end of September?'

'Gorgeous, isn't it?' Judy responded, turning to look out of the window, where the sky seemed improbably blue for the time of year, and the trees and hedgerows were still richly green. 'It's going to be quite a change for her, being in a sleepy backwater like this after her experiences in Afghanistan, I'm sure.'

'Pakistan,' Katie corrected.

'Of course, sorry.' Judy turned back. 'You know, we should ask her to give a talk at the village hall, tell us all about it. Do you think she would?'

'I expect so,' Katie responded, glad that sinking feelings weren't visible, for she was experiencing a particularly horrible one now at the prospect of her sister's popularity. 'Actually, the vicar's already suggested it,' she said, 'and Mrs James wants to know if she'll open the fête next month.'

Judy's eyebrows rose. 'Seems she's already quite in demand,' she remarked. 'I suppose it's inevitable, but we shouldn't forget the real reason she's coming, should we? I'm sure she won't.'

'You know, she's not quite the saint you're all

making her out to be,' Katie responded, wanting to quash it now, before it really took hold. 'To begin with, she's got a son who she just abandoned when he was five.'

'Really? You've never mentioned that before. What do you mean, abandoned?'

Katie's eyes moved away, for she knew it wasn't quite as black as she was painting it, though to serve her own purposes right now she almost wished it was. 'She left him with his father so she could go on with her calling,' she said, knowing very well it had broken Michelle's heart when Robbie had chosen to live in Los Angeles with Michael and his new wife.

'How old is he now?' Judy asked.

'He must be nine, maybe ten. We never see him, because Michael, his father, almost never comes to England now. The point is though, Michelle is totally addicted to her work, which frankly is why I'm so anxious about her coming. If some other crisis pops up in the world between now and when I go, I'm afraid you won't see her for dust, and then what's going to happen to Molly?'

'I'm sure she won't do that,' Judy responded.

'I wish I had your confidence.'

Judy was watching her with a mixture of curiosity and concern. 'I didn't realize this was going to be so difficult for you,' she said gently. 'I mean, I know you don't see each other often, but you've always kept in touch.'

'Only on birthdays and at Christmas. As a matter of fact she's forty today, so I'd planned a bit of a celebration tonight. It won't happen now, of course, because she's not going to be here, is she?'

'You surely can't blame her for a flight being delayed.'

'No, of course not, but this is what it's like with her. Something always comes up or goes wrong, or gets in the way. Nothing's ever straightforward, and even though it might not be her fault, she always manages to let me down somehow, and I've got a horrible feeling it's not going to be any different now.'

Molly was sitting cross-legged on Allison's bed wearing only her bra and a thong. Her eyes were closed, her arms were folded across her breasts as candlelight flickered like tiny wavelets over her skin. Allison, Cecily and Donna stood at the foot of the bed, dressed in these wigs and stuff Cecily had brought, holding hands and chanting softly. The sound of their girlish voices mingled with the haunting melody on the CD, the rhythm fading and building, the heady perfume of incense and oils making Molly feel a bit sick.

'We accept you Molly Kiernan,' they intoned, over and over. 'We accept you Molly Kiernan.'

After a while Allison moved forward, her black crinkly wig glinting like silvery wires in the candlelight. 'I am your sponsor, Molly, so do you promise never to let me down?'

'I promise,' Molly responded, eyes still closed.

Cecily said, 'Molly, do you swear to obey the rules of the Goddess Lilith?'

'I swear,' Molly said. It was like, really hot in the room, but for some reason she kept shivering, and feeling afraid of forgetting her lines, even though she didn't have very many.

'Do you understand that if you break the rules you will be banished, never to return?' Cecily asked.

'I understand.'

'Do you swear to put our Goddess before all others?'

'I swear.'

'She will be your one true mother now.'

'My one true . . .' Molly swallowed, '. . . mother,' she finished.

Cecily picked up a bottle. 'Lie down, Molly Kiernan,' she instructed.

Obediently Molly unfolded her legs and lay back on the bed, arms at her sides. She felt like, dead embarrassed now, being the only one in her underwear, so she kept her eyes closed, and tried to pretend she was having a dream.

Cecily held the bottle over her and poured. The oil was soft and cool as it pooled on to her skin. 'Lilith has decreed that your heart and womb will be torn from your body if you betray us,' she warned. 'Your tongue will be cut from your throat, your eyes plucked from your head.' She poured more oil on to Molly's skin and began gently to massage it in, while Molly kept her doubts about Lilith to herself.

'Do you swear you are a virgin?' Cecily asked.

'I swear,' Molly responded.

'Do you promise to lose your virginity as laid down by our rules?'

'I promise.'

'Open your legs, Molly Kiernan.'

Feeling like, totally freaked out now, Molly parted her legs an inch.

Donna stepped forward, hands clasped together as though in prayer.

'I, Donna Ringwold, do honour your virginity,' she said, bowing before Molly. She moved aside and Allison took her place.

'I, Allison Fortescue-Bond, do honour your virginity,' she echoed, bowing too.

Cecily continued to massage. 'Your virginity is honoured by us all,' she told Molly. 'There are six steps to be taken before you can lose it. Are you willing to take them?'

'Yes,' Molly answered.

'Then recite now from the Oracle of Lilith.'

Obediently Molly began to chant the words she had learned by heart.

> '"I dance life for myself,
> I am whole, I am complete.
> I live my sexuality to please myself
> and pleasure others.
> I express it as it needs to be expressed,
> from the core of myself.
> I am female, I am sexual, I am power."'

'Now speak the name of the man you have chosen to take your virginity,' Cecily said.

A quiver of nerves stole Molly's voice. She tried again. 'Brad Jenkins,' she whispered.

'We call upon the great Goddess Lilith to hear Brad Jenkins,' Cecily cried. There was a moment's silence, then she said, 'Our great Goddess hears and approves Brad Jenkins. Together with Lilith we will help you to achieve your goal. You are one of us now. Your desires are ours, your passions shall be fulfilled, your loves achieved. You will dress, think and speak according to our rules. You will follow the Six Steps. Get up Molly Kiernan and seal your solemn vows.'

Molly got up and stood next to the bed.

'You may dress now, except for your shoes,' Cecily told her, eyeing Molly's new trainers. 'They are the token of our commitment to you, so in gratitude you will say a prayer of thanks to us, before putting them on.'

When she was dressed Molly dropped to her knees, and putting her hands together she recited the prayer Cecily had given her to learn. 'I thank you Daughters of Lilith for making me a member of your exclusive society. I honour and respect you. I promise to obey the rules, and I will always treasure this token of your commitment.' As she finished, she picked up the trainers, feeling a tremor of pure pleasure, for they were sooo cool.

The others applauded and Cecily put a hand on Molly's head. 'You are now a full member of the Daughters of Lilith,' she declared, 'which entitles you to all privileges our secret club offers, starting with . . .' Her eyes were shining, her smile wide, as she threw back her head and cried, '*Getting drunk!*'

The others cheered and clapped, Deepest Blue went on the CD, and Bacardi Breezers were whisked from the fridge.

'So, was that cool, or what?' Allison demanded, linking Molly's arm and pulling her down on to one of the sofas.

'Totally amazing,' Molly responded, actually thinking it was, though still relieved to be dressed.

'I told you, Cecily's like, wild,' Allison went on.

'She made it all up herself. I mean, she got some of the stuff online, you know, from Lilith web sites and places, but the whole ceremony thing, you know, with the oil and chants and stuff, that's totally hers.'

'We've just got to get you up to speed with the steps now,' Cecily told her, 'because we're all on Step Three. So, have you ever kissed a boy?'

Molly kept her eyes down and nodded.

'So that's Step One taken care of,' Allison declared. 'Step Two's kissing with tongues. Have you ever done that?'

Since Molly had already confessed she hadn't, she could only shake her head.

'No big deal,' Allison told her. 'I reckon she can do two and three together, don't you?' she said to the others.

'So what's Step Three?' Molly asked.

They all started to giggle. 'It is like so out there,' Allison informed her. 'You are going to just die when we tell you.'

Chapter Three

The following day Katie was standing in the back car park of Chippenham station, watching the train pull away to continue its journey to Bristol. She checked her watch. Yes, this was definitely the train Michelle had insisted she'd be on, but no more than a handful of people had got off, and none of them was Michelle.

With a bitter, disappointed sigh she unlocked her old Fiesta and slid into the driver's seat, unable to stop herself remembering the last time this had happened, when Michelle had failed to turn up for their mother's funeral because, apparently, a bunch of total strangers in Mogadishu had needed her. So Katie could only wonder what insurmountable obstacle had thrown itself in her path this time to prevent her from being on that train.

As she turned out of the station slip road the Westinghouse traffic was already clogging up the one-way system, and there, right behind her, all of a sudden, was white-van man, that peril of the English roads, whom she'd happily force to slam into the back of her car if she could be bothered with the insurance hassle that came with it. Anyway, at least she hadn't gone to too much trouble for dinner, just a roast-in-the-bag chicken from Sainsbury's and a bottle of mediumly expensive white wine. The spare room was made up, of course, and she'd put some fresh flowers in a vase to brighten it up a bit. She'd even ironed the sheets before putting them on the bed, something she never did for herself and Molly.

Deciding to switch on the news, she hit the button, then almost had second thoughts when she realized it wouldn't surprise her to discover Michelle was in the headlines, for it was the kind of thing her sister usually managed to pull off without too much effort. Thanks to her earlier fame as an actress, people hadn't quite forgotten who she was yet, so maybe that was the cause of her delay, she was still up there at Heathrow, filling the press in on how many babies she'd managed to save since the last time she was in overprivileged, don't-know-where-we're-well-off England, and how many hungry mouths she'd helped feed while the British were wasting enough every week to feed several African nations for an entire year.

The lead news story turned out to be more on the debacle in Iraq, a situation that fascinated and infuriated Katie, for she loathed the hawkish elements of the US regime that had somehow dragged Britain into this, and she still couldn't believe the gullibility of half the American people who just weren't getting that they'd been sold a lemon. Next on the agenda was the story of two British girls who'd disappeared while on holiday in

Croatia. Apparently they'd gone to a nightclub sometime over the weekend and no-one had seen them since, though some pretty sinister details were starting to emerge now, about a couple of local men they'd become involved with. Katie's heart went out to their mothers, for the girls were only just nineteen, not that much older than Molly. The very idea of what the families must be going through now made her long for her old column which she'd frequently used to reach out to people in their times of need.

Finally breaking free of the snarling Chippenham logjam she drove across Bumper's Farm roundabout on the outskirts of town and spotting a neighbour coming the other way, waved out and wished she hadn't told anyone Michelle was coming. By six o'clock it would be all round the village that Mrs Parsons had seen Katie Kiernan driving back from the station alone.

Katie wasn't going to allow herself to dwell on that, though, she was just going to focus on the moment, which right now meant enjoying this next part of the short drive home. It was her favourite stretch, for it entailed cutting through the wide open Wiltshire countryside. The sky seemed so vast, and the fields so enticing and green as they spread out to the far horizon that it made her heart sing. As she approached the Farm Shop she considered stopping off to pick up some eggs for the morning, but then just drove on by. They could always have toast.

'I don't want bloody toast.'

She could hear Molly grumbling now. No matter what she served up lately, Molly never wanted it.

Eventually the road split, and she indicated to turn left, then almost immediately right at the old plane tree, into Mill Lane. A couple more miles of winding country lanes and she'd arrive at Membury Hempton. She'd like just to go on driving for a while, twisting and turning, dreaming and forgetting, pretending she didn't care where the hell Michelle was, refusing to admit that she was now more worried than ever about what was going to happen to Molly when she'd gone.

When she drove into the small parking bay outside their cottage she could already hear the music blaring from an upstairs window. She wondered which she dreaded most, the bone-jarring beat, or silence. It had to be silence of course, because at least when the music was on, she knew Molly was at home.

As she stepped out into a full assault from the latest boy band, she could only feel thankful that Mr and Mrs Preddy next door were hard enough of hearing not to be disturbed by the noise. Not so the neighbours who lived in one of the bigger houses, at the start of Sheep Lane, for they'd already been in touch with the local council and had even persuaded Reg Killet, the local bobby, to come and have a word. If any one of them could talk Molly into turning her damned stereo down, no-one would be happier than her mother, but so far no-one had succeeded. Taking the thing away hadn't worked either, because Molly had simply run away from home. OK, she'd only gone to Allison Fortescue-Bond's, and had come back the next morning, but not until Katie had agreed to return the stereo and never take it away again.

Sighing, she pushed open the gate and paused to pull a few dead fuschias from the baskets hanging either side of the kitchen window. The most pressing issue she faced with Molly right now was whether or not to give her some condoms, because if she was getting up to no good with boys over at Allison's she needed some protection. On the other hand, she didn't want Molly to think she was condoning it, and since it actually might not be happening, she just couldn't make up her mind what to do. Fourteen and already having sex. Her heart twisted with dismay, though she knew it happened, of course, she just hoped to God not to Molly.

As she opened the door Trotty came bounding up to greet her. She gave her a cuddle, threw her ball across the garden, then bracing herself went to check the answering machine. To her surprise there was no word from Michelle, but it was stupid to start getting upset and angry when something awful might have happened, so she should at least make an attempt to find out if it had.

She'd just turned up an old mobile number for Michelle when she realized the music had stopped, and almost at the same instant Molly came thundering down the stairs.

'So where is she?' she demanded, as she reached the bottom.

'I don't know. She wasn't on the train, and there are no messages. Has she called since you've been home?'

Molly shook her head. 'Why are you looking so bothered?' she demanded. 'I thought you didn't care if she came.'

Katie shook her head dismissively. 'Where are you going?' she asked, wanting to change the subject and trying to keep the disapproval from her tone as she eyed the low-slung jeans that all but revealed Molly's young pubes, and the too-tight bra that pushed her overdeveloped breasts into a womanly cleavage.

'Allison's. She's going to help me with my history, because she's already done it at her school.'

'What about something to eat?'

'Why don't you have something, you're too thin.'

'Charming,' Katie responded. 'This is supposed to be my Kate Moss look.'

'Well it's uniquely Katie Kiernan. And don't start sending me text messages while I'm out, they're embarrassing.'

Katie couldn't help but laugh.

It took a moment, then Molly was fighting off a smile too. 'Stop it!' she protested. 'You always do that.'

'What?'

'Make me laugh, and you are so not funny.'

'Have something to eat before you go,' Katie pleaded.

'I'll take an apple,' Molly dug into the bowl, and was about to leave when Katie noticed her trainers.

'Where did you get those shoes?' she demanded.

Molly looked down. 'In a shop,' she answered. 'Where do you think?'

'But we couldn't afford them,' Katie reminded her. 'So where did you get the money?'

Molly's face was puckering into resistance. 'Allison bought them for me, if you must know,' she said. 'Her parents are generous with her pocket money, unlike you.'

'If I had more, I'd give you more,' Katie said, though she might not, for she was afraid of what Molly might spend it on, 'but you know we don't have it these days.'

'We would if you hadn't stopped work.'

Katie sighed. 'I'm not going to argue,' she said. 'Just be back here by eight thirty. You've got school in the morning.'

'Yeah, like I'm really going to be back that early,' Molly sneered, and crunching into the apple she waltzed out of the door.

Katie stood at the window watching her until she disappeared from view, then returning to her address book she began dialling the mobile number she'd found for Michelle. After five rings Michelle's recorded voice came down the line asking the caller to leave a message.

'Hi, it's me,' Katie said. 'I was wondering what happened to you. Please call and let me know.'

After ringing off she popped the chicken in the oven. Might as well cook it anyway. Trotty was nothing if not a willing dinner companion, generally ending up with most of Katie's food, and Molly could always have it cold with a salad when she came in, hopefully by half past eight.

Out of habit she turned on Radio 4 to listen to the news, in case something new had developed in the last half an hour. Of course it hadn't, but by the time the headlines were over she realized there was no point going on avoiding how worried she was about Michelle. 'I know she always manages to let me down somehow,' she said to Judy on the phone, 'but she called from Karachi last night to tell me what time she was arriving at Heathrow, and which train she'd be on, provided there were no more delays. If there were she said she'd let me know, so I don't understand what can have happened.'

'Have you checked with the airline that she was actually on the flight?'

'No. They don't give out that kind of information normally. Oh hang on, someone's trying to get through, with any luck it'll be her,' and switching over the lines she said, 'Hello?'

'Oh hi, Katie. It's Audrey Wilkes here, just wondering if you're going to be at the parish council meeting later. I'm afraid I can't make it, and we really need someone to force it home about clearing those footpaths. It's a disgrace the way they've been allowed to grow over since the foot and mouth ep . . .'

'Yes, yes of course,' Katie interrupted, knowing all about it, since she was the one who'd first introduced it. 'I'll be there, if I can. I'm afraid I have to go now though,' and switching back to Judy she said, 'I'm going to contact the police at Heathrow. I'm not sure what they can do, but . . . Oh God, there's someone else on the line now.'

'Call me back when you've finished,' Judy said. 'I'm in the middle of cooking the boys' tea.'

'Hello?' Katie said, taking the next call.

'Katie, it's Tom. Is this a good time?'

'Tom! No, yes, it's fine. Have you spoken to Michelle?'

'No, but I was hoping to. Didn't she get there yet?'

'No, and I haven't heard from her either. When did you last speak to her?'

'She called me from the airport in Karachi, just before she took off this morning.'

'Not since?'

'No, she can't. My apartment in Lahore's been turned over and one of the things they took was my cellphone. I'm in Karachi now, in a hotel. Let me give you the number.'

Quickly she grabbed a pen from the table drawer, jotted down the number and said, 'I was about to call the airport police.'

'Do that,' he told her. 'I'll try the airline, see if I can find out if she actually got on the flight. Call me back as soon as you have any news.'

'Same goes for you, if you hear anything, please let me know.'

A few minutes later Katie was being put through to the duty officer at Heathrow. After explaining why she was calling, she was left on hold for what felt like an eternity, until the same voice came back on the line saying, 'I'm sorry madam, her name's not appearing on our records anywhere, and as she's not a minor, or a danger to the community, I'm afraid there's not really anything we can do to help you. Maybe you should try the transport police to see if there have been any accidents. I can give you the number.'

Michelle spun round as the door opened and the customs officer who'd brought her to this room almost three hours ago came back in. 'For God's sake! What's going on?' she demanded. 'My sister's waiting. No-one will let me use a phone . . .'

71

'I'm sorry to have kept you,' he interrupted, apparently unfazed by her outburst. 'If you'd like to follow me you can collect your bags and be on your way now.'

Startled, but needing no further prompting, she was almost at the door before she said, 'Can you tell me why I've been held all this time?'

'It was merely procedure,' he responded, standing aside for her to go out ahead of him.

'You mean everyone who comes in from Pakistan has to go through this?'

He merely gestured for her to cross the office where two uniformed women were working at the computers, and a Middle-Eastern-looking man was seated in the waiting room beyond.

Back down in the arrivals hall she found her luggage and holdall, still on its trolley, and looking very much as though it hadn't moved since she'd been parted from it.

'Just one question before I go,' she said, turning to the officer. 'Has there been any sign of my lost bag?'

'I'm afraid not,' he replied, and with a polite nod he disappeared behind the screens, leaving her to make her way out.

Immediately she was through she delved into her holdall to look for her phone. Unable to lay a hand on it, she eased her trolley out of the traffic, and started to pull everything out. To her annoyance it didn't seem to be there. She checked again, then, wondering if it had somehow got transferred to her suitcase while it was being searched, she started to rummage in that too. It wasn't there either, but since she had no intention of going back to confront anyone, she steered her trolley to a payphone, dialled 192 and prayed Katie wasn't ex-directory, even though as an ex-columnist, she almost certainly would be.

As it turned out she didn't even get that far, because it seemed 192 wasn't the number to call any more. Since she didn't have a pen handy to make a note of the alternatives, she banged the phone down and decided to go and hire herself a car rather than start messing around with coaches and trains now.

By the time she drove out of the airport she'd managed to grab herself a sandwich and rent a mobile phone along with the car, which meant she could call Tom and get Katie's number from him.

'Hi, it's me!' she cried, hearing his voice, then groaned as she realized she was speaking to a recording. After the bleep she said, 'Tom, are you there? Pick up if you are. It's me.'

She waited, but nothing happened, so she rang off and tried his mobile.

'Hello?'

'Tom?' she said curiously, almost certain the voice wasn't his.

'Who is speaking please?'

'Sajid? Is that you?'

'Who is speaking please?' the voice repeated.

'I'm sorry, I must have the wrong number,' she said, and rang off.

She tried again, and got the same voice.

'Damn!' she muttered, dropping the phone back on the passenger seat. Either his phone had been stolen, which happened all the time over there, or for some reason she kept connecting with another number.

Well, the only thing to do now was continue on to Katie's and hope she could find the way. As far as she remembered it was fairly simple once she left the M4, though in the dark it might prove a bit of a challenge.

The parish council meeting had gone on much longer than Katie had expected, so it was almost nine o'clock by the time she hurried out of the village hall, needing to get back to take her medication. She was hoping Michelle might have turned up by now, or at least left a message, but apart from Trotty the house was empty when she got there, and there was no blinking light on the machine.

After taking her morphine, she stood against the sink, catching her breath after a long swallow of water, and tried not to be worried about Molly. She often came back half an hour later than she was supposed to, so she wouldn't text her yet. She just wished she knew what she got up to over there at Allison's, but no amount of asking ever seemed to elicit a straight answer, and she didn't really have any grounds to ban her from going. For the moment at least, she just had to live with it.

Sighing, she took her nightly dose of senna and was just wondering what to do next about trying to track down Michelle when she heard a car pulling up outside. Praying it wasn't the police bringing bad news, or Molly with a boyfriend old enough to drive, she watched from the window, waiting for the headlights to go out so she could see who it was. When a tall, dark-haired woman got out she didn't recognize her immediately. It was only when she waved, cheerfully, that she realized it was Michelle.

Relief quickly gave way to annoyance at the light-heartedness of Michelle's manner, as though she were expecting a hearty welcome in spite of being four hours late without so much as a phone call. So instead of going to greet her, Katie turned from the window and set about making herself some tea.

There were three knocks on the back door before Michelle put her head round. 'Hello, can I come in?' she said, managing to look gorgeous, sheepish and playful all in one go, until she registered the tremendous change in Katie and was unable to hide the shock.

'Yes of course,' Katie responded, spooning tea into the pot.

After closing the door Michelle dropped her backpack on the floor and stood looking awkwardly around. The place seemed bigger than she remembered, but every bit as English and homely, though Katie's attitude was causing a bit of a chill.

'Sorry I'm late,' she said, trying to ignore it. 'I was . . .'

'It's all right. It doesn't matter,' Katie cut in.

Michelle took a breath and tried again. 'So how are you?' she asked.

'Fine, thank you.'

When she didn't look up Michelle glanced around again. 'I wasn't quite sure what to expect,' she said, 'your letter . . .'

'Is that all you have?' Katie enquired, looking down at the backpack.

'No. There's a suitcase in the car. They've lost my other one.'

'I see. So that's why you're late?'

'Not really, no. I had a strange thing happen at the airport, they . . .'

'It's OK, you don't have to explain. I'm used to you not turning up when you say you will.'

'Listen, I'm sorry,' Michelle said, colouring slightly. 'I'd have called if I could, but my phone . . .'

'I said you don't have to explain,' Katie reminded her. 'Tom called. He wants you to call him back.'

Michelle looked at the phone and felt uncertain about what to do.

Katie picked up the kettle and poured hot water over the tea. She knew she should be trying harder to be more welcoming, but right now she just couldn't. 'What happened to your hair?' she asked, glad that the glowing blondeness wasn't going to be dazzling her into constant reminders of her own grey fuzz.

'I had it cut, and it changed colour,' Michelle replied, running her fingers through it. 'It just went darker.'

'It doesn't suit you. You looked better before.'

Michelle smiled and shrugged. 'Oh well,' she said, and shoved her hands into the back pockets of her jeans.

Tearing her eyes away from the long, shapely thighs and gently rounded hips, and thinking there was no contest which of them was the skinniest now, Katie tugged open the fridge door to take out the bowl of salad she'd made for Molly. It was unlikely Molly would want it anyway, and if she was hungry when she came in she could always have a chicken sandwich, or beans on toast.

'Is Molly here?' Michelle asked.

'No. She should be back any minute though. Why don't you sit down? Or you can go and freshen up. You probably remember where the bathroom is.'

'Actually, I will if you don't mind,' Michelle answered, picking up her backpack. 'I'll just be a couple of minutes.'

'No rush, it's only salad, and the tea needs to brew. Your room's the one at the end, where you stayed before.'

A few minutes later the back door opened and Molly wobbled in.

'Ah, just in time,' Katie told her, unable to stop herself looking for love bites or syringe marks. Fortunately there were none, however her eyes seemed much too bright and unless Katie was mistaken she'd just got a whiff of alcohol. 'Would you like some salad with your chicken, or would you prefer a sandwich?' she asked.

'Salad in a sandwich,' Molly answered, tugging open the fridge door. 'What juice have we got?'

'Apple or passion fruit.'

Molly took down the carton of passion fruit, filled a glass then slumped down at the table.

'So, did you have a nice evening?' Katie enquired, buttering some bread.

'Yeah, it was cool.'

'Did you do your history?'

'Yeah, whatever,' Molly answered.

Katie glanced over her shoulder. 'I hope you didn't walk back across the fields. You know I'd rather you use the main road at night.'

'I used the main road, *all right*. Honestly!'

Katie put the sandwich on the table, and topped up Molly's juice. 'Have you been drinking?' she demanded, catching the glass as Molly almost knocked it over.

'*No-oh!*'

Katie stared at her hard, but said no more as Michelle was coming back down the stairs.

'Is that Molly?' Michelle said, stepping into the kitchen. 'My goodness, you're so grown-up, and so pretty.'

Molly scowled and finished a mouthful of food before saying, 'So you came then? We thought you weren't going to bother.'

'Molly!' Katie snapped.

Michelle smiled over her surprise. 'Of course I came,' she responded. 'I said I would. I just got a little held up.'

Molly shrugged and got up from the table. 'I'm going to bed,' she told them. 'Excuse me.'

Michelle stood aside.

'Don't be up till all hours on that computer,' Katie called after her.

No reply, just the heavy tread of footsteps and slam of a bedroom door.

Michelle looked at Katie, but her expression was stony, so judging it best not to comment, she merely walked to the teapot and started to pour. 'Nice flowers,' she remarked lightly, carrying the cups to the table. 'Are they from your garden?'

Katie glanced at them. They were the ones she'd removed from Michelle's room earlier. 'No. They were on offer at the supermarket,' she answered crisply.

Michelle waited for her eyes to come back to her. 'Katie, I'm really sorry I was late,' she said gently. 'There was nothing I could do about the plane being delayed, and when I arrived this afternoon . . .'

'You should call Tom,' Katie said, cutting her off. 'He was worried when we didn't know where you were. He left a number. It's next to the phone. Apparently his flat was burgled and they took his mobile.'

Michelle frowned. 'I guess that will account for someone else answering it,' she remarked, picking up the number Katie had jotted down. 'What's he doing in Karachi?' she said.

'He didn't say.'

'OK. I'll use my mobile, save your bill.'

'It doesn't matter. You can use that one.'

Though Michelle would rather have spoken to Tom in private, she didn't want to offend Katie, so pressing in the number she got through to a hotel operator and asked for him by name. After one ring his voice came down the line saying, 'Tell me it's you.'

She smiled. 'It's me,' she said, wishing beyond anything that she was with him now. 'What are you doing in Karachi?'

'Long story. Are you at Katie's? When I called . . .'

'Yes, I'm here. I got stopped at the airport, and couldn't contact anyone.'

'What happened?'

Seizing the opportunity to explain to Katie too,

79

she said, 'Well, they searched my luggage – apart from the bag that didn't turn up, which means my laptop is still in transit somewhere – then they searched me, not a pleasant experience, and after that I was taken to a custody office and questioned.'

'What about?'

Regretting Katie was there now, she said, 'They wanted to know if I'd been working with certain . . . groups, or had any connections . . . Obviously I said no,' she added for Katie's benefit, knowing she'd probably seen straight through the euphemisms. Then, wanting to get off the subject, she said, 'Katie told me about your apartment. Was much taken?'

'Cellphone, computer, books, all my papers.'

'Any idea who it was?'

'No-one's admitting to seeing anyone, but there's not much doubt what they were after. You remember the hand-delivered package that turned up when we came back from the airport? It was from Josh Shine.'

Michelle's eyes widened with interest, for they'd always suspected Josh Shine, the US Embassy's Political Officer in Islamabad, of some very shady connections. 'So what was in the package?' she asked.

'It's probably best you don't know. You've got enough going on over there, and the last thing you need is to be associated with something like this. Though I'm guessing that's why your bags were searched today, to find out if I'd slipped you anything.'

'So do you think they've held on to my computer and phone too?'

'Probably. They'll want to see who you've contacted in the last few days, whether or not I've emailed you anything that might concern them, that sort of thing.'

'So does any of this confirm what we've always thought about Josh?'

'That he's CIA? If he is, then the fact that he's passed this on to me would suggest he's broken ranks. I just wish I knew where the hell he was. We talked briefly on the phone yesterday when he told me to meet him here in Karachi. No sign yet. No word either, but tomorrow's another day, and right now I'm more interested in you, and how the hell I'm going to get along without you?'

Feeling her heart warming she said, 'I've been wondering the same thing.'

'We have to talk, sort something out,' he told her. 'When I'm done here, I'm coming over there. I'd kind of like to see Katie again anyway. How is she?'

Remembering the shock she'd felt on seeing her, and acutely aware of her being there now, Michelle said, 'Why don't you say hi?'

'Sure.'

She turned and held out the phone. 'He wants to say hello.'

Appearing surprised, and even a little pleased, Katie took it and said, 'This is becoming a habit.'

'I hope you're not complaining.'

She smiled. 'No, not at all. So I hope your mind's at rest now, she's arrived in one piece.'

'I'll sleep better,' he confessed.

Unable to stop herself wishing someone cared about her the same way, she said, 'I've only heard

81

Michelle's end, but it sounds as though you've got your hands on something you shouldn't have.'

'That's about the gist of it,' he responded dryly. 'It's pretty dynamite, if it's genuine, and I'm beginning to think it must be, given the fuss it seems to be causing.'

'Then don't do anything stupid.'

'I'm touched you should care.'

'Stop flattering yourself on my phone bill,' she retorted.

Laughing, he said, 'Can I say goodnight to Michelle?'

'Of course,' and getting up from the table she passed the phone back.

'Hi,' Michelle said softly.

'I miss you,' he told her.

'I'd believe you if it weren't too soon to be true.'

'OK, then I'll miss you tomorrow.'

'I doubt it. You've got a lot going on.'

'Jesus, what does a man have to do to make a woman believe he loves her?'

'You could always tell her,' she responded.

'I thought I just did.'

She waited.

'OK, how about I save it till I see you?' he murmured.

'Then don't make it too long.'

After putting the phone down she went to join Katie at the sink, picking up a tea towel to dry the dishes, her mind still full of Tom, and how much she wished she was with him.

'So, I take it you two are an item now,' Katie commented, failing to keep the tartness from her voice.

82

'I can't say I'm surprised, it was always on the cards.'

'It only happened just before I left,' Michelle confessed.

'Really? Then it must have been particularly inconvenient having to come here. Perhaps I should apologize.'

'Katie, for heaven's sake! Of course I'm sorry to leave Tom, but there's nothing to apologize for. I'd never have let you down. Surely you must know that.'

'Because you're worried about what other people might think.'

Shocked, Michelle slammed down the tea towel. '*Katie!* Where on earth is all this coming from?' she demanded. 'I know we haven't always . . .'

'I'm just saying, if you and Tom only got together recently, you can't be too thrilled about having your future with him wrecked by a teenager who's not even yours, can you?'

'She's my niece, so I'd say that makes her mine.'

'But it would be perfectly understandable if you resented us for needing you when you'd obviously rather be elsewhere.'

'If that's what you think then you're wrong. I don't resent you, but I'm not going to stand here arguing with you either.'

Though further cutting remarks were on the tip of Katie's tongue, she bit them back and ran more hot water into the bowl to start cleaning the roasting pan. It wasn't as though she wished something bad had happened to Michelle on the way here, but she might be finding all this a lot easier to cope with if it had. She just hoped the new and now thwarted romance wasn't going to be rubbed in her face by daily phone calls, because that would make it very hard to stand. 'I think you should tell me a bit more about these terrorist groups,' she said crisply.

'There are none,' Michelle responded. 'I was just asked about it at the airport, presumably because I'd flown in from Pakistan.'

'But whatever Tom's getting involved in is terrorist-related.'

'It sounds that way, yes.'

Katie's face was pinched and angry as she turned to look at her. 'This is what makes me so sick about you,' she said tightly. 'You turn up here, four hours late, with all your baggage and intrigue, and you haven't given a single thought, have you, to the kind of position you might have put me and Molly in.'

'That's absolutely not true!' Michelle cried.

'If they questioned you about terrorist connections at the airport, don't you think that's something you should have mentioned by now?'

'Katie, I tried to tell you what happened, but you wouldn't listen.'

'That's right, blame me! You're the one involved with terrorists, but it's my fault . . .'

'Stop being ridiculous,' Michelle cut in. 'I can't help what's happening with Tom, but it's got nothing to do with me . . .'

'What's the matter with you?' Katie seethed, throwing out her hands. 'Your bags were searched . . .'

'But they didn't find anything, so there's not a problem. I'm not involved.'

'How can you say that?'

Michelle took a breath and held out her hands. 'Katie, listen,' she said, trying to calm things down, 'I understand why you're angry, and you have a right to be, but I've already apologized for being late, and I've told you I'm here for you . . .'

'But you don't *want* to be, do you? You'd much rather be over there with Tom, and who can blame you? No-one in their right mind would want to be stuck here with me, least of all you . . .'

'Stop putting words in my mouth!' Michelle shouted. 'Now I don't want to hear any more. I'm jet-lagged, homesick – yes, homesick *and* missing Tom, for which I will not apologize, so I'm going to get my suitcase, say goodnight and go up to bed. With any luck we'll both be in better moods in the morning.'

As she stormed out of the back door Katie stood where she was, smarting and hurting, and detesting her own behaviour to a point where she could actually howl with shame. However, her pride wasn't about to allow any kind of climb-down, so letting the dishwater run out of the sink, she dried her hands and before Michelle came back she took herself off up the stairs to bed.

Chapter Four

Tom and Josh Shine, a short, thin man in his early sixties, were seated either side of the coffee table in Tom's hotel room, going over the documents Josh had sent in the package. Two were different maps of the same location, the other three were mainly lists of names, some of which were of people or political groups, while others detailed various types of arms and explosives. Virtually everything was written in Punjabi or Arabic.

'It seems pretty clear what it is,' Josh was saying, his long, narrow face appearing pinched and tired as they pored over the documents that bore no proof of origin, or even a suggestion of where they might have come from. 'It's still going to need a good translator, but I'm guessing the names refer to sleeper cells and their locations, while the map has got to be the target area for a terrorist hit.'

Tom had studied it all very closely over the past thirty-six hours, so he knew he could be on to a major story here. However, he wasn't going to get too excited yet, for Pakistan's bazaars and madrasas – Islamic schools – were rife with plots, and too many of his colleagues had shelled out small fortunes for information that ended up leading them straight down a dead end. 'Where did you actually get this?' he asked.

Josh's eyes were impenetrable as he said, 'That's about the most prudent question you could ask, and the answer is, it came to me in the bag from Washington, with your name on it.'

Tom was taken aback. 'But if it's genuine this is a plot with some huge potential, which I'm guessing the CIA is on to or you wouldn't be sitting here, so why give it to me?'

Josh reached into his inside pocket, drew out a folded sheet of paper and handed it over.

It was an email dated two days ago from a dot-gov address and headed 'Making the Link'. It consisted mainly of web-site hotlinks with three short lines at the bottom that read

P2OG
Package arriving tomorrow.
Pass to Tom Chambers.

Tom looked up. 'Who's it from?' he asked.

'I tried replying to get more information,' Josh answered, 'but my message just comes back undeliverable.'

'It's a government address though.'

Josh nodded.

Unable to work out whether he knew more than he was telling, Tom looked at the email again. 'Have you tried accessing any of these sites?'

'I didn't want to alert anyone at the embassy.'

Tom was slightly incredulous. 'If you're right about it being Pakistani intelligence who emptied my apartment, then we could assume it was someone at the US Embassy who tipped them off,' he pointed out.

Josh didn't argue.

'What about P2OG? What does it mean?'

'I'm guessing those web sites will answer that.'

Tom put the email aside and returned to the handwritten lists. At the top of one was a date, several months hence. 'If this is the date of the planned attack,' he said, 'then it's of major significance.'

Josh nodded agreement. 'Just prior to the next presidential election,' he said.

'So someone in Washington's planning to use this to their advantage in some way,' Tom commented, as his eyes travelled on down the list. 'Hell, even without a full translation,' he said, 'I can tell you that some of these names belong to Jaish el-Mohammed.'

'Which is probably the most extreme Islamist group operating in this country,' Josh expounded. 'Do your contacts go that deep?'

Tom fixed him with a coldly penetrating stare. 'Even if they did, I'd need a lot more than this before I'd start messing with those guys.'

Josh didn't argue.

'I want to pull Farukh Hassan in on this,' Tom said, referring to a Pakistani journalist whom both he and Josh knew well.

Josh nodded. 'A wise decision.'

They both looked round as someone knocked on the door.

'Who is it?' Tom shouted.

'You order coffee?'

Tom's eyes went to Josh. A second later they were stuffing the documents back in the envelope.

'No, no coffee,' Tom called out.

They heard a room-service trolley rattle away.

'Call Farukh now, get him over here,' Josh said, dabbing the sweat from his neck. 'And tell him to take a good look round before he comes in.'

After switching on the TV to drown his voice, Tom made the call and turned back to Josh. 'If this information really has come from a Washington insider – and for the moment I won't dispute that – then I'd like to know how reliable they are.'

'I wish I could tell you,' Josh responded. 'But I don't know who sent the package or the email, I'm just doing as I was requested, and passing it on to you.'

Tom's expression was grim as his gaze returned to the package. 'You know what this is starting to look like?' he said. 'An inside job on the US government. The CIA, or Defense Intelligence, or someone, presumably including the White House, has got knowledge of a possible terrorist attack, which for some reason they're not acting on, or making public, presumably because they can see some future use for it, either by letting it happen or choosing their own time to block it. However, someone else in Washington's trying to get news of it out there now, someone who clearly doesn't want to be identified as the source.'

'It doesn't have to be someone in Washington,' Josh responded. 'It could be someone in London.'

Tom's eyes narrowed. 'But this here came in the bag from Washington,' he reminded him.

'The maps are pinpointing a British location,' Josh stated, 'and I don't see anyone in Washington holding this back from their best buddies, do you?'

Tom merely continued to stare at the maps. What this current administration would and wouldn't do had long since ceased to inhabit an area of moral certitude for him.

'If someone in London does know about this plot,' Josh continued, 'and say we're right about it being used as some kind of leverage in the presidential elections . . .'

'But how?' Tom interrupted.

Josh shrugged. 'This is all surmise,' he said. 'I'm just running with the theory that someone in London might want this exposed, and is working with a contact in Washington to do it. Whichever way, I'd say the goal is to undermine the current administration.'

Since there were no grounds for arguing with that, Tom got up and started to pace. With so little to go on it would be easy to let the imagination run riot and come up with the biggest story of his life here, but just as easy would be to get it spectacularly wrong and end up as one very dead victim of some extremist jihad cell. So if he did go any further with this – and he knew already it wasn't in him to resist it – he must never lose sight of the fact that he was almost certainly being used in some deadly political game, or that he was an American in a deeply hostile land.

'Which is why you should leave Pakistan now,' Farukh told him, after he'd arrived and Tom had brought him up to speed with it all. 'It is impossible for you to penetrate any of these organisations to the level that's needed, and even if you could, if the Americans want this hushed up for some reason, it'll make no difference who they use to stop you. Jaish el-Mohammed or Pakistani Intelligence, or their own undercover operatives, the result will be the same.'

Having half expected this response, Tom looked at Josh Shine.

'I've got nothing to add to that,' Josh told him.

It was a sobering thought that could easily daunt a lesser man, and Tom had to admit, he was taking some pause.

'While you make up your mind,' Farukh said, 'we could at least have a look at some of these web sites to find out what P2OG actually means, because it's probably some kind of key.'

As Farukh unpacked his laptop Tom picked up the maps and looked them over again. 'There has to be some kind of British involvement here,' he said, thinking of Michelle's experience at Heathrow. 'The question is, do they have the whole picture, or are they just being used by the Americans in ways they know nothing about?'

'A quick answer to that is, it wouldn't be the first time,' Josh said. 'But no matter what the Americans have got going down, experience has taught me never to underestimate the Brits.'

Tom cocked an eyebrow, and after a moment or two a slow smile began to curve his lips.

Michelle jumped at the sound of a gunshot as it ricocheted across the fields. It took only a second to remember where she was, and that there was no need to dive for cover, or rush to the aid of someone who might be hurt, but nevertheless her heart was already pounding.

Ignoring it, she continued clearing weeds from a flower bed, while attempting to listen to the portable radio she'd perched on the edge of the lawn. When in England, like Katie, she generally tuned to Radio 4, but right now she was applying herself to a local pop station in an effort to learn a little about Molly's world. She might be doing better were she able to stop her mind drifting to Tom, wondering what he was doing now, and hoping there wasn't a sinister reason behind his failure to call in the last few days. From the little he'd told her on the phone, it would be easy to start tormenting herself with all kinds of imagined horrors that weren't even close to the truth, so she had to stop putting herself through it, and try to stay focused on why she was here.

Almost immediately her heart sank, for it had been three days now and neither Katie nor Molly, who was clearly taking a lead from her mother, had yet shown any signs of welcoming her. Not that there had been any repeats of the horrible explosion the night she'd arrived, but her efforts to make friends since had mostly met with a stony resistance, and even the gifts she'd brought had been treated with a cursory disdain.

'I'm not wearing any of that crap,' she'd heard Molly remark scathingly to her mother, as they'd taken the jewels upstairs. 'It's gross.'

'It's all right, you don't have to,' Katie had responded.

'And you can't wear those earrings. You'd look like a tart.'

'Ssh, she doesn't have much of an idea what we like here,' Katie said quietly, 'so just put it away in your bedroom and hope she forgets all about it.'

It wasn't so much the ingratitude, or even condescension, that Michelle was finding difficult, it was more the way they were shutting her out. She really had come here to help, but she was almost starting to regret it now, and if it carried on much longer like this the temptation to take the next plane back to her own world might just turn itself into a ticket.

However, she was hopeful of some kind of breakthrough in the next hour or so, for Katie was inside now, composing an article for the *New Statesman*, which, apparently, was the first commission she'd been able to take up in months. From the way she'd responded when the call had come earlier, there was no doubt the request had been a much-needed boost for her morale.

'And there was me thinking I'd been written off as dead already,' she'd laughed after putting the phone down to the editor, and she'd looked so delighted to be remembered that Michelle had instantly forgiven her for the jewels, and wanted to hug her. Instead she'd offered to take over walking the dog and tidying up the garden so that Katie could work in peace for the rest of the morning.

The church clock hadn't long chimed midday when Katie emerged from the kitchen and took a deep, restorative breath of the Indian summer air. 'You know, I'm feeling on quite a high,' she confessed, coming across the lawn to join Michelle.

'Concocting a few thousand words for the *New Statesman* beats the hell out of writing a pain diary, which is about all I'm ever called upon to produce these days.'

Michelle sat back on her heels, shielding her eyes as she looked up at her. There was a flush of colour in Katie's cheeks and a lightness about her that had been missing until now, which just went to prove, Michelle thought, how important it was to feel needed. 'Is it very bad?' she asked.

Katie seemed baffled. 'Oh, the pain,' she said. 'No, no! All under control.'

Realizing she didn't want to discuss it, Michelle said, 'So what did you write about?'

Katie's smile turned wry. 'Would you believe, the pros and cons of preaching teenage abstinence?' she replied. 'It's proving pretty effective in the States, apparently, but as I'm generally suspicious of anything that comes from the religious right, which includes most of the current US policies, I'm reserving judgement and calling for a public debate here. Parents, teachers, children, unmarried mothers etc.'

'Sounds a good idea. What about Molly? Have you talked to her about sex at all?'

Katie sighed. 'Not recently,' she answered, perching on the arm of a wooden bench, 'she insists she knows all about it, which I'm sure she does, because God knows she's surrounded by enough of it, at school, on TV, in the teen magazines, on the Internet, and as far as I can make out half her friends are already doing it. In fact, I'm trying to decide whether or not to give her some condoms, because the last thing we need is another ghastly disease in the house, or, heaven forbid, a baby.'

'Does she actually have a boyfriend?'

'Not that I've been told about, but she's so keen to be a part of Allison Fortescue-Bond's crowd these days that I can't help thinking there's a boy involved somewhere. That's usually when we go off the rails, isn't it? And they're all in such a raging hurry to divest themselves of their innocence these days . . . I suppose we were too, though I was eighteen before I went all the way, and if I remember correctly you were about that age too.'

Michelle nodded. 'Nineteen, actually,' she said, 'and I'd been going out with Clive for about a year by then. God it was awful. I hated the first time, didn't you?'

Katie grimaced. 'I don't even want to think about it,' she responded. 'As I recall it was all lily-white thighs, goose-bumps and grunts in the back of an old Morris.'

Michelle laughed and groaned. 'Oh the romance of it,' she said, her mind drifting back to the many embarrassments and mistakes she'd endured over the years. Then, encouraged by how they'd finally managed to pass a few minutes without having it all collapse in a heap of old grudges and new fears, she tugged off her gloves and followed Katie inside.

'So, no more calls from Tom,' Katie commented, as Michelle began washing her hands.

Wishing she hadn't sounded quite so pleased about it, Michelle said, 'He'll be caught up in the story he's working on.'

Katie sniffed and nodded and unhooked a couple of mugs from the overhead beam. 'Still, you must feel a bit miffed that he hasn't made any contact at all since the other night, if your romance is so new.'

'Concerned more than miffed,' Michelle corrected. 'But I have to get used to the idea that I'm here now, and that he's going to carry on with his work, the way he always has.'

Katie dropped two tea bags into the mugs. 'So he's not planning to come and visit?' she said, going for the milk.

'Actually, he wants to, but I've no idea when it might be.'

A silence followed in which Michelle wondered what had happened to stir up the tension again, and Katie wished she could stop being snippy and just tell Michelle that she was sorry for the other night, and for coming between her and Tom, and for all the other injustices she'd done her over the years, but for some reason the words were stuck in her throat. Maybe she was just too much of a bitter and twisted old stick to be able to admit she was wrong, or maybe she was still too angry with Michelle for having a love life and a whole history of adventures with Tom when they'd had the freedom to be themselves and do the kinds of things Katie had only ever dreamt of. Whatever it was, she had to get her feelings under control, because being like this certainly wasn't going to change anything for her now, nor was it going to make life bearable while they were all living under the same roof.

'Can I read the article?' Michelle asked, genuinely interested, though using it as another attempt to be friendly.

Katie was about to answer when the sound of someone running across the garden made them both turn round.

'Mum! Mum!' Molly cried, swinging round the door. 'I forgot my phone this morning, like major crisis, and my thingy's started, so I've had to come home.'

'There's a new packet in the bathroom cabinet,' Katie told her, 'and don't throw the wrappers down the toilet.'

'Nag, nag, nag nag,' Molly muttered, running up the stairs.

Katie shot Michelle a glance. 'Well there's a relief,' she commented quietly. 'She's still irregular and I'm paranoid, not a soothing combination.' Then with a smile, 'I thought I was long past the days of waiting for a period, now here I am again. My own, if you're interested, have stopped altogether. Hysterectomy, instant menopause and chemotherapy. It's been a lot of fun around here these last few months.' Her eyes moved back to Michelle. 'It might even account for how edgy I've been with you, women in my hormonal condition aren't known for rational behaviour.'

More than willing to accept the olive branch, Michelle smiled and said, 'I probably haven't helped, so let's just put it behind us, shall we, and have that cup of tea.'

Ten minutes later Molly still hadn't reappeared, so Katie went upstairs to find out what had happened.

'Molly!' she cried, finding her at the computer.

'Go away!' Molly shouted. 'This is private.'

'I hope you're not in one of those chat rooms.'

'I said go away.'

'Don't speak to me like that. Now, you have to go back to school, so turn that thing off and get going.'

'I will when I've finished,' but she was already logging off, and after waiting for the screen to go dark she leapt up from her chair and came to give Katie a hearty hug and resounding kiss on the cheek.

'And how did I manage to deserve that?' Katie asked suspiciously.

'You just do. Can I take the charger to school, because my mobile's nearly flat?'

'Kissed for a charger. Go on, and try to say something nice to Michelle on your way past.'

'What for?'

'Just do it.'

'I'm not wearing those jewels . . .'

'Stop it.'

'You're laughing.'

'I am not. Now go.'

Michelle was sitting at the table reading Katie's article when Molly thundered down the stairs and unplugged the charger.

'Has your lost bag turned up yet?' Molly asked.

Surprised she'd remembered, Michelle said, 'No. Not yet. I called this morning to see if there was any news, they said they'd get back to me.'

Molly shrugged, and apparently satisfied with her attempt to be nice, sailed off out of the door to where the PE teacher was waiting in her car.

'Well, seems we're not devil-spawn today,' Katie remarked, coming into the kitchen and watching Molly go. 'Honestly, I thought my mood swings were bad enough, hers make me feel positively centred. Speaking of which, it's about time for my meditation, so I'll leave you to it. Feel free to try calling Tom if you like.'

Michelle glanced at the clock. 'Actually, I wouldn't mind checking my email, if I can use your computer. Robbie's probably sent a message, and some of the kids at the camp . . .'

'Help yourself,' Katie told her, gesturing towards the laptop she'd left open on the table, and she was about to start up the stairs when a car caught her eye out of the window. 'Is that someone coming in here?' she said, frowning.

Michelle peered over her shoulder and watched two middle-aged men in jeans, shirtsleeves and dark glasses getting out of a silver saloon car.

'Anyone you know?' Katie asked, as they headed towards the gate.

Michelle shook her head. 'I don't know anyone,' she reminded her.

'Then we must have won the lottery,' Katie decided, 'which would be a miracle since we don't do it. Do we have any long-lost relatives who might have passed on? They look a bit grim.'

'As far as I know it's just us,' Michelle answered, starting to feel vaguely uneasy.

'OK, let's find out who they are and what they want,' Katie declared, as the front doorbell rang, and walking round the side of the house, she said, 'Hello. Can I help you?'

The shorter and stockier of the two men reached into his pocket and started towards her. 'Detective Inspector Wilding,' he told her. 'This is FBI Legal Attaché Fellowes. We're looking for Michelle Rowe. Is she here?'

Katie turned as Michelle came to stand next to her.

'I'm Michelle Rowe,' she said, praying this wasn't going to be about Tom, while knowing it must be – just please God let him be safe, and don't let it be something to send Katie off the deep end again. 'How can I help you?'

Wilding hadn't removed his sunglasses, so it wasn't possible for her to read anything beyond his words. 'We're making enquiries about a friend of yours, Tom Chambers?' he told her.

'What about him?'

'The Pakistani authorities are interested to know when you were last in contact with him.'

Michelle's eyes flicked to the other man – and he needs an FBI agent to hold his hand while he asks this, she was thinking. 'Why would they want to know?' she enquired politely.

'He's been reported missing,' Wilding answered.

A pang of fear hit her heart. 'By whom?' She was looking straight at Fellowes. 'Who's reported him missing?'

Once again Wilding answered. 'The Pakistani authorities are trying to locate him,' he replied, which was actually no answer at all.

Wishing she'd made Tom tell her more about Josh Shine and the documents so she'd have a better idea of what she was dealing with now, she said, 'Why are they looking for him? Has he done something wrong?'

Ignoring the question again he said, 'Do you know where he is?'

'I assume still in Pakistan, but I can't tell you exactly where.'

'When was your last contact with him?'

Willing Katie not to contradict her, Michelle said, 'The day I left Pakistan.'

'You haven't spoken to him since?'

'It's only been five days.'

He allowed several seconds to elapse, then said, 'Are you aware that he has connections with certain fundamentalist groups in Pakistan?'

Her hands began clenching at her sides. 'He would call them contacts, or sources,' she responded.

'I'm sure he would, but if there's anything you can tell us about these *contacts* you'd be wise to.'

She said nothing.

He sighed. 'Miss Rowe, I doubt you need me to remind you what can happen to American journalists who get tied up with the wrong people in Pakistan,' he said.

Michelle knew very well what he was alluding to and felt disgusted that anyone would use the tragic and barbaric murder of one of Tom's colleagues in such an invidious way. 'Can I see your ID again, please?' she said, wanting them to know that she wasn't quite as intimidated as they'd no doubt like her to be.

Wilding reached into his pocket. After scrutinizing his badge, she turned to the FBI agent and waited for him to produce his. 'Thank you,' she said, satisfied that they were who they were claiming to be.

'Don't you want to help him?' Wilding enquired.

'If I thought he needed it, of course I would,' she replied.

'Oh, where he is, he needs it,' Wilding assured her.

Her face was taut as she said, 'I thought you didn't know where he was.'

'You understand what I'm saying. You know the territory. You know it's not a good place to disappear.'

Her only response was to stare at him, while the fear inside her grew. However, she and Tom had had too many run-ins with the likes of Wilding and Fellowes over the years for her to tell them anything until she'd tried tracking Tom down herself first.

Wilding shook his head in dismay. 'You're not doing him any favours,' he warned.

Still she said nothing.

He turned to Katie.

Michelle tensed, but to her relief Katie stayed silent.

'There comes a time,' Wilding told her, 'when it's wiser to reveal the identity of a source, or the whereabouts of someone who's in danger, who might not even know they're in danger, than to keep it hidden.'

'I'm afraid I don't know who his sources are,' Michelle responded. 'And I've already told you, I don't know where he is.'

Finally the FBI legal officer spoke. 'If you suddenly recover your memory,' he said, removing a card from his shirt pocket, 'my cell is on twenty-four/seven.'

Taking the card she folded it in her palm and watched as both men turned to leave. Katie remained at her side, watching too. The sun seemed suddenly very hot, and neither of them spoke until the car had reversed from its parking spot and disappeared up the lane, leaving them with birdsong and butterflies and the bizarre tranquillity of an idyllic country setting.

Michelle was on the point of turning round when Katie said, 'OK. I want you out of my house now.'

Michelle took a breath to protest.

'I don't want to hear it,' Katie raged. 'You just lied to them. They're police for God's sake, and this is the second time terrorism's raised its head since you've been here. I'm not waiting for the next. So just go upstairs, pack your belongings and go back to wherever the hell you came from.'

'Katie! Will you just listen?'

'I've heard enough. I don't want you here, Michelle, with all your lies and secrets and covering up for Tom. Now just take whatever's yours and please be gone by the time I get back,' and before Michelle could utter another word she marched across the garden and slammed out of the gate.

'I'm sorry,' Katie sobbed as Judy hugged her. 'I know I'm probably overreacting, but I was so incensed when I heard her lie . . .'

'Sssh, you don't have to apologize,' Judy soothed. 'You know my door's always open, and I'm glad I was here.'

'I just don't know what to do,' Katie said, pulling away and attempting to calm down. 'I thought we were getting somewhere, I started to open up and then the next thing I know the police are on my doorstep – what am I talking about, the *police*, like

103

it was Reg Killet on his pushbike just popped over from Chippenham nick. It was the anti-terrorist squad, or Special Branch or . . .'

'You don't know that . . .'

'I saw her face, Judy. And the other one was American. FBI, no less, and she damned well lied to them.'

'You need to talk to her,' Judy said. 'Let her explain what's happening, why she said what she did, and I'm sure it can all be sorted out.'

'Judy, for God's sake, we're talking about terrorism here. I know that's hard to digest when we're in the middle of Membury Hempton where the worst explosions we get are from George Arnold's rear end in church on Sundays . . . Don't laugh, it wasn't supposed to be funny. She's brought it with her, Jude. Whether she meant to or not, it's here, and I can't deal with it . You must understand that. Molly has to have someone she can feel safe and secure with, and while Michelle is . . .'

'Katie, stop! Take some deep breaths and count to ten. Make it a hundred, I'm in no hurry. No! Just do as I say. In, out, in, out. This is probably nowhere near as bad as you think, and if you just give her the chance to explain I'm sure you'll find she's needing to take a few deep breaths too. After all, she's the one who's just been told someone she loves is missing, or whatever he is, and we all know what happened to that poor American boy they took captive over there, so she's probably got the fear of God in her now. Keep breathing, then take some time to think about how she's feeling right now, and if, after you've discussed it, you still feel it's better for her to go, I'm sure it'll be a mutual agreement. I'm absolutely certain the last thing she wants is to cause you and Molly any more stress than you're already going through.'

Katie looked at her with tired, haunted eyes. 'You're right, of course,' she said. 'I'm too afraid of everything these days . . . I never used to be like this . . .'

'Stop being the victim,' Judy gently chided.

Katie's eyes closed and after a few moments she started to shake her head. 'It scares me half to death, but . . . I don't know. I'm glad she's here, and I don't actually want her to go . . .'

'Then talk to her. Find out why she lied, listen to what she has to say without going off the handle, and try to remember, this was the kind of intrigue you used to thrive on in your heyday, so go and start living again, girl, because, not to put too fine a point on it, you're going to be a long time dead.'

Michelle was sitting at the kitchen table when Katie returned, her face bloodless and strained, her whole demeanour showing the turmoil she was locked in.

She looked up as Katie came in, bracing herself for another onslaught of anger, but Katie merely came and sat down opposite her, bunching her hands on the table, and fixing her with eyes that were still wary, but a lot less hostile than before she'd stormed off.

'Are you OK?' Michelle asked.

'Yes. Are you?'

Michelle nodded. 'I want you to know,' she said,

105

'if I thought for one minute that I posed any kind of risk to you and Molly I wouldn't even dream of staying.'

Katie swallowed and nodded to show that she appreciated the words. 'Then tell me what that was all about,' she said. 'Why did you lie?'

'Because I didn't want them to think that we know anything about what Tom's involved in. It doesn't concern us . . .'

'But what *is* he involved in? Just what are we covering up here?'

'All I know is that someone we've long believed to be a CIA operative passed him some documents that, considering the fuss they're causing, must be classified. I don't know what's in them, Tom wouldn't tell me because he doesn't want us to get dragged in.'

'So Wilding and his federal friend. Who were they, exactly?'

'Wilding's badge was from the Metropolitan Police, so he could be anti-terrorist, Special Branch, or MI5 using the badge as a cover. And the FBI agent is presumably London based, because he was calling himself a legal attaché. That's the term they use when they're stationed outside the US.'

'So do you think Tom really is missing?'

'I don't know. He could just have gone underground for a while. There are people I can call, or email. Without my computer . . . I can go into town and find an Internet café if you'd rather I didn't use yours.'

'You can use mine,' Katie told her.

Michelle looked at her uncertainly. 'Are you sure? I mean, I don't want to . . .'

'Don't argue, I'm as keen as you are to know he's all right, so just use it.'

As Michelle typed in her emails Katie sat with her, wishing there was someone she could contact too to help in the search, but it wasn't a part of the world she knew. So she reconciled herself to being a sounding board for Michelle, as she ran through the list of those who were most likely to know where Tom was.

By seven that evening Michelle had tried just about everyone she knew from Karachi, Lahore, Islamabad, even the camp at Shamshuta, but no-one had heard from Tom in the last few days, not even Sajid, his fixer. This was alarming her more than anything, for he rarely went anywhere without taking Sajid, or at least informing him of where he was going.

'I am very sorry,' Sajid was telling her now, speaking to her for the fourth time in as many hours. 'I try hotel in Karachi again, and someone say he is leaving without paying the bill.'

'Then he must have left in a hurry,' Michelle cried, unable to stop herself running with the implications of that.

'I go to Karachi to learn truth.'

'Yes, Sajid, do that. Please do it,' she told him, 'and call me as soon as you can.'

As he rang off she looked at Katie across the table, then buried her face in her hands. 'I'm sorry about this,' she murmured, 'I'm really, really . . .'

'Stop it,' Katie chided, glancing at her watch. 'It's important to know he's safe, so I say we give it until morning, and if we still haven't managed to find

107

out anything by then, you should call our federal friend who left his card, to ask for an update.'

Michelle nodded and wiped her hands over her face. 'Shall I pour us some wine?' she said, as Katie began packing up her laptop. 'I think we could both do with it.' Then, remembering Katie probably wouldn't be allowed to have alcohol while on so much medication, she winced and said, 'Sorry. That was insensitive.'

Katie looked startled. 'Why? I'd love a glass,' she responded, 'but we'll have to save it until later, because I'm supposed to be at a parish magazine meeting in less than five minutes. If I weren't this quarter's editor I'd trade their front page for what seems to be taking shape in our kitchen, but I can't let them down. I'm afraid I'll have to take the computer with me too.'

'It's OK,' Michelle assured her. 'It's past midnight over there anyway, so it's unlikely there'll be any more news tonight. Shall I make some dinner for when you come back?'

'We ate an hour ago,' Katie gently reminded her.

Michelle shook her head and laughed dryly. 'Of course,' she mumbled. 'What about Molly? Shouldn't she be home by now?'

'She sent a text from Allison's saying she was doing her homework there, but could I record *EastEnders*.' She rolled her eyes and chuckled. 'That's what I love about my daughter,' she commented, 'she has this unfailing ability to focus you right back on everything that's trivial and tosh, and make it seem like the most important thing in the world, which to her, I suppose, it is.'

*

Uncertainty was quivering in Molly's smile as she turned from the computer screen and looked up at Allison.

'You know the rules,' Allison told her tartly. 'If you want to go on being a Daughter of Lilith you've got to meet someone off the Internet. Everyone else has done it, we're just waiting for you now so we can all move on.'

Molly still looked hesitant.

'For God's sake!' Allison exclaimed. 'You're only in because I really stuck my neck out for you, so don't let me down now. You want to go out with Brad, don't you? Well, no way are any of us going to help you if you don't do this.'

Molly turned back to the keyboard.

'All you've got to do is meet him!' Allison cried when she didn't start typing. 'You don't have to do anything else . . .'

'Why don't I give him your email address?' Molly suggested, referring to the boy they were instant-messaging.

Another message started coming through.

```
Are you still there, Sexxy? Have
you got any clothes on?
```

Though shocked, Molly joined in Allison's shriek of laughter.

'Tell him no,' Allison demanded.

'No way am I going to arrange to meet him if I do that,' Molly told her.

'All right. Just tell him anyway.'

Feeling off the hook for meeting him, Molly immediately went to it:

I am totally naked. Are you?

The reply came back:

Completely.

'Oh wow!' Allison shouted. 'Tell him to send a picture.'

Molly typed it in, and the message came back:

What's your email address?

'Oh my God, he's going to send one!' Molly gasped, turning hot and shaky.

'Give him your email. Give him mine too. I've got to have this.'

Without thinking Molly did as she was told, then waited for a reply.

Check your email.

'Out of the way!' Allison cried, pushing her off the chair. 'He must have sent a picture,' and opening her inbox she found the message, complete with attachment.

Both girls' eyes rounded like saucers as the picture started to download.

'OH MY GOD!' Allison gulped.

Molly just stared at it, speechless.

Allison turned to her, brimming over with excitement. 'Do you think it's his?' she said. 'He could have cut it out of a magazine.'

Have you got it yet?

Feverishly Allison turned back to the keyboard, and carried on as though she were Molly.

Yes. It's HUGE!

It's all yours, Sexxy. What are you going to do with it?

'Allison! Is that you up there?'

'Oh shit, it's my mother,' Allison gasped, and right in the middle of the reply she shut the computer down. 'Yeah, it's me,' she shouted back. 'I thought she was going to be out all evening,' she hissed to Molly. 'Make out like we're doing some homework or something.'

'Oh, you're busy studying,' her mother said, coming in the door. 'Good girls.' Her bloodshot eyes moved to Molly. 'Hello dear,' she said, taking a sip of heavily spiked tea from the mug she was holding. 'How are you?'

'Fine thank you, Mrs Bond. How are you?'

'Oh, you know,' she sighed.

'Can you leave us alone now,' Allison said. 'We're trying to finish this.'

Janice took another sip. 'I thought you might like to know that Toby's asked to have a party the weekend of his birthday,' she told her. 'I said we could make it a combined one, for both of you. He's got some very handsome friends,' she added, winking at Molly. 'Might find yourself a boy-friend.'

'Muuum!' Allison pleaded.

Janice smiled at Molly. 'How's your mother, dear? I saw her the other day, she's looking

111

splendid. Do you know if she used the Atkins diet? I've been thinking about it myself . . .'

'Shut up!' Allison snapped.

'But darling, I'd love to lose some weight . . .'

'Just stop talking stupid and go!' Allison raged.

'I'm only saying, we girls need to make the most of ourselves, even at your age . . .'

Allison leapt to her feet. 'If you don't get out now, I'll throw you out,' she warned.

Janice's eyes boggled. 'Goodness, do you speak to your mother that way, Molly? I'm sure you don't.'

'She's even worse than I am, if you must know,' Allison yelled, 'because you're all the same, you stupid middle-aged cows, who can't hang on to your husbands and get drunk on gin every day, and fall down the stairs and behave like total slappers. Look at you! Who can blame Daddy for never coming home, when you're such a fucking mess! I'd never come home if I didn't have to. I hate it here. All you ever do is drink and try to get off with Toby's friends. You're a fucking embarrassment, so just take your *tea* and get the bloody hell out of here.'

Janice's face was white with shock. Anger was sparking in her eyes, though no words were forming as she swayed slightly and tried to keep focused on what her daughter had said. When she finally opened her mouth to respond a hiccup emerged.

Allison turned away in disgust, and continued to fume as the door closed behind her mother, and footsteps sounded on the stairs. 'Can you believe that stupid cow?' she hissed. 'I hate her. I mean it, I

112

really hate her. As soon as I'm sixteen I'm getting my own flat and I'll never come back to this place again. You can come with me, if you like.'

Molly's eyes were wide.

'Oh for God's sake!' Allison spat. 'I don't know why I bother with you. You are like, so dumb and immature and if it weren't for me you wouldn't have any bloody friends, so learn to be grateful.'

'I am,' Molly assured her.

'Then you've got to meet someone off the Net,' Allison snapped. 'If you don't, you'll be out and then you won't be able to come to Toby's party, and Brad's bound to be there . . .'

'I just don't want to meet this creep,' Molly said. 'Not after all the emails and stuff. Can't I meet someone else?'

Allison was going back online. 'Suit yourself,' she said, busy on the keyboard, 'just hurry up and do it, or you won't be one of the Daughters any more. Shit! I've run out of paper,' she complained, leaning over to her printer. 'I want to take that picture to school to show the others. You'll get some cred for that, Molly, so print it out when you get home and bring it over tomorrow. And don't let us down with everything else. You've got to the end of the week to achieve Step Three, or the wrath of Lilith will be upon you, and you definitely won't be coming to the party.'

Michelle was wrapped in towels as she crossed the narrow landing from the ornate Victorian bathroom to the tiny box bedroom that was hers. Her suitcase was still taking up almost as much space as the bed, and what few things she'd unpacked were cluttering up the surface of the antique chest that had once belonged to her parents. It made her feel nostalgic to look at it, as did the photograph of Molly as a toddler on the window sill, where she didn't appear very much different to how she was now, behind the make-up and scowl. Her niece's need was so great, Michelle was thinking as she gazed at it, greater than she could even begin to imagine, for Molly had no idea of how to survive without her mother, and why should she? No-one ever did until it happened, and now it was going to happen to Molly, in a different way to the many other children Michelle had seen lose theirs over the years, but no less tragically. Molly's impending loss was why Michelle wouldn't leave, not even to try and find Tom. She and Molly needed all the time left to them now to forge a relationship that would allow Katie to go as peacefully as she deserved.

Letting the towel pool at her feet, she reached for her thin white dressing gown, and had just finished belting it when the phone started to ring.

Thinking immediately of Tom and those who had yet to call back, she ran into Katie's room and grabbed the phone.

'Hello! Is Sajid here,' he said. 'I am calling from Islamic Republic of Pak . . .'

'Sajid. It's Michelle. What's happened? Where are you?'

'In Lahore. I go to Karachi tomorrow, but I receive email from Mr Tom.'

'When?' Michelle cried. 'What does it say?'

'Few minutes ago. I check and there is email. Not earlier. Only now.'

114

'What does it say, Sajid? Do you know where he is?'

'He ask for money. He tell me to take money to a place.'

'What place? How much money?'

'One hundred thousand rupees. He say he will send me name of place tomorrow.'

'One hundred thousand rupees! Where are you going to get so much money?'

'Do you have it, Miss Michelle?' he asked sheepishly.

'No! I mean I can get it, but when does he need it by?'

'Email not say. I forward on to you, so you can read too.'

'Good. Listen, I'm going to look at it now, and I'll call you back. Are you on your usual number?'

'At my brother's carpet shop,' he answered. 'Yes, I am there.'

Immediately she rang off and ran downstairs to turn on the computer. 'Damn!' she cried, remembering Katie had taken it with her. At the same instant she recalled Molly's. She rushed back upstairs, threw open Molly's door, ploughed through the discarded clothes, CDs and magazines on the floor, and turned on the computer. It seemed to take an eternity to warm up, but once there she clicked on Outlook Express and to her relief it made an automatic connection.

She wasn't interested in Molly's emails, only in getting to her own, so she quickly went through to hotmail and typed in her user name and password. She was just watching her messages download when a voice shrieked from the door.

'What are you doing in my room! How dare you go on my computer?'

Mortified, Michelle swung round. 'Molly, I'm sorry, it's an emergency,' she cried.

'You've got no fucking right coming in here. No-one comes in unless I say so, so get out, NOW!'

Her anger was so palpable it almost felt like a blow. 'Molly, I'm sorry,' Michelle cried, starting to get up. 'I'm really, really sorry.'

'I don't care. Just go.'

'I am, but please, will you just let me check . . .'

'*No!*' Molly screamed. 'My computer's private . . .'

'What on earth's going on?' Katie demanded, appearing behind Molly in the doorway.

'*She* was on my computer,' Molly raged. 'I never said she could come in here. That computer's private, and you've got no right . . .'

'All right, all right,' Katie cut in.

'She better not have been snooping around my private stuff . . .'

'I haven't, Molly, I swear,' Michelle told her. 'I was just . . .'

'Why don't you go back to where you came from!' Molly hissed. 'We don't want you here. You're in the way and . . .'

'Molly, you're grounded for a week,' Katie cut in.

'No fucking way!'

'If you use that language again it'll be two.'

'Fuck!' Molly spat.

Ignoring her Katie turned to Michelle.

'Sajid's had an email from Tom,' Michelle quickly explained. 'He's forwarded it on . . . Molly, I swear I haven't been prying into . . .'

116

'All right, let's go downstairs and check on my computer,' Katie said, putting an arm across Molly to let Michelle past.

Molly was glaring furiously, but before she could start snarling again Katie thrust her into the room, grabbed Michelle out of it, and quickly closed the door. 'I think you've just learned never to touch a teenager's computer,' she said, wryly.

Still sobered by the experience, and not yet able to see the funny side, Michelle merely followed her sister down the stairs and waited for her to unpack her laptop.

A few minutes later she'd reconnected with the Internet and was reading the email Tom had sent to Sajid.

```
Bring 100,000 rupees to place in
next email. Tom.
```

```
M. YTNQQJ QQJXXZW
```

Katie looked at Michelle. 'What do all those letters mean?' she asked.

'It's a code we use,' Michelle answered. 'The M is for Michelle, the rest is going to take some working out. Do you have a pen and paper?'

After taking both from a drawer and passing them over, Katie went to the fridge and took out a bottle of wine.

'How much is one hundred thousand rupees?' she asked, watching Michelle count on her fingers, then jot something down.

'About two thousand dollars. A virtually impossible sum for someone like Sajid to raise, so the answer to where he should get it is probably here.'

Katie filled two glasses and carried them to the table. 'Can I help at all?' she asked.

'I'm almost there. I wonder if there's any significance to the amount,' Michelle continued, almost to herself. 'It doesn't sound much to buy himself out of prison, or a kidnap . . . XWVUT – S,' she said, and wrote it down. Finally, she sat back, and turned the notepad round so that Katie could read it.

Katie frowned. 'Toille Llessur,' she said. 'Would that be a rare form of Punjabi, or some kind of exotic undergarment?'

Chuckling, Michelle took a sip of wine, and turned the notepad back. 'Actually, it's a name,' she said, 'but not one I know. Elliot Russell?'

Katie's eyes opened wide with astonishment. 'Elliot?' she said. 'He's a journalist, here in England.'

'Tom must have guessed you'd know him,' Michelle responded. 'And presumably he wants to make contact.'

Remembering that Tom had lost all his personal belongings in the raid on his flat, Katie said, 'If he's pulling Elliot in on his story then there must be a British connection.'

Michelle regarded her warily.

'He couldn't have chosen anyone better,' Katie informed her. 'I've known Elliot a long time, and he's good. He lives with Laurie Forbes, another journalist who produces an investigative report programme . . . Or he did. They were supposed to get married, about a month ago, but something went wrong, something to do with another woman, and the wedding was called off. Rumour has it they're back together now, but I'm rather out of the loop these days, so I don't know how true that is. What matters to us though, is getting hold of Elliot's email address so we can pass it on to Tom.'

'Do you have his number?' Michelle asked, not wanting to waste any more time.

Katie glanced at the clock. Ten past eight. 'The home number I have for him is out of date now,' she answered, 'but there's a chance he might still be at his office.'

As she got up from the table, she could feel a stirring sense of excitement. 'It's been a long time since I've needed my old contacts book,' she confessed, opening a dresser drawer, and feeling as though she were reconnecting with a lifeline. Her eyes came up to Michelle's and began sparkling as she said, 'You know, there's probably not much we can do to help out, being stuck here, but if there does turn out to be something, like making phone calls or doing some background research, I wouldn't mind giving it a go.'

'Do you think that's wise?' Michelle responded, clearly not thinking so. 'It won't have been what Tom intended when he sent the email.'

'I'm sure he didn't,' Katie said, 'but I'm equally sure that I don't want the rest of my life to be all about dying, so if this gives me the opportunity to be involved again, to focus on something beyond my own little world, I want to take it.'

Michelle was still uneasy. 'What about Molly?' she said.

'I'll still be here. I'm not going anywhere, and it's only a small role I'm talking about. Something that makes me feel as though I'm living again.'

Not having the heart to refuse when she could see how much it meant to Katie, Michelle smiled and refilled her glass as she sat down at the table to dial Elliot's number.

Chapter Five

It was just after eight fifteen as Elliot Russell knocked on the front door of his own apartment. He was late, which wasn't a great start, but his timekeeping never had been a strong point, so with any luck Laurie wouldn't be expecting him till now. He had his own key, of course, but after recent events he wasn't too sure when he'd be given the go-ahead to use it again.

As he waited his strong, forbidding features were set in an even deeper scowl than normal, while his imposing height and physique somewhat belied how he was feeling inside. Indeed he was silently cursing the nerves that were making him feel like a damned schoolboy, for of all the difficult, even dangerous situations he'd faced in his life, and there were plenty, he didn't recall ever feeling as anxious as this. He guessed that wasn't true, since there were instances when he'd come very close to losing his life, but that, he'd learned recently, came second to losing Laurie.

He wondered why it was taking her so long to

answer. It wouldn't be like her to stand him up, or not call if she'd been delayed getting home, so she was presumably there. Maybe she was in the bathroom, or outside, on the wide balcony that overlooked the river and Tower Bridge. It was a nice evening, warm for late September, so she could have taken a drink out there and got caught up on the phone.

He was about to knock again when he heard the sound of the latch turning.

'Hi,' he said, as she opened the door.

'Hi,' she responded, standing back for him to come in.

He could see by her flushed cheeks and tousled blonde hair that she'd just woken up, which wasn't surprising for she'd still be jet-lagged after the flight back from Bali two days ago. She was beautifully suntanned too, and if he'd ever seen her looking more desirable he was at a loss to recall it right now.

She left him to close the door and follow her into the huge, open-plan sitting room that included a state-of-the-art Poggenpohl kitchen, an open-tread staircase that rose to the mezzanine level and all their furniture, books, pictures and memorabilia from over the years. No matter that he wasn't living here any more, it still felt like home. He'd give almost anything to come back, to be as they were just a few short months ago, together and happy and turning this fabulous old warehouse apartment into a uniquely styled home just for them. How could he have put it all in jeopardy? How was he ever going to make her understand the depth of his regret?

'What would you like to drink?' she asked, stifling a yawn.

'Whatever you're having.'

She walked round to the kitchen and took a bottle of vodka from the freezer. If she made Cosmopolitans he'd take it as a good sign, for they'd drunk a lot of them whilst in Bali on what should have been their honeymoon, but wasn't, thanks to his betrayal. In fact, considering the magnitude of what he'd done, just weeks before they were due to get married, it was nothing short of a miracle that she'd agreed to go with him. She'd made it clear before they went, though, that it wasn't instant forgiveness, nor was she offering any guarantees that it would eventually come. She'd merely accepted that they needed to talk without the pressures and interruptions of their everyday lives, and as the honeymoon was already booked and paid for it had seemed a reasonable idea to go.

How much easier it had been, all those thousands of miles from home, to feel that they were recapturing at least some of what they'd lost. He could only wish it felt that easy now, but after two days of being back it was already clear to them both that they needed to find a new way forward based on the reality of their lives here in London, not on the romantic idyll of a faraway island.

'Did you go to the office today?' he asked, relaxing a little as he saw the cranberry juice and triple sec going into the shaker.

She nodded, and licked the juice off her fingers. 'Yes. Rose wasn't there though,' she said, referring to her partner. 'She's been invited to Baghdad by an

Iraqi family who have a story to tell – don't ask me what exactly, because I don't know yet – so she's out there now, and won't be back for at least a month. She left the cuttings for the last programme though. We had some great reviews.'

'I've seen them. Congratulations.'

She smiled. As a documentary film-maker with her own small production company, based just along the river in Limehouse, she'd recently made a programme exposing the plight of a group of Indian women who'd been smuggled into the country and forced into prostitution. It had aired while they were away so she was only now catching up with the response.

'What about you?' she said, after shaking the drink and filling two Martini glasses. 'Did you go to your office today?'

'Not difficult,' he responded, with no little irony, for he was currently staying in the small studio flat attached to his Canary Wharf office, which he and his research team used for grabbing catnaps when they were on particularly long shifts.

'Of course,' she said. 'Sorry. So how is it? Are you comfortable enough there?'

'It's OK for the time being. I should probably start looking around for somewhere to rent though.'

'You can always come back here, and I'll go to stay with Rhona,' she offered.

He shook his head. Returning was an option he'd only accept if she were going to be here too. 'This place is yours as much as mine,' he told her, 'and I'm the one who screwed up, so it's only right that you should keep your home.'

'Hair shirts don't really suit you,' she told him,

'but I won't argue,' and bringing the drinks round she handed one to him. 'What shall we drink to?' she asked, looking up into his eyes.

'Forgiveness?'

She smiled and nodded. 'OK. To forgiveness.'

They touched glasses and drank. They were standing very close, and when she lowered her glass he so badly wanted to kiss her it was almost impossible not to, but this was the first time, since their return, that he'd come to the apartment, and he didn't yet know the rules.

'I love you,' he murmured, remembering the passion with which they'd made love while in Bali, and wondering if it was as hard for her to hold back now as it was for him.

Her eyes remained on his as she lifted a hand to his cheek. 'I love you too,' she said, as he kissed her palm, 'I just wonder if it's enough.'

Having no answer to that, he watched her go to curl up on one of the large downy cushions scattered between the sofa and coffee table.

'You can sit down too,' she said with a playful light in her eyes.

Attempting to reflect her humour, he sat on the chair that was close enough for him to touch the soft silkiness of her hair, but though he wanted to, he didn't. 'Are we going out to eat?' he asked.

'I thought we'd stay in,' she answered. 'I bought some salmon steaks, we could make a salad.'

He nodded. Why couldn't he focus his mind on anything but the image of her suntanned and naked in Bali, lying beneath him, sitting astride him, her face clouded with lust, her passion urging him to heights he'd rarely reached with anyone else. He wanted her now, though he understood it was not being able to have her that was making the need so much more intense.

She looked up at him and as she began to talk about other things, he fought the urge to tell her again how sorry he was. He still didn't fully understand what had compelled him to hurt her the way he had. It had to have been some kind of aberration, for now the mere thought of Andraya Sorrantos, the Brazilian artist he'd been unable to resist, filled him with dismay and even a degree of revulsion.

'And what will you do, now we're back?' she was asking. 'Are you going to continue with your memoirs?'

His heart sank. 'I guess so,' he answered, 'but this enforced sabbatical is half killing me now. With so much going on, the insanity in Iraq, the intelligence scandals, the wall through Palestine . . . I should never have agreed to keep silent about the Phraxos dealings, or let them force me into taking this time out.'

'You did it to save a lot of people's lives,' she reminded him. 'If you'd gone public with your findings, and that giant conglomerate had gone under, we'd still be feeling the repercussions now.'

'Aren't we anyway, if you consider how many people have died in Afghanistan and Iraq since I was paid for my silence? As the world's biggest defence investor, the Phraxos Group is cleaning up thanks to these wars, and what makes me sick to my stomach is that I know they're involved in writing the war plan.' He shook his head and took a sip of his drink. 'This is a bad time we're living in,' he said, 'and if they go into Syria, or Iran . . .' He looked round as the phone started to ring, and felt annoyed that she reached behind her to answer it.

'Hello?' she said into the receiver. 'Oh hi, how are you? Yes, we got back two days ago. We had a lovely time, thank you.' She turned away and spoke more softly as she said, 'Listen, it's not a good time right now. Can I call you tomorrow?'

She didn't ring off straight away, and though Elliot had no way of knowing for certain, he had a horrible feeling she was speaking to Nick van Zant, the foreign correspondent who'd ridden Galahad-like to her rescue after he, Elliot, had walked out to be with another woman.

'OK, I'll have to go now,' she said into the phone, 'there's someone else trying to get through. Yes, I promise I'll call tomorrow.' She clicked over the line and said, 'Hello? Oh, hi Murray. Yes, we had a great time thank you. He's here, I'll pass you over.'

As she handed him the phone Elliot felt irritated with his office manager now for interrupting him while he was here. 'This better be good,' he said shortly.

'I've just had a call from Katie Kiernan,' Murray told him.

Elliot blinked and instantly mellowed. 'Katie? How is she?'

'I was afraid to ask,' Murray confessed. 'But she sounded OK. She wants you to call her – tonight if you can.'

'Any idea what about?'

'Kind of, but it's better that she explains. I've got her number.'

As he looked round for a pen Laurie passed one

over, together with a Post-it pad. 'OK, shoot,' he said to Murray.

'I've checked and it's a Wiltshire number,' Murray told him after he'd written it down. 'Just in case you were wondering.'

'She moved there about a year ago,' Elliot reminded him. 'Anything else?'

'No. That's it.'

After clicking off the line he said to Laurie, 'Apparently Katie Kiernan wants me to call and before you ask, Murray didn't have the guts to enquire how she was.'

'I'll bet she encounters a lot of that,' Laurie responded, 'people not wanting to mention her condition, and we're not exactly in a position to criticize, when we've hardly been in touch since she gave up her column.'

'Well we will be now,' and clicking the line back on he started to dial.

'Let me say hi first,' Laurie said, holding out a hand for the phone.

A few moments later someone at the other end said, 'Hello?'

'Katie?' Laurie asked.

'No. I'll get her,' and as the receiver clattered on a surface the same voice yelled, 'Mum!'

Seconds later Katie was saying, 'OK, Molly, I've got it.' The extension went down and Katie said, 'Hello?'

'Katie. It's Laurie Forbes. I know you want to speak to . . .'

'Laurie! How lovely to hear you. How are you?'

'I'm great. How are . . .'

'I saw your programme on the Indian women.

128

Thank God you saved so many, but what a terrible tragedy.'

'Terrible,' Laurie agreed. 'But how are you?'

'Not bad. Actually, I'm fine. Is Elliot with you? I guess he must be if you're calling, so does this mean you're back together?'

'We'll chat another time about that,' Laurie replied. 'I just wanted to find out how you are. I'll put him on now.'

Elliot took the phone, saying, 'Katie. I kept thinking my life wasn't quite complete, and now here you are, the missing piece.'

'Just like you to call me a piece,' she responded tartly. 'Never did have any respect for someone who was madly in love with you.'

'If I thought that were true I'd ask you to marry me,' he joked.

'Yes, well, maybe the less distance we travel down that road right now, the better,' she retorted in a tone so dry it made him laugh. 'Anyway, enough of all this persiflage, my sister, Michelle, has received an email from Tom Chambers – you do know him, I take it?'

'I certainly do.'

'He wants to be in touch with you, so I'm calling for your email address, which I know Murray could have given me, but I wasn't about to deprive myself of an opportunity to speak to you.'

'I'm glad you didn't,' he said, frowning. 'Is there a problem about Tom contacting me direct?'

'It would seem so. We're not entirely sure what's happening over there . . .'

'Where?'

'Pakistan.'

Elliot pulled a face. Of all the countries to be facing a problem in, that had to rate as one of the worst.

'Everything was taken from his apartment about a week ago,' Katie continued, 'so he probably doesn't have your number any more. The trouble is, we don't have one for him either. Only an email address. Actually, you need to speak to Michelle, she can fill you in on what she knows.'

Elliot was looking at his watch. 'Ask her to put it in an email,' he said. 'I'll give it a read, and if need be I'll come down there tomorrow and talk to her in person.'

After ending the call he dialled his office number, told Murray to use their contacts in Pakistan to start trying to track down Tom Chambers, then handed the phone back to Laurie.

'So are you going to tell me what that was all about?' she prompted. 'Or am I to be kept in suspense?'

After filling her in on the little Katie had told him he said, 'Why don't you come with me if I go down there tomorrow? Katie would love to see you, I'm sure, and depending on what this is all about, there could be something in it for you too.'

'OK,' she responded. 'I don't have much on at the moment, and a day out in the country is always a treat.'

He tapped his glass to hers and got to his feet. 'If your computer's on,' he said, 'I'll go and send a couple of emails to the States, see if there's anything going down about Tom over there, and pick up Michelle's when it comes through. Then how about some dinner?'

'Your wish is my command, oh master,' she responded. 'I'll also refresh the drinks and put on some music if that would meet with your desires.'

'It'll do for a start,' he told her, with a look that made her laugh.

As she walked over to the CD player and he went into her study she knew he'd be hoping she'd choose an opera, for it was a signal they often used to let the other know they wanted to make love. However, it wasn't going to happen tonight, not because she didn't want to, for it was rare for her not to want to make love with Elliot, but because the call she'd received earlier was from Nick van Zant. The way she'd responded to the sound of his voice had confirmed what she'd suspected while in Bali, that it wasn't all over between her and Nick yet. In fact, considering how persistent and erotic her thoughts had become about him while she was away, and how unsettled she was feeling now after speaking to him, she was starting to wonder if what she'd believed to be a brief and almost convenient affair while she was trying to come to terms with Elliot's betrayal had been the start of something much deeper, and maybe more threatening to their relationship even than his affair with Andraya.

Molly was still smarting at the way her mother had made her apologize to Michelle this morning, like Michelle was her mum's best friend now, when she hadn't been able to stand her before. Well, see if Molly cared that they were like all interested in something going on in Pakistan now and totally leaving her out. She didn't want to talk about all their dumb stuff anyway, it was bad enough having

131

to listen to it over breakfast. And no, she didn't want to go shopping with Michelle later on, thank you very much, she'd probably have a meeting of the Daughters to go to, and even if she didn't, no way did she want to spend any time with someone who shouldn't even be in their house anyway.

She was sitting near the back of the chemistry lab, half-slumped across the bench as the teacher blabbed on and on about different kinds of bondings and stuff, like anyone gave a toss. Even when she didn't have so much else on her mind she found chemistry the most boring subject in the world, because it had nothing to do with anything she'd ever need to know in her life, and who in the whole Universe gave a fuck about ionic or covalent bondings anyway? They were hardly going to help her sort out what she was going to do about meeting someone off the Internet, were they? They weren't even going to help her get a job one day, because no way was she carrying on with this bloody crap when it came to GCSEs.

Sighing, she changed arms to slump on the other side, and was midway through formulating a plan to fake Step Three when Mr Glover suddenly took off across the lab in a really scary way and snatched something out of Kylie Green's hands. Kylie's face turned beetroot, so did Sophie Turner's who was sitting next to her, but it was nothing to the colour Mr Glover's turned when he saw what he'd grabbed.

'Where on earth did this come from?' he demanded, his whiskery eyebrows going all weird and prickly.

Molly's insides turned to ice as she realized what

it was. Oh my God, she was like in such big trouble now, because it was the picture she'd printed out for Allison, to take over there later. And what she wasn't going to do to the slag who'd stolen it out of her bag, once she found out who it was. *Just don't say where it came from, Kylie, or I'll kill you.*

'It belongs to Molly Kiernan, sir,' Kylie told him.

You are dead, Molly thought furiously.

Mr Glover turned in her direction. 'Where did you get this, Molly?' he asked, in a seriously dangerous tone.

'I – uh, it came in an email, sir,' she answered, knowing there was no point denying it because the addresses were there at the top.

Folding the picture into quarters he stuffed it into his lab-coat pocket and returned to the front of the class. 'We'll continue our lesson now,' he said, 'but this will go to the headmaster when we've finished, Molly, who I'm sure will want to speak to you himself, and probably to your parents too.'

Not bothering to point out that she only had one, who didn't even care about her anyway, Molly dropped her head and wished all kinds of evil on Kylie Green and everyone else who was staring at her, including the two retards opposite whose giggling just now had obviously got Glover's attention.

At the end of the lesson she fled the lab, grabbing Rusty Phillips on the way and dragging him with her. He might be like the most seriously rank boy in the class with his greasy ginger hair, biscuit-sized freckles and metal teeth, but he had a crush on her that was hopefully big enough to help her with Step Three.

By the time they came to a stop on the far side of the sports field she'd filled him on what he had to do, and sinking down on the grass she said, 'So have you got it? Do you understand everything I said?'

He shrugged. 'You want me to go on my computer and instant-message you,' he said, obviously wondering what could be simpler.

'That's right. Here are the details, addresses and stuff,' she said, handing him the notes she'd furtively scribbled in class. 'I've written down what you've got to ask me, and what I'll say back.'

He started to read, his pale skin turning pink under his freckles as he got the gist of what it was about. 'You're not supposed to meet anyone from chat rooms,' he told her.

'I know that,' she cried, 'it's why I'm asking you to meet me. If you don't, I'll have to do it for real, and if I end up getting murdered it'll be your fault.'

His brown eyes gazed anxiously into hers. 'But why have you got to do it?' he asked simply.

'Because if I don't I'll be thrown out of my group, and don't ask anything about it, because it's secret and based on the Goddess Oracle, which you won't know anything about.'

Looking wretched he read over her notes again. 'So I've got to arrange to meet you on the bridge in Chippenham, to go for a walk by the river?' he said.

'That's right. Then later, I want you to instant-message me again to go on about what a fantastic time we had and how we snogged with tongues. I've written it all down. Just stick to it, and everything'll work perfectly.'

'But why can't it be for real? You know, I could be like your boyfriend.'

'That is so never going to happen,' she retorted haughtily.

He looked back at the notes, his shoulders hunching in defeat.

'All right, listen,' she said, realizing this was going to take some extra powers of persuasion, 'if you do it, I promise to let you snog me. Like really quick, half a second, and *definitely no tongues*.'

His pallor brightened as his head came up. 'Snog first, then I'll do it,' he said.

Wanting to gag, she said, 'How do I know I can trust you?'

'I always keep my word. You know that.'

'And you won't tell another living soul?'

'I swear.'

'OK. It's a deal.' She held out a hand to shake, then realizing he was leaning in for his snog, she shoved him back. 'Not here, you idiot!' she hissed. 'Everyone'll see. Meet me in the end bower after school, and make sure you file any sharp edges off those braces before you come, I don't want to end up having stitches.'

As she got up, Kylie and several other girls from the chemistry class were coming towards her. 'Molly Kiernan, you are such a slapper, carrying pictures like that around in your bag,' one of them sneered.

'You are so in trouble now,' another one loftily informed her.

'Do you think I care? Just because you're too stupid to know what any of it's about . . . None of you can even get a boyfriend . . .'

'Look who's talking, hanging out with Rank Rusty Phillips,' Kylie spat.

'He's helping me with my homework. My boyfriend's someone you don't even know. His name's Brad and he's eighteen.'

'You are such a liar.'

'Believe what you like, but you'll feel pretty stupid when he comes to pick me up from school on his motorbike,' and hiking her bag higher on her shoulder, she pushed past them to go and sit somewhere on her own. She composed a text to her mum saying she was sorry again and that she loved her, which would hopefully soften her up a bit before she found out about the email Glover had snatched. She even considered saying she'd go shopping with Michelle, but no, she definitely didn't want to do that. Leaving it out, she sent the message and stuffed the phone back in her bag, free now to imagine how being Brad's girlfriend would be like the coolest, most amazing thing ever.

It was a little after one as Michelle hurried up through the village of Castle Combe, barely registering the picturesque cottages either side of the narrow street, or the old market cross at the top just outside the inn she was heading for.

Pushing the door open she looked around, trying to spot someone who could be Elliot Russell amongst the locals and tourists who were crowding the stone-walled bar with its two open fireplaces, deep casement windows, and collection of photographs from films that had been shot in the village.

Spotting her first, Elliot got to his feet and came

across to meet her. 'Michelle? Elliot Russell,' he said, holding out a hand to shake. 'We're over here, by the window.'

Following him to a table set against the curved stone wall with views down over the village, she watched an extremely attractive blonde woman rise to meet her.

'Laurie Forbes,' Laurie said, shaking Michelle's hand. 'It's lovely to meet you.'

Michelle smiled, liking the warmth in Laurie's eyes. 'Thanks for coming,' she said, 'and for meeting me here.'

'Isn't Katie joining us?' Laurie asked, as they sat down.

Michelle's eyes showed a wry humour as she recalled Katie's voluble disgust at being forced to stay at home. 'I'm afraid not,' she said. 'She wanted to, but the Macmillan nurse is coming today. She sends her love though, and says she'd love to see you if you've time to drop in before you return to London.'

Beneath the tan Laurie's face had paled. 'Macmillan nurse?' she echoed, understanding very well what that meant.

Knowing that she'd be dropping something of a bombshell with that, Michelle spoke softly as she said, 'Yes, I'm sorry. Her care changed from curative to palliative about three weeks ago.'

Laurie looked at Elliot, who appeared equally as shocked. 'We'd kind of presumed, after her call, that she was on the mend,' he said.

Michelle shook her head. 'It's why I've come back to England,' she explained. 'She hasn't told many people, so if you wouldn't mind keeping it to yourselves for now . . . She knows I'm telling you, but she hasn't actually broken it to her daughter yet.'

'Oh no, this is so awful,' Laurie responded, clearly very upset. 'How old is Molly now?'

'Fourteen.'

Michelle watched their faces as they looked at each other, and tried to assimilate this unexpected news. It was plain to see how fond they were of Katie, which touched her deeply, but feeling the need to lighten things a little now she said, 'If you happen to have any tips on how to bond with a teenager, I'd love to hear them, because I'm clean out of ideas myself, and I haven't even got started yet.'

Laurie turned to Elliot. 'Drinks,' he declared, taking the only way out. 'What are you going to have?'

'Lemonade for me,' Michelle answered. 'Katie and I rather overindulged last night, I'm afraid.'

'Same for me,' Laurie said. Then, turning back to Michelle, 'You know, if there's anything we can do . . .'

'That's very kind of you,' Michelle responded. 'I think we're managing for the moment, in fact, once you get over the shock of how she looks, you could almost forget there's anything wrong with her, she's so like her normal self.'

Laurie's eyes were imbued with affection as she said, 'It must be very hard for you.'

Michelle took a deep breath. Actually, it was, but she didn't really want to discuss her own feelings when Katie's mattered much more. 'We'll get through it,' she said, with a smile to show her appreciation for the thought. Then, glancing over at Elliot as he stood at the bar ordering drinks, she said, 'You have a lovely tan, both of you. Have you been away somewhere?'

'Bali,' Laurie answered, with a wry expression. 'It was our honeymoon, but Elliot met someone else just before the wedding, so we didn't actually get married.'

Though Katie had already told her that, Michelle felt it polite to feign surprise.

'He claims he's over the other woman now,' Laurie continued, 'but I guess time will have to be the proof of that.' Looking up as Elliot rejoined them, she said, 'Now let's get down to why we're here. We got your email, but we should probably go over it, make sure we're understanding everything correctly.'

Michelle took one of the menus a waiter was passing out, but neither of them studied it as she began expanding on her email, filling them in on the details of what had happened since she'd arrived in England. She began with her detention at Heathrow, her missing bag and mobile, then related what Tom had told her during their phone conversation. She went on to the visit from the police, and most recently the email to Sajid.

'Yes, we got that,' Elliot told her. 'I'm assuming his accounts have been frozen, preventing him from accessing his own funds, or he's gone into hiding and doesn't want to risk tipping anyone off to where he is. When we put that together with the little else we've got, there doesn't seem much doubt that he's trying to avoid the intelligence services – US, Pakistani, and possibly British, because they're obviously operating out there too. So, someone wants their classified documents back, which leads us to the big question, what's in them? For the moment we don't know, so let's start with Joshua Shine. Is there anything else you can tell us about him?'

Michelle shook her head. 'Everything's in the email,' she answered. 'He was Political Officer at the US Consulate in Lahore for at least ten years, until they were all recalled to Islamabad at the start of hostilities. Tom's long suspected him of being a CIA case officer for the region, but we don't have any proof.'

'I spoke to someone at the embassy in Islamabad this morning,' Elliot informed her. 'Apparently Mr Shine is no longer in Pakistan, so I've asked my partner in Washington, Max Erwin . . . ?'

Michelle nodded. 'I know the name,' she confirmed.

'He's making enquiries that end,' Elliot continued. 'Now, do you know a Pakistani journalist by the name of Farukh Hassan?'

Michelle looked surprised. 'Yes, very well. He's a good friend of Tom's. They've worked together a lot in recent years. In fact, he was one of the first people I tried to get hold of.'

'Me too,' Elliot said, 'and I had a call about an hour ago telling me that Farukh was at the hotel in Karachi with Tom and another man – possibly Josh Shine – before they took off in a hurry. My contact also informed me that the hotel was then closed down for several hours while it was searched by the police and ISI.'

'ISI?' Laurie queried.

'Pakistan's Intelligence service,' he elaborated.

Michelle's face was showing her concern. 'That was three days ago,' she said.

'So they're obviously in hiding somewhere, and my guess is, Tom needs that money to get himself out of the country. It would be the only sensible thing to do under the circumstances, because no-one in their right mind would hang around to be arrested by the Pakistanis. Bad things happen behind their closed doors, which you probably know even more about than I do, so we won't go there.'

'What do you think of the possibility that they *have* managed to find him and that he needs the money to bribe his way out of jail?' Michelle said, voicing one of her worst fears.

'We can't dismiss it,' Elliot responded, 'but my gut's telling me that's not the case. Nor do I think he's fallen – or been pushed – into the hands of a terrorist group,' he continued, addressing her other worst fear, 'because it's unlikely he'd have got an email out, and the amount isn't big enough for a ransom.'

Laurie said, 'We sent an email back to Tom this morning, with a copy to Sajid, letting them know that the money will be there as soon as they tell us where and when they need it.'

'Are you sure?' Michelle said. 'I mean, I can find the cash . . .'

Elliot put up a hand. 'It's easier if we do it,' he said. 'Now let's move on to the visit you had from the anti-terrorist squad and the FBI . . .'

'It was definitely anti-terrorist?' Michelle interrupted.

Elliot nodded. 'We established that last night. This morning we learned that the FBI agent is the Acting Legal Attaché with a fierce ambition to secure the job, always a dangerous type. What's significant is that he came to see you himself, and didn't send one of his deputies.'

'He hardly spoke,' Michelle told him.

'He didn't need to, his anti-terrorist chum was doing it for him, and this isn't his jurisdiction.'

Laurie said, 'Did either of them say anything to give you an inkling of what might be in those documents?'

Michelle was thinking hard. 'Nothing at all,' she said. 'They hardly stayed above five minutes, and everything they said I put in the email. Katie checked it, it was how she remembered it too.'

Elliot was looking pensive. 'OK,' he said, 'now let's go over it all again to make sure we haven't missed anything.'

By the end of lunch Michelle was so relieved to have Elliot in charge that she actually felt physically lighter as they wandered back down through the village and over the bridge to where they'd parked their cars.

'What next?' she asked, as they came to a stop at Elliot's Porsche. 'Is there anything Katie and I can do? You know how well connected she is in London, and she's longing to do something . . .'

'I can imagine,' Elliot responded dryly, 'and I can't think of anyone I'd be happier to have on board. For the moment though we're in Tom's hands, so until he gets in touch again, there's not much more any of us can do. Just keep us informed if you hear anything, or suddenly remember something you might have overlooked.' Turning to Laurie he said, 'I need to head back to London now. I'm guessing you'll want to stay and see Katie.'

'Absolutely,' she confirmed.

'OK. If you drop me at the station I'll take the train and leave you the car, then I can use the phone as I go.' To Michelle he said, 'Send Katie my love, and tell her I'll definitely call in on her next time. And she knows my number if she needs anything.'

'Thank you,' Michelle replied, liking the way he sounded as he spoke about Katie. 'Thank you for everything.'

'Good luck with your niece,' he added.

Michelle groaned and laughed. 'I think I'm going to need it.'

After giving Laurie directions from the station back to Katie's, Michelle got into her hire car and pulled out behind them as they started heading towards Chippenham. Though she was as eager as Katie to help in any way they could, now that Elliot seemed to think that Tom was safe – at least for the moment – she felt able to start focusing more on Molly and how to win her over. It was going to be an extremely delicate process, she knew that, and it was already off to a bad start, though she was daring to hope that this new détente with Katie would turn out to be lasting enough to bring about a mellowing effect in Molly.

When she pulled up outside the cottage everything appeared quite normal and quiet. No sign of the nurse's car, though she'd have been long gone by now, and Katie's Fiesta was in its usual place with a flyer from a local car wash trapped against the windscreen. Finding Trotty at the gate waiting

143

to greet her, Michelle scooped her up and stopped a moment to look around at the fields beyond the garden, the trees that overhung the lane, the vast blue emptiness of the sky, the sunlight sparkling on the duck pond. It seemed, strangely, as though everything was taking a pause, inhaling a last breath of summer before finally allowing the leaves to start changing colour and the storms to gather. Suddenly struck by how it could be a metaphor for Katie's life, she quickly refocused on Trotty and walked across the garden and in through the open back door to find Katie sitting at the table in front of her computer.

'Are you all right?' she asked, wondering why she thought she wasn't.

'Yes, I'm fine,' Katie answered, looking up. 'Just bringing myself up to date on Pakistan, and realizing that while the world's eye is on Iraq, we're missing where the real danger lies.'

Michelle nodded and going with it said, 'It's where terrorists are most likely to get their hands on nuclear weapons.'

Katie looked at the screen again. 'I wonder if they already have,' she murmured. Then seeming to detach from it, she said, 'So how was lunch?'

'What did the nurse say, first?' Michelle asked, putting her purse down and wondering if Katie really did look worse than she had a couple of hours ago, or if it was simply that she wasn't wearing her wig.

'Oh, my supplier,' Katie answered flippantly. 'She's giving me a bigger fix of morphine, and wants me to go and see Dr Simon next week. Nothing serious. Just a check-up.'

Michelle felt a beat of unease. 'I don't believe you,' she said.

Katie laughed in surprise. 'Why ever not?'

'Why are you seeing the specialist?'

Katie was on the brink of delivering another flippant reply, until realizing that Michelle was seeing straight through her bravado, she sighed and looked away. 'All right, the nurse thinks I need more symptom control, so she's recommending some second-line chemo. She says it'll ease some of the pain.'

Michelle went towards her and wrapped her in her arms. 'I hadn't realized it was that bad,' she said. 'You're too good at hiding it.'

'It's not, not really,' Katie responded. 'Just now and again.'

Michelle drew back to look at her. 'Don't keep things from me,' she said. 'Whatever it is, I need to know.'

Katie smiled, but as she tried to pull away she found herself holding on tighter, and then her frail, emaciated body began to shake as a dreaded wave of self-pity broke through her resolve.

Michelle tightened her embrace and felt her own tears welling too, as the sharpness of Katie's bones pressed up against her own, and her feathery hair brushed her cheek. She felt so helpless and angry that this should be happening, so confused by the world and all the pain it visited on the undeserving.

'I'm sorry,' Katie said, pulling away to dry her eyes. 'It just comes over me sometimes. I'm fine now.'

'You don't have to say sorry to me,' Michelle told her gently.

'But I do,' Katie replied, looking into her eyes. 'I've treated you so badly, not just recently, but over the years . . .'

'Ssh,' Michelle scolded. 'Sisters are like that with each other sometimes.'

A smile trembled on Katie's lips. 'I wish I'd allowed myself to get to know you better before all this,' she said. 'I really think we could have been friends.'

Touching her face, Michelle said, 'What's important is that we are now,' and pulling her into another embrace she kissed her fuzzy hair and felt the bond that had lain dormant for too long finally starting to enfold them.

Reaching for another tissue to blow her nose, Katie said, 'You still haven't told me about your lunch.'

After checking that she really was steadier now, Michelle let her go and went to fill the kettle. 'I can understand why Tom wants Elliot involved,' she said. 'He hasn't wasted any time. Laurie's coming to see you, by the way. She's just dropping Elliot at the station.'

Katie immediately brightened. 'Then I'd better put me 'air back on,' she quipped. 'Can't have her seeing me like this, or I'll scare her off.'

Michelle smiled. 'From how fond she seems of you, I think that's unlikely. I really liked her. Him too.'

'So did you get the gossip? Are they back together? Or are they being all grown-up and twenty-first century by not letting personal issues get in the way of matters professional?'

'No, I think they're together.'

Katie seemed pleased, though she was shaking her head. 'If they are, then frankly it's a miracle she's taken him back after he went off with that Brazilian tart. Gorgeous and irresistible as he is, I'm not sure I'd have taken him back if he'd put me through that.'

'I got the impression it's not altogether resolved.'

Katie's eyebrows rose. 'I'd be amazed if it was,' she said. 'It can take years for a relationship to recover from that kind of betrayal, and even then it's never forgotten. Anyway, I'd better go upstairs and sort myself out before she gets here. The computer's still connected if you want to check your email.'

There turned out to be nothing from Tom or Sajid, though Michelle guessed they'd contact Elliot direct now, so she'd have to wait to hear from him. However, there was a message from another quarter that seemed to confirm at least one piece of information that Elliot had been given by the US Embassy in Islamabad.

Spoke to Josh Shine ten minutes ago. He's in Frankfurt on way back to Washington. Wouldn't discuss Tom or anything else. D.

'D?' Katie asked, when she read it.

'Daphne Soliman. She's an Egyptian lawyer, based at their consulate in Karachi,' Michelle explained, after forwarding the message to Elliot. 'I should probably call to let him know I've sent it.'

Katie stood back as she disconnected, and enjoying the sense of intrigue was about to pick up her tea when the phone started to ring.

Being the closest, Michelle answered.

'Mrs Kiernan?' said the voice at the other end. 'It's Mr Webb here, Molly's headmaster.'

Michelle's heart paused in its beat, for there was almost never a good reason for a head teacher to be in touch with a parent. 'Uh, it's not Mrs Kiernan,' she said, wishing she could pretend to be in an attempt to spare Katie what might be coming. 'I'll put her on.'

As she handed over the receiver she mouthed who it was, and felt even worse as she saw Katie's spirits draw into a knot of fear.

'Hello Mr Webb,' Katie said into the phone. 'Is everything all right with Molly?'

'She's fine,' came the hasty reply. 'No accidents. Perfect health, but I would like you to come to the school for a little chat, if it's not too much trouble.'

Wasting no time on relief that Molly's physical being was intact, Katie's concern instantly took off in another direction. 'What about?' she asked. 'Is there a problem with her work?'

'Not exactly, but something has come up that we need to bring to your attention. Could you come tomorrow, around three?'

'Yes, yes of course. Around three.' As she rang off her anxious eyes went to Michelle. 'He wants to see me,' she said. 'I hope to God she hasn't gone and done something stupid.'

'He didn't give you any idea what it was?'

Katie shook her head. 'The question now,' she said, stuck in the nightmare of a hundred different horrors, 'is do I interrogate her when she comes home so I'll know what I'm walking into tomorrow? Or do I save myself for Mr Webb?'

Closing her eyes, she put her hands over her face and groaned. 'I love her with all my heart and soul, I swear I do, and I know already I'm going to regret saying this, but sometimes, just sometimes, I wish I could forget I was a mother and throw myself into an orgy of unadulterated self-indulgence.'

Michelle smiled. 'The plaintive cry of a million mothers around the world,' she reminded her.

Katie shot her a look that made her laugh.

'I could always go to the school for you,' Michelle offered.

Katie hesitated, seeming to like the idea, but then she was shaking her head. 'No. You two should reach more of a rapport before you get involved in any difficulties at school, otherwise the embarrassment factor could raise its ugly head, and I'm sure you'll agree, one monster less is what we need right now, not one more.'

Chapter Six

Molly was shoving her way past the queue of children waiting to go into the village shop when her mobile bleeped, letting her know there was a text. Having to put her can of Coke and crisps on a wall next to some moron's bike, she fished the phone out of her bag and clicked on to read.

```
5.30.
Mtg of DOLs.
```

Feeling totally cool about being a DOL, and cooler still that she was going to be late for the right reason, she quickly sent a message back saying,

```
Mtg sm1 fm net @ 5.
Wl b thr aftr.
Hope nt rank.
```

Not wanting to think any more about rank, and how she'd just snogged it in the shape of Rank Rusty – *hurl, gag, vomit* – she tucked her mobile back in her rucksack, picked up her Coke and crisps and crossed the road towards the pub.

She was rounding the corner into Sheep Lane when a text came back asking her where the meeting was so they could be nearby to make sure no-one tried to rape or kill her.

Relieved she hadn't made anything up she texted back the details telling them to be on the bridge – out of earshot but close enough to see – and was just putting her phone away again when she noticed the Porsche parked right outside their house. A Porsche! Like how cool was that? Who did her mother know who owned a Porsche? They used to know loads of people who had smart cars in London, but never anyone round here.

Dreaming of how lush it would be if it were Brad's car and he'd just come round to pick her up, she sauntered in through the gate. Downing the last of her Coke, she meandered round the corner of the house to find her mother and Michelle sitting at the garden table with some blonde woman she kind of recognized.

'Molly, here you are,' Katie said.

'No, I'm like somewhere else,' Molly retorted.

'Well I won't argue that,' Katie said dryly. 'Come and say hello to Laurie. Do you remember her?'

'Molly,' Laurie smiled, getting up to greet her. 'You've grown up a lot since I last saw you. How are you?'

'Oh, I know who you are,' Molly said, remembering now. 'You're Laurie Forbes, off the telly. Is that your car?'

'My boyfriend's actually.'

'It is like, so cool,' Molly told her. 'That is so what I want my boyfriend to drive, when I get one.'

'You mean you don't have one now?'

Molly really wanted to say she did, but her mother was there and she was the last person she could tell about Brad. Already she was looking at her all like, curious, as though she was expecting some huge revelation or grandchildren or something. Bloody hell. Why did anyone have to mention boyfriends?

'I can take you for a spin if you like,' Laurie offered.

Startled at first, Molly's eyes quickly lit up, then realizing she probably didn't have time before she was due to meet Rank Rusty, she said, 'I've got to go out. My friend's helping me with my homework,' and shooting her mother a look that Katie instantly mirrored, she tried not to laugh and started inside.

'There you are,' Katie said to Michelle, 'all you need is a Porsche.'

'I heard that,' Molly snapped as Michelle laughed.

'It was just a joke,' Katie assured her.

'Yeah, well you make me sick when you do that,' Molly said sulkily, 'and you're drunk.'

'I've had one glass of wine,' Katie cried in protest. 'Well, maybe two.'

Molly's eyes narrowed, but she said no more, merely opened the fridge and took out a Twix. 'Did you get my magazines this morning?' she shouted as she started up the stairs.

'They're on your bed.'

Bloody good job, Molly was thinking, or there really would have been a row, because *Sugar* was giving away a poster of Busted this week and she had to have it. At least that was one good thing about her mother, she didn't get her knickers in a twist about the posters any more, and it was like, so brilliant lying on the bed totally blissing out as she looked at them all and listened to her CD and imagined she was being snogged by Brad.

Out in the garden they were keeping their voices low as they talked about Molly. 'She's a stunner,' Laurie was saying, 'and quite developed for her age.'

'Tell me about it,' Katie groaned. 'I just wish her mind was as developed. Or do I? Maybe not.'

They laughed, and Katie picked up the bottle to refill their glasses.

'Now where were we?' she said, casting her mind back to what they'd been discussing before Molly arrived. 'I know, you were about to fill me in on this Sherry person you hired as a researcher and who ended up being arrested for trying to off you.'

Laurie winced and laughed, though she supposed it was an accurate enough precis, but as she began recounting the story she was thinking more of how relaxed and even peaceful Katie seemed, in spite of the terrible havoc that had been wrought on her looks, as well as her body, so what had it done to the rest of her? On the surface, she clearly wanted everyone to think she was still the same, for the way she'd greeted Laurie had been vintage Katie, saying she knew she looked like a Halloween ghoul, but be thankful she'd remembered the wig and hadn't gone for the lipstick, because that was really scary, and now Laurie must feel free to be horrified while she got on and opened the wine.

Laurie could hardly begin to imagine the kind of courage it must take to come to terms with what she was facing, never mind being able to make light of it. How would she feel, she wondered, if she were in Katie's shoes? How would she deal with the terrible knowledge that soon she would have to let go of the people she loved, and the life she treasured? It seemed so unreal. It must be changing her perspective on everything, perhaps in ways she hadn't yet realized. And what was it like for Michelle, watching it happen, feeling powerless to ease the pain, or lessen the suffering. Having lost her own sister, though to a very different kind of death, Laurie's heart went out to Michelle. Her position she could more easily imagine, knowing how utterly shattered she'd been when Lysette had taken her own life.

'So, are you going to tell us what you're working on now?' Katie demanded, after she and Michelle had finished enjoying Laurie's behind-the-scenes story.

Laurie inhaled the crisp afternoon air, loving how peaceful and relaxing it was here, light years away from the usual chaos of her life. 'Well, Rose is in Iraq,' she said, taking another sip of wine, 'and one of our researchers is looking into the number of girls who go missing from Eastern European resorts each year, so that about has our overseas quota covered for the moment, which leaves me trying to come up with something on the domestic front. And as a matter of fact, I'm wondering if I might have found it.'

Katie frowned. 'You mean Tom's story?' she said, not certain how it fitted into the definition of domestic.

'No, though I guess it could turn out to be part of

it,' Laurie answered. Her eyes dropped to her glass as she continued to think through her idea, while wondering if it was acceptable even to suggest it.

'Goodness, I'm intrigued now, aren't you?' Katie remarked to Michelle when the pause continued.

Michelle was watching Laurie closely.

Laurie glanced at her and, to her surprise, caught a very brief widening of the eyes, almost as though Michelle had read her thoughts and was telling her to go ahead.

'Actually,' Laurie said to Katie, 'I was thinking about you, and what an excellent subject you'd make for a programme.'

Katie blinked, took a breath and found herself speechless.

'You'd be a tremendous inspiration to women in your position,' Laurie explained. 'Your humour, your courage, the way you're dealing with all you're having to go through. It's asking a lot, I know, but there are thousands, if not millions of people out there who'd get so much from your story, who're genuinely interested in how you are, and how Katie Kiernan is dealing with the very disease we all live in such fear of.'

Katie was still stunned.

'You had a huge and loyal following with your column,' Laurie reminded her. 'People from all walks of life used to read you every week, take in what you said, and often act on it . . .'

'Or try to sue me,' Katie cut in with a laugh.

'Being controversial was your trademark. We all expected it and you never let us down. You've been sorely missed, Katie, and I think everyone would like to know how you are now, and to see that the old spark is still there, despite what you're going through.'

Katie merely looked at her. Didn't she realize it was all a front? There was nothing brave or inspirational about her, she was a coward, a weakling, a sham. In the end she turned to Michelle.

Michelle smiled and said nothing.

'I know this has come right out of the blue,' Laurie went on. 'I had no idea before I got here that I was even going to suggest it, but I truly think it would make a fantastic programme. Naturally, I'd only shoot what you want us to, and I'd give you editorial control. Look, I'm probably going too fast. Take your time to think it over. There's absolutely no pressure, and even if you decide to go with it and change your mind later, we'll stop right away.'

Katie was looking slightly flushed as her eyes returned to Michelle. 'What do you think?' she asked, feeling a bit dazed.

Michelle was about to answer when music suddenly started to blare from Molly's bedroom window. She glanced up, then speaking slightly louder than before, she said, 'I think you should do as Laurie says and not make a decision right away. There's a lot to consider, and while I agree you'd be a tremendous inspiration for other women in your position, it's not what we think that counts. It's what you think, and how you'd feel having a camera right there when the nurse is around, or when the pain's particularly bad, or when you're not quite as mobile as you are now.'

'But it would be here when we help with Tom's story,' Katie pointed out. 'I mean, if we do. I'd like people to think that I was involved to the last, particularly on something with all of you. I'd be going out on a note to feel proud of – and for Molly to feel proud of too.'

'What about Molly?' Michelle said gently. 'Would you want her to be a part of it?'

Sobered by the prospect, Katie's eyes moved out across the lane. She was thinking of the summons from Molly's headmaster, and how it would be to have a camera there while she dealt with something like that. She needed to go no further, for as much as she might want this for herself, she knew already she had to turn it down. It just wouldn't be fair to subject Molly's turmoil to any kind of public scrutiny, particularly when she didn't even know yet that her mother was going to die.

'She wouldn't have to be in it, if you don't want her to be,' Laurie said.

Katie considered that, but it would mean shutting her daughter out, and she wasn't sure that was a good idea either. On the other hand, she could at least give it some more thought, because she didn't want to turn Laurie down flat, and there might be ways round it with Molly. She wondered how deep Laurie would want to go though. Showing her on the phone or computer, researching and briefing as Tom's story unfolded, was one thing; seeing her in the bedroom, or at the hospital, or watching her dosing up with morphine, that could be another altogether.

'Please believe me,' Laurie said, as her mobile started to bleep, 'we'll only do whatever you're comfortable with.' The text message came up:

                    Call me when you
                    can. N.

   Thankful no-one could see the way she reacted
inside, she cleared the phone, saying, 'Sorry, where
were we?'
   'Tossing me around on the horns of a dilemma,'
Katie reminded her. 'And it's very tempting, I have
to admit, but I'll need more time to think about it.'
   'Of course. It'll take hours of discussion anyway
to come up with the right format and how deep
you want us to go, though at this stage, I'm
already inclined to say that Molly should be off
limits.'
   Katie nodded.
   'Personally I think we should keep an open mind
about that,' Michelle said. 'There might come a
time when she wants to contribute, and as it's
about her mother . . .' She broke off as Molly
suddenly cranked up the volume.
   'Westlife,' Katie informed her. Then to Laurie,
'Tell you what, why don't you stay for dinner?
We've still got endless gossip to catch up on, and
we can talk some more about this. Unless you have
to get back . . .'
   'No, there's no rush,' Laurie assured her. 'So
thank you, I'd love to.'
   Katie's delight beamed from her smile. 'I wish I
could offer you a bed for the night to save you the
drive later,' she said, 'but there's only a sofa spare,
I'm afraid. Tom slept on it when he came though,
and if it's big enough for him . . .'
   Michelle laughed. 'Laurie can have my bed,' she
said.

'Or Molly could sleep in with me,' Katie suggested.

'No, no,' Laurie protested. 'I'm not taking anyone's bed. I can book into the pub where we had lunch. It's a hotel too, so I'll give them a call and see if there's room.'

By the time she'd made her reservation Michelle had gone into the kitchen to start sorting out what they could eat, while Katie tottered about with a hose and glass of wine. 'I'm so glad you came,' she said to Laurie, watering a large blue hydrangea. 'It's perked us all up no end, even Molly, having a Porsche parked outside.'

Laughing, Laurie said, 'Before I have any more to drink, I should go into Chippenham and pick up a few things for the night. Do you think Molly might like a lift to wherever she's going?'

'Are you kidding? In that car? Go on up and ask her, but be careful to knock first, then wait for permission to enter.'

Totally disgusted with everything she'd heard, Molly turned her music up even louder, so there was no way she could hear them now. Like, did they think she was deaf, or something, going on about making her mum the star of some programme, like they were the stupid Osbournes, or something? Mrs Cool with her Cancer who could inspire the nation. *Ugh! No!* Molly's hands pressed hard against her ears, as though to block it all out. She rolled over on the bed and pressed her face to the pillow, drawing her hands and elbows in even tighter against her. She hated the world. Hated it, hated it. Why couldn't it just go away and leave her alone? Why didn't everyone go? Michelle, Laurie Forbes, everyone. She felt like running and running and ending up somewhere they'd never ever find her. If Brad was her boyfriend she could go to him and he'd make them all leave her alone, stop them saying stupid things that just got on her nerves and made her so angry she wanted to thump the bed, and thump them and scream and kick . . .

Someone was knocking on the door, but they could just *go away*! She didn't want anyone in here. This was her room. It was private and they could just *fuck off* and leave her alone.

They knocked again so she drew the pillow tighter over her head.

'Molly!'

She didn't recognize the voice, but then realized it was Laurie Forbes. What was she doing up here? Just because she had a Porsche didn't give her the right to come banging on people's doors. And anyway, this was all her fault, talking to her mum as though she was like, dying, or something, when everyone knew the treatment was over so she was getting better now. So why didn't she just get lost? Go back to London where she belonged and take Michelle with her?

Katie and Michelle were both in the kitchen as Laurie came back down the stairs.

'I don't think she can hear me over the music,' she said, 'but I took your advice not to go in.'

'She probably thought it was me,' Katie responded.

'Or me,' Michelle added.

'Well I've got a Porsche, so it couldn't be me,'

Laurie quipped, making them laugh.

At that instant Molly came thundering down the stairs and started shoving her way past.

'Where are you going in such a hurry?' Katie demanded.

'Out!'

'Where? Molly! Come back here.'

Molly kept on going, out the door, over the garden fence, sprinting up the lane towards the village, and disappearing from view.

Katie sighed in exasperation. 'Please excuse my daughter's manners,' she said to Laurie. 'She will apologize before we have dinner, which should be . . .' She turned to Michelle. 'Around seven?'

'Seven thirty,' Michelle amended. 'I need to pop over to the supermarket for a few things.'

As she and Laurie walked out to their cars together, Laurie said, 'Tell me, what do you think about doing a programme? Was I inappropriate to suggest it, or would it work?'

Michelle looked round at the sound of childish chatter, over by the pond. 'I think it would be wonderful for Katie,' she said. 'She's really missed being in the cut and thrust of it all, as you can tell, and you know how she loves the limelight. The problem is, we have no way of knowing how the next weeks, or months, are going to unfold, and with Molly being so unpredictable . . .' She sighed. 'I don't know. My instinct says yes, but then I'm not so sure.'

Laurie smiled. 'Well, we don't have to make a decision right away, and anyway, it's up to Katie in the end. Now, I'll just check my email before I go to see if Elliot's heard anything from Tom,' and taking out her Blackberry she clicked on to see what was there. 'Nothing,' she said, putting it away again. 'I'll give him a call from the car, and let you know if there's any news.'

As she drove away Laurie turned on Elliot's digital phone, already tensing in dread of discovering a message from Andraya. To her relief there were none, so selecting the speed dial for their home she turned into the village and waited for him to answer.

'Hi, it's me,' she said, as his voice came over the speaker. 'Anything from Tom yet?'

'No. But following on from Michelle's email that Joshua Shine was in Frankfurt, I've just learned that he's now on his way to Washington. Max will take over from there. How was Katie?'

'Amazing, actually. She said to tell you she loves you.'

The smile was audible in his voice as he said, 'I hope you told her the feeling's mutual.'

'No, but I will. I'm thinking of doing a programme about her.'

He took only a moment to respond. 'That's a great idea,' he said. 'Is she up for it?'

'She has some reservations, but we're going to talk it all through, which means I'm going to stay down here tonight. I've booked in at the pub where we had lunch.'

There was a pause before he said, 'I see.'

Knowing what he was thinking, she said, 'Is there a problem? Do you need the car?'

'No. I was just wondering if you'd called Nick back yet.'

Despite the immediate flare of guilt, her voice

was quite neutral as she said, 'What do you mean, called him back? Has he left a message?'

'Wasn't that him on the phone last night?'

Almost missing a sign for the town centre, she veered sharply to the left and narrowly avoided a ditch. How had he known it was Nick last night? She hadn't mentioned him, nor had he asked at the time. 'Actually it was Rhona,' she said, blurting out the lie without thinking. 'And no I haven't called her back yet.'

'Oh.'

She waited.

He said nothing.

'What on earth makes you think it was Nick?' she demanded.

'I just get the feeling it's not quite finished between you two.'

Starting to feel slightly angry now, she said, 'I don't think this conversation's getting us anywhere so shall we change the subject?'

'If you like.'

She struggled for something else to say, but was still too thrown by his suspicions over Nick, and annoyed with herself for lying.

'Actually, I was going to call Nick myself,' he said. 'He's written several pieces about US intelligence in the last couple of years, so depending where this leads us, he could turn out to be helpful.'

Stiffening, she said, 'It's up to you if you get him involved, it has nothing to do with me. I just called to let you know my plans for tonight, and to say, why don't you stay at the flat, seeing as it's going to be empty.'

'Thank you,' he responded. Then, quoting a line from *La Bohème*, he said, '*All 'uom felice sta il sospetto accanto,*' and a moment later the line went dead.

Suspicion forever jogs the happy man's elbow.

Was he happy, she wondered, and her heart contracted with guilt, for she knew he wasn't, and he was right to be suspicious, because it wasn't all over between her and Nick. But what did he expect, that everything would change for her just because he'd decided he didn't want Andraya any more? It didn't work like that. She couldn't just forget what he'd done, any more than she could pretend that nothing had happened with Nick. She didn't know where she wanted it to go with Nick, or if she should even see him to find out, though of course, she would. Was this how it had been for Elliot with Andraya, she wondered? Wanting to resist, while all the time knowing he wouldn't.

Deciding to call Michelle to update her on Joshua Shine's movements, she parked the car alongside a small rank of shops in the town centre, and spoke to her on the mobile as she crossed the bridge on foot towards a pedestrian precinct.

It didn't take long to pick up the few essentials she needed for the night, and with her mind still full of Elliot and Nick, she was on her way back across the bridge when she spotted Molly dawdling along the riverbank with a boy. They weren't close enough for her to get a particularly good look, but even from where she was the geeky-looking creature with his awkward gait, peculiar ginger hair and puny physique didn't seem at all the type she'd have imagined Molly to go for. However, they were probably just friends, since they weren't holding hands, nor was Molly appearing very happy about being there. A moment later they ducked in under some overhanging branches, and were lost from sight.

Laurie continued on to the car, past a trio of giggling girls, across a mini roundabout towards an Oxfam shop, where she hit the remote on the keys and was just sliding into the car when her personal mobile started to ring. Seeing Nick's name on the readout her heart gave a powerful jolt. For a moment she even tried to resist answering, but in the end she couldn't.

'Hi. How are you?' she said.

'I'm good,' he answered. 'Is it OK to talk?'

The sound of his voice was already having the effect she was dreading. 'Yes,' she said, managing to sound much more in control than she was feeling. 'Actually, Elliot wants to be in touch with you about a story he's getting involved with. Do you happen to know Tom Chambers?'

'Tom? Sure I do. Do you know what it's about?'

'I should let Elliot fill you in.'

'OK, I'll give him a call.'

Realizing that really wouldn't be a good idea, she said, 'Maybe you should wait till he calls you.'

'Anything you say,' he responded, seeming to understand. 'So, you had a good time in Bali?'

Wishing she wasn't actually sitting in Elliot's car while having this call, she said, 'Yes, it was lovely, thank you.'

'Lovely in the sense it's all worked out with Elliot? You're officially back together?'

Not entirely sure how she wanted to answer that, she said, 'Let's put it this way, we haven't

165

given up on each other yet, but we've still got a way to go.'

There was a pause, then his voice seemed to steal right into her as he said, 'So there's some room for hope?'

Oh God, how was she going to answer that when she truly didn't know?

'He doesn't deserve you,' he said softly.

She took a breath. 'Nick, I . . . I'd like us to be friends . . .'

He gave a sharp intake of breath, as though he'd been stung. 'Not what I wanted to hear,' he told her.

'OK, if you want to know the truth,' she said, 'I do still have feelings for you, but Elliot and I . . .'

'Listen, you don't have to explain. I get the picture, and I shouldn't be putting this pressure on. So consider it off, and tell me where you are now.'

Closing her eyes in relief she said, 'Wiltshire. Actually, I'm looking into making a programme about Katie Kiernan, so I could be here for a few days.' She wondered if that had sounded like an invitation, and even thought it might be.

'I'm going to be down that way myself tomorrow,' he said. 'Well, GCHQ Cheltenham, which isn't a million miles away.'

'About an hour, I think,' she answered, not daring to allow her mind to go any further than that.

'Listen, I'm sorry, I've got another call coming in,' he said. 'It could be one I'm waiting for. I'll get back to you.'

As he rang off she dropped the phone on the seat beside her and heaved an unsteady sigh. At least she hadn't actually suggested they meet tomorrow, nor had she let him think Elliot was out of the picture. Which he wasn't. Far from it, but if Nick wanted to see her when he was down this way, was she really going to say no? And if he came to her hotel . . . She cut the thought off there, for she knew only too well what would happen, and if it did, where the hell was that going to leave her relationship with Elliot?

The Daughters of Lilith were hanging out in Allison's bedroom, listening to the latest CD from Beyoncé, while painting their nails and brushing each other's hair. The TV was on too, showing pop videos with the sound turned down, and the computer was logged on so they could go in and out of chat rooms when they felt like it.

'. . . so then the bloody teacher grabbed the picture,' Molly was saying, 'and now I'm in deep trouble. He's even got the diary stuff me and Allison wrote.'

'I bet it makes him all randy and yuk,' Donna giggled, pulling a face.

'Just say someone planted it on you,' Cecily advised, dipping a brush into a pot of purple nail polish. Then dismissing Molly's concern, she said, 'So now Molly's met someone from the Net we can move on to Step Four. Oh God, whose phone is that?' she grumbled, as one started to ring.

Afraid it was hers, Molly quickly checked, but then Donna was saying, 'Ugh, vomit. It's my mother.'

'Sssss,' they all hissed. 'The enemy. Sssss.'

Molly laughed the loudest and sank down on to the bed. She'd sent a text to her mother on the way over to say she wouldn't be home for dinner, as if she'd care, with all her friends there keeping her happy.

'Right, forget Step Four for the moment,' Allison declared when Donna had finished on the phone, 'I reckon we should give Molly the good news now, don't you?'

Molly's eyes opened wide with surprise. 'What's that?' she said, already excited.

Allison looked at the others. 'Shall I tell her?'

'No, keep her in suspense,' Donna teased.

'No!' Molly cried, throwing a cushion at her. 'What is it? I want to know.'

'It's about Brad,' Allison told her.

Molly's heart turned over, and the smile dropped from her face. 'What about him?' she said, feeling sick and hot and like really strange. 'Is he seeing someone? Oh God, please don't tell me he's seeing someone.'

'We just said it was good, didn't we?' Allison scolded. 'So no, he's not seeing someone – though he *might* . . .' her eyes swivelled round the others and came back to Molly, 'be seeing you.'

Molly's breath caught as her heart tried to catapult out of her chest. 'Oh my God,' she murmured, feeling herself start to shake. 'Why? Did he say something? Oh my God! Oh my God!'

'He asked Toby to get your mobile number off me,' Alison told her.

'Oh no! Oh no!' Molly gasped, pressing her hands to her cheeks. 'He's going to call me?'

'Why else would he ask for your number?' Allison laughed, glancing at the others. 'You are like, so lucky, because you're not going to have any

168

problem with Step Six if he's interested in you already. And he thinks you're sixteen, so don't go telling him your real age or you'll blow it.'

'And don't go missing out Steps Four and Five,' Cecily reminded her, 'because remember, we all have to achieve Step Sex – *sex*!' And she screeched with laughter at the slip of the tongue. 'I said sex! Can you believe that? I said sex instead of six.'

'What she means,' Donna continued, 'is we all have to make Step Six on the same night, and as we've designated the night of the party, you've got to wait, Molly. OK? So don't go letting him do anything before. I mean you can like snog, and he can feel you up and stuff, just don't go all the way.'

Feeling almost faint at the idea of it, Molly flattened herself on the bed and stared up at the ceiling.

'Right,' Cecily said, 'so we all know what we're doing for Step Four, but we've still got to come up with an idea for Step Five.'

'I reckon it should be more like Step Four,' Molly said. 'You know, nothing to do with boys. Stealing something's good. It's got high risk, and gets us something we want, so for Step Five, why don't we do something more like that?'

No-one seemed to have a problem with that, but as they all started to discuss it Molly couldn't think about anything except Brad. He wanted her number. She just couldn't believe it. This was like, really amazing. People would talk about her in shops and places when she walked in, saying things like 'That's her, Brad Jenkins's girlfriend,' or 'He's really crazy about her,' or 'She is *so* lucky,' and she'd just pretend she hadn't heard, and go on looking through the clothes rails, picking out something to wear to a party she was going to with Brad that night.

'Are you listening, Molly?' Donna cried, poking and tickling her. 'You want to know what Step Five is, don't you?'

Molly sat up, ready to listen.

Allison started to speak, and as Molly registered the words her eyes dilated. 'I can't do that,' she protested. 'No way. I'm not doing that.'

'Mothers are the enemy,' Donna reminded her. 'So what's the problem?'

'I'm just not doing it,' Molly replied, getting up.

'But you hate your mother. You said so.'

'I know, but I'm not doing that to her.' Molly was picking up her belongings now, preparing to leave.

'Are you a Daughter of Lilith, or are you a snivelling coward who's cheated her way in, and who we'll now have to expel?' Cecily snarled.

Molly swung round, green eyes blazing. 'My mother's been really sick, and she's only just getting better,' she cried, close to tears, 'so no way am I going to push her down the stairs. That's a really mean thing to do to anyone . . .'

'Actually, her mum has been sick,' Allison said to the others, 'so maybe we should think of something else. I mean, mine's falling down the stairs all the time, she's so drunk, but Molly's mum's a bit different.'

Cecily tore her eyes from Molly and blew on her nails.

'Come on, Mol,' Allison said, going to put an arm round her. 'The pizzas'll be here any minute, so you can't leave now.'

170

Allowing herself to be led back to the bed, Molly tried to say something, but was still too close to tears.

'So what was the matter with your mum?' Donna asked.

'Nothing,' Molly answered, wiping her nose with the back of her hand. 'She's all right now,' and desperate to change the subject, she said, 'let's go online and see if we can find some ideas for Step Five.'

As she and Donna started to surf, Cecily beckoned Allison over to one of the sofas.

'I'm telling you, she's not for real,' Cecily whispered. 'I reckon that dork she met by the bridge was someone from school, and she's definitely making it up about hating her mother.'

'Listen,' Allison said, keeping her voice down, 'if you start upsetting her, or think about throwing her out, we won't be able to pull this off with Brad, will we, and you said yourself, it is going to be so completely awesome if we can.'

Cecily's eyes travelled in Molly's direction. 'All right,' she said, finally, 'we'll give her one more chance, but I'm telling you this, whatever Step Five turns out to be she has to do it, no excuses, no tantrums, or she's out.'

It was gone midnight by the time a taxi arrived at Katie's to take Laurie back to the inn. Before she left, she made one last call to Elliot to find out if Tom had been in touch yet.

'Still no word,' she said regretfully to Michelle as she rang off.

Knowing Elliot would have contacted them right

away if there had been, Michelle covered her mounting concern with a smile. 'We'll see you tomorrow?' she said, going to the door with Laurie.

Laurie nodded. 'I'm sure he'll have been in touch by then,' she said encouragingly.

'I'm sure he will too,' Katie said, as she and Michelle walked upstairs together a few minutes later, and after checking Molly's light was out, she went into her bedroom. Michelle went into hers where she passed a sleepless night tormenting herself with all the dangers Tom could be facing.

Chapter Seven

Deborah Gough was waiting patiently for the rest of the committee to take their seats around the conference table. As the chair, she was at the head, ageing hands clasped loosely on the blotter in front of her, a stack of files to her right, a fresh cup of coffee to her left. Her benign, somewhat attractive features masked the full force of her intellect and lethal drive of her ambition. However, there wasn't a man present who was unaware of how ruthless she had been in achieving her position, or of how powerfully connected she now was.

Already she was sensing a degree of resentment at her appointment as head of this hastily formed Special Operations Executive, which was made up of the most senior-ranking advisors, experts and analysts from both the US and Britain's intelligence services. She'd spoken to each of them individually over the last two days, so knew who her most dangerous enemies were. Ronald Platt of the National Security Council, and Daniel Allbringer of the Defense Intelligence Board.

Once everyone was settled and the support staff had closed and secured all doors, she cut through ceremony and came straight to the point.

'As you know, gentlemen,' she began in a raspy Southern drawl, 'our purpose is threefold. First, we must identify the actual source of the leak. Who, in the upper ranks of the intelligence community, or Government, arranged for those documents to reach a member of the press?' She looked swiftly around, knowing that everyone was wondering if the culprit sat right here in this room.

She allowed her eyes to alight on no-one in particular and continued. 'Joshua Shine is now back in this country and has been taken to Camp Peary, where he will be interrogated. Should he prove unhelpful it will become necessary to investigate ourselves and our own departments. As each of you has already assured me that you are fully prepared to do this, we'll move on our second purpose, which is to retrieve the documents. So far we have no evidence to say that the journalist, Tom Chambers, actually has them in his possession – his computer revealed no communications referring to the P2OG, and his cellphone records showed no contact with anyone to give us immediate cause for alarm. However, it's been almost a week since his personal belongings were taken from his apartment, and as it's a matter of record that he met with Josh Shine at least twice in that time, we're going to be working on the assumption that Chambers does have the documents, or has already passed them on.' She looked across the table to Michael Dalby, Director of Operations for Britain's Secret Intelligence Service, whose very name was unknown to the British public, and his colleague, Sir Christopher Malton, who was chairman of Britain's Joint Intelligence Committee.

Understanding what was expected of him, Dalby, a short, trim man with grizzled grey hair and a neat moustache, said, 'I can report that Michelle Rowe did not transport the documents into the UK, nor did any emails on her computer refer to them.'

'Phone calls?' Deborah Gough prompted.

'None on her mobile to cause any concern. Apparently, she's in the country to take care of a dying sister who, I feel it prudent to mention, is a journalist of some repute in the UK.'

'Name?'

'Katie Kiernan.'

After noting it down, Deborah Gough looked up again. 'Considering the state of the woman's health, I don't see her as a potential cause for concern, but before we dismiss the possibility, would anyone like to comment?'

Daniel Allbringer immediately said, 'I think we should run a background check, get an update on her health and current political affiliations.'

Gough nodded and noted it down.

Allbringer wasn't finished. 'Going back to Michelle Rowe,' he said, 'we know what a powerful force she and Chambers have proved in the past in their efforts to expose corruption, fight for human rights and bring world focus to areas that most need it. We can highly applaud a lot of their work, however they've made no secret of their views concerning the current US administration and its foreign policies in the past few years, so I don't think we should dismiss Michelle Rowe on account of her sister's health.'

Deborah Gough regarded his smooth, handsome features, showing none of her dislike, only close interest in his opinion. 'I agree,' she said, finally, 'but I don't believe her to be a high-risk priority. However, Chambers is, which brings me to our third purpose, that of damage control. We of course hope that it won't get that far, but as a pre-cautionary measure I've ordered a highly aggressive campaign to be drawn up ready to discredit Chambers and his motives for exposing a covert intelligence and military operation that is, in fact, entirely fictitious.' She waited for someone to challenge the last comment, but to her satisfaction it received not even a murmur of surprise. She'd always found that believing totally in the message you were trying to get across was a strategy that worked well, and it appeared her fellow Executive members agreed.

'Before we go any further,' Allbringer said, 'can we just backtrack to the retrieval of the documents? There's nothing about them, as far as I'm aware, to establish their origin, so as I see it, Chambers's biggest problem is going to be how to connect them to the P2OG, if he indeed knows that is what he needs to connect them to.'

Deborah Gough was nodding. 'You're right, of course,' she said, 'but unlike the courts, the media doesn't bear a burden of proof. He can put it out there for public scrutiny and speculation, and we'll immediately find ourselves on the back foot having to explain. That is something we'd prefer to avoid, which could be done by mounting our own campaign first, which is why I've already had one drawn up. However, let's continue to aim for the best-case scenario, which is to apprehend Chambers and get the documents back.'

There was a general grunt of agreement with that, and after completing the notes she was making, Gough moved on. 'As you know,' she said, 'our own agents, working in conjunction with Pakistani intelligence, failed to apprehend Chambers at the hotel in Karachi. Since then, the only lead we have is a failed attempt to access one of his bank accounts in Peshawar three days ago. We're going to assume that he'll raise funds from another quarter, and use them to purchase a fake identity. We know that he manages to blend into Islamic communities with some ease, using the aliases of Omar Qureshi or Asif Karim. Counterfeit passports in these names were seized from his apartment, so he will be unable to use them to leave Pakistan – if that is his intention, and the prevailing opinion right now is that it is.'

'Do we have an arrest warrant out for him?' Platt asked the FBI chief.

'Not at this time. It'll only alert other members of the press, but the situation will be reviewed hourly.'

Allbringer said, 'We all know that a large element of Pakistan's intelligence service is in the pockets of the country's terrorist network, and as history tells us how they treat American detainees – journalists in particular – might we assume, if they manage to track down Chambers, that there will be an end to this matter in a much more decisive manner than the ones we are proposing?'

Gough smiled at his coyness. 'It's true, assassination is not currently a part of our mandate,' she responded. 'However, I'm afraid I can't speak for our Pakistani colleagues, so we shall have to wait and see what develops over the next few days.' She smiled pleasantly, and leaving Allbringer to wonder if an order had already been given to execute Chambers, she turned to Michael Dalby. He was expressing concern over the UK's position should this highly sensitive P2 operation come to light – and since the maps in Chambers's possession were of a British site, Deborah was willing to concede that he had good reason to be worried.

Michelle was speeding through the country lanes, driving Molly to school after they'd all overslept. It was the first time they'd been alone together, but from the instant they'd got into the car Molly had been firmly barricaded behind the pop station she'd tuned into. Now she was tapping madly on the keys of her mobile phone. It was almost as though she were in a taxi, or on a bus, with no obligation even to acknowledge there was anyone else around, never mind attempt any kind of conversation. It had been easier, Michelle was thinking irritably, to communicate with children whose language she didn't speak, though she had to admit if she weren't so worried about Tom she might be trying a little harder herself.

'So what's on the agenda today?' she finally ventured, as they turned out of Mill Lane to join the main road.

Though Molly's eyes remained fixed on her mobile, she didn't sound particularly hostile as she said, 'Usual lessons.'

'Do you have a favourite?' Michelle asked.

Molly shrugged. 'French is OK. So's history.' She finished tapping into her mobile and turned to look at Michelle. 'So how long are you staying?' she asked bluntly.

Michelle kept her eyes on the road. 'Oh, I'm not sure yet,' she answered breezily. 'A few more weeks.'

'Aren't you missing it over there?'

'Yes, but I'm enjoying being here.'

Molly sniffed, as though not really believing it, and turned to stare out of the window. 'What about Robbie?' she suddenly blurted. 'Don't you miss him?'

'Of course,' Michelle answered.

'So why aren't you over in America with him?'

'He lives with his father and stepmother, but I visit as often as I can.' Then, after a pause, 'Have you ever been to America?'

'No. Why doesn't he live with you?'

'It's a long story, but between you and me, I wish he did.'

Molly fell silent again, leaving Michelle to reflect on the subtext of their short exchange, which had been all about Molly finding reasons for her to leave. She wasn't surprised, but it added to her concern that Katie still hadn't told her the truth.

Molly suddenly sat forward. 'This song is *wicked*,' she declared, and up went the volume.

By the time they arrived at the school, Molly was already clutching her bag, eager to jump out.

179

'I can pick you up later, if you like,' Michelle offered, as she prepared to slam the door.

'No need. Thanks.'

'Do you have everything? Money? Homework?'

'Got it. See you,' and throwing the door closed she ran to catch up with the other late arrivals.

Michelle sat watching her, envisaging a time in the future when it would be her, instead of Katie, being summoned to this sprawling, ugly mass of Sixties buildings. Such an event seemed to have no place in reality, nor did she want it to, for it would mean that Katie was no longer with them, so detaching from the thought, she turned the car around. Her mind drifted to another place, another world, where she and Tom had spent so much time together, and wasted so many opportunities to become as intimate as they had on her final afternoon. She longed for him now, and prayed to God that there would be some contact soon, something to tell her where he was, or at least that he was safe.

After picking up the day's papers, she returned home to find Katie sitting in front of her laptop, still in her dressing gown and apparently engrossed in whatever she was reading on the screen.

'Something interesting?' Michelle asked, coming to look over her shoulder.

'I'm not sure. It's just the first web site that came up when I typed in P2OG,' Katie answered.

Michelle frowned. 'What's that?'

Katie scrolled down. 'It was in the message from Tom.'

Startled, Michelle said, 'You mean he's been in touch?'

'Yes. Elliot called about twenty minutes ago.'

Michelle took a breath. 'And you didn't think to call me?' she said.

'I assumed Elliot would.'

Michelle waited for her to look up.

Finally registering the silence Katie sat back. 'I'm sorry,' she said, realizing how upset Michelle was. 'When Elliot told me there was an email I just went straight online to read it.'

'Then I'd like to see it, if you don't mind,' Michelle said.

'Yes, of course.' Katie immediately stood up for her to sit down. 'He's safe,' she quickly assured her.

Bringing the email on to the screen Michelle started to read, still slightly thrown by the last few seconds, but quickly able to focus on Tom.

```
Elliot


thanks for arranging money. Will
pay back soonest. Sajid will
contact you with details of bank.
Farukh will meet him and bring to
me. Intend to leave P. in next few
days. This is looking big.
Intelligence driven. Start with
P20G. Need all the b/g we can get.
Other web addresses to follow. Not
in my keeping right now. Will fwd
soonest.

M. ? ZX & ZP HTAJWY TV NS QNP B
OJR?

QTAE DTZ
```

It took Michelle a few minutes to unravel the code, which ended with the two words 'love you', then turning the pad round for Katie to see the rest of it, she said, 'I should put it in an email to Elliot.'

As she typed it in, Katie read the words aloud. '"?US and UK covert op in link with JEM?" Who's JEM?'

'It's a fundamental Islamist group based in Pakistan,' Michelle answered, sending the message then reaching for the phone.

Katie's eyes opened wide. 'Is he saying that our intelligence services are in cahoots with terrorists?' she asked incredulously.

'He's suggesting it. The question marks mean he isn't sure. What did you get from P2OG?'

'I still haven't read much, but I'll go back to it now. Was Molly OK, by the way? Did you get there on time?'

'Yes, she's fine. She wants to know how long I'm staying.'

Katie's head came up again, but before she could respond, Elliot had answered the phone.

'Hi, it's Michelle,' she told him. 'I've just sent you a translation of the last line. I think you'll find it interesting. What are you getting from P2OG?'

'It's an acronym for Proactive Pre-emptive Operations Group,' he told her, 'which seems to be a secret counter-intelligence unit for dealing with terrorists and rogue states, though I haven't come up with anything yet to say it actually exists. It just seems to be a recommendation from the Defense Science Board to the US Defense Department dating back to early 2002. I've sent it all on to Max, in Washington, to see what he can come up with.'

'But essentially, if it does exist, what would it be?'

'A kind of elite task force comprising intelligence and military whose primary function, as I see it, would be to stimulate terror attacks in order for the US to stage a quick response in any country it chose.'

Immediately registering the horrific potential of that, Michelle's eyes moved to Katie, who could hear what was being said. 'So do you think Tom's found proof of its existence?' she asked.

'That's not what he says. If anything, it's what he's looking for.'

'What about the UK connection?'

'I haven't found one yet, but looking at your email, Tom obviously thinks there is one.'

Speaking loudly enough for Elliot to hear, Katie said, 'Is it worth making a few calls to see if P2OG rings any bells here?'

'Let's hold fire for the moment,' he answered. 'Tom's saying he should be out of Pakistan in the next few days, and we don't want to alert anyone to the fact we're on to this until we know what we're actually dealing with.'

'Of course,' Katie responded.

'Listen, I have to go now,' Elliot said. 'Don't do anything until you hear from me again. Is Laurie with you by any chance?'

'No, but we're expecting her any minute,' Michelle replied.

'OK. If I haven't spoken to her by the time she gets there, ask her to call.'

After ringing off Michelle went to pour herself a coffee.

'I'm sorry,' Katie said, watching her and sensing she still wasn't quite forgiven. 'I should have called you the minute I knew he'd been in touch.'

'Yes, you should,' Michelle responded. 'But we'll let it go now, mainly because you're looking very pale. Are you all right?'

'Hung-over,' Katie confessed, 'which you must be too.'

'A bit.'

Katie smiled and nodded towards the dresser. 'There's a letter for you from the airline,' she said.

Breaking it open Michelle read the few lines quickly, then tore the page into small pieces and stuffed them in the bin. 'They're sorry they haven't been able to find my suitcase,' she said, 'so perhaps I'd like to get in touch with my insurer.' Her voice was taut with anger. 'That's all my personal records gone, not to mention the computer itself and everything else that was in the bag.'

'Don't you need the letter to make a claim?' Katie asked, glancing at the bin.

'Do you seriously think I was insured?'

Katie inhaled, not entirely sure what to say next, partly because she knew that a lot of Michelle's anger was still directed at her. 'I should go and make myself presentable before Laurie arrives,' she said, and getting up from the computer she left Michelle to continue reading the scant information she'd found so far regarding the P2OG.

Laurie had accessed Tom's email through her Blackberry before leaving the hotel and was now on the phone to Elliot as she drove into Membury

Hempton, sunglasses on to protect her eyes from the dazzling sun, and the windows half open to let in some air.

'The fact that Tom's getting out of Pakistan,' Elliot was saying, 'means he's happy to leave that end of it to Farukh, who'll be able to go deeper into the mosques and madrasas than he can. So my guess is, he's decided there's more to be gained from being here, or in the US, but until I've spoken to him we can't know anything for certain.'

'So you're waiting for Sajid to be in touch now with the bank details?' she said.

'That's right. The money's already in Pakistan so it'll only require a local transfer. Hang on, let me check who this other call's from.' A moment later he was back on the line. 'No-one important,' he said. 'Now, since this is taking on all the hallmarks of a highly suspect joint-intelligence operation, I'm questioning the wisdom of allowing Katie to be involved.'

Laurie's eyebrows went up. 'Why? Her contacts will be as good as anyone else's. Possibly even better, and besides, with Michelle in the same house, I don't see how we can avoid it.'

'You might find Michelle agrees with me,' he responded. 'These guys don't play by the rules, she knows that better than most, and considering Katie's condition . . .'

'Elliot, Katie's a grown woman who can make her own decisions, and I, for one, am not about to stand in the way. I doubt Michelle would either, because Katie's clearly seeing this as her last opportunity to be involved in something big, and what harm do you think she's going to come to, stuck down here in Wiltshire, making a few calls and surfing about on the Net?'

'Location's got nothing to do with it. If the US is planning to pre-empt another war and get this country involved, then we're all in a vulnerable position, because they're going to do everything they can to stop it going public before they're ready.'

'I take your point, but I still don't think we can exclude Katie, unless she herself decides that we should.'

'OK. I've expressed my concerns, and I'll come back to them if need be, but until then, let's move on.'

'Happily, but I'll tell her you were worried, it'll be sure to please her, because she's very fond of you.'

'As I am of her. What progress did you make on the programme front last night?'

'Actually not much. She's avoiding making any kind of commitment, I think mainly because of Molly. So I'm going to pull back from the personal, and see if she's more comfortable with the political.'

Elliot laughed. 'That's like asking a man with one leg if he's more comfortable sitting down,' he commented.

'I know, but I think it's the kind of swan song she's more likely to go for, laying into our Government for all its failings, particularly over this last year, which she was too ill to comment on – and now we have this added bonus of a new situation unfolding around us. I think hearing it from her, as it happens, could have a profound effect on everyone, including us.'

'I won't argue with that,' he responded.

'Good. Right, I'm outside the house now, so I should ring off. Just tell me, have you contacted Nick since you received the email? If this P2OG group has morphed into a reality, he might know something about it.'

There was a moment's pause before he said, 'I want to consult with Tom before I open it up any further. Unless you've already mentioned something to Nick?'

She was feeling slightly breathless now, and wondering why she'd even brought it up. 'No, I merely told him that you might be in touch,' she said.

'I see. So you've spoken to him? Or perhaps you've seen him?'

'We spoke on the phone yesterday.'

There was another drawn-out silence before he finally said, 'Are you coming back tonight? I only ask to know if I need to vacate the flat.'

'No, you're asking to find out if I'm seeing Nick.'

'Wrong, but you can answer that anyway, if you feel the need to.'

'My focus right now is on making a programme about Katie,' she reminded him, 'which means I will be spending the day with her and Michelle. How that goes will dictate whether or not I come back to London tonight.'

'Then I'll wait to hear from you,' he said, and as the line went dead she knew he'd have been only too aware of how she'd avoided a direct answer to his question.

'You know, I sometimes see us all as gazelles,' Katie was musing aloud as she strolled into the village with Laurie and Michelle. 'There we all are supping innocently at our personal little watering holes of life, getting on with things and doing the best we can, while all the while, out of sight and out of mind, dark forces are stalking. Those forces, to my mind, are the American neo-conservatives with their projects and think tanks and ambitions of global dominance that affect every single one of us. Our country's at war because of them, and they're quite obviously behind this P2OG initiative to provoke others. OK, we have no proof that the P2 exists other than on paper, but do any of us really doubt it? To quote Gore Vidal, they're operating a policy of "perpetual war for perpetual peace" and while they're at it, they're managing to brainwash certain elements of our Government into believing it's the right way to go. I'm telling you, if I still had my column I'd be using it to demand that we have a vote in the next US presidential election, because if we're going to be any further subjected to that neo-ninny's right-wing agenda, I think we need to have a say.'

Though Laurie was laughing, she was in perfect agreement as she said, 'There aren't many who'd argue with that.'

Warming to her subject, Katie said, 'Did you happen to hear the Foreign Secretary on the radio earlier? He opens his mouth and out comes all this neo-con guff about Article 51 of the UN Charter giving the right to take pre-emptive action. That is utter bollocks, excuse my language. Article 51 only allows for self-defence in the event of armed attack. Nowhere, in the entire Charter, does it even refer to the right to take pre-emptive action, so the man told a bare-faced lie.'

'Which, when scrutinized in the light of what Tom seems to be suggesting,' Michelle said, 'leads us to wondering if the ground is being set for another illegal war.'

As they reached the war memorial on the village's central island they paused to look at the names that had been chiselled into the stone. 'Seems rather inauspicious that we should find ourselves here while having this conversation, doesn't it?' Katie remarked.

'These men died for the greater good and freedom,' Laurie said. 'What are our men and women dying for now?'

'It's a good question with several answers,' Katie responded, 'and one is to grab control of as much oil as possible to feed the gas-guzzlers of the United States. They need to be taxed, the way we are, watch their consumption drop then.'

'Anyone who did that would be thrown out of office,' Laurie commented, as they walked on across the road towards the pub.

'Of course, which is why it won't happen. And then shall we get into how many billions the arms industry is making out of this war? And the next question is, how many members of the US cabinet are heavily invested in that nasty conglomeration of genocide pedlars? It stinks, the whole lot of it, but as much as I might want this little voice of mine to be heard, I don't think it's going to make a lot of difference now. We're too deeply in the pockets of that ghastly hanging-chads regime.'

'It's only by speaking out that we can make a change,' Laurie reminded her. 'And I'm offering you a platform.'

Katie smiled. 'Oh, I can go on and on,' she assured her, 'but I thought you wanted a more personal slant for the programme.'

'I do, but being who you are, it has to include your political and societal views, and an involvement in Tom's story, if it happens, will bring another dimension to what we're trying to achieve.'

'Which is actually what?'

'To see how Katie Kiernan's playing the end game.'

They were outside the pub now, though none of them attempted to go in as they came to a stop. Katie was looking pensive, so Michelle and Laurie waited, watching her until she said, 'You know how much I want to be a part of Tom's story, if I can, but I have to confess to being anxious about how it might affect Molly. Am I going to be putting her at any kind of risk?'

Laurie looked at Michelle, feeling she should be the one to answer that.

'If it were gangs or terrorists Tom was seeking to expose, I'd be a lot more concerned,' Michelle said. 'But Western intelligence organizations don't target their own women and children. OK, it's possible, depending how this plays out, that someone might decide to put a little pressure on you at some point . . .'

'Let them try,' Katie interjected.

Michelle smiled. '. . . but it almost certainly wouldn't involve Molly, and once they know you're sick, it's highly unlikely they'll come anywhere near you either. They just couldn't afford the publicity if it got out, and of course, by the very nature of who you are, it would.'

Katie was nodding. 'That's more or less what I thought you'd say,' she responded, her gaze drifting over to the old manor house that was currently being converted into three separate dwellings.

'The instant something doesn't look or feel right,' Laurie said, 'we'll cut you completely free of the political story, but remember you're not going to be playing that big a role. None of us are. It's only Elliot and Tom who'll be in the firing line, and that's not what this programme is going to be about. The focus is on you, as a woman first, then a mother, then a journalist.'

Katie's eyebrows went up as she turned back.

Matching the irony in her expression, Laurie said, 'Why don't we try putting a couple of things on tape? No camera, just sound. If nothing else, it could help establish the parameters of how personal or controversial you want to get.'

Katie nodded and pursed her lips. 'OK, on that basis, I don't see any reason not to give it a try, if you have the time.'

'Of course I have. Look, why don't I stay on till the weekend? That way I'll be close at hand if you feel like chatting, and when you don't, I can either talk to Michelle who would obviously be an integral part of the programme, or recce the local area for some dreamy countryside shots.'

Katie smiled and glanced at Michelle. 'You're very tempting,' she told Laurie, slipping a hand into Michelle's, 'and because I love having you around I'm going to say yes, please stay till the weekend.'

Laurie immediately hugged her. 'I'll call Elliot and ask him to courier down my laptop and tape recorder,' she said, 'then we can get started any time you like.'

Katie grimaced. 'I don't think it can be today,' she responded, glancing at her watch. 'I'm going to love you and leave you now, while I toddle off to the doctor. Then I have my spiritual counselling group at one thirty, where I'm currently bottom of the class because I'm so pissed off this is happening to me, which isn't supposed to be the attitude, and I can't seem to find the right one, but I keep on trying. And at three I'm due to see Molly's headmaster, which I'm actually trying not to think about, but I should at least be nice and mellowed out after my session with Heather the Healer. I suppose we could meet after that, but I'm a bit anxious about how it's going to go with aforementioned headmaster, and anyway, I should be meditating somewhere between four and six, if I'm not having to have a serious chat with Molly. Then at seven I've got my line-dancing class, which you should come to, I think you'll like it.'

Michelle was laughing. 'She's winding you up,' she told Laurie. 'Can you honestly see her line dancing?'

'Don't scoff,' Katie told her. 'I've actually tried it you know, and OK, I was as bad as you might expect, but at least I had a go. It's a lonely world out here in the country, so you have to do what you can for a bit of entertainment. Is that your phone, Laurie?'

'Yes,' she answered, pulling it out of her bag, and feeling her nerves starting to churn, she clicked on to read the text.

192

```
At GCHQ. Where r
u? N.
```

Resisting the urge to send a message straight back giving him the name of her hotel, she clicked off and put the phone away.

'Are you OK?' Michelle asked, noticing how flushed she suddenly was. 'Not bad news, I hope.'

'No! No, not at all,' Laurie answered. 'In fact it was someone you might know. Nick van Zant?'

Michelle nodded. 'Not well, but I've met him a couple of times with Tom.'

Katie was regarding her through narrowed eyes. 'Didn't I read somewhere that you and he . . . ?'

'Yes,' Laurie jumped in, 'you did, and we were, while Elliot was having his affair with the Brazilian bombshell. Frankly, he saved my life, because I honestly thought I was going under after Elliot walked out.'

'But Elliot's back now, so where does that leave you and Nick? Actually, you don't have to answer that, your body language is doing it for you.'

Michelle's eyes were simmering with laughter. 'She doesn't miss a thing,' she warned.

Laurie's cheeks were burning.

Katie grinned. 'OK, I can't hang around here with my knees going weak as we gossip about two Titans of the journalistic world, three if we're going to include Tom. I'm due at the doctor's in five minutes, so keep in mind the sizzling account I've just given you of my day, and I'll try not to be offended if you decide it's simply too risqué for a pre-watershed show.'

*

Molly was doodling love hearts and entwined initials in the back of her Religious Instruction book, wondering how she and Brad could work out the Bodhisattva Concept so that they could be reborn together, or maybe even escape samsara completely to get out of suffering, because like, who wanted that? Anyway, it was all Hindu, or Buddhist, or something eastern and exotic that didn't count in Chippenham, where she was like just blissing out over the text messages Brad had sent at lunchtime.

> Toby gave me yr
> nmbr. Hope thats
> OK. Brad.
>
> Yes, OK. I'm glad.

She was just starting to panic that saying she was glad wasn't cool, when he texted her again.

> R u on instant
> message?
>
> Yes.
>
> What's yr adrs?
> Let's chat ltr.

Immediately she'd sent her address, then forwarded the entire exchange to the DOLs, who'd texted her back like crazy, giving her all kinds of advice. She had to turn the phone off in lessons, but she was just dying for school to end now, so she could call them and go over everything he might say and what she should say back, and then what he might say again, and what she should say to that. This was like, just the best thing that had ever happened to her. She'd never had a boyfriend before, and her eyes closed as a wave of nerves rushed through her so fiercely she almost needed the loo, but then Kelly Milne nudged her hard, and told her to look out of the window.

'Isn't that your mum coming up the drive?' she whispered.

Molly's eyes grew large as a cold dread opened up in her chest. It wasn't just because she was afraid her mum was here about the stupid picture Glover had snatched, but because from up here her mum looked all thin and like weird, as though the chain had come off her karmic cycle.

'Did you know she was coming?' Kelly asked.

Molly shook her head, then abruptly turned back to pay attention to the lesson. She wanted to get in Buddha's good books so he'd make Brad call tonight.

Chapter Eight

After leaving the school Katie drove straight home, left the car in its usual space, and carried the evidence of Molly's disgrace into the house. There was only Trotty to greet her, and a note from Michelle saying she'd gone to the supermarket with Laurie, but Laurie wasn't staying for dinner. Katie barely registered the words, for she was still so upset by her meeting with the headmaster, and disconcerted now by how empty the house seemed, that for a bewildering, disorienting moment she felt almost afraid.

Scooping Trotty into her arms, she buried her face in the dog's lovely soft fur, and carried her upstairs. In her bedroom she dropped Trotty on the bed, with the proof of her motherly neglect, and sat down in front of the three oval mirrors of her antique dressing table. She looked as dreadful as she felt, ashen-faced, hollow eyes, sunken cheeks. Ironically, only her wig seemed to exude any semblance of life.

But what did she, or the way she looked matter,

when she'd obviously gone so terribly wrong with Molly that her young life was heading fast towards disaster – if it wasn't there already. Fear was tightening a stranglehold round her heart even though her instincts seemed to be telling her it was all a game, something Molly and her friends got up to, the way teenagers did. However, if she'd learned anything in her years as a columnist, it was how wrong parents could be about their own children, how often they failed to read the signs even when they were staring them in the face.

Fighting to hold back the tears, she covered her face with her hands and felt the pain of it all pressing so hard into her heart she could barely stand it. No amount of spiritual counselling, understanding or meditation could make this any easier to bear. Molly was her baby, her own flesh and blood, the most precious part of her life, and she was failing her completely. With all her might she was trying not to be bitter about her fate, to be, instead, one of those women who was noble and brave, who accepted their lot with equanimity and forgiveness, but there was no light from God shining in her soul today, no inner peace to smooth the way. She didn't want to die. She wanted to be here for her daughter, to go on being a mother, and show her how deeply she mattered.

'Please God,' she choked, starting to break down, 'please, please, please, let me stay with her. Even if it's only until she's old enough to cope on her own.'

Her head fell into her hands as she sobbed. It wasn't for her that she needed to live, it was for Molly, couldn't God see that? She'd go freely and happily if there was no Molly, but how could she just give in and accept her fate, focus her mind on the now, or anything else, when Molly's whole future was at stake?

It was a long time before she was able to pull herself together and stumble into the bathroom to rinse her face, but mercifully she managed it in time, for she was just coming back out on to the landing when the sound of the back kitchen door opening brought her to a stop. She hoped it was Michelle, *please God let it be Michelle,* but the thud of Molly's school bag hitting the floor told her that God wasn't listening.

Downstairs Molly was banging about in the fridge, turning on the radio, pouring herself a drink.

Katie stayed where she was, caught in the dilemma of whether to postpone confronting the issue to give herself more time to think it through, or whether to address it now and get it over with. The second stair creaked and her heart contracted. She put her towel on the banister and continued to stand where she was, outside Molly's room, almost as though barring the way.

As Molly reached the top she stopped, her face draining as she saw her mother.

'What's the matter?' she demanded, already on the defensive. 'What are you standing there like that for?'

'I have to talk to you,' Katie said.

Molly scowled and started towards her room. 'I've got homework to do,' she retorted.

'I've been to the school today,' Katie said quietly. 'What you had confiscated in the chemistry lab needs a lot of explaining. Now I'm prepared to listen, but I don't want any lies, or . . .'

Molly's eyes flashed. 'Why do you just assume I'm going to lie?' she cried.

'All right, I'm sorry. I shouldn't have said that, but it doesn't get us away from the fact that it has your email address at the top . . .'

'Yeah, exactly, which makes it my personal stuff, so you should all just mind your own fucking business and give it back.'

'Don't you dare speak to me like that!'

'I'll speak to you how I want.'

'Molly. I want you to swear to me that you've never met this man.'

'All right. I've never met him!' She had such a sullen, defiant look on her face that Katie could have slapped it.

'I don't believe you,' Katie said.

Molly threw out her hands. 'See, I can't win, can I?' she cried.

'Are you charging boys to do things to you?' Katie demanded. 'Is that how you afforded those shoes?'

Molly's eyes flew open in shock, then her face went dark with rage to think her mother could actually believe she'd do something like that. 'So what if it was how I got them?' she challenged. 'I never get anything around here, so . . .'

'It would make you a common whore,' Katie cut in.

'So what? Who cares what I am? Definitely not you.'

'Molly, that is not true.'

'Yes it is, now get out of my way.'

'You just stop right there,' Katie said blocking her. 'Now you listen to me, I love you more than anything else in this world, but that doesn't make having pictures like that acceptable. Mr Webb is reporting it to the police, did you know that?'

Molly turned pale.

'Well, what did you expect?' Katie cried. 'You know about the dangers of the Internet and you've left me with no alternative but to confiscate your computer . . .'

'Like hell,' Molly cried, barging past. 'You touch that, and you'll be sorry.'

Katie grabbed her, but she was too strong and pushed her away.

'Don't you dare go in that room!' Katie warned.

'I need my computer . . .'

'Not for the Internet you don't, so I'm having it disconnected. You can go online at school, or on my computer, but your privileges are revoked.' As she finished she was starting down the stairs.

Molly thundered after her. 'If you do anything to that phone line, I'll smash your head in!' she screamed.

Katie turned back, appalled by the threat, but as she started to respond her foot slid off the edge of a stair and though she tried to grab the handrail she wasn't quick enough and fell to the bottom, cracking her head on the flagstone floor below.

Molly gaped at her in horror. 'Mum?' she whispered.

Katie could only lie there, too dazed to focus.

'Oh my God, oh my God,' Molly muttered.

Katie blinked and reached out for the leg of a chair.

The door opened and Michelle came in. 'Katie!' she cried, running straight to her. 'What happened? Are you all right?'

'Just give me a hand up,' Katie croaked.

Michelle grabbed her, then heard Molly saying, 'I didn't do it! I *didn't do it*.'

Seeing the stricken look on Molly's face and registering her words, Michelle's heart turned to ice. 'Molly, what happened?' she demanded.

'I didn't do anything,' Molly cried. 'It wasn't my fault!'

'OK, calm down,' Katie said as Michelle helped her up. 'No-one's saying it was your fault . . .'

'Yes you are. *She* is. She's blaming me, and I didn't do anything.' Molly's face was turning puce with rage. 'You don't belong in our family,' she yelled at Michelle, 'so why don't you just go back to where you belong? We were all right before you came along . . .'

'Molly, stop it,' Katie cried.

'No, I won't. I'm getting out of here. I hate this house. And I hate you . . .'

'Molly, please,' Michelle implored as Molly came flying down the stairs.

'Get out of my way,' Molly seethed, elbowing her way past. '*Just get out of my way*,' she screamed as Michelle tried to take hold of her, and grabbing her bag she banged a fist against a pile of dishes and ran out of the door.

'Molly! Come back!' Michelle called, going after her, but as she got outside Molly was already leaping the fence and racing as fast as she could up the lane towards the woods.

Still in the kitchen, Katie was holding on to the

edge of the sink feeling as though she were about to throw up.

'Are you hurt?' Michelle asked, coming back in.

'No, just a bit shaken.' She took a deep breath and let it out slowly. 'She'll go to Allison's,' she said. 'I'll call in a minute to make sure.'

'So what happened?'

Katie's eyes closed as the spinning in her head became faster. 'I think I'm going to faint,' she whispered.

Quickly Michelle sat her down and rubbed her back as she put her head between her knees. She stayed there for almost a minute, before sitting up again. 'That's better,' she sighed, as her vision started to clear.

'Have you eaten anything today?' Michelle asked.

'I'm fine.'

'Katie. What have you eaten today?'

Katie's smile was weak. 'First it's me having a go at Molly, then it's you having a go at me. What a happy house.'

Michelle's humour wasn't responding. 'If you don't eat, you're not going to have any energy, and if you have no energy how can you even begin to think you're capable of dealing with Molly?'

Katie shot her one of her famously dry looks.

'You're not taking the megace are you?' Michelle stated.

'Sometimes.'

'Katie, you have to eat, and if appetite stimulants are the only way . . .'

'Can we just get drunk? I'm feeling in need.'

'Not on an empty stomach.'

'OK. You cook, I'll take the megace and open the wine, and then you can tell me all about Laurie's triangle . . .'

'No. You can tell me all about Molly and how you ended up on the floor with her halfway up the stairs.'

'She didn't push me, so I've no idea why she thinks I think she did. What I do know, though, is I've made a terrible mess of everything with her, and right now I haven't got the first idea how to put it right.'

Michelle's eyes were dark with concern. 'I could suggest you begin by telling her the truth,' she said, softening her tone, 'but you obviously need to let this settle down a bit first. What happened at the school? I take it that's what this was about?'

Katie nodded. 'I think, *hope* I overreacted, so I want you to take a look at what I brought home, and tell me what you think, how you would handle it from here. Whatever we decide though, I'm going to have to tell Laurie that the programme can't happen, because after this . . . I have to focus totally on Molly now, and forget my pathetic, selfish bid for a last grasp at fame.'

Molly ran and ran – across the horse and pony field, over the next stile, through Bell Woods and finally up the drive to Allison's house.

Spotting her coming, Allison bounded out of the stables to meet her. 'What's up?' she cried.

'I had a terrible row with my mum,' Molly gasped, dashing away the tears. 'She's threatened to take my computer away, and Brad's instant-messaging me tonight. You've got to let me use yours.'

'No problem. Come on. Let's go to my room. What was the row about?'

'She's seen the picture that was confiscated,' Molly explained, following her into the big farmhouse kitchen where Mrs Bond, phone in one hand, glass in the other, flashed a sweet smile as she passed.

'Oh shit,' Allison groaned. 'Have you been grounded?'

'We didn't get that far, she fell down the stairs, and it was like, so surreal, because it was like Step Five before we abandoned it, and maybe I pushed her, but I know I didn't. I was going to help her up, but then Michelle came in and you could tell she thought I'd done it. She is such a bitch. I hate her. Everything's gone wrong in our house since she came. I wish I knew how to get rid of her.'

'We'll work something out,' Allison assured her, pushing open her bedroom door.

'Someone's texting me,' Molly said, her heart giving a jump in case it was Brad.

```
Please let me
know where u r.
Mum.
```

'Oh God!' she cried, throwing a quick glance at Allison.

Allison was busy lighting a cigarette and turning on the computer, so Molly hurriedly typed a message back.

```
At A's.
```

'Oh God, it's her again,' she seethed, as her mother messaged back.

```
R u OK?

Yes. R u?

Yes. Love you. We
need to talk.
```

Molly sighed and tutted and tossed the phone on the bed. 'God, this is like so unreal, with Brad texting me today, and then her exploding at me when I got home. Who needs it?' she grumbled, glad her mum was all right.

'What time's he instant-messaging?' Allison asked.

'Six. Are the others coming over?'

Allison was already dialling. 'Cecy? It's me. My house at six. Tell Donna. Molly's going to chat to Brad from here, and she's got a problem she needs solving.'

'What problem?' Molly asked as she rang off.

'With your aunt. You said you want to get rid of her.'

Molly sat up. 'Yes, that's right,' she confirmed. 'I just know she's like, responsible for everything that's going wrong in our house, and she hates me, so I've got to find a way of making her go back to where she came from.'

'OK, we'll put our heads together and come up with something,' Allison responded. 'That's not your mother again is it?' she snapped impatiently as Molly's phone started ringing.

Molly looked at the name on the display, blinked, then her mouth fell open as she realized who it was. 'Oh my God! Oh my God!' she gasped. 'It's him. It's Brad. And it's not a text.'

Allison stared at her, dumbfounded, then a grin spread across her face. 'Well go on, answer it!' she cried. 'Oh my God. This is like, so cool. And I am like, so jealous. Molly, *answer it*.'

Dying with nerves, Molly clicked on the line. 'Hello?' she said softly, deafened by her own heartbeat.

'Hi. Molly? It's Brad.'

Her mouth opened wide again as she gave a silent scream of elation. 'Hi. How are you?' she asked.

'I'm cool. How are you?'

'Yeah, I'm cool too.'

'It's OK to talk, is it?' he asked. 'It's not a bad time?'

'No! No, it's cool.'

'Good. It's just that something's come up so I can't make it to a computer at six. I was going to send a text, but then I thought it would be like, kind of good to hear your voice.'

Molly swallowed hard, and tried to stop herself going into orbit. 'That's cool,' she said.

'Stop saying cool,' Allison hissed.

Molly blushed and turned aside as Brad said, 'So you're the Molly I saw at Toby Bond's house.'

'Yes,' she whispered.

'Do you go to the same school as Allison?'

'No. I go to the local one in Chippenham. I used to go to one in London, but then my dad . . . Then

206

we had to come and live here. Where do you live? I mean, when you're not at school.'

'In London. Kensington. Do you know it?'

'Yes! It's where we used to live. That is so awesome. We were neighbours.'

He was laughing, and then they got into which street he lived in, and discovered they'd been about ten minutes from each other. Then they chatted about all the places they knew, or went to, so it turned out to be amazing they'd never met before.

When finally they rang off Molly threw aside the phone, clapped her hands over her face and kicked her feet up and down. 'Oh my God! Oh my God!' she cried. 'I don't believe it. I've actually spoken to him! Oh my God. Allison. This is like so unbelievable.'

Laughing, Allison crushed her cigarette in an ashtray. 'So come on, what did he say?' she demanded. 'Start from the beginning and tell me everything.'

By the time the others arrived at six they'd been over it a dozen times, and Molly was more than happy to go over it another dozen for Cecily and Donna. In the end Cecily got bored and wandered over to the computer.

'What are you doing?' Allison asked.

'I'm trying to find this web site I heard about,' she answered, keeping her eyes on the screen. 'Apparently there's a chat room for all these sad sacks who want to commit suicide. I thought it could be a bit of a laugh to find out what they're saying.'

'You are like, so warped,' Allison told her.

Molly was smiling, still basking in the glow of

her phone call, until another text came through from her mother.

> Dinner's almost
> ready.

'Is it him?' Cecily demanded, spinning round.
'No, it's my mother.'
'Ssss,' they all hissed.

> eating at A's
>
> Home by 8 pls.

Molly's face darkened. 'Like hell,' she muttered at the phone. 'No way, if you've taken my computer.'

'She won't,' Allison said confidently. 'They always threaten, but they never actually do it.'

'Yes, but Michelle might talk her into it.' She threw out her hands in frustration. 'See! That's what I mean, everything's going wrong because of her. So you've got to help me come up with a way to get rid of her.'

'Cecily!' Allison barked. 'You're always full of ideas.'

'I'm thinking,' Cecily responded, tapping away at the keyboard. 'Just let me finish this, then we'll start an elimination conference.'

Molly wrinkled her nose as she looked at the others, but they didn't seem to know what Cecily was talking about either, so she just went back to dreaming about Brad and what she was going to say the next time he called.

Taking the bottle of wine and glass the barman was handing her, Laurie started upstairs to her room. She wasn't quite sure who she was trying to fool, herself or the barman, that she'd be drinking alone, but what did it matter? The barman had no interest in her conscience, and she was only eager to find a way of shutting it down. Yet she wasn't thinking about Elliot now, only about Nick, and how long it might take him to get here.

Going into the bathroom she turned on the shower and started to undress. When she was ready she'd go back down to the bar to wait, make sure they stayed in sight of other people, so they wouldn't even be able to hold hands. She wondered why she was telling herself such nonsense, but went on doing it anyway. Once she saw him she'd probably find that the attraction was all in her mind, that it just needed some reality to steal the power from the fantasy. They'd be glad to see each other, naturally, but he would leave after a leisurely dinner and drive back to Cheltenham, while she returned to her room alone.

Just before he was due, she glanced around the cosy, old-fashioned room with its muted wallpaper, leaded windows and solid oak beams, then she turned off the overhead light, so that only two lamps were casting a warm, amber glow over the bed, and went to close the curtains. In one corner was a tall, free-standing mirror, where her reflection showed none of the turmoil inside her, only a slender, blonde woman, wearing jeans and one of the new T-shirt tops she'd picked up in Chippenham yesterday. It was plain white with buttons that ran right down the front, many of which she hadn't yet fastened. It accentuated her tan beautifully, particularly in this light, and because she'd chosen to save the new bra and panties she'd bought for tomorrow, the generous fullness of her breasts wasn't only visible through the top's partly open front, but through the tightly clinging fabric that hinted at the darkness of her nipples, while revealing all of their prominence.

She felt breathless and flushed by the wine she'd already drunk, and though there was plenty of time to do up her buttons and put a jacket over the top, she'd done neither by the time he knocked on the door.

With her heart pounding violently, and her limbs feeling like liquid, she turned away from the mirror and walked across the room. As her hand grasped the latch she tried to will herself out of what almost felt like a trance. She needed to appear friendly and casual, and though she knew she wasn't even close to achieving it, she told herself she was and finally opened the door.

He was tall, blond, devastatingly handsome, and the instant she saw him she knew there was no point trying to fool herself any longer.

'Hi,' he said, his voice sounding gruff, as his gaze seemed to penetrate all the remaining layers of her resolve.

She attempted a smile. 'Do – do you want to come in?' she offered, almost feeling as though her breasts were naked. 'Or shall we go down to the bar?'

Staying with her eyes, he said, 'Your call.'

Leaving the door open she walked back to the

bed to pick up her bag. As her hand reached it she heard the floorboards creak behind her, then the door click closed. She stopped breathing, waiting for him to move, but for long, agonizing seconds there was only the power of him standing there and the tension that was charging the air. He moved up behind her, and she groaned aloud as he reached around her to cup her breasts roughly in his hands. Her head fell back on to his shoulder, and his hands tightened their hold as he buried his face in her neck. She turned her mouth to his and as he pushed his tongue deep inside he pressed his erection hard up against her.

'I've been thinking about this all day,' he told her roughly.

'Me too,' she gasped, loving the feel of his cock against her buttocks, so big and ready, and his hands moving under her T-shirt on to her skin. She raised her arms and he tore the top off. His fingers closed on her nipples, squeezing and pulling so hard that the urgency in her spilled over, making her reach for the zip in his jeans, so she could feel him too. Within seconds their clothes were on the floor, and he was bending her over the bed, opening her legs wide.

'Tell me this is what you want,' he growled.

'Yes, oh yes,' she gasped as he began moving into her. 'Oh God, yes.'

He held her hips as he rocked back and forth in short rapid strokes, then suddenly he plunged all the way into her.

'Oh my God!' she cried. 'Nick, please . . .'

He did it again, and again, thrusting and pounding, moving his hands all over the front of her, from her mouth, to her breasts, to between her legs. She sobbed and gasped, pushing her buttocks higher, to take him in even deeper.

She'd wanted this too much, was too ready, and so was he, because within minutes they were caught up in the mounting force of the other's climax. The sensations were so intense there was no holding back. They had to let go, there was no other way.

'Oh Jesus Christ,' he gasped, banging into her again and again. He was coming and coming and couldn't stop. The hunger of her orgasm was devouring him, twisting and pulling, taking him into a madness of fulfilment that was going on and on.

'Oh yes,' she almost screamed, as she finally went over the edge with him. She pushed her face into the pillow and sobbed and gasped at the power of so much sensation. His chest was pressed to her back, his thighs clamped against hers. She could feel him all over, inside and out.

At last he came to a shuddering, breathless halt, every muscle in his body on fire. He held her close and kissed her hair, then turned her lips so he could kiss them too. 'Not quite the welcome I was expecting,' he murmured. 'But God, I hoped.'

She laughed softly, and turning beneath him, put her arms around him and searched for his mouth. He kissed her hard, squeezing her in even tighter to his body, as though somehow he could make them one.

In the end, he raised himself up on his elbows and gazed down at her face. 'You were different tonight,' he told her.

She smiled and brushed her lips against his. 'I was broken-hearted before,' she reminded him.

His eyes searched hers, speaking in a way that words wouldn't allow, until finally he lowered his head and kissed her again, moulding her tongue and her lips with his own, letting all the tenderness in his heart flow into the embrace. It was a long time before his mouth moved from hers, and began moving slowly down to her neck and on to her breasts. He covered them with kisses, licked and gently bit them, before sucking first one, then the other big, rosy nipple into his mouth.

Her eyes fluttered closed as he continued to kiss and tease, using his lips and his fingers, his tongue and the hard tips of his nails, until each nipple stood out so large and swollen, so tender and moist, that even the feel of his breath was like an intense caress. His fingers moved downwards, trailing a tantalizing path over her navel and hip bones, to the join in her legs where they slid into the moistness.

'Don't stop,' she murmured, arching her back towards him, 'please don't stop.'

His fingers moved back and forth, gently, but insistently, then harder and faster. His mouth was tight on her nipple, and became even tighter as she opened her legs wide. Then his tongue was where his fingers had been, and her head rolled from side to side as the exquisite sensations rushed through her like a river of fire.

Moving his mouth back up to hers he prepared to enter her again. 'Are you ready?' he asked.

Her vision was blurred by sensation as she nodded.

213

He sank into her slowly, filling her and feeling her. 'Is this good?' he asked, gently riding her.

'Oh yes,' she whispered. 'Oh yes, oh yes.'

'Harder?'

She nodded, and her eyes closed as he increased the pressure.

'Tell me when you want more,' he murmured.

'I want more,' she told him. 'I want you all the way in me. I want you to fuck me . . . *Oh God*,' she cried as he jerked in so hard it jarred her all over.

'Like this?' he growled, and did it again.

'Yes. Yes.'

He rammed her again and again, pumping her with all his might, and feeling her body go weak beneath his. 'I can't take any more,' she gasped.

'Yes you can. You want it. I'm in you, fucking you. This is what you want.'

'I'm going to come,' she moaned.

'I'm right with you. Just hold on. Oh *yes*, *oh yes*!' he cried as her fingers found his balls.

'Nick. I'm there, I'm there,' she choked.

He was pounding her harder than ever, muscles straining, sweat pouring, until finally his climax broke too, and as everything rushed into her he clung tightly to her, feeling every last pulse of an orgasm so sublime and so encompassing that it surpassed even the last.

For a long time they lay in each other's arms, waiting for their heartbeats to calm and the aftershocks inside to finally fade. The very smell of him was still intoxicating her, and she inhaled deeply as though drinking him in. His hand was on her face, his thumb close to her mouth, so she drew it between her lips and kissed it. Their legs were entwined, he was still inside her, but gradually the power was leaving him. She turned to look at him, and found his eyes on her, but as he started to speak she put her fingers on his lips, then leaned in to kiss him.

Finally he rolled on to his back to lie with one arm over his eyes, and his legs wide apart. She looked down at him, and touched her palm to the flat, hard plain of his abdomen. His thighs were long and powerfully muscled, his feet were slender and almost as female as a woman's. She pressed her mouth to the damp hair on his chest, then slid quietly from the bed and went into the bathroom to fetch a second glass for the wine. As she looked in the mirror she saw the reflection of a woman who was sated and flushed, still dazed by the power of a relentless climax and tanned all over. She thought of Elliot and wondered if this was how it had been with Andraya. She waited for the guilt, but it didn't come, and turning round she went to stand in the doorway, so he could see her naked.

'Shall we go down for dinner before they stop serving?' she said.

Raising his arm, he turned his head to look at her. 'I guess they don't do room service,' he said, letting his eyes move all over her.

'No.'

'You're beautiful,' he told her softly.

Walking back to the bed, she took his hand and pressed it to her lower belly. 'Will I have had enough of you by morning?' she asked.

'There's only one way to find out,' he murmured, and pulled her back into his arms.

*

Katie was fast asleep. The first rays of dawn were barely over the horizon, the house was dark and still, and not even Trotty deigned to open an eye as Molly came quietly into the bedroom. Seeing her mother's slight frame beneath the covers Molly stood looking at her for a moment, as though unsure whether to wake her, then lifting the covers she snuggled herself in like a spoon.

Katie's eyes remained closed as she put an arm around her daughter and kissed the back of her tousled dark head.

'Mum?' Molly whispered after a while.

'Mm?'

'I've never met that man in the picture.'

Katie squeezed her. 'I didn't think so,' she said. 'I just went off the deep end.'

The digital clock flicked on to five twenty. A thrush started to sing in the apple tree outside; a distant cockerel crowed.

'Sorry,' they said together, and smiled into the darkness.

Now wasn't the time, Katie decided, to pursue anything else. This was a special moment, just the two of them together, so why let anything spoil it?

Chapter Nine

'So the money's now on its way to Tom,' Katie was saying to Laurie as they strolled up the lane towards the woods. 'Which means we might hear from him in the next day or two.'

'We should, if all goes to plan,' Laurie confirmed, stifling a yawn.

'It'll make a big difference to Michelle if we do,' Katie remarked, 'because she's finding this a lot harder than she's admitting. She's used to being in the thick of it, or at least able to do something to help when he gets himself in a fix. Anyway, there's nothing to be done until we hear from him, so I guess we should . . . Is that mine?' she said as a mobile started to ring.

'I think so,' Laurie answered, swallowing her disappointment that it wasn't hers, for she was hoping Nick would call, if only to say hi.

'It's the doctor's surgery,' Katie said, clicking on. 'It won't take a second.'

As she took the call, Laurie's mind returned instantly to Nick, and all they'd done last night.

Even to think of it was flaring responses through her that were almost as erotically charged as the reality. Her body still ached from so much love-making. They'd hardly been able to tear themselves away from each other, had been so inflamed by passion that they'd barely made any time to talk or even eat.

'Just confirming my hospital appointment next week,' Katie said, ringing off. 'So where were we? Ah, yes, I was about to tell you what happened at the school yesterday.'

As she began to explain about Molly, Laurie tried desperately to stay focused, but now she was worrying about Elliot and how the hell she was going to face him when the time came. Speaking to him on the phone this morning had been bad enough, for her conscience had returned with such a vengeance when she'd heard his voice that she'd barely been able to register what he was saying. Then Nick had come out of the bathroom and started to remove the robe she'd covered herself with, leaving her with no choice but to cut the call short. So what was Elliot thinking now, she kept asking herself. Had he guessed what was happening? Was he tormenting himself with images of her and Nick, the way she had with images of him and Andraya?

Forcing herself to concentrate, she watched Katie lean over a five-bar gate to stroke the muzzle of a sleek, golden horse.

'So if you'd called last night,' Katie was saying, 'I'd have told you a programme was completely out of the question, but on reflection I probably did overreact when I saw that picture, and I'm angry with myself now for thinking the worst of Molly, when I should have known it was just kids messing around.'

'Are you going to punish her anyway?' Laurie asked, thankful that she'd managed to absorb enough to know what Katie was talking about.

'I don't know. I'd rather trust her to not do anything like it again, but I'd be fooling myself if I thought she was never going to succumb to peer pressure, particularly when she's been so lonely since we came here. She's happy to have friends again, and when you take into consideration what she's going to be facing soon, I don't want to start making her miserable now.' She sighed and watched Trotty skimming across the field after a rabbit she was never going to catch. 'Now,' she said, turning back with a twinkle in her eye, 'I'm starting to form the impression that you didn't get much sleep last night.'

Laurie quickly covered her mouth again, and grimaced an apology. 'I didn't,' she confirmed, feeling the burn of Nick's hands as though they were still on her. 'Sorry, it's annoying when people keep yawning.'

Katie smiled.

After a moment Laurie smiled too, but resisted the urge to discuss her dilemma, for easy as Katie was to talk to, she had enough of her own issues to deal with. 'So what would you like to do about the programme?' she asked. 'You know how keen I am, but as I told you before, it's your decision.'

Turning to track the stately progress of a fully plumed pheasant as it plodded dumbly towards Trotty's lair, Katie said, 'I think I'd like to carry on as we agreed yesterday. As you said, it doesn't commit me to anything, and we're here now, so why don't we go ahead with whatever you had planned for today and see how it goes?' She cast her a droll look. 'If you can remember what you had planned, that is.'

Laurie laughed and blushed. 'Michelle's right,' she said, 'nothing ever gets past you.'

'Nothing,' Katie confirmed.

Still laughing, and having to remind herself once again that they weren't here to discuss her, Laurie said, 'OK, why don't we kick off with something nice and easy like what you'd most like to achieve in the time you have left.'

Katie's eyebrows rose. 'Nice and easy,' she repeated dryly, and leaning her elbows against the gate, she murmured the question softly to herself, then added with a laugh, 'You mean apart from an end to global warming, overthrowing the current US regime, and getting laid?'

'You missed out world peace.'

'No, that's covered under number two. Actually getting rid of those power-crazed maniacs who've set up shop in the White House would probably sort out most world issues, but I don't think this is the kind of answer you had in mind.'

Laurie shook her head.

'OK, so let me see. Well, I suppose after making sure Molly's OK and taken care of, which is obviously what Michelle's here for, probably what I'd most like to achieve is the kind of inner peace that makes it all right to go.'

Laurie felt mildly surprised. 'You give the appearance of already being there,' she told her.

Katie gave a scoff of laughter. 'Not even close,' she assured her. 'If you could see me lying in my bed at night like a petrified virgin, listening to the incessant babble in my head as I go over and over everything my spiritual counsellor advises, madly trying to channel my thoughts into the now so that I can overcome my resistance and accept what's happening, which I'm told is the path to inner calm . . . Believe me, it's chaos in here, but I try and sometimes it actually works, for a minute or two, until the demons start parachuting in again, and my fears light up like beacons to guide them straight to the hot spots.'

Laurie watched her as she seemed to drift for a while.

'Actually, if you want to know the truth,' she went on, 'I'm absolutely terrified. Not of dying particularly, or of what comes next, though I can't say I'm thrilled about the one-way part of the deal. No, what I'm most afraid of is leaving Molly. I know that without her I'd be empty, so my fear is that's how she'll feel without me. She's still so young and it frightens me to think of her in the world without me, even though I know Michelle will love and take care of her.'

Laurie was thinking of all the other mothers who were facing the same nightmare, as well as the millions who weren't, for no-one could be immune to the agony of having to say a premature goodbye to a child.

'I still haven't told her,' Katie said, her eyes following the pheasant as it flapped and clucked over a hedgerow and disappeared from view. 'I keep waiting for the right moment, but I guess I'm going to have to accept that for something like this, there is no right moment.' After a while she turned to look back down the lane, and spotting Michelle coming to join them, gave her a wave.

'They say,' she continued, 'that knowing you're going to die gives you an appreciation of life and the people around you that you didn't have before, and it's true, in so many ways. One of them, for me, is how I've finally allowed myself to see Michelle for who she really is. I used to tell myself she was selfish and conceited, unreliable, inconsiderate and far, far too pleased with herself, when actually I was just jealous of how beautiful she is, and the way everyone adores or admires her. She's reached a place inside herself where she doesn't sit in judgement of others, the way most of us do, she doesn't even shove scene-stealers like me out of the limelight so everyone can get a good look at her, because she doesn't need to. She's happy with who she is, and feels no need to prove herself to people who aren't really listening anyway. Whereas I've always been one of those loud, opinionated types who underneath it all are horribly threatened by people like her.' She shook her head in dismay. 'All these years I've been coveting her spot on the stage, while forgetting to look at my own, which means I've missed out on so much. I was only seeing the false picture, where I'd painted her accomplishments in such dazzling and magnificent colours that next to them mine could only wither and fade.' She gave a protracted sigh of exasperation, as though amazed she hadn't seen all this before, when it seemed so clear to her now.

'You look very intense,' Michelle commented, as

she joined them. 'I hope she's not boring you.'

'Actually, I was going to leave that to you,' Katie retorted, turning to stroke the horse as it nudged her.

Michelle laughed, then frowned curiously. 'Katie? Why have you got a duster on your back?'

'Because I had a notion to clean up the neighbourhood,' Katie responded glibly. 'What duster?'

Michelle peeled it from the belt of her sweater and passed it over. 'This one,' she said.

'Now why don't prattish things like that happen to you?' Katie wanted to know, tucking the duster in her pocket and enjoying watching Laurie laugh.

'It's only one per family,' Michelle responded. 'So, where were you up to?'

'I was just about to drown in a swamp of self-pity,' Katie informed her. 'You see, I have to feel sorry for myself,' she explained to Laurie, 'because no-one else around here does.'

'You'd get a lot more sympathy from me if you'd eat,' Michelle told her.

'Actually, I've taken my megace today, and while you were immersed in all the P2 stuff this morning I trotted off to get myself a new prescription. So how good does that make you feel?'

'Almost as good as the smile I got from Molly before she went off to school.'

Katie's eyes immediately showed her pleasure. 'You see, behind the snarling, snapping trainee dragon is a winning little creature just dying to get out. It's all those hormones that are doing it, rampaging around in jackboots one minute, in fluffy socks the next, so carry on taking the hornbeam is what I say, it'll keep you nice and chilled out.'

223

'Hornbeam?' Laurie echoed.

'Ah yes, my secret weapon, it has magical powers in times of stress, so you might want to take some with you when you leave here later.'

'I'll take as much as you can spare,' Laurie responded dryly.

'Am I missing something?' Michelle said, as Katie laughed.

'She's trying to change the subject,' Laurie answered, 'so she's no longer the focus. Now come on, stop trying to pretend you're a retiring violet, because no-one's convinced, and tell us about *you*. What is it really like to be Katie Kiernan these days? Who is she? What's driving her? How does she want to be remembered? When will she ever tell us the real truth about *her*?'

Katie looked at Michelle. 'Could that qualify as bullying?' she demanded.

Michelle nodded. 'Absolutely. So how does it feel to be on the receiving end?'

Katie's eyes narrowed. 'You're in a conspiracy, you two,' she declared. 'And you're rushing me.'

'Well, if you will wait till you're moving out before you invite us in, we don't have much choice,' Michelle responded.

Katie's eyes lit up. 'That's good,' she told her. 'I like it.' And in order to savour it, she repeated it.

Laurie watched her familiar, animated face, and found herself caught for a moment in a strange displacement of time, as though she were looking at a photograph, and this was all a memory. It was a disturbing, upsetting feeling, for though she'd never been in any doubt that losing Katie would be extremely hard to bear, it was as though the fact that it really was going to happen was only just hitting her.

'Are you all right?' Katie asked.

'Yes, yes I'm fine,' Laurie assured her, smiling again. 'Just a bug, or something,' she added, blinking her eyes.

'She's been up half the night making the beast with two backs,' Katie informed Michelle. 'What?' she demanded as Laurie and Michelle spluttered with laughter.

'The beast with two backs?' Michelle repeated.

Katie sighed. 'That's the trouble with you airheads, you just don't know your Shakespeare,' she complained.

Laurie was still laughing. 'Please say you'll do this programme, Katie,' she implored. 'Please, please.'

'You'll have to talk to my manager,' Katie responded haughtily as they started walking on towards the woods. 'She's right beside you. I don't do anything without her approval these days. She's got me all carefully managed and mapped out, so that I'm scared of moving without her.'

'Did you ever hear such nonsense?' Michelle demanded. 'Can you imagine anyone ever managing *her*? You'd have to get yourself a lion-taming degree to begin with, not to mention a flak-proof jacket, gold-star health coverage, and regular top-up courses in emergency first aid for the soul.'

'That's the old me,' Katie retorted. 'The new me doesn't do soul-bashing any more, unless it happens to be of the neo-con variety. I'd happily churn that around the axis of evil a few times to get it to change its foreign policies, and turn our

225

gorgeous little planet into a dandy old place to be. Of course, if you're me, with an expiring membership, it seems pretty dandy already, but I'm thinking ahead now, and trying not to be selfish. Oh Laurie, there goes your phone.'

Laurie's heart had already gone into free fall. 'Sorry, I should have turned it off,' she said, taking it out of her pocket. Seeing who it was, her nerves churned up all over again. 'It's Elliot,' she told them. 'I'll let it go through to messages and pick it up later. Have you spoken to him this morning?' she asked Michelle.

Michelle shook her head. 'Just an email saying Sajid's passed the money on to Farukh, who wants me to know that Tom's very much alive and itching to get out of there. But before we become side-tracked again, I'll hand back to you, oh gracious Wonder Wit in white slacks and wonky wig.'

Katie's hands flew to her head.

Laurie burst out laughing.

'You've got a nasty little streak in you,' Katie told Michelle.

Michelle grinned and walked on along the footpath towards Bell Wood.

'Molly and I used to come here a lot, when we first moved in,' Katie told Laurie as they followed. 'We'd talk about all our dreams, the adventures we'd have, the crazy things we wanted to be, then go home, write them down and pop them into our dream box.'

'What a lovely idea,' Laurie commented.

'What were yours?' Michelle asked.

Katie smiled. 'Actually, I never used to tell Molly the truth, because I didn't want her to feel that I'd

226

missed out on something because of her, or that she was standing in my way, but my big dream, my real-life ambition, was always to be an investigative reporter. I was already off to a good start before Molly was born, but when she came along, and then her father ditched us for a roulette wheel . . . Well, babies and in-depth research don't make for happy bedfellows, so one had to go. I'm not complaining, please don't think that, I've loved writing my column and being involved in all the perks and spins-offs that came from it. I'm just saying my real dream never actually made it to the box.'

'So what did?' Laurie prompted.

Katie thought for a moment. 'I think I said I wanted to be a lap dancer, or something like that,' she confessed.

'What kind of mother is she?' Michelle demanded with a laugh.

Katie was grinning. 'I also dreamt about being an explorer in India, and a Nobel prizewinner . . . Oh, I had one where I wanted to dance at a Viennese ball.'

'You always wanted to do that,' Michelle reminded her. 'We used to watch them on TV when we were teenagers and imagine ourselves there in those flowing white dresses and tiaras, gliding about in the arms of some dashingly handsome young stud.'

'Corny, but still very appealing,' Katie responded. 'I don't suppose I'll ever get to one now though. Anyway, hopes and dreams are probably a good area to get into, if we do make the programme,' she said to Laurie.

Laurie nodded agreement. 'So talk to me about hope,' she said. 'How does it fit in with everything now?'

Katie didn't have to think for long. 'Hope,' she said, 'is a man. One minute it's there, making you feel all cosy and safe, the next you don't know where the heck it's gone. Of course, it's off with someone else, making them feel all secure and upbeat while you plunge around in the depths of despair, until it suddenly swoops back in again to give you another little perk-up. For two pins I'd give it up altogether, chuck it out on its ear and tell it to go turn someone else into a basket case, but just as I get to the point of doing it, I'm suddenly being seduced all over again into believing I can beat all the odds and win. No, he's a dreadful rogue is hope, uncrushable, untamable and totally irresistible.'

Laurie hadn't missed the key admission that was wrapped up in all the playfulness, so steering her gently back in that direction, she said, 'So there are times you believe you can conquer this?'

'Of course,' Katie admitted. 'I wouldn't be human if I didn't, and miracles do happen, so why not for me? I just try to keep a fix on reality too, because no matter how hard I try to rise above it, the fact is, I do have a disease that isn't responding to treatment, and when it stops doing that, it's time to make sure your insurance is paid up.'

'So what do you say to those who read, and write, the self-help books on how to achieve your own miracle healing, or how to put positive thinking into action?'

'I say keep writing and keep reading, because

they do so much good. Those books are a miracle in themselves, and if I hadn't read any of them I'd be in a far worse state than I am now, that's for sure.'

'And alternative medicine?'

'Give anything a go. At this stage, you don't have anything to lose, so why not?'

'Have you tried it?'

'Of course, and I'll probably keep on trying, because the point is never to stop exploring, and never to give up hope. See, there he is back again, and I didn't even hear him knock. Actually, I think it's a part of the conspiracy you two have got going, to keep inviting him in when I'm not looking, and he seems to be hanging around a lot longer while you're here, so watch out, or he'll start convincing you I can beat this . . .'

'I don't need any convincing,' Michelle cut in.

'Me neither,' Laurie added, having to swallow another yawn.

'Careful,' Katie cautioned. 'He's obviously getting to you already, so make sure you keep him at a distance, or it'll all end in tears when he just dumps you and walks out the door.' She put on a bright smile and planting her hands on her hips, said to Laurie, 'OK, I've had enough of all this for today. I want to know about you now, because I believe you're in need of some pastoral care and Michelle and I are just the people to give it. Are we not, Michelle?'

Michelle blinked. 'Oh, absolutely,' she agreed.

'So let's assume that you were with Nick van Zant last night?'

Deciding just to go with it now, Laurie nodded.

'And that Elliot doesn't know anything about it?'

229

Laurie shuddered and shook her head.

'And that you're now avoiding Elliot and . . . What? Where's Nick actually fitting into this picture?'

Laurie swallowed and sighed in confusion. 'I only wish I knew,' she answered. 'It's hard to base anything on one night . . .'

'But you were seeing him before.'

'It's different now though. I'm not quite sure why, or how, it just is. Or it felt that way last night. In some ways it's like I've lost all reason, because even now, as I'm standing here talking to you, a part of me is willing him to call, or send me a text, or be in touch somehow to let me know that he'll come back to the hotel tonight. Or I'll go to him. Whatever, as long as I see him.'

Katie glanced at Michelle. 'Does he feel the same?' she asked.

'I think so. I don't know. We haven't discussed anything, there's hardly been time, and anyway, I don't have the first idea what I want from this. All I know is I can barely keep my hands off him. Even over breakfast in the pub lounge this morning, I was saying to myself, if he wanted to take me right here, in the middle of the room, I'd let him.'

Katie's eyes opened wide. 'My, that would pull in the tourists,' she remarked.

Laurie erupted in laughter.

'I'm sorry, I shouldn't jest,' Katie said, 'because it's obviously serious, and if it goes on like this it's likely to cause you a lot of heartache. So, Michelle, what should she do?'

Michelle turned to stare at her. 'Why didn't I see that coming?' she demanded.

'I can't imagine.'

Michelle slanted her a look, and turned to Laurie. 'Do you think,' she said, 'that on some level, this could be more about punishing Elliot than actually being in the throes of an infatuation with someone else?'

Laurie frowned and Katie looked impressed. 'To me the two seem quite separate,' Laurie answered, 'though obviously I can understand why they seem linked to you.'

'That's because you're right in the middle of it,' Katie chipped in, 'so it's not possible for you to be objective.'

'Does that mean you agree with Michelle, that it's all about punishing Elliot?'

Katie nodded. 'I think it's highly probable,' she answered.

'A part of you must still be extremely angry over what he did,' Michelle said, 'particularly if it only happened a couple of months ago. Can you honestly say you've forgiven him?'

Laurie stared at her, but it didn't take her long to shake her head. 'I know I haven't,' she admitted. 'I want to, because I know I still love him, and in truth I want to spend the rest of my life with him, but it's a question of trust, and the fear that he'd ever do something like that again.'

'Is this other woman completely off the scene now?' Katie asked.

'So he says.'

'But you don't believe it?'

'Sometimes, but then I start wondering what he'd do if she suddenly decided she wanted him back again.'

Katie frowned. 'I thought he ended the relation-ship.'

'So he tells me, but I keep asking myself, why would he give up someone like that? She's got to be the sexiest woman on the planet . . .'

'Perhaps because he came to his senses and realized he was still in love with you?' Katie suggested.

Laurie looked sceptical.

'Well, I can't imagine any other reason,' Michelle said.

'But the damage has been done,' Laurie pointed out. 'There's no going back now. We can't pretend it didn't happen, and I just don't know how we're going to build a life together with something like that at the foundation.'

Katie was looking thoughtful as she leaned against a tree and folded her arms. 'Let's go back to Nick for a minute,' she said. 'Do you think it's just lust you're feeling, or could it be something deeper?'

Laurie's eyes closed as a shudder of nerves went through her. 'I don't know,' she replied. 'He would be a very easy man to love, and to live with, whereas Elliot probably has to be one of the most difficult. But that's a part of his attraction, a very large part in fact, because he's always a challenge and God knows, life is never dull with him, even if it can be painful at times. But it wouldn't be dull with Nick either . . . Oh God, I just don't know. I'm very confused and if I could, I'd give them both up and go and join the VSO where I might actually . . .'

'. . . meet Tom Chambers, another Titan of world reporting,' Katie picked up. 'Now that would be a really interesting development, wouldn't it?' she declared, cocking her head thoughtfully to one side.

'Only you would think so,' Michelle responded dryly.

As all three of them laughed, they turned to stroll on through the sun-dappled glades, absorbing the nostalgic scent of fresh earth and bitter grasses mingling with the faintly intrusive pong of farmyard spread.

'Well, this is clearly going to take some sorting out,' Katie stated, as they began circling round to take the path home. 'So a full and interesting time ahead, I would say, what with Laurie and her two men, Michelle and her crazy one, and me with my hormones. In fact, all we need now is Molly to fall in love and things could start seriously hotting up around here.'

Chapter Ten

Molly's face was pinched and pale, her temper ready to fly as she surged ahead of the crowd, out of the school building, and across the yard. The instant she was past the gates she switched on her mobile, and watched with pained, anxious eyes as it spurted into life.

No messages, no texts, no missed calls.

She was starting to panic. There must be something wrong with her phone, because Brad had promised to ring. So why hadn't he? What had she done wrong?

'Hey, Molly!'

She turned abruptly away. She didn't want to talk to anyone, she only wanted to cry, or call Brad to find out why he hadn't texted her when he'd said he would. Everyone knew she was waiting, which was her own stupid fault for telling them about him in the first place, and now she wanted to smash their ugly faces for staring at her and snickering and bitching behind her back the way they were.

'Get lost,' she raged as Rank Rusty came up to her.

'I thought you needed some help with your homework,' he said, turning beetroot.

'Well I don't. Now just fuck off!' she shouted, and stuffing her mobile back in her bag she started to run for the bus.

She sat on her own, but Kylie and Greta were only a few rows back, talking loud enough for her to hear, and make everyone else laugh.

'Oh Brad, Brad, I love you,' Kylie was chanting.

'I love you too,' Greta smooched, pretending to be Brad.

'Kiss me, darling. Oh kiss me.'

'What's the matter Molly?' Kylie shouted. 'You're not crying are you, because he didn't call?'

'Why don't you just leave her alone!' Rank Rusty shouted.

'I don't need you sticking up for me,' Molly raged, as everyone jeered and booed and told her Rank Rusty was all she could get. 'And actually, if you must know,' she snarled, eyes flashing with fury, 'he did call, and we're going to instant-message tonight.'

'Oh yeah!' Kylie sneered. 'Like we really believe you.'

Too close to tears to take it any further, Molly turned round again and stared out of the window. She hated this school and everyone in it, and she hated the stupid policewoman who'd come and lectured her today about giving out her email to people in chat rooms, and she hated the head-master for telling the police in the first place, and she hated the whole wide world, because it was just a horrible, mean and stupid place to be, where everyone always let you down, and nothing ever went right, especially not for her.

By the time the bus finally lumbered to a stop next to the war memorial in Membury Hempton, she was ready to jump off. As she landed on the pavement she started to run, desperate to get home now to check her email. Please God don't let her mum have disconnected the Internet, but this morning, when they were having a cuddle, she'd said she'd give her one more chance, and she didn't usually go back on her word.

As she burst into the kitchen Katie looked up from the table, cheeks flushed, eyes bright with laughter. Michelle and Laurie Forbes were there too, and there was an open photo album on the table.

'Hello,' Katie said. 'Have a good day?'

Molly scowled at her.

'Oh, that sort of day,' Katie responded.

Molly continued to glare, so Katie glared back, then her mouth started to wobble, and all of a sudden everyone, except Molly, burst out laughing.

'Why don't you just grow up?' Molly shouted, and shoving past them she dashed up the stairs.

'This is starting to feel like Patsy and Edina's house,' Katie commented.

'Whose house?' Michelle responded.

Molly slammed her bedroom door, threw her bag on the bed, and jabbed on the computer, then the CD. Just how stupid could Michelle get? How could she not know about *Ab Fab*? What bloody planet had she been on for the last hundred years?

And why didn't she just get lost and go back to it, and take Laurie Forbes with her, because it was like she was moving in too, so maybe Molly should just move out and make room for them all.

Please God let there be an email. I'll do anything. Anything.

She watched the connection download. If there was no email she was going to go straight on the suicide site Cecily had found the other night and look up a way to kill herself. That should make everyone happy, because they didn't care about her anyway, especially not Brad, because there wasn't an email and now she really, really did want to die.

Grabbing her mobile she pressed in Allison's number. 'I don't understand it,' she wailed. 'Have you spoken to Toby today? Did he say anything?'

'I haven't spoken to him,' Allison answered. 'But don't get yourself in such a state. Boys are like that. They're always saying they'll do something, then ending up not doing it.'

'So you think he'll call?'

'Of course. He asked Toby all about you, didn't he, so he's obviously like really interested, and . . .'

'Tell me what he said to Toby again. No listen, I don't have much credit left on my mobile, so can I come over?'

'No problem. I'll have finished this stupid homework by the time you get here, *and*,' she said, dragging the word out, 'I've got a surprise for you.'

Killing the music and computer, Molly grabbed her bag and raced back down the stairs.

'Where are you going?' her mother demanded.

'Out!'

'Molly!'

'Allison's, *all right*,' Molly yelled.

'It's starting to rain, you can't go out without a . . . Molly!' she shouted, as Molly tore open the door.

'I'll give you a lift,' Michelle offered.

'I don't want a lift!' Molly screamed. 'I don't want you to come near me. None of you, so just leave me alone.'

She ran all the way to Allison's, her mobile clutched in one hand, ready in case it rang. Her stupid mother and Michelle and Laurie, they just didn't know what it was like waiting for someone to call. It was like, the worst feeling in the world. It made her feel all panicky and afraid and like she wanted to be sick.

'You've got to call Toby, find out what's happening,' she demanded the minute she arrived in Allison's room.

'No problem,' Allison said, picking up her mobile. 'There's a towel on the bed if you want to dry your hair.'

Molly picked it up, but barely knew what she was doing as she watched Allison dial.

'I was thinking,' Allison said as she waited for an answer, 'that we could make Step Five to break into Toby's school.'

Molly's heart did a horrible plunge, then soared wildly up again. She didn't want to do that, but she did. It was like too far out, but really, really cool if she got to see Brad. 'How would we get down there?' she asked.

Allison shrugged, then hearing her brother's voice said, 'Tobes, it's me? What are you up to?' She listened, wagged her head back and forth, rolled her eyes at Molly, then said, 'OK. See you.'

'What?' Molly cried, as she rang off.

'They've got a load of work on and he doesn't have time to talk to me now. Anyway, listen, Cecy's been giving some serious thought to how we can get rid of your aunt. She's been going online getting all these like, spells and things that are really supposed to work, she's even found out what kind of plants are poisonous and how you can put them in food or . . .'

Molly was staring at her in horror. 'I don't want to kill her, for God's sake!' she cried. 'What, is Cecily insane, or something? I just want her to go back to her own country, well that's here, but I mean the one she's just left.'

Allison frowned. 'I told her poisoning was too drastic,' she said, 'but you know what she's like. I'll tell her she has to come up with something else. Oh my God! That's your phone. Is it him?'

Molly's heart was in her throat as she grabbed it and looked. 'Oh my God, it is!' she gasped. 'Oh Allison, it's him. Oh I can't believe it. What am I going to say?'

'Start with hello,' Allison laughed. 'Go on, answer.'

Molly clicked on. 'Hello?' she said.

'Hi,' he responded. 'How are you?'

'I'm cool. How are you?'

'Like really stressed out,' he answered. 'I've had just the worst day, which is why I haven't been able to call till now. We're just taking a break before we go back again, so I wanted to say hi.'

'You haven't finished lessons yet?' she asked.

'Oh yeah, we're just getting ready for this like, major debate tomorrow night, and I'm like president of our team, so I've really got to be on the ball. What have you been doing today?'

'Oh nothing, just the usual. I was going to send you an email . . .'

'Why don't you? Not sure about instant-messaging tonight, we're like, so bogged down, but when we finish, around midnight, I'll send you one then.'

'OK,' she said, blushing and grinning at Allison.

'Cool. I'd better get back to it now.'

'OK. Bye then.'

'Bye.'

Molly clicked off, let her head fall forward and felt such a rush of elation that she sank to her knees. 'I am just like, so, so much in love,' she told Allison in a shaky voice.

Laughing, Allison sank down next to her and drew her into a madly squealing embrace. 'All right, now time for the surprise,' she declared. 'Close your eyes and hold out your hand.'

Molly did as she was told, her insides going wobbly and tight like they were made of elastic. Then feeling something drop into her palm she looked down and saw a lipgloss.

'That's the right one, isn't it?' Allison said.

Molly nodded.

'So Step Four accomplished by Allison Fortescue-Bond,' Allison announced, beaming with pride.

Molly was starting to feel all sick and giddy again, because she knew she had to accomplish it too, and she didn't dare say she couldn't, but she really didn't want to steal anything from a shop, because what if she got caught? Her mum would go totally ballistic, and she still hadn't told her yet about the policewoman who'd come to the school today about that stupid picture. She wanted all that just to go away now, but if she ended up being arrested for stealing . . .

Molly took a breath, then closed her eyes as a wave of emotion washed all over her. 'Do you reckon we could really go down to the school for Step Five?' she said, needing to change the subject.

Allison's eyes widened and she shrugged. 'Sounds cool to me,' she responded. 'Except, it might get in the way of Step Six a bit, you know, make things happen in the wrong order, if we see the boys before the party.'

Molly was instantly downcast. 'I don't think I can wait that long,' she confessed.

Laughing, Allison said, 'Yes, you can. It's only like, three weeks, and you haven't done Step Four yet, so get cracking, you slapper, I'm waiting for my bracelet.'

Since returning to the hotel Laurie had spent almost an hour on the phone talking to her partner, Rose, who was still in Baghdad. Having finished the call she immediately dialled Elliot's number, knowing she couldn't go on avoiding him, and at the same time using it as an excuse not to think about Nick and the fact that he hadn't been in touch all day.

'Hi, it's me,' she said, when Elliot answered.

'I'm on the other line to Max in Washington,' he told her.

'What news from his end?'

'Apparently Joshua Shine's back in the States,

241

but no-one seems to know where, exactly. And still no word from Tom.'

'OK. Before you go, did you remember to courier my laptop?'

'It's ready to go. Sorry, I forgot to take it to the office. It'll be with you first thing tomorrow,' and he went back to his other call.

For a while she stood staring down at the phone, imagining him at their apartment, and wishing she was with him, back how they used to be, secure in their relationship, unwavering in their love – until Andraya had come along. He'd been her whole world up until then, she'd never even dreamt of looking at another man, yet now here she was, longing for Nick in a way that made a mockery of her longing for Elliot.

She drew a deep breath, and tried to get a grip on what she was really feeling, but her mind was filling up with thoughts of Nick pushing Elliot aside, much as he'd pushed her aside to be with Andraya. She couldn't understand why Nick hadn't called today. She'd felt so certain he would, for he'd seemed to find it every bit as difficult to tear himself away from her this morning as she had from him. Of course, she could always call him, but she needed the reassurance of knowing that this was as important to him as it was to her, so he had to make the next move.

Sighing again, she walked across the room to go and look out of the window. The rain had stopped now, but it was a dull, overcast evening, as flattening to the view as it was to her spirits. What she wanted now was Elliot to come walking up through the village, as though to rescue her from herself, but she knew he wouldn't. Anyway it was a lie, because she was so very, very close to reaching for the phone, and knew, in her heart, that she didn't really want to be stopped. Maybe Nick needed the same reassurance. After all, she was the one in a relationship, and with someone he profoundly respected. That would make it extremely difficult for him to call, now they'd gone this far. Or what if he'd been involved in an accident? Was he even now lying somewhere on a life-support machine? How was she going to feel if she hadn't even tried to call?

He answered on the second ring, clearly already knowing it was her from the way he said, 'I was just thinking about you.'

Though it lifted her heart, she wanted to ask why, if it were true, he hadn't called. The intimacy of his tone was already reaching her, however, so all she said was, 'I was thinking about you too.'

She heard him stretch and yawn. 'Sorry,' he said, 'I didn't get too much sleep last night.'

She couldn't help but smile. 'Funny, nor did I. What were you doing?'

'I was making love to the most beautiful woman who just couldn't seem to get enough,' he told her softly.

Feeling her body growing warm, she murmured, 'Funny, but she still can't.'

His only response was a chuckle as he stretched again, and she felt the heat of embarrassment spread over her, that he hadn't admitted to feeling the same.

'Where are you?' she asked.

'Still in Cheltenham. Because of the late start I didn't get finished until an hour ago, so I've checked myself into a hotel here, before heading back to London tomorrow.'

She felt herself turning dizzy. Why had he checked into a hotel there, when he could have come here?

'Where are you?' he asked.

'The same place I was last night,' she answered, and to her undying shame heard herself adding, 'I was hoping you might come and join me.'

There was a slight pause, before he drawled, 'Mm, were you now? Well, that sounds like an offer I can't refuse.'

Relief eased the tension inside her, allowing her to manage a lighthearted tease as she said, 'Shall I meet you down in the bar, so we can at least eat this evening?'

'The answer to that is yes, if you want me to fuck you there.'

Desire shot through her so savagely that it took the smile from her face. 'Come as soon as you can,' she replied, and put the phone down.

Going to the bathroom she turned on the shower, then turned it off again as she decided to order champagne. She was just about to pick up the phone when it started to ring. Dreading it might be him changing his mind, she was almost tempted to ignore it, but of course she couldn't.

'Hello?' she said, cautiously.

'Hi. It's me.'

Everything in her stopped, then slowly started to swirl. It was Elliot, and the guilt was so awful she almost couldn't bear it. 'Hi,' she responded, turning to sit on the edge of the bed. 'All finished with Max?'

'Yes.'

She waited for him to say more, and knew when he didn't that he was expecting her to explain why she hadn't returned his calls today. 'How are you?' she asked, knowing that avoiding the issue was only making it worse.

'I don't know,' he answered. 'Finding this difficult, I guess.'

So was she. Oh God, so was she.

'What are you doing this evening?' he asked, filling the pause.

More guilt swept up into the shame she was already feeling. 'Uh, just having dinner, then watching some TV,' she answered, unable to gauge how truthful she sounded, while detesting the lie. 'What about you?'

'I'm waiting to hear from Tom.'

'Of course.' What was she going to do if he offered to come and join her? How would she put Nick off? But she wouldn't, because she couldn't, for even speaking to Elliot was not lessening the need to repeat last night.

'Tell me how you got on with Katie today,' he prompted.

Knowing there was time, and only too willing to move on to safer ground, she began relating the comments and humour of the day, and gradually felt herself becoming more animated. It was as though Katie's energy had somehow remained in the words, so that they only had to be spoken for it to be released. Then she recalled Michelle's suggestion that she was sleeping with Nick to punish Elliot, and felt her heart sink in despair. If that were true, then she was punishing herself too, because just to think of how much it would hurt him if he knew that in less than an hour she would be utterly betraying him, was as painful as it had been when he'd betrayed her. So why was she doing it? She couldn't answer that, all she knew was that as soon as the call was over it was almost as though it hadn't happened, for she was picking up the phone again· to order champagne, while blanking everything else from her mind beyond Nick and the evening ahead.

By the time he knocked she'd already drunk a full glass of champagne – to calm her nerves and give herself the courage to go through with the way she'd planned to greet him.

'Is it you?' she called softly.

'I hope you're not expecting anyone else,' he responded dryly.

With her heart pounding she pulled open the door and felt an intense flare of heat between her legs as his initial surprise was quickly darkened by lust.

'Come in,' she said, almost politely. 'Would you like some champagne?' and not waiting for an answer she went to fetch the two glasses she'd already filled, leaving him to close the door.

She smiled as she held out his drink, as though playing the hostess at a cocktail party full of people. His eyes remained fixed on hers as he came towards her, then holding the glass aside, he pushed his fingers roughly between her legs and his tongue deep into her mouth. She moaned and gasped as the sensations shot through her, then almost staggered against him as he pulled abruptly away.

Sucking in her lips, she continued to gaze into his eyes as they touched glasses. They sipped the champagne, then taking his hand she led him to the bed.

As he sat down she took his drink and set it on the nightstand with her own.

He was entranced by her nudity, and inflamed by her intention as she dropped to her knees in front of him, causing an enormous surge of desire to course through him. Carefully she unzipped his jeans to release his achingly hard erection. She held it, and regarded it, seeming fascinated by its size and potential for pleasure, then her eyes came up to his, blue and utterly brazen, as she began stroking him with her tongue, making him smooth and moist before finally drawing him deeply into her mouth. Groaning, he slid his hands into her hair and let his head fall back as she tightened her grip around him and reached under his shirt to rake her nails over his chest. The intensity was building too quickly, so raising her up he kissed her fully on the mouth until the immediate threat of release subsided.

She placed his hands on her breasts, clearly as aroused as he was, and let her head fall over his as he stooped to suck her nipples into his mouth. Then lying back on the bed he took her with him, making it easy for her to come astride him. He slipped into her slowly, filling her and filling her as she sank right down on to him, raised her hips, then sank down again. He gazed up into her face, his eyes clouded with lust, his hands smoothing up and down her inner thighs, until finally he touched her where she longed to be touched.

She gasped, arched her back and began riding him faster.

'Yes,' he murmured. 'That's it. Oh Christ, Laurie . . .'

His fingers were relentless and ruthless, forcing her on, taking her beyond pleasure into pain and into new realms of pleasure. His hips pumped to meet hers, her breasts yearned for his mouth and hands. She cupped them herself, pulling and twisting the nipples and becoming more aroused than ever as he urged her to keep going.

'I'm there,' he suddenly gasped. 'Jesus Christ, I'm there,' and as the first rush exploded into her, she felt the searing power of her own orgasm starting to break.

'Hold me,' he growled, 'just hold me.'

She wrapped herself around him, pressing her face to his neck as wave after wave convulsed her. He held her tight, feeling every contraction as it gripped him, while his own climax threw its might into the very depths of her.

It was a long time later, as they lay in each other's arms, breathing less rapidly, but still coated in sweat, that he smoothed back her hair and looked into her eyes.

She smiled. 'You're not even undressed yet,' she teased.

'Maybe because a certain beautiful woman didn't give me the chance,' he responded with irony. 'But it's a situation soon remedied.'

She watched him remove his clothes, then slipped back into his arms as he lay down with her again, loving the feel of him against her, and the way he kissed and held her close. She listened to the beat of his heart, and rhythm of his breath, and tried not to think of anything beyond this moment. He was here, they'd made love again and for now that was all she wanted.

Chapter Eleven

'Elliot. Tom Chambers.'

Elliot came immediately awake and turned on the light. Four fifty-five. 'Tom. Where are you?' he said into the phone.

'About to board a plane for Manila. I'll call you again from there, but I want you to know how much I appreciate what you're doing. I'll pay the money back in the next couple of days.'

'No rush,' Elliot assured him. 'So what's it all about?'

'You've got a handle on the P2OG?'

'An elite and highly covert task force to stimulate terrorist attacks,' Elliot responded. 'Does it exist?'

'Almost certainly, but we need to find proof. The documents Josh Shine gave me don't make the link, but there's no doubting what they are. A planned terror attack on Britain.'

Elliot was so taken aback it took a moment for him to respond. 'Do you want to run that by me again?' he said.

'You heard me correct,' Tom told him, 'but I

think it's just been made to look that way, probably for the jihad guys, to get them to buy into it. My hunch is, it goes a lot deeper, and has an end game that's a whole lot more serious.'

'Can you fax me copies of what you have?' Elliot asked.

'Right now it's in a mailbox Farukh keeps in Manila where we sent everything for safekeeping. Once I have it, we should meet. It'll probably be safer that way.'

'Of course. Do you want me to come out there?'

'No. I've got myself an Italian passport, so I can come to Europe. Farukh's staying in Pakistan, but he's not optimistic about turning up much that's reliable, because the kind of people we need to talk to are going to say anything to damage the Americans. Now tell me, have your background checks led you to the Project for America in the Twenty-first Century?'

'The 21 Project. Absolutely,' Elliot confirmed. 'Once I knew P2 was a neo-con invention, it was where I started.'

There was irony in Tom's tone as he said, 'So there you have it. Everything you need to know about US plans for world dominance. Interesting reading, huh? But I'm told the version that's online was revised in 2002. Apparently certain names and various sections of the text have changed since the original was issued back in '97, so we need to find out what and who, by getting hold of copies of both.'

'How's this relating to what you have?' Elliot asked.

'I'm guessing the original contains information

that will help to prove P2's existence. So far I haven't been able to locate the '97 version anywhere online, which is definitely ominous.'

'We'll keep on it. Max should be able to turn up something through his contacts in Washington. He's running into a brick wall over Joshua Shine, by the way, but he got wind yesterday of some recently formed committee that's supposed to be investigating a specific leak. No details yet, but the coincidence is intriguing.'

'I'll say,' Tom commented. Then, 'Listen, my plane's going to take off any minute, so just tell me, how's Michelle? Any more visits from the Feds?'

'No, but she's found an interesting web site that could give us several leads. She'll be relieved I've heard from you.'

'Tell her I'm fine, and I'll call when I can. How about Katie?'

'She seems OK. Challenging times with Molly, I hear. Do you have a number we can reach you on now?'

After giving it to him, Tom said, 'I've got to run. I'll be in touch when I get to Manila and we'll set up a place to meet.'

After ringing off Elliot went straight through to the bathroom and turned on the shower. There was no point trying to get back to sleep now, the call had brought him wide awake, and left him with a lot to think about. He'd ring Max as soon as he'd put on some coffee, then he'd send emails to his research team instructing them to start tracking down the original version of the 21 Project as soon as they got to the office.

With all that done, he found Laurie's car keys in

their usual place, picked up her laptop and a holdall he'd packed for her, and after locking the front door, he took the lift down to the underground parking.

It was only a little after six a.m., so as he drove out of the building and across Tower Bridge the build-up of morning traffic was hardly under way. It took no more than forty minutes to drive through London, where the M4 was much slower due to an accident. However, he calculated he should still make it to Wiltshire by eight, which was too early to give Michelle Tom's news in person, but hopefully just about right to surprise Laurie with breakfast in bed and personal delivery of her computer.

Laurie was gazing wantonly into Nick's eyes and making him laugh as they waited for their breakfast to arrive. They were alone in the lounge, so felt free to murmur lovers' intimacies, and even kiss, as the memory of last night stole erotically between them, and the promise of the next hour added its own tantalizing frissons to the quietly mounting desire.

'So tell me why you didn't call yesterday,' she said in mock reproach, while entwining her fingers in his.

His eyes were resting on hers, showing the depth of his feelings and the pleasure her touch was giving him. 'The truth? I was afraid you might be having second thoughts,' he responded.

She was surprised, then sceptical. 'I don't believe you,' she challenged, biting gently into his fingers.

'And I got caught up,' he confessed. 'But this is

253

pretty powerful for me, and I wasn't sure it was the same for you.'

As though nothing existed beyond them, she leaned forward to put her lips against his. 'Well it is,' she whispered, and kissed him deeply.

When finally she drew back to look at him a light of humour came into his eyes. 'I think you only want me for my body,' he teased.

'Absolutely,' she murmured, and circled his lips with her tongue. 'Don't you want me for mine?'

'Let's put it this way,' he responded, 'whenever I look at you I want to put my mouth on yours and my hands all over you.'

This time the desire cut through her so sharply that she might have abandoned breakfast had the waiter not arrived at that moment to set down his tray.

Trying not to laugh, Nick sat back to make room for the dishes, and watched as each one was laid out on the pristine white tablecloth. 'So what's on your agenda today?' he asked, as much for the waiter's benefit as his own.

'More talks with Katie and Michelle,' she answered, her cheeks still flushed as she shook out her napkin. 'What about you?'

He thanked the waiter, and lifted the cafetière to pour. 'I think I'll go back to GCHQ, give it one more shot,' he told her. 'There's someone I'd really like to talk to there, but he's playing extremely hard to get.' He buttered a triangle of toast and offered it for her to eat.

She bit into it, meeting his eyes, and loving the mild charge she felt at being fed from his fingers. 'What's it about?' she asked.

'He heads a team that apparently knows a lot about how certain elections are being rigged in the States.'

'You mean, they're a part of it?' she asked in surprise.

'Not necessarily, but they could be assessing it.'

'To implement here?'

'Or not, if they conclude it won't work here.'

After making certain no-one was around he slipped a hand inside her shirt and gently massaged her breasts.

Loving the feel of it, so doing nothing to stop it, she said, 'But even if you do get to speak to this person, he's surely not going to admit to any plans for electoral subversion.'

'Of course not,' he said, removing his hand, 'but I happen to know he's spent a lot of time at CIA HQ these past two years, and was regularly wined and dined by people in some very high places, so I'm interested to hear his explanation of why he was there.'

'And your theory would be?'

After eating the toast she was offering, he said, 'I'm not sure yet, but there's a presidential election coming up, and our own a few months after, so it could be worth looking into.'

'Yes, it could,' she responded, and would have said more, had his hand not disappeared under the table at that moment.

'I want you very badly right now,' he told her gruffly.

'The feeling's mutual,' she murmured, parting her thighs to allow his hand to move higher.

He touched his mouth to hers. 'I think I should tell you exactly what's in my mind,' he whispered.

Loving the idea of verbal foreplay, she gazed into his eyes, and said, 'Yes, I think you should.'

As he spoke she watched his mouth and felt herself melting in the heat of his words, for it was easy to imagine him doing everything he was describing. In the end she put her lips against his and with her eyes fluttering closed pushed her tongue into his mouth.

To her astonishment he pulled sharply away and rose to his feet.

'Elliot,' he said hoarsely.

She spun round in horror, so shocked that she couldn't believe what she was seeing. It was a nightmare. It couldn't be true. Elliot was standing at the door, watching her. She started to get up, but found she couldn't. How long had he been there, how much had he seen, though the very fact she and Nick were together was enough. She started to shake, and found herself almost unable to breathe.

'I was on my way to see Michelle, so I brought the things you asked for,' he told her, coming to put her laptop and holdall on the floor next to the table.

'I thought you were going to send them,' she said, absurdly, as though it had somehow given her licence to be here like this.

'It would seem I probably should have.'

She could see his pain in the paleness of his face, hear it in his voice and even feel it in his heart. How could she be doing this to him? Why had she even considered it, when he was the only man in the world she'd ever really wanted or loved?

To Nick he said, 'I left a message on your

machine, about an hour ago. I'd appreciate it if you could give me a call when you can.'

Laurie stared at him, dumbfounded.

'Of course,' Nick responded.

Elliot turned his eyes back to her, and her heart seemed to stop as he dropped a set of keys on the table. 'I brought your car,' he said. 'It's parked at the end of the village. I'd like to take mine now.'

Too shaken to know what else to do, she picked up her bag, and put the keys into his hand. 'Elliot, we have to talk,' she said.

He turned to walk out.

'Elliot!' she cried.

She caught up with him out in the street. 'Elliot! We have to talk,' she insisted.

'There's nothing to discuss,' he said, refusing to look at her.

'Of course there is. Elliot, don't go like this. *Please,*' she cried, grabbing his arm.

'Where's the car?' he asked.

'Just over the bridge. Listen, I'm sorry, Elliot, I . . .'

'I don't want to hear it,' he said, and shrugging her off he walked on down through the village.

She stood watching him, the terror of losing him pounding in her heart, the horror of the last few minutes still reeling in her head. She could hardly believe it was real, that he'd found out like this, or that she'd even done it. Nothing seemed to be making any sense. She had to talk to him, but not now, while they were both still caught up in the shock. Besides, what was she going to say when she had no words to explain her feelings for Nick, or promises to offer that she wouldn't see him again?

Turning back into the pub, she found Nick still standing beside the table, obviously as shaken as she was, though his eyes reflected more concern for her than for himself.

'Are you OK?' he asked.

Feeling suddenly overwhelmed, she covered her face with her hands, as though to block out anything more. 'I've hurt him so much,' she said, too appalled even to cry. 'He might not be showing it, but there's no-one better than Elliot at disguising his feelings.' She shook her head, still unable to accept just how detached he had seemed. 'I can hardly believe he wants you to call him,' she said, looking up.

'Me neither,' he responded.

She frowned in confusion. 'It's as though none of this means anything.'

His tone was dry as he said, 'Would you rather he'd decked me?'

'Maybe I would,' she confessed, so thrown by it all that she hardly knew what she was thinking.

Coming to her, he pulled her into his arms and kissed the tip of her nose. 'Maybe I should leave,' he suggested.

She nodded. 'Yes, you probably should,' she responded. 'I'll wait here while you go up to get your things.' It wasn't that she didn't want to be near him, it was more a fear that even now she wouldn't be able to resist him.

By the time he came back, carrying his jacket and overnight bag, she'd tried calling Elliot on his mobile, but he wasn't answering, so she'd rung off without leaving a message. She looked at Nick, saw the uncertainty in his eyes, and walked into his arms.

'Will you call?' she asked, as he kissed her.

'Of course,' he promised, and after kissing her again he said, 'he doesn't deserve you, you know.'

At that her heart contracted, but though her instinct was to defend Elliot, she said nothing, only watched him open the door. She stood looking out of the window as he walked down through the village, until finally he disappeared from view. And still she remained where she was, locked in such a turmoil of emotions that she could hardly begin to reach the truth of what any of them were.

'When I saw the Porsche pull up I assumed it was Laurie,' Katie smiled, as she walked across the garden to greet Elliot. 'I was going to say,' she added, as he scooped her into a warm embrace, 'if I'd known it was you, I'd have rushed upstairs to get my kit off, but something's telling me you're not in the mood.'

'I'm always in the mood for Katie Kiernan,' he assured her with a smile.

Unconvinced, she tilted her head to one side and regarded his darkly handsome features closely.

'So how are you?' he asked, planting a kiss on her nose. 'And give it to me straight.'

'Well, I'll give you this,' she responded, 'you managed to cover up your shock better than most, because I know I'm not a pretty sight these days, and don't try telling me otherwise.'

'You're gorgeous, and that's not an answer.'

She shrugged. 'OK, try this one: if you come back next week, you'll probably find Michelle's got me spreadeagled on a stick at the end of the garden to scare off the crows.'

Chuckling, Michelle came to welcome him. 'How lovely to see you,' she said, kissing both his cheeks. 'We've just finished breakfast, but there's plenty left and the coffee's still warm.'

'Coffee sounds great,' he told her, as she led the way inside.

'Is Laurie joining us?' she asked, glancing back over her shoulder.

'Uh, no . . . I'm not sure,' he replied, and pretended not to notice Katie's eyes slanting in his direction.

'The music's Molly's,' Katie told him, still intrigued by his reply. 'You're lucky she's feeling sentimental this morning, it's usually blasting the roof off. Ah, speak of the devil,' and Molly came charging down the stairs, school uniform half-buttoned, one sock on, one off.

'Didn't you hear me?' she demanded. 'Where's my mascara?'

'You've got that the wrong way round,' Katie informed her. 'The mascara's mine, the eyelashes are yours, and this is Elliot, would you care to say hello?'

'Hello,' Molly said sweetly.

Katie rolled her eyes. 'She's got a dental appointment,' she told Elliot, 'or she wouldn't still be here.' Then to Molly, 'The mascara's in the bathroom cabinet with the rest of *my* make-up – and there's still plenty of time, so calm down.'

'I don't need you to come with me,' Molly protested, as she flounced back up the stairs. 'I can go on my own.'

'Did I say I was coming?' Katie retorted. She shook her head and turned back to Elliot. 'Dentists, daughters and doctors, whoever knew life was going to become so thrilling?' Then breaking into a smile of pure pleasure she reached for his hands. 'It's good to see you,' she said warmly. 'I miss our sparring. You always kept me on my toes.'

'While you were running me round in circles,' he responded, managing to push some irony through the heaviness of his thoughts.

'Coffee,' Michelle said, putting a mug on the table next to the milk jug and sugar. 'Help yourself to a croissant, feel free to avail yourself of my sister, but please don't keep me in suspense any longer. You've heard from Tom. That's why you're here.'

'Yes, to both,' he responded, as he sat down on the chair Katie was directing him to. 'We didn't talk for long, but he's OK, and on his way to Manila.'

Relief immediately softened Michelle's expression. 'Why Manila?' she asked, sitting down too.

He explained about Farukh's mailbox, its contents, and what else Tom had managed to tell him, adding, 'He should be in touch again once he's in the Philippines. I've got a number for him now, but for the moment I'd recommend not using it, because mobiles are easy to trace, and I think he wants to deal with the authorities in his time, rather than theirs.'

Though disappointed, she was used to this with Tom, so she merely nodded and noted the number down as Katie said, 'Let me give you my understanding of the 21 Project, then you can tell me if I'm right.'

Elliot signalled with his coffee for her to go ahead.

'Basically, it's a document that spells out how to achieve American world dominance,' she began. 'It was compiled back in the Nineties, I believe, and its goals are to throw out any international treaties that don't further US interests, to militarize outer space, assume total control of cyberspace . . . Let me see . . . Yes, to drastically increase defence spending, and to use nuclear weapons where necessary to deal with rogue states.'

He nodded.

'Its authors,' she continued, 'are the much despised neo-conservatives who are now running the White House and Pentagon – and, by dint of unswerving support for pre-emptive military strikes, elements of our own government too, some might say.'

His eyebrows were up. 'That about covers it,' he told her.

Michelle said, 'So the P2 task force is a spin-off of this Project?'

'Almost without doubt,' he confirmed.

'And what Tom has is documentary evidence of one of their missions, which *appears* to be the funding and plotting of a terror attack on Britain?'

Again he nodded. 'Appears being the operative word,' he added, 'because he thinks there's actually more to it, and I'd go along with that, because why would the US help launch an attack on its biggest ally?'

Katie scoffed. 'There are certain parties in that regime who'd stop at nothing to secure the next election,' she reminded him.

'But how would a terror attack on Britain do that?'

'Well, it would stir up enough fear in the US electorate to make them leery of a leadership change – *oh my God they've hit our best mates, thank God our leaders have managed to protect us. Mustn't dare change them now, the next lot haven't had any experience, so we've got to stay with who we know . . .*'

Elliot wasn't unimpressed. 'It's certainly a theory that could hold water,' he conceded, 'but we've a long way to go before we could prove anything like that, and besides, it's unlikely anyone in Whitehall would support an attack on our soil, and for the moment at least, we're presuming someone this side of the Atlantic is party to this project.'

Wishing she shared his faith in their government, Katie merely shrugged and picked up her coffee, as Michelle said, 'So what do we do next?'

'Find the original 21 Project document,' he answered. 'It seems to have been withdrawn from circulation, so it could take some tracking down. Max is on it in Washington, I've got my researchers on it too, so what you could do is familiarize yourselves with the later version, so that when the time comes you'll be quick to spot any inconsistencies with the original. There's also the web site you found the other day, listing the names of everyone involved in the recommendation for an elite pre-emptive task force, i.e. the P2OG. Most of them are going to be supporters of the 21 Project, possibly even neo-cons themselves.'

Michelle was already reaching for the printout which she'd put in the dresser drawer. 'There are dozens of names,' she said. 'Most seem to have scientific, military or nuclear backgrounds.'

As they began going through the list Katie got up to answer the phone. 'Hello?' she said, still half-listening to Michelle and Elliot.

'Katie. It's Laurie. Is Elliot with you?'

Katie hesitated, for Laurie's tone was reminding her of Elliot's tension when he'd arrived. 'As a matter of fact he is,' she replied. 'Shall I pass you over?'

'If you wouldn't mind.'

'Laurie,' she told Elliot, holding out the phone.

'Tell her I'll talk to her later,' he responded, still focusing on Michelle's list.

Katie put the phone back to her ear.

'I heard,' Laurie said. Then after a pause, 'Has he told you he walked in on me and Nick this morning?'

Though Katie had already guessed as much, with Elliot sitting right there all she could say was, 'Are we still meeting today?'

Laurie took a breath. 'Would it be a problem if I had to postpone until tomorrow?'

'Don't worry. It looks as though Michelle and I are going to have our work cut out beavering around the Internet now Tom's finally given us a direction.'

'I thought he must have been in touch,' Laurie said. 'That's why Elliot's there?'

'Yes.'

'When's he heading back to London?'

Katie turned to Elliot. 'When are you heading back to London?'

Once again he said, 'Tell her I'll speak to her

later,' and he continued listening to Michelle.

'Sorry, I'm putting you in a horrible position,' Laurie said. 'I'll ring off now and call you later. Or perhaps you could call me when you can.'

'Of course,' Katie promised, and regretting that there was no more she could say or do for now, she rang off. 'So where are we?' she asked, returning to the table and knowing Elliot would want to continue as though the last few minutes hadn't happened.

'We were just posing the question,' he answered, appearing slightly more strained than before, 'which elements of the British Establishment would be supportive of American world dominance?'

Katie frowned. 'I think, if we put it in the context of gain, we should come up with a few answers,' she replied.

'Personal or political?'

'Either way, it definitely wouldn't be good.'

Smiling at the understatement, Michelle said, 'I think we need to fire up your computer, my darling, and start this ball rolling. There's more coffee if you'd like some,' she told Elliot.

'No, one is fine,' he replied, carrying his empty cup to the sink. 'There's going to be a lot to plough through,' he warned, 'it could take days, and even then you'll still be pulling up articles, comments, reports, you name it, that are going to have some relevance. The important thing is to stay focused on the P2OG and anything that might prove its existence.'

'What about calling some of the names on that list and asking them to comment?' Katie said.

'Yes, but not yet. A call from any of us is going to

confirm that Tom's running with the story, and we don't want to do that until he's ready.'

Acknowledging the logic of that, she said, 'It'll be interesting to see what lengths they go to to try and stop him, because that in itself will tell us a lot.'

Elliot nodded agreement.

'You look as though you're about to leave,' Michelle commented.

'I need to get back to London,' he responded, glancing at his watch.

Getting up to give him a hug, she said, 'Stay in touch, and thanks for coming all this way.'

His smile was sardonic as he said, 'It was worth it, just to see Katie.'

Beaming with pleasure, Katie linked his arm and walked outside with him. 'It's a beautiful day again,' she remarked, gazing up at the mostly blue sky. 'We've been so lucky with the weather this year. The forecast says it's about to change though.'

He made no comment, merely turned to look at her as they reached the corner of the house.

'I know what's happening between you and Laurie is none of my business,' she said gently, 'and I'm not about to embarrass you by trying to make it so, I just want to say this: she's obviously still finding it very hard to come to terms with what you did. It was a terrible shock, and probably hurt her even more deeply than you fully realize. You're getting a taste of it now, but I don't think it's revenge she's after. I think it's much more complicated than that, and a part of it will be about who she feels secure with – and he hasn't let her down the way you did.' She put a hand on his chest and smiled. 'I know it's going to be devastating thinking of her with another man, but instead of trying to force her to give him up and stay with you, I would suggest that you make sure she knows she's loved, then give her some space to work out what she really wants. It could take you a lot closer to forgiveness than you think. No promises, that's just my opinion, and it goes without saying, if there's anything I can do you know where I am.'

He continued to look at her, absorbing her words, and seeing a woman who was a shadow of the one he'd known and admired for so long, yet somehow seemed to be burning brighter than ever. 'How did I ever let you get away?' he said softly.

A roguish twinkle stole into her eyes, signalling an end to the seriousness. 'Oh, I'm still hooked,' she warned, 'but before you let it go to your head, my weirdy old hormones have got my libido whirling around all over the place these days, and I'm afraid any old trousers will do.'

As he laughed, a disgusted voice shot from behind, 'Mum! You are just *so* embarrassing!'

'Oh God, I forgot you were still here,' Katie groaned. 'I'm sorry, OK?' And to Elliot, 'You're not allowed to be human if you're a mother.'

Elliot turned to Molly. 'I could be going your way, if you'd like a lift?' he offered.

Molly's eyes rounded. 'Is the Porsche yours?'

'Pff, transparent as air,' Katie scoffed, 'at least I play a bit harder to get.'

'Maybe that's where you go wrong,' Molly retorted, planting a kiss on her cheek.

Katie's eyes were wide as she watched them waltz off towards the gate. 'Did you hear that?' she said to Michelle, going back inside. 'That waspy little zinger she just shafted me with could have come straight out of your low-voltage repartee.'

'Correction,' Michelle said mildly, 'straight out of yours, which is where we all get it from. Now, we've got work to do, and since you're far better at this kind of research than I am, why don't you take over the controls?'

Katie was about to sit down at the computer when she suddenly changed her mind. 'No,' she said, decisively. 'I've been doing that ever since you got here, keeping myself in the spotlight, always running the show as though I'm the only one with make-up and a script. I think it's time you came out of the wings to share the stage, because, crushing as it might be to someone of my dazzling talent, your part in the finale is going to be far more relevant than my own.'

Michelle was looking at her with a mix of wry amusement and affection. 'You don't half talk a lot of twaddle sometimes,' she commented.

Katie was unabashed. 'No, I'm standing aside,' she insisted, still warming to her theme. 'You're in charge now and I'm happy to fade off into the background so everyone knows who the real star is.'

Michelle cocked an eyebrow, but said no more, for Katie could be as theatrical or as generously intentioned as she liked, it just simply wasn't going to happen that she'd stand aside and let someone else take over. It wasn't in her nature, never had been, and never would be, nor would Michelle ever want it to be.

Chapter Twelve

After putting the phone down to Katie, Laurie had decided that the only way she could hope to think straight was to take herself out of the hotel and lose herself in the countryside, where there would be no phones, and no temptation to call either Elliot or Nick, while she tried to sort out the dreadful mess she was in.

She'd started out walking down through the village to an old stone bridge that crossed the river and yielded to a footpath the other side that crept in a dry, cracked strip through the reeds and bushes along the bank. After a while she climbed a stile and followed the slope of the path, away from the river, up into a meadow, where it unravelled like a ribbon into the tempting depths of a wood beyond. She found it colder amongst the trees, but somehow more restful. The way the sunlight played on the leaves and streamed in misty bands across the pathway filled her with a sense of timelessness and beauty that gradually began to loosen her tension and allow some calm to return to the frantic racing of her mind. But it still wasn't easy to face the questions that needed to be answered when even to form them was painful, and the prospect of how much hurt she could cause all three of them was as daunting as the thought of facing Elliot again.

It should have been so straightforward, for in her heart she knew she'd never loved anyone the way she loved him, nor could she imagine her life without him, but perhaps it wasn't about imagining, perhaps it was about accepting that life was unfolding the way it was now to show her that the time for them was drawing to an end. Even to think it was making her panicky again, and want to hold on even tighter, but in a steadier, more rational part of her mind she knew that was the natural instinct for anyone who felt about to fall. But what if letting go was the right thing to do? She'd found it impossible when he'd left her for Andraya, she'd held on so tight then that the pain and fear had become like a living force inside her, possessing her, and pushing her so relentlessly and mercilessly towards the edge that if Nick hadn't been there, she dreaded to think now what she might have done.

She remembered only too well how long Elliot had made her wait before he'd discuss why he'd left her, the terrible agony of self-doubt he'd put her through before he'd finally confronted his actions. And even then he hadn't told her about Andraya. He'd said he couldn't marry her because he didn't love her the way she deserved to be loved. The truth about Andraya hadn't come out until later.

In the end, dazed with grief and devastated by

rejection, she'd seduced Nick while barely know-ing what she was doing. He'd tried to resist, afraid of how deeply she might regret it later, but she'd so desperately needed the closeness, as well as the reassurance that someone could want her the same way Elliot wanted Andraya, that he'd finally given in. It had been beautiful and tender, he'd given everything of himself, despite knowing that for her it was only a partial escape, because even then she'd hardly been able to get Elliot and Andraya out of her mind. And it was no different now. The very thought of them together filled her with so much pain and jealousy that she had to instantly close it down. She wanted to think only of Nick, to make love with him and know that his passion burned with the same strength as her own, and that when he was with her he was there completely, not torn between her and a woman who was so exotically sensuous and exciting that it could only be a matter of time before Elliot went back to her.

She walked on and on, across fields and meadows, over stiles, through more woods, until eventually she rejoined the river, a long way from where she'd started. She stood for a long time staring into the bubbling, swirling current, feeling her thoughts moving with it, rising and turning, falling and moving on, until finally she found the courage to admit that in spite of everything she was telling herself about Nick, it still didn't change the way she felt about Elliot. No matter that he'd betrayed her so cruelly, or that he'd let her down in so many ways, the love they shared was still there in her heart. However damaged and changed it was, until everything was resolved between them she had to accept that it simply wasn't fair to carry on using Nick in this way.

When she finally returned to the hotel she went straight to her room, picked up the phone and dialled Nick's number. He answered on the third ring, and even though he was half way to London, he agreed to turn round and come back.

As she waited she considered trying to call Elliot again, but decided against it, for right now she wouldn't know what to say. She wondered where he was, how much thought he was giving to this morning, and how he was dealing with the hurt. Knowing him as she did, it was easy to imagine him blocking it out by immersing himself in Tom's story, indeed he'd already demonstrated it this morning, when he'd asked Nick to call him. Had they spoken yet, she wondered.

It was just after five thirty when she saw Nick's car pulling up below her window, next to the market cross. As she watched him get out her insides were folding into a chaos of nerves, though, for the moment at least, her mind seemed calm, and her resolve more or less intact. She'd rehearsed what she was going to say, even though she knew it would probably all come out differently, because she had no idea how he was going to react, or even how she was going to feel when it came time for him to leave. Right now she truly didn't think she'd be able to let him go, so she tried just to focus on the few minutes ahead, because how she greeted him would, she believed, set the tone for how she handled everything else.

When the knock came she closed her eyes and tried to ignore the hammering of her heart. Maybe they should have met in the bar, or somewhere else completely, far away from the hotel and the intimacy they'd shared in this room, but it was too late now, and finally steeling herself she went to open the door.

He said nothing as he looked at her, and as she looked back her heart turned inside out, for his expression told her that he already knew what she was going to say, but he'd come anyway, driven all this way back to hear her tell him it was over, when he could so easily have put it off, or made her tell him on the phone. She took a breath, maybe to invite him in, or maybe just to say hello, she wasn't entirely sure, she only knew that all her words had gone, and that she was moving into his arms because it was the only place in the world she wanted to be.

The door closed behind them and their embrace grew deeper and ever more needful, as though the fear of parting was drawing them tighter together. They made love with more tenderness than they had before, never taking their eyes from each other as their bodies moved rhythmically together, allowing them to feel each sensation as exquisitely as if it were the first. There was no urgency, only an intensity that seemed to flow between them with as much ease as the physical part of their pleasure. Their climax was a long and deeply sensuous time in coming, building with excruciating power to a point where neither of them could hold back any more. Only then did he kiss her again, catching her cries in his mouth, while the full force of his release cascaded into the tightly pulsing depths of her very being.

Neither of them moved to break the embrace,

they simply lay together, bound in each other's arms, kissing, holding on tight and feeling every last moment of the love they had shared. She pushed her hands into his hair, and over his back, kept her legs wrapped around him and his penis inside her. He whispered softly that he loved her and put his mouth to hers again, as though to stop her responding.

She gazed up into his eyes and saw her own feelings reflected there. 'I don't understand what's happening,' she whispered, 'I just know I can't let you go.'

'Ssh,' he whispered, as tears rose in her eyes.

As they kissed again he rolled carefully on to his back, parting their bodies, but taking her with him so that she was still in his arms.

'What are you thinking?' she asked, winding her fingers through the dark hair on his chest.

He smiled and in the end said, 'Crazy thoughts of having you all to myself.'

'Why crazy?'

He glanced down at her, but didn't answer, only kissed the top of her head.

'It's not a good time to be making any promises,' she said, 'but . . .'

'Then don't make any,' he broke in softly. 'Let's just accept that this is how we feel, and whatever needs to be done will be done when the time is right. It doesn't have to be now.'

Her heart filled up with emotion, and turning her face to his she said, 'I feel as though I'm using you, and that's not fair when . . .'

'Hey,' he said with a smile, 'do I look like I'm complaining?'

'No, but . . .'

'Laurie, we'll get through this,' he told her gently. 'I'm going to make it as easy for you as I can, and if that means having to wait, or only being able to see you in secret, then I'd rather that than not see you at all.'

Her eyes closed as she swallowed the lump that had risen in her throat. 'Elliot knows now,' she said, 'so there's no reason for it to be secret.'

'Have you spoken to him since this morning?'

'No. I don't know what I'm going to say . . . I don't even want to think about it . . .' She sighed unsteadily and turned her face into his neck.

'I picked up his message,' he told her, stroking her hair. 'He wants me to do some digging around in New York while I'm there.'

She drew back. 'You're going to New York?'

'Tomorrow,' he answered. 'I guess I didn't tell you, but is that surprising when we never seem to give ourselves much time to talk?'

'I want that to change,' she said earnestly. 'I want to know everything about you.'

'You pretty much already do,' he smiled.

'Not true, but tell me why you're going to New York.'

'I'm taking Julia back,' he answered, referring to his thirteen-year-old daughter. 'She's been over here on a school trip, so she's staying with me tonight, before I take her back to her mother.'

'So where is she now?'

'With my cousin, the one who has the house above my apartment.' Lifting an arm so he could see his watch, he said, 'I was on my way there when you called, so I'll have to be leaving soon.'

Feeling an almost overpowering urge to try and stop him, she fought it back by reminding herself that she'd have plenty of time to see him in the coming weeks, while he probably didn't know when he was going to see his daughter again. Even so, she hated the thought of him leaving her here now.

'So did you actually speak to Elliot?' she asked, as he shifted slightly to make himself more comfortable. 'Or did you just pick up the message?'

'We spoke, and before you ask, no he didn't mention anything about this morning. It was almost as though it hadn't happened, though I admit he didn't sound too friendly. Just business-like. He wants to get hold of the original version of the 21 Project, and thought, with all my contacts in the States, I might be able to help.'

'Can you?'

'Possibly. I'll give it a try, anyway. I'll meet up with Max Erwin while I'm there, and he'll probably brief me some more.'

'So Elliot didn't get into what Tom said when he called?'

'No, and I didn't ask. The call was difficult enough, and to be frank I'm surprised he's pulling me in on this.'

So was she, but only to a degree, for Elliot was often unpredictable, and certainly not given to letting his emotions stand in the way of a story. 'How long are you going to be away?' she asked, dreading it, yet in a way almost welcoming it, for it would give her the chance to think some more.

'About a week.'

'I'll miss you,' she murmured.

'You could always come with me,' he said.

Her heart jumped at the prospect, but though she'd have loved to be in another city with him where they could feel free to be themselves, she remembered how utterly broken she'd been when Elliot had gone off to Tuscany with Andraya. That was when her affair with Nick had started, in the very depths of such unimaginable pain that had Nick not been there to hold her it would probably have swallowed her completely. So no matter what Elliot had done, she wasn't going to make him suffer like that. She must speak to him first, only then could she consider going anywhere, even any further in the relationship with Nick.

Smiling as he pulled her on top of him, she gazed down into his face and felt a quiet surge of love filling her heart. His hands were moving down her back and over her buttocks, and as he began kissing her neck she could feel herself becoming aroused again, until his mobile rang and groaning with annoyance he let his head fall back on the pillow.

'It'll be Julia,' he murmured.

'Then you should answer. Have you told her you're going to be late?'

'Yes, but she'll want to know if I'm on my way yet.'

She rolled off him, and as he reached for his jeans she drew her nails gently down his back, pressing her lips to his skin, then settling into his arms again as he put the phone to his ear.

'Hi sweetheart,' he said, pulling Laurie in closer. 'Yes, I'm just on my way out to the car now.' He paused, then smiled. 'You're cooking dinner with candles? Won't that take a long time?' He laughed as both she and Laurie groaned at his joke. 'OK,' he said, 'I'll be there as soon as I can,' and clicking off he dropped the phone on the bedside table.

'OK, beautiful woman,' he said in a seductively low voice, 'I want you to stay right where you are, so that I can look at you as I get dressed, then for the whole of next week I can think of you all mussed and flushed and looking so goddamned sexy I want to ravish you all over again.'

'No-one's stopping you,' she murmured, feeling his hardness pressing against her.

He kissed her lingeringly and deeply, then broke abruptly away. 'I have to go,' he said firmly, and slapping her playfully on the buttocks, he got quickly up from the bed.

She lay back on the pillows, putting her hands behind her head, and watched as he dressed. 'You know, it turns me on as much watching you put your clothes on as it does when you take them off,' she told him.

His eyes narrowed, and after zipping his jeans with some difficulty he picked up his mobile and stood looking down at her. 'No-one else in the world could drag me away now,' he told her gruffly.

'Go,' she whispered, linking her fingers through his.

Leaning over her he kissed her first on the mouth, then on each nipple, then slowly and deeply between the legs.

'That's not fair,' she told him as he stood up again.

He smiled. 'I'll call you later,' he said, and touching his fingers to his lips, he left.

After he'd gone Laurie lay where she was, staring up at the ceiling, reliving the last hour and how they'd seemed to move into a deeper and stronger sense of each other that felt every bit as powerful as the physical allure. But even as she allowed the quiet contentment to steal over her, like a mist it started slowly to fade, until it had vanished completely, leaving her feeling strangely raw and sad. It was as though he'd abandoned her, which was nonsense, and she knew it, but for some reason she couldn't seem to stop the feeling. As it intensified she felt herself being pulled back into all the pain and confusion she'd managed to bury while he was here.

Getting up from the bed, she went to take a shower, as though she could somehow wash away all the turmoil. Then she pulled on her jeans and a T-shirt, and plugged in her laptop.

She sat for a long time staring at the screen, thinking about Elliot, what he might be doing and where he could be. Though she detested even the thought of it, she understood now how he'd got caught up in a passion for another woman. Even so, it was no easier to bear, and betraying him was proving just as painful as when he'd betrayed her. She tried composing an email to him, but nothing sounded right, and deciding that this was hardly the way to communicate, she closed the computer down and turned on her mobile. There were several texts and voicemails, but none from him. She could feel angry at his silence, but just felt anxious and more alone than she ever had.

Deciding she should call Katie to fix a time for tomorrow, she was searching for the number when the landline started to ring. Immediately her heart leapt. It could be anyone, of course, but her mind had gone instantly to Elliot, and in spite of the terrible nerves that could easily prevent her from answering, there was still a part of her that desperately wanted it to be him.

'Hello?' she said into the receiver.

'Hi,' he responded.

The sound of his voice moved through her like a physical pain. 'How are you?' she asked, sinking down on to the edge of the bed.

'I'm OK. How are you?'

'Yes, fine. Where are you?'

'At home. Is Nick there with you?'

Her eyes closed. 'No,' she answered. It wasn't a lie, but God knew it felt like one.

'I know I deserve this,' he said, 'but . . .'

'I'm not punishing you, Elliot,' she told him, only realizing after she'd said it that maybe he needed to think she was. 'I'm really sorry,' she said softly. 'Really, really sorry.'

His voice was horribly strained as he said, 'Does that mean it's over between us?'

No, she wanted to scream, but then she thought of Nick and didn't know what to say. 'It means,' she whispered in the end, 'that I don't want to hurt you, but I – I don't know how to stop.'

'So it wasn't just something you had to get out of your system?'

'Elliot, please don't do this.'

'I love you, Laurie,' he said, his voice thick with emotion. 'You know that.'

'I love you too,' she cried in despair. 'Oh God, I don't know what to tell you. I hardly understand it myself, but I know I don't want to lose you.'

'You can't have us both.'

'That's not what I'm saying. I – I don't know what I'm saying, but we do need to talk. I'll come home tomorrow. Will you be there?'

'No. I'm leaving at midday to meet Tom.'

She wanted to ask him not to go, but she couldn't. 'How long will you be gone?'

'Probably until the end of the week.'

'Where is he?'

'En route to our rendezvous point by now. Have you spoken to Katie and Michelle today?'

'No, not really.'

'They'll be able to fill you in on what's happening. There are several people here I want to talk to. I was hoping, if you're able to fit it in . . .'

'Of course,' she said, only too ready to help, as though, in some way, it could make up for everything else she was doing.

'I'll email you a list,' he said, 'and the kind of line you need to take. Once you've talked to Katie and Michelle you'll have a good idea anyway, but I should be contactable, at least for some of the time.'

She thought of the week going by without either him or Nick being here, and though she knew she should be thankful for the respite, she wasn't. Speaking to him now was filling her with such a fear of being without him that she had to accept she was still a very long way from knowing what she really wanted.

'We'll talk when I get back,' he said.

'OK.' She swallowed, and pressed her fingers to her lips as her eyes filled with tears. 'I love you,' she whispered, the words coming out on a sob.

'I love you too,' he responded, and after letting the silence stretch for a while, he put the phone down.

As she rang off too, she put a hand to her head and tried to understand why she found it so easy to tell him she loved him, yet seemed unable to say it to Nick, when she was so certain she felt it. Was it because her conscience wouldn't allow her to take that next step until everything was resolved with Elliot? Or was it because her feelings for Elliot were truer, and so more easily spoken? Right now, she had no answers, all she knew was that she'd never felt so wretched, nor more in need of confiding in someone. She thought of how she'd always turned to Elliot before, they'd discussed everything, kept nothing secret and were always each other's greatest support, but his betrayal had changed that, and now hers was driving them even further apart. In her heart she knew that wasn't what she wanted, but she couldn't see any way of stopping it. No matter how sorry he was about Andraya, or how hard he tried to convince her that it was her he loved, it was never going to make what he'd done just disappear. It was always going to be there, and though it hadn't stopped her from loving him yet, she wondered if, in fact, it was slowly starting to happen.

It was early evening as Elliot waited inside Pisa airport for Tom's flight to come in from Rome. Though they had a lot to get through over the next few days, right now his thoughts were entirely dominated by Laurie and what the hell he could do to save their relationship. Somehow he had to find

282

a way of persuading her not to give up on them yet, for he could feel her slipping away, and it was scaring him half to death. He'd thought a lot about Katie's advice to give her some space, but though he could see some merit in it, he wished to God he knew how he was going to heed it. His instinct was to hold on to Laurie so tight she could never break free – or to damn well kill Nick van Zant if he ever went anywhere near her again.

Glancing up as passengers from the Rome flight began trickling through, he looked around for Tom, but there was no sign of him yet. The phone in his hand started to ring, and seeing it was Laurie he immediately clicked on, knowing the call would be story-related. They'd agreed not to discuss their relationship until he got back, and they'd already spoken several times today as she updated him on the research she was carrying out with Katie and Michelle.

Not until the call was almost over did her voice soften as she asked how he was. It caused such a wrenching in his heart that it made his eyes close as he said, 'Do you want the truth?'

'Of course,' she whispered.

'Then I don't know if I've ever felt more helpless or afraid in my life.'

'I'm sorry. The last thing I want is to hurt you.'

'I wouldn't care as long as you came back to me. Just tell me what I have to do, Laurie, and I'll do it.'

Her voice was shredded with pain as she said, 'I wish I knew.'

A silence passed that seemed to fill with everything else they wanted to say, but it wasn't the right time, they needed to be together, not at opposite ends of a phone line. He just wished he didn't feel as though he was handling this all wrong.

In the end she was the first to speak again. 'Michelle's wondering if Tom's with you yet.'

His voice sounded hoarse as he said, 'He's just about to come through. I'll put him on as soon as he does.'

'OK. She wants to talk to you anyway, so I'll pass you over.'

The next few minutes were taken up with more detail from the day's research, until finally he spotted Tom striding towards him in black jeans, tatty leather jacket and a two-day beard. 'He's here,' he told Michelle.

'Hey,' Tom said, shaking his hand. 'Everything OK?'

'Everything's good. Michelle wants to talk to you,' and passing the phone over he reached for Tom's luggage.

Tom's eyes were showing his pleasure as he said, 'Hey, am I finally speaking to the woman I love?'

Giving him some privacy Elliot walked on outside, where the sun was well on its way to setting now, shrouding the surrounding Tuscan hills in a deep golden glow and glinting off windscreens in dazzling pools of light.

By the time they were both in the rental car and driving out of the airport towards the autostrada, Tom had finished his call and was updating him on the ease with which he'd come into the country on his fake Euro/Italian passport. 'It was a grand well spent,' he said, scratching his beard, 'which reminds me I've arranged for funds to be put on standby for release from my bank in the Caymans

– my US accounts are all frozen, surprise, surprise, but this is one they didn't manage to find, so I should be able to pay you back in the next few days.'

'No rush,' Elliot assured him. 'I brought more cash in case you needed it. Two thousand euros, and half a dozen pay-as-you-talk phones. Has there been any contact from Washington?'

'Nothing, apart from the regular email asking me to report to the nearest embassy regarding a matter of great importance.'

'And you're not inclined to comply?'

Tom's expression filled with irony. 'Let's look at it this way,' he said, 'instead of picking up the phone and politely asking for their documents back, or inviting me in for a spot of tea and cosy chat of the bullshit variety, what do they do? They arrange for someone to turn over my apartment who proceeded to help themselves to just about everything in it. Then they send a bunch of ISI scumbags to pick me up in Karachi, which thankfully failed. They arranged for Michelle to be detained and harassed at Heathrow airport; they whisk Josh Shine off the face of the planet . . . No contact yet, I guess?'

Elliot shook his head.

'So basically they're doing a mighty fine job of convincing me I'm no longer on their best-friend list. Now you might think me fussy, but I don't reckon that's all adding up to a very promising kind of chinwag, and it definitely doesn't make me want to accept any offers of hospitality until I've got a better idea of what's going on.'

Chuckling, Elliot glanced in the rear-view mirror

as a set of headlights zoomed up behind them and hardly paused before overtaking.

'What about your end?' Tom asked. 'Anyone been in touch?'

'Not yet, but they're sure to know I'm involved by now, so I'm expecting something any day. Meanwhile, I've got an ex-SIS guy who's a good friend asking around, seeing what he can find out. He'll get back to us in the next few days.' As he slowed up at a set of traffic lights he looked across at the driver who pulled alongside. It was a woman, alone and oozing the kind of brazen appeal that immediately made him think of Andraya. He turned quickly away, not wanting any reminders of the transient lust that had screwed up his life, then swung the car round hard to the left as the lights made the abrupt change from red to green. 'So what's the next move?' he asked Tom, relieved to see the woman taking the right-hand fork, almost as though it were symbolic of a parting with his own weakness.

'First, I want you to take a look at what I have,' Tom answered. 'There's no mistaking what it is, but the maps are of an area that includes a nuclear power plant, which is fundamentally why I'm convinced there's more to it, because no way is anyone from our side going to gain anything from blowing up a nuclear site in the middle of Britain.'

Finding no fault with that assumption, while still managing to hope it was right, Elliot said, 'So tell me about the source, Joshua Shine. We're assuming he's broken ranks to give you classified information?'

'That's definitely how it looks, but we've got to

remember he's one of them, and in my experience, nothing's ever that straightforward where spooks are concerned.'

'But you're certain he is CIA?'

'He didn't deny it, and everything backs it up, from information he's given me in the past, to the way he lives his life, right down to his recent disappearance. What we need to know is whether he's taken himself into hiding, or if they're holding him somewhere. My guess is the second, given the fact he went back to Washington. However, we should also consider the possibility that he hasn't broken ranks at all, but is part of some elaborate conspiracy to leak information for purposes we're yet to discover.'

'Making us CIA puppets if we go with it?'

'It's possible. The intelligence services have been dumped on from a great height this past year, so they could be after some revenge, and I'd say exposing an outfit like P2OG would do it.'

Finally reaching the autostrada Elliot accelerated hard, heading towards the medieval town of Pietrasanta, where a trusted Italian colleague kept a secret apartment for love trysts and other clandestine needs. 'So why not just give you proof of its existence, and ask you to protect your source?' he said.

'Proof of existence won't have the same impact as details of an actual mission,' Tom pointed out. 'What we need now is to understand that mission, and connect it to the right body, which has to be the P2OG, or why point us in that direction. Any luck tracking down the original 21 Project yet?'

'No, everyone's working on it, but Max is giving

priority to this new committee that's recently been formed, mainly because he's received an anonymous, uncontactable dot-gov email.'

Tom was immediately interested. 'Saying what?' he demanded.

'It gives a list of four names – Daniel Allbringer and Ronald Platt?'

'Allbringer's with the Defense Intelligence Board, and Platt's with the NSC.'

'Michael Dalby, Director of Operations with MI6, which isn't a name in the public domain, so it won't be easy to get through to him. Laurie's going to start with the chairman of the Joint Intelligence Committee, Sir Christopher Malton, if she can get him to take her calls, which he's ignored so far today.'

'Anything else?' Tom prompted.

'The only other detail was "21 Project – 97 version" which we already know we need,' and speeding up to overtake a slow-moving truck, he waited until they were back in the right lane before saying, 'Laurie had an interesting piece of advice from the FBI Legal Attaché in London earlier. When she called to say she'd heard they were looking for you in Pakistan, and had they had any luck tracing you yet, she was told she'd do well to disassociate herself from the matter unless she wanted to join the rest of us on a fast track to the end of a great career.'

Tom's head drew back in surprise. 'Subtle,' he commented, though his expression was turning dark as he gave more thought to the warning. 'I was kind of expecting something like this,' he said. 'With everything they took from my apartment,

288

terrorist training manuals, books on explosives, fake Pakistani passports, jihad tapes, you name it, it won't be hard to spin it so's I end up as the one involved with terrorists, and there are people in Washington who'd like nothing more than to be rid of me. I'm not controllable, and the US Establishment is very prone to eliminating elements it can't control, particularly this current regime.'

Elliot shot him a glance.

Tom raised his eyebrows and grinned. 'OK, eliminate might be putting it a bit strong,' he conceded, 'but they play dirty, these guys, you know that as well as I do.'

Elliot wasn't disagreeing, but as Tom yawned and yawned again he said, 'Let's drop it for now, start afresh in the morning, when we can run every theory to every possible conclusion, and take a look at the backgrounds of all the major players that Katie and Michelle are faxing over to the apartment.'

Feeling only too relieved to let the subject slide for a while, Tom drew a hand over his tired face and turned to stare through his own reflection, out into the night. It wasn't long before his mind was full of Michelle, and picturing her the last time he'd seen her, looking more beautiful than he could bear in only the gaudy jewels. He couldn't even begin to put into words how much he longed to hold her right now. It was a need that was so pressing it was almost impossible to contain, though he knew it often grew stronger with tiredness, and maybe having reduced the six-thousand-mile gap between them to a mere eight hundred was making it seem more profound.

It was after midnight by the time the ancient wall

of Pietrasanta came into view. By then they'd made a stop for dinner and had returned to discussing the story, though were ready to break off again to decipher the directions their temporary landlord had faxed to Elliot's XDA. Luckily, they turned out to be reasonably easy to follow, and the key, as arranged, was found magnetized to the bottom of a fire hydrant on the second landing of a smart, mid-terrace town house set well back from the main piazza. The only payment required was a bottle of good wine when they left and a generous tip for the maid.

Being familiar with their host's famously flamboyant tastes, it came as a pleasant surprise to discover that their home for the next few days had a much more minimalist interior than they'd expected. There were a few intriguing abstracts on the walls, a vast cream-coloured sofa strewn with bronze pillows and throws, and a long oak-veneer dining table that crossed both sash windows and would double nicely as a desk for them both. The bedroom, with its garishly ornate four-poster bed, lavish silk drapes and faux-fur spreads was much more in keeping with their expectations, and created a few moments of amusement as each insisted the other make themself at home.

In the end it was Tom who won the more highly prized sofa, though he couldn't escape one of the fur spreads to cover him. He wondered why it made him think of Michelle, and decided it was because almost everything did if he allowed it, and being this exhausted he wanted nothing more than to absorb himself in memories of her as he sank into oblivion.

'I'll leave this with you so you can look it over in the night, if you wake up,' Elliot said, coming out of the bedroom with the fifteen-page fax Katie and Michelle had sent across. 'There's a note at the end you might want to look at now though.'

When he received no response, he put the fax down on the floor next to Tom so he'd see it when he woke up, and returned to the bedroom, feeling pretty tired himself. Since Nick was in New York, and therefore not with Laurie, he felt hopeful that tonight he might actually be able to sleep.

Chapter Thirteen

It was Tuesday afternoon. Over the weekend autumn had finally made its bow, turning the skies over Wiltshire belligerent and gloomy, while buffeting the countryside with fierce bursts of rain and random hits of wind as though to remind everyone of just how temperamental this season could be. It was cold too, and definitely not the kind of day to go walking. However, Katie seemed to have it fixed in her head that she wanted to get out of the car, so Michelle obligingly pulled into a layby that curved in a half-moon across the front of a small, lonely-looking copse and turned off the engine.

'Where are we?' she asked, gazing through the smeary windscreen for a clue as to why they'd stopped, but all she could see were trees that seemed about to be smothered by sky.

Despite the paleness of her cheeks and creeping weariness in her bones Katie was smiling. 'We're in my secret place,' she answered with a playful lilt in her voice. 'Come on, I want to introduce you to my friend.'

Intrigued, though concerned, because they'd just left the hospital where Katie had been given more chemo to compress her swollen tumour, Michelle got out of the car and followed her along a narrow muddy path into the wood.

'Don't you think it's beautiful here?' Katie said, gazing around, and barely noticing the fat blobs of rain that plopped down from the leaves on to her face.

Seeing the light in her eyes Michelle felt more curious than ever, though she had to admit that the stillness of the air, and a strange feeling of watchfulness in the trees, were somehow entrancing.

The smell of damp wood and earth filled the copse as they trudged on along the path, pulling back brambles to pass, and ducking under low-hanging branches. Birds were singing and somewhere, a long way overhead, a plane passed by. Michelle looked at Katie's slight frame in front of her, and hoped that it would soon fill out, for since taking the megace again her appetite had returned, and even now she was carrying a packet of biscuits that she was crumbling to share with the wildlife.

'There,' Katie declared, coming to a stop in a tiny clearing.

Puzzled, Michelle looked around, wondering what exactly she was supposed to be looking for.

'That tree, right there,' Katie told her, using both hands to present the giant, greying trunk that soared upwards into a golden tangle of leaves and branches. 'It's mine.'

Michelle followed her eyes, surprised and quite taken by the notion that Katie was laying claim to a

293

tree that looked like a beech, though actually might not be.

'Isn't it magnificent?' Katie said. 'It's a hornbeam, and I want you to promise me that when I go, you'll make it yours. I'm serious,' she insisted, when Michelle turned to look at her. 'It doesn't cost very much, only two pounds fifty each month and you'll be helping to save our countryside. I think it's a worthy cause, don't you?'

Unable to give any other reply, Michelle simply said, 'Of course.'

Katie smiled and winked. 'Never imagined myself as a tree-hugger,' she confessed, 'but that old fellow there . . . Come on,' she said, taking Michelle's hand to lead her closer. 'Come and touch it and tell me if you feel anything, because I know I did.'

Obediently Michelle traipsed through the undergrowth to the tree, and put her hands to the brittle grey bark. Then, copying Katie, she closed her eyes. For a long time she felt only the girth of the trunk, and the smear of damp on her cheek. Then she became aware of a distant stirring sensation very deep inside her, followed by a soft rush of emotion that moved into her heart and swelled gently in her chest. Immediately her eyes opened.

Katie was smiling, though her eyes remained closed as she inhaled the musky scent of the wood. 'The day the doctor gave me the bad news,' she said, 'I came here, and when I saw this old hornbeam I just knew it was special.' She breathed deeply again, absorbing the heady power of the tree as though it were able to transpose its magical healing directly into her skin. She looked up, her slightly jaundiced eyes moving amongst the jagged, pointed leaves and tiny catkins of the female flowers. 'It was green and proud and in full bloom the last time I came,' she said softly. 'Now the leaves are starting to yellow.'

Unable to escape the symbolism Michelle put her arms around the tree again, as though to pull in the strength she needed to get through the next few minutes without breaking down.

'When you feel something like this it's hard not to believe there's a God, isn't it?' Katie murmured.

'Have you told Molly about this?' Michelle finally managed to ask.

'No, not yet. I wanted to show you first, because it's something I knew you'd understand, and probably feel too, being the exceptionally sensitive soul that you are. I don't think everyone would feel it.'

Smiling, Michelle drew her into an embrace. 'I love you Katie Rowe,' she said, using the name she'd been born with.

'I love you too,' Katie responded, 'even though you've just crushed my last chocolate biscuit.'

Laughing, and swallowing the lump in her throat, Michelle said, 'Come on, we need to get you home.'

Katie took a last, lingering look at the hornbeam, then linking Michelle's arm she said, 'You see, I feel all charged up and able to cope again now. I thought I might, if I came here.'

Knowing she was probably referring as much to the looming scene with Molly as to her own physical challenge, Michelle hugged her arm in tighter, and said, 'I'm glad it's helped, but I still don't think you should confront Molly today. You're just not up to it.'

Katie sighed deeply and looked down at the soggy leaves and damp, broken twigs they were treading underfoot. 'You're probably right,' she said. 'I just wish she'd told me the police had talked to her about the picture she had confiscated, then the call this morning might not have come as such a shock.'

'Well at least this monster, whoever he is, has been arrested,' Michelle said comfortingly. 'And what you have to do now is stop tormenting yourself with what could have been. I know it's hard, but she's OK, and thank God, she didn't ever meet up with him.'

'But if he'd been closer to home she might . . .'

'Stop!' Michelle broke in, gently but firmly. 'She didn't, and that's as far as you need to go.'

'She has to be told who he is though,' Katie persisted.

'Of course, but not today. Give yourself some time to recover from this first.'

'What about taking her computer away? I really think I should . . .'

'That's going to be hard when you've told her you trust her not to use the chat rooms any more. And for all you know she's kept her word.'

'The police have asked to see the computer . . .'

'Katie, why don't you leave this to me. I'll deal with Molly and the police, while you just concentrate on you.'

Katie's eyebrows rose, but she said no more until they were back in the car and pulling out on to the road. 'You're going to deal with Molly?' she said, sounding intrigued and even amused.

'Do you have a problem with that?' Michelle responded.

'No, not at all,' Katie assured her, opening another packet of biscuits, 'but I think Molly might.'

'Then Molly will just have to deal with it.'

Katie crunched into a ginger nut and offered the packet to Michelle. 'Yes, she will,' she decided, as Michelle shook her head. 'I said I was going to stand aside and let you take over, so that's what I'm going to do. In fact I've been creating the problem all along, by not letting you establish a relationship with her, so what better way to do it than to tackle her head on? Yes, I can see there's some merit in setting off all the fireworks at once . . .'

'Katie.'

Katie finished her biscuit, took out another and was halfway through that when she said, 'Aren't you scared?'

'Stop it,' Michelle laughed.

'I know I would be,' Katie confessed.

'I've just had a hornbeam fix,' Michelle reminded her, 'so I'm fearless.'

'You must have OD'd – either that, or you're more in touch with your inner twig than I am. But I'll say no more. You're in charge now, and I can't tell you how wonderful it feels to let go.'

Suspecting that a creeping exhaustion had forced that admission, rather than the truth, Michelle glanced over at her, and seeing how tired she looked, she gently removed the biscuits from her hand and told her to lie back.

Without a murmur of protest Katie turned her head to one side and rested it on the seat belt. She really was worn out, which was a pity, because she'd felt so alive at the weekend while they were researching for Tom's story and talking to him and Elliot on the phone, but she'd be right on top of it again just as soon as she'd had some sleep – and after Laurie had reported back on the interviews she was conducting in London.

'Did you manage to talk to Laurie before she left on Sunday?' she asked, turning blearily back to Michelle.

'You mean about her bringing a camera next weekend?'

'No, about this situation with Elliot and Nick van Zant.'

'Yes, but only briefly.'

'It's not good, is it?'

'No, but it's not for you to worry about. She'll cope.'

Katie sighed. 'I like worrying about other people, it takes my mind off me.'

'Ah, but we need your mind on you if we're going to pull off a miracle,' Michelle reminded her.

Katie's eyes remained closed as she smiled. 'Miracles do happen, don't they?' she said softly.

'Yes, of course,' Michelle answered.

Still smiling Katie finally relinquished herself to the arms of sleep, while Michelle continued to drive, tears spilling on to her cheeks as she prayed silently and fervently to God to prove her right.

'Where's Mum?' Molly demanded, coming to stand in the doorway.

Michelle looked up from where she was sitting at one end of the big, downy sofa, with a cascade of paperwork between her lap and the floor. She'd been so engrossed in the files they'd printed out over the weekend that she hadn't heard Molly come in. She was certainly standing there now though, all bristling five foot four of her, with a school bag clutched in one hand, a damp raincoat shrugged half off her shoulders and a super-charged attitude that brooked no ignoring.

'She's upstairs, having a lie-down,' Michelle answered. 'Can I get you anything?'

'No thanks. I'll go and see her.'

'She's asleep.'

Molly's face tightened. 'So? I can still go and see her.'

'I'd like to have a little chat with you first,' Michelle said, gathering up the papers to stack on an arm of the sofa.

Molly's defences couldn't have shot up faster. 'I've got homework to do,' she blurted, already backing off.

Undaunted, Michelle rose to her feet. 'The police were in touch today,' she said, 'about the person you were emailing.'

Molly's eyes blazed, but Michelle could see a goodly amount of unease clouding up the anger.

'He was found in possession of child porn-ography,' Michelle told her, sounding perfectly matter-of-fact, 'so the police were able to arrest him.'

'It's got nothing to do with me,' Molly snapped. 'I never went anywhere near him . . .'

'No-one's trying to say you did, but you should

299

have told your mum that the police had talked to you . . .'

'What's it got to do with you?' Molly retorted rudely. 'I'll tell her what I want to tell her . . .'

'I don't think you understand the position you put her in,' Michelle said. 'If the police think you're hiding things from her, which obviously they do now, it makes it look as though she's not paying proper attention at home, and forces them to wonder what else you might be hiding. As a result, they want to see your computer.'

Molly's eyes opened wide with shock. 'No way!' she shouted. 'That is my private property and no-one but me goes anywhere near it.'

'They're not insisting, but Molly, you have to realize, that kind of refusal only raises suspicions.'

'Yours, maybe, but I couldn't care less what you think. You've got no right talking to me about any of this anyway. It's none of your bloody business . . .'

'Actually, it is my business. You're my niece, and I care about you very much, so I don't want . . .'

'That is such crap! You don't even care about your own son, so how can you say you care about me?'

'Of course I care about Robbie, but we're talking about you . . .'

'Not any more, we're not.'

'Molly! Come back here, and keep your voice down . . .'

'I'll shout all I want, this is my house, not yours, and she's my mother, so if she wakes up . . .'

'All right, if that's how you want to play it,' Michelle cut in, and almost before Molly knew what was happening she was being marched back into the sitting room and turned round to face Michelle. 'Now you can listen to me,' Michelle said firmly. 'You are behaving like a spoiled, selfish, distinctly unintelligent brat, with no consideration for anyone but yourself, and we both know that is *not* who you are, or the way you've been brought up. You're fourteen now, Molly, so it's time to act your age and start facing some responsibilities.'

'Don't you dare . . .'

'A good way to begin,' Michelle cut across her, 'would be to apologize to your mother for the worry and upset you caused her this morning – if you don't, then I'm afraid I won't defend you any more, and your computer will be taken away.'

Molly was beside herself. 'I don't need you to defend me,' she shouted. 'I can defend myself. So why don't you just get out . . .'

'And go back to where I came from? Yes, I know how it goes. Well, as it happens, this is where I came from, this very family, and if you can't see that the people you're hurting most by resisting me are you and your mother, then perhaps I'm wrong and you aren't very clever.'

'Well perhaps I'm not,' she snarled, jutting her face out.

Ignoring the temptation, Michelle said, 'Now you can either apologize for your outrageous rudeness and we'll start over again, or you can go to your room and stay there until you're able to demonstrate what a reasonable and worthwhile human being you actually are.'

Molly's lips were curled in a snarl. 'You can't make me do anything I don't want to do,' she spat.

'Oh yes I can, and if you want to put it to the test . . .'

Molly drew herself upright. 'You lay one hand on me and I'll smash . . .'

'Don't be ridiculous, I'm not going to hit you. Now I've given you your choices, apologize, or go to your room.'

'I'm going to talk to Mum. She needs to be told what an absolute cow you are . . .'

Michelle was unbending. 'Molly, don't disturb her,' she said sharply. 'She's had a difficult day . . .' She drew back as Molly suddenly rounded on her like a hissing cat.

'She's my mother!' she spat. 'If I want to disturb her then I bloody well will.'

'I've just told you, she's had a difficult day so she . . .'

'No she has not!'

Michelle blinked.

'She has not had a difficult day! She doesn't have difficult days any more. Everyone knows that.' Her face was horribly stricken and Michelle had rarely seen such a struggle to cover so much fear. It made her want to pull her into her arms and swear to her that it would be all right, but how could she? She was in no position to make such a promise, and affection was clearly the last thing Molly wanted from her right now.

'Listen, Molly,' she said gently, 'I understand how hard this is for you, but you know your mother's sick, and running away from it . . .'

'She is *not*!' Molly almost screamed. 'Stop saying that.'

It was hard, but Michelle knew she had to keep

pushing, for it was the only way to start breaking the defences down. 'Molly, you know it's true,' she said, 'and you know it's why I'm here . . .'

'No! She's all right. She doesn't need you . . .'

'Molly, please try to understand . . .'

'Shut up! Just *shut up!*' Her hands were over her ears, tears were rolling down her cheeks, but though she turned away, she didn't leave the room. She just stood in front of the fireplace, still blocking her ears, her young shoulders shaking as her body convulsed with sobs.

Going to her, Michelle wrapped her tightly in her arms, wanting to convey the feeling of safety she needed. But Molly couldn't accept it. If she did, it might mean having to admit the real reason why Michelle was here.

Michelle winced as a sharp elbow jammed into her side. 'Get off me,' Molly raged, 'don't touch me,' and shoving her out of the way she ran into the kitchen and up the stairs.

Michelle remained where she was, one hand to her head, the other to her side where Molly had dug her. It had been a far from easy encounter, though really no worse than she'd expected. Even so, her heart ached with as much pity as it did frustration at her inability to ease Molly's pain.

Upstairs in her room Molly was so enraged she wanted to lash out and hurt someone really, really badly. She had scissors and nail files that she could stab into her arms and legs, or Michelle's face, or anyone who tried to stop her doing anything. She hated them all, the police, the teachers, her mother, Michelle – especially Michelle. She was going to ring Cecily and tell her she wanted her poisons, or her witchcraft, or anything else she could think of to get rid of her. She had to instant-message with Brad first though, and she was already late. Oh my God, she was late! What if he hadn't waited?

As she connected to the Internet she dashed away her tears, as though pushing them off her face could push them out of her heart. Please let him still be there. If he wasn't it would be stupid, fucking Michelle's fault, for keeping her downstairs. And Rank Rusty's, because she'd stayed behind to try and persuade him to shoplift the bracelet Allison wanted, but he'd refused to do it, and had even threatened to tell if she did it herself! Stupid, idiot fucking moron! She had to have that bracelet to get through to Step Five, which was going to happen on Friday night, when they all got together to contact Lilith and smoke some weed. Allison had said it was the best idea for Step Five, because there would be lots of weed at the party, so they could get in practice, and Brad definitely smoked weed, so she had to do it too, or he'd think she was a delinquent and wouldn't want any more to do with her.

He wasn't there! She was too late. Bloody, fucking Michelle. She hated her so much. He'd sent an email though, saying he couldn't wait any longer, but would instant-message later, if she could make it at ten.

Yes, she could make it at ten, as long as they didn't take her computer away. They wouldn't though, because she wouldn't let them. She just wished she knew what to do about the bracelet, because she'd promised Allison she'd take it over there on Thursday and she had to revise for a major maths test tomorrow, so tonight was the only chance she had to get it. She kept trying to think of excuses for not having it, but whatever she said she knew they wouldn't believe her. They'd call her a coward, say she wasn't fit to be a DOL, and then throw her out, which meant Cecily wouldn't help her get rid of Michelle, she'd be banned from the party, she wouldn't be Brad's girlfriend any more, and she wouldn't have any friends either.

It couldn't happen. It just couldn't. She had to get that bracelet or she might as well go on the suicide site again now. Unless . . . Oh my God! Unless . . . No, she couldn't. It wouldn't work. They'd find out and then it would be even worse than if she hadn't got the bracelet at all. But how would they find out? Who was going to know if she bought it? All she had to do was make sure no-one was around when she went into the shop, then she could hand over the money and come out with the bracelet. Which was all just like, brilliant, if she had the frigging money. But she didn't, did she? All she had was five lousy quid, and the bracelet was ten ninety nine.

Well, there was nothing else for it, she'd just have to steal the money. She could take it out of her mum's handbag, which was probably in its usual place, hanging on the back of a chair in the kitchen. The thought of that slowed her up a bit, making her feel slightly dizzy and sick. Her mum would go like, totally ballistic if she ever found out, but she wouldn't find out if Molly took the whole purse, would she? She'd think she'd dropped it somewhere, which she might have, because those sorts of things happened all the time.

Disconnecting from the Web, she picked up her coat and bag and tiptoed out on to the landing. The place was dead quiet, except for her heart which was banging about like a drum. Her mum didn't snore, which was a shame, because then she'd know if she was asleep, and Michelle didn't watch TV – like, was she for real? – so there was no noise downstairs either.

Hardly daring to breathe, she took the stairs one at a time, wincing and waiting after each creak of a floorboard, though there were hardly any, and none of them were like, really loud.

The handbag was in its usual place, which was perfect, because it wasn't possible to see that chair from inside the sitting room. She skimmed quickly towards it, dipped a hand in, felt around, and finding the purse pulled it out. Her heart was beating so fast now it was like, right out of control. She didn't really want to do this, but what choice did she have? If her mum would give her more money there wouldn't be a problem, would there, so really her mum only had herself to blame. And she definitely wouldn't want her to go out nicking stuff from shops and getting herself arrested, maybe even put in reform school, or prison, so this was definitely what she had to do, because it was the best thing for her mum too.

Opening the top flap of her school bag she slid the purse inside. She was feeling like, so peculiar now, as if she was floating or drowning or something. She tried to breathe and found her chest was like, closed down. She tried again. It worked, but she had to get out of here now. She was just taking a step towards the door when Michelle said,

'Molly.'

She froze, then spun round. To her horror Michelle was standing right there, in the kitchen.

'Put it back,' Michelle said quietly.

Molly's eyes flashed with outrage. 'What?' she demanded.

'You know what I'm talking about, now put it back and we'll pretend it never happened.'

'You're crazy, do you know that?' Molly sneered. 'You're sick up here. I haven't got anything, so I don't . . .'

'Molly, I saw you take it, now put it . . . Molly! Come back here,' she shouted, as Molly flung open the door. 'Molly!'

Molly was leaping the fence. She wasn't listening to anything Michelle was saying. It was all blocked out. She was just running and running, into the lane, up past the duck pond, crashing into Judy as she came the other way, but on she went.

'Molly, are you all right?' Judy called after her.

Molly tore on. She wasn't stopping for anyone, she was going to Chippenham, where she'd buy the bracelet, then she'd catch the bus back to Allison's, or even over to Rank Rusty's and show him she didn't need his stupid help . . .

Judy was still looking bemused as she joined Michelle in the garden. 'What happened?' she asked. 'She seemed in a mighty big hurry.'

Michelle sighed, and shook her head. 'Let's just say I'm starting to get an idea now of how deeply in denial she is,' she said.

'Oh dear. So Katie still hasn't told her?'

Michelle shook her head.

'Well, it's not uncommon for relatives to try and block it out,' Judy said, following her into the house. 'It's a form of self-protection, obviously, so if Molly tells herself forcefully enough that it's not happening, then in her world it's not.'

'Which is clearly why she's having such a hard time with me being here,' Michelle said, filling the kettle. 'Underneath it all she knows what it means, so if she can make me go away then everything will be all right again.'

'Poor love,' Judy said. 'Breaks your heart, doesn't it, to think of what she's going through.'

Michelle nodded, and attempted a smile. 'We'll get there,' she said softly.

Judy put a hand on her arm and squeezed it. 'I came round to find out how Katie got on today,' she said. 'I guess she's asleep, is she?'

'She was, but there's a good chance Molly and I managed to wake her up. If we did, she's apparently decided to be very un-Katie and just let us get on with it.' She didn't add, 'which doesn't bode well for our miracle,' for not intervening in that dreadful scene could be an indication that Katie might actually be starting to let go.

Chapter Fourteen

The small town of Pietrasanta, with its typical Italian piazzas and flatfronted houses was gleaming after a deluge of rain. Elliot was beside the apartment window working on his laptop while half-listening to Tom as he spoke to Michelle on the phone.

'So first they set up the worst of the known terrorist groups to stage a devastating attack on the West,' Tom was saying, 'then, just in the nick of time, the plot gets exposed and paraded down Pennsylvania Avenue. Next thing we know the hawks have been re-elected, then with proof of this terrible plot's origins, the invasion of Pakistan can begin, because America has to get control of those nuclear weapons before they fall into the wrong hands – which they're apt to at any time.'

Michelle was quiet for a moment as she took it all in. 'And if the British believe they were the intended victim of the plot,' she finally added, 'the Government won't receive too much opposition to riding into the next war with their American chums.'

'Exactly. All this is theory, of course, we have no proof, and actually there is a case for the end justifying the means, because the Pakistan situation has to be resolved. It's the iniquitous exploitation of people's fears for re-election purposes that I object to, because we're going to end up with the British public believing they came very close to being nuked, when it was all a ruse to get the Republicans back in power, and their country into another war. It's unconscionable, and if we're right in our assumptions, the neo-conservatives, who are driving this, can't be allowed to get away with it.'

'Hang on,' Michelle said, 'Katie's listening, she wants to say something.'

'Do we have to have proof?' Katie asked. 'You've got the maps and the emails . . .'

'But nothing to connect them,' Tom reminded her. 'As it stands, we'd have a hard job getting anyone to run it, because it's all hypothetical, and the mainstream US press is pretty much Republican-owned, so no-one's going to stick their necks out over something like this unless they're certain their heads won't end up rolling.'

'You'd get it published here, in Britain.'

'Maybe, but they too will probably want something a bit more substantial to go on, and as time's still more or less on our side we can carry on trying to join at least some of the dots, so that when we come to present our case it looks credible, even if not totally irrefutable.'

Reaching for his own phone, Elliot felt a familiar twist of nerves go through him when he saw it was Laurie. 'Hi, any luck?' he said, already knowing what she was calling about.

'Yep. Sir Christopher Malton's agreed to see me for five minutes if I can get there before eleven. I'm on my way now, so it would help to speak to Tom.'

'Of course, I'll put him on.'

'Before you do, have you spoken to Max this morning?'

'Still too early for him. Why?'

'Just that Nick flew down to Washington to join him last night.'

Immediately Elliot's face darkened. 'For a particular reason?' he asked, understanding that she must have spoken to Nick to know where he was.

'I think something came up in New York. He didn't give me any details though.'

Elliot glanced across the table as Tom finished his call. 'Laurie's about to meet with Christopher Malton,' he told him. 'Talk her through the way you want her to play it.'

'I'd say lay it all on the table,' Tom responded. 'We're not the ones with anything to hide.'

As he took the phone, Elliot got up from his computer and went to refresh his coffee. Though he was half-listening to Tom, he was finding it hard to get past the mention of Nick, for even to think of Laurie on the phone to him, never mind everything else they were doing, was tearing him apart so badly it was as though he was losing control.

He was still standing in the kitchen, staring at his empty coffee cup, when Tom came in with the phone. 'She wants to talk to you again,' he said, passing it over.

Taking it, Elliot put it to his ear.

'Are you there?' she asked.

'Yes.'

'When are you coming back?'

'Friday. Possibly Saturday.'

'I'm taking a camera to Katie's on Friday. It's just to give her a feel for it, a kind of rehearsal to help her make up her mind, but I can meet you at the flat late Saturday afternoon, if you like.'

He turned to look out of the window, where the mountains that rose up behind the terrace were misted by rain.

'We need to talk,' she reminded him.

'Sure,' he said. 'I'll see you at the flat.' He was about to ring off when something compelled him to add, 'What about Nick? When's he back?'

'I don't know. I think at the weekend.'

'Will you be staying with him?'

She paused. 'That wasn't my intention.'

Already wishing he hadn't asked, he said, 'Call me when you've spoken to Malton,' and abruptly ended the call.

As he returned to his computer the phone rang again, and seeing the name of his SIS contact and close friend, Chris Gallagher, he gladly clicked onto the diversion.

'OK, this is what I've got so far,' Chris told him. 'They know you're working with Tom Chambers, which won't come as a surprise, but they don't seem to know you're with him now, which means we spirited you out of the UK without hitting their radar. You might have some hassle getting back in if you come the conventional route, they'll want to know where you've been, they might even detain you, so if you can make it to Le Touquet I'll pick you up in the Rockwell, just let me know when.'

'I owe you for this,' Elliot told him.

'I'm glad to be of help. Now listen, there's more. I spoke to Laurie earlier and she's definitely on the right track with Christopher Malton. He's in regular contact with Daniel Allbringer, over in the States, and with Michael Dalby, here in the UK. Dalby's recently been in Washington, so that puts him in the right place when this new committee convened. One of the guys on the ground here in London tells me that orders are coming direct from Dalby himself, but there haven't been many, just to haul Tom in if they find him, and hand him straight over to the Yanks. Ask Tom if he's familiar with the name Deborah Gough?'

'Deborah Gough,' Elliot said to Tom.

Tom's eyebrows rose in surprise. 'What about her?'

Elliot relayed Tom's question.

'I think she's part of this committee,' Chris responded. 'I'll give you more when I get it. Now for the big one. I can't mention any names, but the advice I'm receiving for Tom is to get rid of whatever Josh Shine gave him – burn, erase, nuke, whatever needs to be done, just don't get caught with it in his possession.'

Elliot looked at Tom. 'Why?' he asked.

'If you've seen it, you'll probably be able to answer that better than I can, but I trust the guy I spoke to, so I'm going to add my voice to the advice, get rid of it and move on.'

Elliot said nothing. He didn't have to, Chris would already know how unlikely it was he and Tom would heed the advice.

'You're still supposed to be on sabbatical,' Chris

reminded him. 'If you break that agreement, they'll go after you in ways that'll make you wish you'd never heard of Tom Chambers, which brings us neatly to your contact with our own illustrious round table of spooks – and one in particular.'

Elliot inwardly groaned. 'What about him?' he said.

'Have you spoken to him?'

'No.'

'Then you should probably prepare for a visit. It would make sense, considering his superiors know you're in touch with Tom, and once Laurie starts collaring some very important people with some extremely awkward questions, they're going to presume you're behind it.'

'Laurie's her own person.'

'Of course, but just keep in mind that there are often more effective ways of reaching a person than dialling direct. And on that note, I'll leave you.'

With the ominous meaning ringing in his ears, Elliot disconnected and turned to Tom who was still staring at him, listening to his end of the call.

'Who *was* that?' Tom asked.

'His name's Chris Gallagher,' Elliot answered. 'He's a pilot, an art dealer and ex-SIS. He's also a good friend, and someone I trust implicitly.' He didn't add that in his capacity as art dealer, Chris Gallagher had brought Andraya Sorrantos into his life. This had no relevance to what they were discussing, nor was Chris in any way to blame for the course Elliot had embarked upon as a result of the introduction. All that mattered here was that Chris had access to people and information that was going to prove vital if they continued with this investigation. 'Tell me more about Deborah Gough,' he said, as Tom came to sit at the table.

Tom arched his eyebrows, and rested his chin on one hand. 'The last I knew, she was CIA,' he answered. 'Probably still is, if she's involved in this. I've never met the woman, but I'm told she's pretty impressive. Fearless is the word I remember being used. And extreme. She used to head up Counter Intelligence at Langley, but that was a few years ago. She could have made it to executive director by now, or even higher. We can probably find out easily enough.' He was searching for the fax Katie and Michelle had sent a few days ago, that contained the names of those who'd drawn up the initial recommendation for the P2OG. 'She's not here,' he said, as he looked through, 'but she could have been a member of the commissioning panel, which is classified I see.' He read on for a while, then started to chuckle as he registered some of Katie's comments. 'We should get her to write this,' he said, 'she's good.'

Laurie was seated opposite the arch conservative, Sir Christopher Malton, feeling probably only half as awed as he would like, for there had been no mistaking the condescension that emanated from behind his horn-rimmed glasses as he'd deigned to glance up from his desk upon her arrival.

'I appreciate you seeing me at such short notice,' she said, as the door closed behind his assistant who'd offered neither coffee, nor to take her coat.

'It will have to be brief,' he told her, not bothering to hide his impatience, nor to look up from the notes he was making.

'Then I'll come straight to the point,' she said. 'What can you tell me about an elite military/intelligence task force called the Proactive Pre-emptive Operations Group, or P2OG for short?'

Frowning, he turned over a page and continued to read as he said, 'I believe it was an idea generated by certain members of the US Defense Department back in 2002, and commissioned for analysis by a group of experts.'

Surprised that he'd answered so readily, she said, 'So it doesn't actually exist, except on paper?'

'I believe that is what I said,' he responded, still engrossed in his paperwork.

She noted down his answer, then looked at him again.

'What do you know about the details of a terrorist plot that were leaked to Tom Chambers?' she asked.

A few seconds ticked by before he said, 'Who?'

'Tom Chambers,' she repeated.

'I don't know what you're talking about.'

Noting that he'd said 'what' and not 'who', she asked, 'Are you telling me you've never heard of Tom Chambers?'

Sighing, he put down his pen and linked his long, arthritic fingers on the stack of papers in front of him. 'What is your point, Ms Forbes?' he said shortly.

'My point is,' she said, 'that the US authorities have enlisted the help of our own law enforcement in their search for Tom Chambers, and I was hoping, as a member of the Joint Intelligence Committee, that you could tell me why they are so keen to interview him.'

His steely eyes bored into hers, almost causing her to flinch. 'If you require information concerning the police,' he responded, 'wouldn't you do better to talk to them?'

'I have. They're not very forthcoming either, so maybe I'll ask the question again, what do you know about the details of a terrorist plot that were leaked to Tom Chambers?'

He started to answer, then seemed to rethink, and scrutinized her in a way that was clearly meant to intimidate, and after almost a minute of it came close to succeeding. 'Terrorist plots, or let's say, what appear to be terrorist plots,' he said finally, 'are coming to light one way or another all the time, so unless you can be more specific, I'm afraid I can't give you an answer.'

Realizing he was fishing for information, she said, 'I'm referring to a plot concerning the Sizewell B Nuclear Power Station.'

His eyes immediately widened. 'I can assure you, if any such plot had come to the attention of the intelligence services I would know about it, and as I don't, I think that rather puts your colleague's source into question.'

Grateful for such an accommodating lead-in, she said, 'What do you know about Joshua Shine?'

Not a muscle in his furrowed face flickered as he said, 'I don't believe I'm familiar with the name.'

'He was the Political Officer at the US Consulate in Lahore. We've been trying to reach him, but he seems to have disappeared.'

He merely looked at her, as though expecting her to enlighten him with the relevance of this new subject.

'Do you know where he is?' she asked.

'I believe I just told you I've never heard of him,' he replied. 'And as your enquiries seem to be focusing on Americans, wouldn't you be better served at the US Embassy?'

Laurie was writing in her notepad. ' "Never heard of him," ' she quoted under her breath. Then looking up again, she resumed her smile and ignoring his question said, 'Sir Christopher, how long have you been a member of the British-American Project for a Successor Generation?'

He face turned to stone.

'I'm sorry. Do you have an objection to answering?' she asked. 'I mean, it's not classified information, is it?'

'Of course not, I'm simply curious to know what relevance it has to what we were discussing.'

'That's what I'm trying to find out,' she confessed. 'You are a member, aren't you?'

'I am.'

'And you do meet regularly with other members, both sides of the Atlantic?'

'I wouldn't say regularly, but yes, we meet from time to time.'

'Have you met recently, to discuss Tom Chambers?'

His head drew back. 'I am not about to divulge details of meetings that have absolutely nothing to do with you,' he responded witheringly.

'So you have discussed Tom Chambers?'

'That is not what I said.'

Her heart was starting to thud as she glanced down at her notes. 'But you were with Daniel Allbringer of the US Defense Intelligence Board, in

Florida on October 1st and 2nd this year?' she said.

His face darkened, showing his annoyance at this checking of his movements.

'You were also in Washington, just after that, attending a meeting with several other members of the British and American intelligence services?'

'Yes.'

'But you didn't discuss Tom Chambers, or the leaked details of a terrorist plot that has Sizewell B as its focus?'

Leaning forward he said, 'It was not on the agenda, but even if it were, I can assure you, it is not a matter I would be discussing with you.'

'I see,' she replied, making a point of writing his answer down again, not because she'd forget, but because she wanted to unsettle him. 'Mr Allbringer's considered something of a hawk in his own country, isn't he?' she said. 'No, it's OK, you don't have to answer that, it's a matter of record, as are your own similar views on pre-emptive action.'

The skin round his mouth was starting to pale. 'Where's the question, Ms Forbes?' he demanded.

'Oh, there are plenty,' she responded. 'Perhaps you can tell me how many members of your elite British-American society stand to gain, either financially or politically, by aligning themselves with the neo-conservatives? In fact, what I would really like to know is how deeply the neo-cons are involved, through members of your society, in setting our own political agenda, and to what lengths any of you might go to ensure a continuance of power?'

He was on his feet, face quivering with outrage, but before he could speak she said, 'Please tell me what you know about the terrorist plot that has fallen into Tom Chambers's hands.'

His eyes bulged behind their lenses.

'Have any arrests been made as a result of this plot being uncovered?' she asked.

He didn't answer.

'Is that a yes or a no?' she prompted.

'This interview is over,' he snarled, starting for the door.

'So a terrorist cell is penetrated, a plot uncovered, and in spite of knowing who's involved, no arrests are made.' She wrinkled her nose. 'Something's not right here, Sir Christopher, is it?'

Coming to tower over her, he spoke in a fiercely sibilant voice. 'You may think you're clever with all you've managed to deduce so far, but let me tell you, you're jumping to all the wrong conclusions. The information Tom Chambers has is false. It was planted on him by a rogue agent, who is waging a personal vendetta against his own government. The agent concerned is now under arrest.'

'And this agent would be?'

A quick sharpness in his eyes told her he'd just realized his mistake.

'The man whose name you're not familiar with,' she reminded him.

For a horrible moment she thought he was going to strike her, then quite suddenly his whole demeanour changed. 'Look,' he said, assuming a long-suffering, almost avuncular air, 'I fully appreciate why you and your friends think there's a story here, but let me assure you, there isn't. Let me also remind you that Elliot Russell is bound by an agreement to cease all investigative reporting for the period of one year. I don't believe that time is up.'

'Do I look like Elliot Russell?' she said tightly.

As he started to respond the phone rang and snatching it up he listened to the voice at the other end, then said, 'Thank you,' and rang off.

'That was a reminder that I'm already late for my next meeting,' he told her. 'However, I want to say this before you go – Elliot Russell is a fine reporter, you both are, so you're doing yourselves a grave disservice by becoming involved in crackpot conspiracy theories that are never going to hold up under any amount of scrutiny. So I would suggest, if you want to retain the well-deserved credibility you have earned, that you give up on this nonsense now, before your reputations and your careers become damaged beyond repair.'

The unexpected tone of sincerity startled her, and remained with her as she rode the lift down to the ground floor and stepped outside into the chill, windy thoroughfare of Whitehall. It wasn't that she'd been taken in by it, because she hadn't. However, it was intriguing her that this was now the second time she'd been warned to safeguard her career.

'It confirms,' Elliot responded down the line when she told him, 'that they're already planning to do everything they can to discredit Tom, if he goes public with what he has.'

'Precisely,' she said, hailing a cab as it turned out of Horseguards.

'And he claims Joshua Shine is under arrest?' he continued. 'On what charges?'

'I don't know. He didn't use the name, but it's definitely who he was talking about.'

'I'll get Max on to it. Where are you now?'

'On my way home. Hang on.' After giving the driver her address, she jumped into the back of the cab and slammed the door. 'So, to precis,' she said, as they merged into the traffic, 'Sir Christopher now knows everything Tom wants him to know, and he's definitely worried. More than worried. He also wants me to remind you of your agreement to shut down for a year.'

'As if I'd forgotten,' he responded. 'You sound tired.'

'Not really, just coming down after the adrenalin rush of challenging someone with the power to destroy me.'

There was a smile in his voice as he said, 'It's not going to happen.'

Finding herself wishing he'd be there when she got back, she resisted telling him so and said, 'I'll put everything in an email when I get home. Any more news your end?'

'Nothing you don't already know.'

'I'll talk to you later then.'

'Sure.'

Neither of them rang off, and as she sat listening to the silence she was imagining him at the other end, the sternness of his expression that covered the pain, the stillness of his body that masked the unrest. She wanted so much to tell him she missed him, because it was how she felt, but then she thought of Nick and her eyes closed in despair.

'Better go,' she whispered, and ended the call.

A moment later, as the taxi cut across Trafalgar

Square, her phone rang again. She held on to it, staring out of the window, wanting it to be him calling back, but when she looked at the readout it was Katie's number on the display.

'How did it go?' Michelle asked.

'I'm putting it all in an email to Elliot,' she answered. 'I'll send you a copy, but in a nutshell, when I asked what part the neo-cons are playing on the British political stage I obviously hit a very sore spot.'

'Interesting,' Michelle murmured. 'Did you mention anything about the British-American Successor Generation?'

'Absolutely. Another hit. God they make me sick with all their exclusive societies, think tanks, top secret projects . . . It's all highly suspect if you ask me, downright Masonic even. How to make the very rich even richer, and keep the rest of us in a state of fear, or ignorance or just plain dumb servitude to their billion-dollar empires.'

'I agree with everything you're saying,' Michelle responded. 'But are you all right? You sound a bit flat.'

Laurie sighed. 'I'm fine,' she assured her. 'Just sounding off. How's Katie?'

'Actually, in a filthy mood, but I'm not allowed to say so.'

'Is she there?'

'Her breath is burning my neck.'

Laurie heard Katie laugh.

'She'd speak to you,' Michelle continued, 'but there are three doughnuts currently being masticated right in front of her vocal cords. However, she wants to know if you'd like to stay here on Friday night, because she can either force Molly to sleep with her, so you can have Molly's bed, or she can kick me downstairs on to the sofa. And given the shortness of her fuse at the moment the kicking won't be metaphorical.'

Laughing, Laurie said, '*I'll* take the sofa, and thank you for the invitation.'

'We'll argue that one when you get here.'

'We miss you,' Katie shouted from the background.

'I miss you too,' Laurie responded, realizing how true it was.

There was a click and Michelle said, 'You're on the speaker now.'

'I said, I miss you too,' Laurie repeated. 'Why are you in a bad mood, Katie?'

'Oh, I'm on the ropes again, getting the stuffing beaten out of me by my reluctance to leave this planet, so I've been picking on Michelle, trying to make her think it's all her fault. No luck so far, and anyway I'm about to make a comeback. Seconds out, round six to survival. Doughnuts help, so bring Krispy Kremes when you come.'

'This is your bad mood?' Laurie challenged.

'Speaking to you instantly cheers me up,' Katie informed her. 'I'm really looking forward to the weekend, with or without the camera. Is that someone else trying to get through?' she asked, reacting to a bleep on the line.

'Sounds like it,' Laurie replied. 'I should probably take it,' and after promising to call again later, she switched over to the other line without checking who it was.

'Hi, it's me,' Nick said.

The jolt she felt just to hear him almost swallowed her voice. 'You're up early,' she responded, echoing his sleepy tone.

'It's almost seven o'clock, and I was lying here thinking about you.'

She wanted to ask what kind of thoughts, but forced herself to say, 'I've just come from Sir Christopher Malton's office.'

'Oh?' he responded, sounding intrigued.

'I'll email the details,' she said. 'Have you spoken to Elliot?'

'Not yet.'

'I told him you were with Max. I think he's expecting your call.'

'OK. I'll speak to him when we're finished here. I'm booked on to the red-eye on Friday, by the way, which gets me in early Saturday morning. Will you be around?'

'No, I'll be at Katie's, and I've arranged to see Elliot on Saturday night. We need to talk.'

'Of course. Are you sure you don't want me to talk to him with you?'

'Sure.' She gazed out at the dirty old buildings of Fleet Street, the littered pavements and pale, cross faces of those battling the wind. The world was seeming such an alien place lately, as though she didn't quite belong.

'Can I see you on Sunday?' he asked.

Sunday seemed a long way away. 'Yes. I'll come to your apartment,' she replied.

There was a moment before he said, 'I know it might be a bit soon for this, but if you want to bring a suitcase . . .' He paused again. 'What I'm saying is, I'm ready to make the commitment.'

Her heart immediately contracted, and as her eyes closed the words seemed to float in front of her, not quite reaching her, but there anyway waiting to be understood and accepted. 'I'll call when I'm on my way,' she said in a whisper.

After she'd rung off she sat with the phone in her lap, gazing out at the City, and wondering how on earth she was going to resolve this when she was in no doubt that she still loved Elliot, but it wasn't changing the fact that she still wanted to be with Nick.

Sir Christopher Malton was with Michael Dalby at intelligence headquarters on the South Bank of the Thames. Daniel Allbringer and Ronald Platt were in Platt's office in Washington, where their images were being beamed to the video screen at one end of the darkened conference room in London. All four men were silent as they listened to the recording of Malton's interview with Laurie Forbes.

When it ended, Malton said, 'Copies have already been made and are on their way to Washington.'

Allbringer glanced at Platt. 'I think it's clear that at least part of the purpose here was to let us know the way Chambers has interpreted the information,' he said.

Platt nodded. 'He's so damned close to the truth that this will have to go right to the top,' he stated.

'Of course,' Dalby responded, 'which is why it's a pity Mrs Gough can't take part in this call.'

'She's on the Hill briefing the Senate Intelligence Committee,' Platt told him, 'but we all know she's an advocate of extreme measures, and I don't think there's much doubt this tape is going to get her clock ticking. She wants Chambers here, in the States, in person. Failing that, she wants him silenced.'

'Can I respectfully remind you,' Dalby said, 'that it was her sanctioning of the raid on Chambers's apartment and attempt to arrest him that rapidly exacerbated the situation to a point where damage control is already proving extremely difficult. So before we start overreacting again, please let's stay mindful of the fact that Laurie Forbes made no mention of how the Pakistan connection is facilitating the ultimate goal.'

'Added to that,' Malton interjected, 'is the fact that Chambers still has no way of authenticating those documents.'

'I'm hearing you, gentlemen,' Allbringer assured them, 'I'm just making the point, but now he's reached these conclusions I'd say the election strategy is shot.'

'Again, let's not be hasty,' Dalby responded.

Platt said, 'I requested a status update from Special Operations Command on P2 penetration in Pakistan. I'm told they're in so deep now even their own mothers wouldn't know them if they came up for air, so I can't see the mission being aborted.'

'No-one wants that,' Dalby assured him.

Allbringer got to his feet, walked out of shot, then back in again. 'Mrs Gough is already eager to start the press campaign against Chambers,' he said. 'We're still persuading her to hold off for the moment . . .'

'You have to,' Dalby told him. 'Now that Elliot Russell – and others – are working with him a procedure of discreditation is not the way to go.'

'So what are you recommending?' Allbringer enquired.

'First, that we send another email to Chambers asking him to report to his nearest US embassy.'

'Which he's going to ignore, like all the others we've sent,' Allbringer said impatiently. 'We need to bang it home to him that he's in danger of seriously compromising national security.'

'If we do that, we give him an official link to his documents,' Dalby pointed out. 'Or at the very least we give them credibility, and as Sir Christopher has already planted the suggestion that they're false, we need to stay with it. So I'm going to recommend that for the time being we merely keep Chambers and Russell under surveillance . . .'

Platt came in forcefully. 'First, we don't actually know where they are right now, and second, it's no longer this government's policy to sit around waiting for the bomb to drop. We need swift and decisive action to thwart all attempts of subversion, which is what this is.'

Though they were all acutely aware that the subversion was being led by an unknown intelligence insider, no-one made reference to it, merely listened to Dalby as he said, 'We are dealing with some very highly respected journalists here, who, between them, wield enough influence to make it absolutely vital that we get this right. If we don't the blowback's going to be impossible to contain. So, I'm going to put my recommendations in an email for the entire committee to consider, and suggest we speak again tomorrow.'

'Before we end this,' Allbringer said, 'we need

more background on this Russell character. How controllable is he, because we're not receiving a pleasing picture at this end.'

'We've had some dealings with him in the past, which I'll add to my email,' Dalby told him. 'When he resurfaces, or when we locate him, someone will pay him a visit. I'm also issuing instructions for surveillance to be put on his apartment, his phones and computer, and on the home of Katie Kiernan where Michelle Rowe is still in residence.'

Chapter Fifteen

Michelle was reading Laurie's email as Molly came in the door and plonked her bag on the kitchen table.

'You're home early,' Michelle commented, without looking up.

Molly didn't respond, merely glanced awkwardly around the kitchen, then looked at Michelle again. 'Where's Mum?' she demanded.

'She was in the bath, but she might be out by now,' Michelle answered, still engrossed in the email.

'So. Did you tell her?' Molly challenged.

Michelle frowned and after reaching the end of a sentence, finally looked up. 'You mean about the purse? No. You put it back, didn't you?'

'Yeah. Well?'

'*Well*, you put it back, so I didn't see any point in upsetting her.'

Molly turned away, and went to jerk open the fridge door.

Watching, as she filled a glass with juice, Michelle said, 'What did you want the money for?'

'That is none of your business.'

'If you'd come to me, I'd have given you what you need.'

Molly shrugged and started to drink.

Michelle sighed. 'Look, I'm not going to lecture you on the evils of stealing,' she said, 'because I know you're perfectly aware of them. I'd just like you to promise that if you need anything in future, then rather than raiding your mother's purse you'll come to me.'

Molly didn't answer.

'Do I have the promise?' Michelle prompted, sensing that behind the mask Molly was torn between asking for money now, and resisting the idea that Michelle would be around in the future.

'Whatever,' Molly responded, and picking up her bag she made to push past.

'Before you go,' Michelle said, 'I've had some emails and photographs from the children I was working with in the camp. I was wondering if you'd like to see them.'

Molly turned round, clearly surprised by the suggestion, and even seeming to wonder if Michelle had lost her marbles, because why would she be interested in some kids she'd never even met?

'I told them about you before I left,' Michelle said, 'and they're saying hello.'

Molly glanced down at the computer.

'Some of them are about your age,' Michelle went on. 'I was thinking, maybe you'd like to correspond with one or two, tell them about your life here in England, and find out a bit more about them.'

331

'What would I want to do that for?' Molly retorted. 'We don't even speak the same language.'

'There are translators in the camp.'

Molly shot another quick look at the open laptop, then giving another of her 'whatever' shrugs, said, 'I don't have time. I've got to revise for a maths test,' and hitching her bag higher on her shoulder she stomped off up the stairs.

Michelle waited for the sound of the bedroom door slamming shut, followed by the expected thump of music, then went back to the email, vaguely heartened by the flicker of interest Molly hadn't quite managed to disguise. It would be an irony indeed, she was thinking as she continued to read, if the Afghan children turned out to be a bridge to her niece. More likely though, it would be Robbie's indomitable good nature that would finally break down his cousin's barriers and help to seal a relationship. However, that wasn't going to happen for a while, because Robbie was still in school, and no decisions had yet been made on when he could come – or how long he might stay. Certainly if Michelle had her way it would happen tomorrow, but for the time being she had to content herself with three or four phone calls a week, and the chirpy little emails he regularly sent.

Even before she reached the end of Laurie's transcript of the meeting with Malton, her gaze was wandering to the phone. All she had to do was pick it up and dial Tom's number to hear his voice, but she wouldn't, because Laurie's message had included a caution from Elliot that they should keep calls to a minimum now, in number and duration. Though she fully understood Tom's reasons for staying out of sight so that he could deal with Washington in his time rather than theirs, it did nothing to stop her longing to be with him, or to overcome an almost overwhelming need to lean on him the way she had in the past. Today, for some reason, she was finding it much harder to cope with the growing dread of losing Katie than she normally did, and it would be so wonderful to have him to talk to. However, her problems were not his priority right now, and besides, it was no more than a passing depression that she was already feeling ashamed of, because if Katie could find the strength to deal with it day in, day out, with no respite, then so could she.

Sighing, she tore her eyes from the phone, and deciding to go and check on Katie, she printed out the email to take with her, and went upstairs to knock on her sister's bedroom door. 'Can I come in?' she asked, pushing it open.

'Yes. Yes of course,' Katie answered.

'Laurie's email has come through,' Michelle told her. 'It's an interesting read. Apparently Tom . . . Oh, my goodness, what is it?' she gasped, catching Katie's reflection in the mirror.

'Ssh, shh, it's nothing,' Katie assured her, dabbing her eyes, and attempting to blow her nose.

Michelle quickly closed the door and went to sit next to her on the double stool in front of the mirror. 'What's happened?' she asked, putting an arm around her. 'Why are you crying?'

'I'm not . . . I'm just . . .' She put her head back as though to stop any more tears from rising. 'It just came over me, out of the blue,' she said. 'Well, actually, out of a spot,' she confessed, and pointed to an angry red swelling between her eyebrows. 'I thought it was another tumour,' she added, in a voice that was strangled by laughter and tears.

'Oh you,' Michelle cried, hugging her. 'You had me really worried for a moment there. It's all the sugar you've been eating. We've got to get you on a proper diet.'

'No, please don't. You name it, I've sunk myself in the misery of it, and in the end they proved no more effective than all the spiritual guff I sit here omming with day after day. All right, meditation helps keep me calm and lifts my spirits a bit, but it just doesn't have the same kick as a doughnut.'

Michelle laughed. 'Then doughnuts you shall have,' she declared. 'And spots.'

Katie was frowning into the mirror. 'Ugh! Look at it,' she said crossly. 'It's so big.'

'Volcanic,' Michelle agreed.

Katie's eyes remained fierce, then quite suddenly she put her hands over her face and started to sob. 'I'm sorry,' she gasped. 'I'm so sorry. You shouldn't be seeing me like this . . .'

'Oh, for heaven's sake,' Michelle cried, pulling her into an embrace. 'If you can't let go with me, then who can you . . .?'

'I just feel so pathetic,' Katie gasped. 'I keep trying to be strong, to tell myself I can get through this, but that's the whole point, I'm not going to, am I? And I'm so afraid, Michelle. I'm just so afraid.'

'Oh my darling, my darling,' Michelle soothed, struggling to hold back her own tears.

'It's eating me up, so that I can't think about anything else,' Katie wept. 'I keep telling myself I can fight it, sometimes I even believe I can, but then little spots start boiling up on my forehead, or in private places, and I end up feeling so disgustingly sorry for myself . . .' She struggled to catch her breath. 'I don't want to leave you, Michelle. I love you so much, and I've been so happy since you've been here. I've started living again and . . . Oh heaven help me, make me stop before I totally fall apart.'

'You won't,' Michelle told her firmly through her own tears. 'I won't let you.'

'I've got so much to be grateful for,' Katie choked, attempting to seize the positive route. 'Like I said, having you here, being a part of something . . . It's making me feel so alive. And Laurie . . . She's made such a difference. I'm not sure why, but . . .' She gave an anguished sort of laugh. 'Thank God she can't see me now, eh? This definitely isn't the face I want to show to the world. Oh my God, look at it,' she groaned, turning to the mirror.

Michelle looked at it, and in spite of the blotches and swollen eyes, she couldn't have loved it more. 'The spot doesn't help,' she said gravely.

Katie spluttered with laughter, and reached for more tissues. 'Actually, this is probably the very scene Laurie would like to catch on camera,' she said, blowing her nose. 'And it's the very scene that gives me serious reservations about going ahead with it all. It's not what Molly's going to want to see. It'll be hard enough for her when I've gone, without having to watch how hard it was for me.'

'Then tell Laurie that,' Michelle responded. 'She'll understand.'

Katie sighed and nodded. 'I've promised to give it a go with the camera,' she said, 'so I won't let her down. At least, not before I've given it a chance.' She looked at Michelle's reflection. 'Are you starting to read this the way I am?' she said. 'That I'm using Laurie's interest to keep her coming here because it's a wonderful distraction, and a bit of a boost to my flagging ego? The promise of more limelight is helping me to go on showing off how brave, or clever, or witty I am, even though it's all an illusion.'

Michelle reached for the brush and started to tidy Katie's wispy tufts of hair. 'It's not an illusion,' she informed her gently. 'You're all that and more.'

Katie's eyes closed as she enjoyed the sensation of the brush on her scalp, and neither of them spoke again until the phone started to ring.

'I'll get it,' Katie said. 'I expect it's to tell me my prescription's ready.'

As she walked over to the bed Michelle put the hairbrush down again, and fought the urge just to cry and cry as she dropped the balled-up tissues in the wastebasket.

'Hello?' Katie said into the receiver.

'Katie?' a voice at the other end asked.

'Yes? Oh, Tom, is that you?'

Immediately Michelle's heart reacted. *Please let it be him, please, please.*

'It's me,' Tom confirmed. 'How are you?'

'Fine. Great,' Katie assured him. 'Wishing you were here. We both are.'

There was a smile in his voice as he said, 'You did a great job with your notes. I owe you.'

'It was mostly Michelle. I wrote them up, but she did all the work.'

'Have you read Laurie's email?'

'Not yet, but it's here. I'll read it now, and pass you over to Michelle.'

Taking the receiver Michelle spoke softly as she said, 'Is this wise?'

'A few seconds and I'll be gone,' he told her. 'I just wanted to hear you.'

The echo of her own longing created a surge of warmth inside her. 'How are you?' she asked.

'OK. How about you?'

'Worried about you.'

'Don't be. I'm fine.'

Aware of how little time they had, she said, 'Has anything happened since Laurie saw Malton this morning?'

'A couple of things,' he answered. 'Max has received confirmation of Josh Shine's arrest, which apparently only happened two days ago. We're not sure where he was before that, Max is still working on it, and the charges aren't clear at the moment either.'

'Doesn't he have a lawyer?'

'Yep, who's with Josh even as we speak, so Max hasn't had a chance to talk to him yet. It should happen in the next couple of hours.'

'And the second development?' she prompted.

'Nick van Zant's found someone who can get us a copy of the 1997 version of the 21 Project, so with any luck we should be cooking with gas any time now.'

'That's excellent news,' she said, easily able to imagine his pleasure, for she'd often been with him at the time of a breakthrough. 'I want to ask when we're likely to see you,' she said, 'but I guess you don't know.'

His voice became lower and more intimate as he said, 'Believe me, you can't want it more than I do.' Then he added, 'I had to be crazy to think I could let you go.'

Emotion tightened her throat as the very words she longed to hear stole into her heart, seeming to renew her strength and build her courage in a way only he could. 'I was never going anywhere,' she whispered.

'I guess I know that now,' he said.

Katie was watching her as she put the phone down, and seeing how emotional she was she drew her into her arms. 'He'll be all right,' she assured her.

'Yes, of course,' Michelle agreed, wishing she knew why she was finding it so hard to believe. 'I don't know why I'm reacting like this, I'll have myself together in a minute.'

Katie smiled and hugged her tighter, then they both winced as a voice from next door suddenly yelled, 'Mum! *Mum!*'

Seconds later the door bounced open to admit a smouldering Molly. 'Mum, I've got *three* spots,' she declared in outrage.

'Oh now, that's just showing off,' Katie told her.

Michelle laughed and Molly glared at her. 'I'm serious,' she cried. 'You've got to get rid of them.'

Katie looked at Michelle – and her flawless skin. 'Are you starting to feel left out?' she asked.

'*Mum!*' Molly raged.

'All right. All right,' Katie said hurriedly. 'Let's get you into the bathroom before you start erupting.'

'You are *sooo* not funny,' Molly told her.

'Then why are you laughing?'

'I am not,' Molly responded, as they marched out on to the landing.

'Yes you are. Now, hold your face up to the light and let me see. Oh my God, no wonder you're panicking.'

'Oh, don't say that!'

Katie frowned and peered a little closer. 'Where exactly are they?' she asked.

'Here, on my chin.'

Leaving them to continue their search, Michelle walked on along the landing to her room and closed the door. Though she wanted to be a part of the light-hearted moments, Molly still wasn't ready yet, and right now, feeling as troubled as she did, she wasn't able to think of a way to help things along.

Tom and Elliot were on the main piazza in Pietrasanta drinking coffee outside one of the cafés, while Elliot talked to Nick van Zant on the phone.

'It turns out there have been two revisions of the 21 Project,' Nick was telling him. 'One in 2000 and the other in 2002.'

'What about the original '97 version?' Elliot asked.

'I've got the first twenty pages. They're not giving us much so far, but my contact's not happy about sending the entire document all in one go.'

'OK. Can you email us what you have?'

'Sure.'

'Tell him to copy it to Michelle and Katie,' Tom reminded him.

Elliot passed the message on and said, 'Laurie tells me you're back in England at the weekend.'

'That's right,' Nick responded. 'You too, I hear?'

Assuming that was van Zant letting him know he'd spoken to Laurie, Elliot resisted the urge to hurl the phone against the nearest wall, and submerging his feelings beneath a neutral tone he said, 'That's right. I need to start talking to a few people myself, find out what they know about this P2 project.'

'Everyone I've spoken to is convinced it's a spin-off from the 21 Project,' Nick told him. 'No-one can confirm it's ever made it off the page though.'

'I don't think we're in much doubt of it now,' Elliot retorted.

'No, of course not. Let me know if I can be of any help.'

'Thanks. I will.' He wanted to add, *just stay the hell away from Laurie,* but what he actually said was, 'How's Max doing with Josh Shine's lawyer?'

'He's over at his office now, so no more news on that front yet. Something that did come up before he left though, was an email from an anonymous dot-gov source which I'll forward on to you.'

'Tell me what it says.'

Nick read it out. ' "Look for missing names and facilitating factor." '

Elliot frowned, and repeated it to Tom. 'What does it mean?' he said to Nick.

'We haven't figured it out yet. Does Tom have any suggestions?'

Tom shook his head. 'I'll need to see it,' he said, 'but it sounds like another guiding hand from our secret source. Does Max have any more on this confidential committee?'

'It's calling itself a Special Operations Executive,' Nick answered when Elliot asked, 'and Deborah Gough's chairing it. Apparently the FBI's counter-terrorism chief is also on it, along with the other names Max gave you.'

'And their brief?'

'Codeword/top secret,' Nick replied, quoting the CIA's highest classification level.

'OK, call if there's any more news,' Elliot said, and clicked off the line.

Trying not to run with how pissed off he was that van Zant had been the one to connect with the '97 version, even though he'd known he'd be the most likely to, he turned to Tom as Tom said, 'If it weren't for the Sizewell issue, I'd be inclined to back off this now, because the situation in Pakistan has to be addressed. But if they are setting it up like this, letting an entire nation believe they came within a cat's whisker of nuclear disaster as a means of getting re-elected, then going on to an end game that fits in with their world-dominance Project just fine and dandy . . .' He shook his head in disgust. 'You know what makes me really mad?' he said. 'The case for sending the military into Pakistan is a slam dunk in comparison to going into Iraq. The Pakistanis have got nuclear weapons for God's sake, and no-one's denying it – and nowhere else on earth are they more likely to fall into the hands of terrorists.'

'If you're a neo-conservative with global ambitions, then manipulating the situation this way will be seen merely as a matter of expediency,' Elliot stated. 'Or killing two birds with one stone.'

Tom slanted him a look. 'We've got to get proof

this is happening,' he said. 'We need to be able to lay it out that the P2OG has morphed from paper into reality, and this is the kind of operation they're being briefed to carry out.'

'I'm not going to argue with that,' Elliot responded, 'but what's bothering me is why our anonymous source isn't providing the proof. Can it be that difficult?'

Tom picked up his coffee and drank. 'It's bothering me too,' he confessed, 'because the answer could be that it doesn't exist in a form that's usable. Or that it'll be an obvious trace back to him if he does provide it.'

Having come to much the same conclusions Elliot said, 'OK, so back to Christopher Malton. His interview with Laurie will have permeated through to the right channels by now, so the question is, how are they going to respond?'

'Tell me what you're thinking,' Tom said.

'I'm thinking that apart from issuing you with another invitation to an embassy near you, and reminding me I'm supposed to be writing my memoirs, they're either going to try and brand you some kind of terrorist sympathizer with what they found in your apartment, or they'll start a serious manhunt to track you down and bring you in.'

Tom was nodding thoughtfully. 'There are a lot of charges they could cook up against me right now, yet they haven't run with any of them. Why?'

'We could be about to enter some kind of stand-off,' Elliot suggested. 'They won't go for you, if you don't go for them.'

Tom was still pensive. 'It's a pity,' he said, 'that they haven't played the "compromising national security" card yet. I thought they would have by now.'

'Not if it can be used in evidence against them,' Elliot pointed out, 'and it could, if it's in print, because it'll suggest an eagerness to get those documents back that would seem overstated for something that's supposed to be false.' As he finished he was using his XDA to access his email. Frowning as he saw the messages from Nick, he said, 'There are two dot-gov messages here. Another must have come through since we spoke to him.' He opened the first to find it was the one they already knew about. Then after opening the second his eyes started to widen with interest.

'Read this,' he said, handing the organizer over to Tom.

' "Deduction of election strategy correct." ' Tom turned back to Elliot. 'Laurie's reference to that was pretty subtle,' he said, 'but someone's picked it up right away – and that someone hasn't wasted any time letting us know we're on the right trail.'

'Coming this soon after the meeting with Malton,' Elliot said, 'it has to be someone on that executive, or pretty damned close to it.'

Tom was nodding agreement. 'So what do we do now?' he said, starting to assess the significance of the message.

'Right now, apart from analysing the pages being fed through to Nick, there's nothing we can do,' Elliot answered. 'The next move has to be theirs, though it might be a good idea to start working on our own strategy in the event they do manage to pick you up before we're ready.'

Tom seemed only to be half-listening as he

focused on something across the piazza. Then turning back to Elliot, he said, 'Talk to me about your pilot friend, Chris Gallagher. Just how trustworthy is he?'

'Daughters of Lilith, are you ready to communicate with our Mother?' Cecily asked in a low, preacher-ish tone. Her richly charcoaled eyelids were respectfully lowered, while her sparkle-glossed lips gleamed in the candlelight that cast tall, spooky shadows around Allison's bedroom.

'We are ready,' Allison, Molly and Donna responded.

As they joined hands to form a circle around the ouija board spread out on the floor, Molly felt Allison's pearl bracelet drop against her own wrist. She'd bought it with the ten quid she'd stolen from her mum's purse, which she was definitely going to pay back once she'd managed to save up enough.

Cecily gazed down at the order of ceremony that she'd carefully devised by pulling information from the Net and writing some of it herself. Incantations were burbling from the CD that she and Donna had recorded the previous night, while outside a rumble of thunder shuddered in the heavens, making Molly's skin go all goosey.

After checking that the others were studying their copies of the ceremony, Cecily began. 'Allison, Daughter of Lilith, please bring fragrance to our Mother,' she instructed.

Letting go of Molly's and Donna's hands, Allison quietly opened a box of matches and lit the tiny wands of incense that were arranged like a bouquet at one end of the board. When she'd finished, she retook the other's hands and solemnly bowed her head.

'Donna, Daughter of Lilith, please bring beauty to our Mother,' Cecily gently commanded.

Getting silently to her feet, Donna scooped an armful of flowers from the bed, and scattered them randomly around the group, before kneeling and retaking Cecily's and Allison's hands.

'Molly, Daughter of Lilith, prepare yourself to receive the advice of our most Wondrous Mother,' Cecily said.

Obediently Molly turned around and picked up the flowing red wig that Cecily had brought for her. After settling it over her own hair, she smoothed it back from her face, and bowed her head. Cecily had said she should wear it because she was to play a bigger part in the ceremony tonight than the others, and the goddess wig, according to Cecily, was the highest form of respect.

Cecily began to chant from her notes. 'Oh Most Divine Mother, Lilith, the misunderstood and maligned creator of the feminine, the limitless source of our power, the one true goddess, we gather to worship you on the night of the full moon so that we can feel the true might of your eternal spirit.' She squeezed Molly's and Donna's hands to give them the signal to respond.

'Oh Most Divine Mother we are gathered and await your guidance and blessings,' they all said together.

'We are now at Stage Five of our Six-Step journey to womanhood,' Cecily continued. 'Each of us has faithfully complied with the challenges we have set for each other, which have included acts of bravery, female domination, and a rejection of our earthly mothers, for you are the only true Mother. It is now necessary to cleanse ourselves before going any further by confessing our mortal weaknesses and transgressions, whereupon we ask you to grant us absolution, and to show us the way forward.' She lifted her head, and with eyes closed, said, 'Allison, Daughter of Lilith, please begin.'

Allison took a breath, felt her mouth tremble slightly with the urge to laugh, then reading from the notes, she said, 'Oh Divine Mother, I am guilty of still being a virgin, so I am not yet empowered to harness the male ego. I understand that it is my duty to tame him and return his lost soul to his Divine Mother Lilith.'

'Please tell our Divine Mother what you intend to do about this failure,' Cecily prompted.

'On the night of the twenty-eighth I will rectify the failure using your own methods of seduction, oh Mother,' Allison responded, keeping faithfully to the script. 'My subject is chosen. His name is Miles Greengross.'

'Divine Mother,' Cecily said, 'please indicate your approval of Allison's chosen subject.'

In accordance with the instructions laid out, they waited for Cecily to clear the incense and flowers from the board, then leaned forward to place a finger on the upturned glass at the centre of it. Almost instantly it started to glide towards the word yes.

'Thank you, Divine Mother,' Cecily said, returning the glass to the centre. 'Thank you, Allison.'

Allison relinked her hands with Molly's and Donna's and listened as Donna was invited to

346

make the next confession. Her chosen subject was Martin Quayle, and Lilith readily gave her approval.

As they all rejoined hands Cecily let her head fall back, as though an ecstatic trance had befallen her, then she began to speak softly, making her own confession. 'Oh Most Beautiful and Compassionate Mother Lilith,' she said, 'my own virginity still afflicts me too, but I seek to rectify the failure on the same day as the others. My subject is Toby Fortescue-Bond. Please indicate your approval or not, as the case may be.'

Once again the glass moved to yes, and as they all sank back on to their heels the rain outside began hammering against the window, while the wind whistled like a whip.

Molly waited, knowing it was her turn next. She was starting to feel a bit anxious now, for there were no more words on the page, and it was turning kind of spooky in here, with all the candles and incense and weirdy chants from the CD. She told herself she wasn't really bothered by the glass moving around the board, because she knew Cecily was pushing it – she had to be, because no way was it moving on its own – but that wind outside was like, seriously scary and for all they knew it could be the devil trying to get in. The trouble was, she had to get approval for Brad, and there was no other way, or not according to Cecily.

'Dear and Bountiful Mother,' Cecily began, her voice rising like a wave in the storm as she continued with a script that only she had a copy of now, 'we humbly present the last of your daughters. I know, because you have spoken privately to me, that you have reservations about Molly, but I ask you to be patient with her, and accept our undertaking to keep her in the Way. Yes, she has lied, yes, she lacks faith, and yes, she has a false heart . . .'

Molly was horrified. Why was Cecily saying those things? How could she know that Molly hadn't done all she was supposed to? She hadn't been there. She didn't know anything, so she was just being mean, trying to frighten Molly, because she'd never really liked her, and had always wanted to get rid of her. Fear began jabbing at Molly like sticks. This could be leading up to a ban from the party . . .

'. . . but we can save her, Dear Mother,' Cecily was saying. 'And she wants to be saved, which is why she has changed her hair to match yours. She understands the power of the Feminine, and that you alone are that power. Do you see her, Great Lilith? She awaits your blessing, and she also asks for your help. Please tell us, Mother, if you are willing to forgive her faults and offer that help.'

Molly was breathless, as following Cecily's lead everyone leaned in to the glass.

'Not you, Molly,' Cecily told her.

Anxiously Molly took her hand away, and watched with big, worried eyes, as the glass started to move. To her horror, it set off in the direction of no, but then it seemed to teeter, and almost before she knew it, it had doubled back towards the yes.

'Thank you, Lilith,' Cecily said. 'We value your answers, and shall abide by them. Now, please tell us if you approve Molly's chosen one. His name is Bradley Jenkins, and though her passion has made her vulnerable to his male aura, so that she is handing him all her power, I promise we can help her to bring him to you. So will you approve him, Divine Mother?'

Molly was almost dizzied by the drumming in her ears, for she wasn't sure what Cecily meant about Brad's male aura, or handing him her power, but at least this time she was allowed to touch the glass. When it moved to yes she almost collapsed with relief.

'Now we come to Molly's request for help,' Cecily said. 'There is a person in her life, Divine Mother, a relative, who is an evil presence, and Molly seeks your assistance in obliterating her.'

Molly's heart gave an uneasy thud. Obliterating was a really strong word, and all she wanted was for Michelle to go back to where she came from, not to die or anything. She'd told Cecily, no poisons, or murder or anything, but the trouble with Cecily was she was always so extreme, and if Molly didn't do as she said she'd probably get her revenge by messing everything up with Brad.

'The Divine Lilith is ready to speak,' Cecily informed them.

Once again they put their fingers on the glass. For several seconds nothing happened, until finally it began inching slowly across the board towards the letter A.

Molly almost snatched her hand away as the word assassinate shot to the front of her mind. She glanced at Cecily but her eyes were firmly closed as she announced the letter A.

The glass edged to the right and came to a stop in front of the letter B.

Abstract. Absent. Abseil. What did it mean? What was it spelling?

'B,' Cecily pronounced.

Molly was leaping from Aberdeen to abstain, when once again the glass started to move. This time it hesitated in front of the W, then proceeded on to the U.

Molly was perplexed. *Abu . . . Dhabi. Abundance.* She looked up, caught Allison's eye, then returned her gaze to the glass as it started off again, this time travelling the short distance to S.

Abus. A thud of fear banged in Molly's chest. Was it trying to say 'A bus' as in push Michelle under one? Well, just no way was she going to do that, not even if it meant she couldn't go to the party. She glanced at Allison and saw that she was looking baffled too, then feeling the glass setting off again, she watched as it crossed the full width of the board and stopped at E.

Abuse. She blinked. What did that mean, exactly? Abuse what? She looked at Cecily as she spoke the letter aloud, then waited to see if the glass would move again.

Seconds ticked by and nothing happened. In the end, Cecily said, 'Divine Mother, do you wish to continue?'

The glass wobbled, stilled, then skated all the way back towards the letter A.

Was it going to spell the same word again? No, because the next stop was at C, and immediately Molly started to get worked up again in case it was 'accident', and when the glass backed off an inch, then returned to the C, she was convinced. However, to her relief, the next

350

letter turned out to be U. Then came S, then finally E.

Abuse. Accuse. Molly looked at Cecily.

Cecily closed her eyes, drew in a deep breath, then let herself go limp. 'The Divine Mother has spoken,' she finally told them, 'and now she has left us.'

They all sat back on their heels, glancing at each other, then turning to Cecily to await further instructions.

'The Mother is gone,' Cecily confirmed, and began packing up the board.

'But what does it mean, abuse, accuse?' Allison demanded.

'It means,' Cecily answered, keeping her eyes on what she was doing, 'that to be rid of your aunt, Molly, you should accuse her of abuse.'

Molly's insides turned to liquid. 'But I can't do that,' she protested. 'It's not true.'

Cecily's patience immediately thinned. 'It doesn't have to be true to be effective,' she stated haughtily. 'It's the one sure way of making her leave your house, because no-one will let her stay if you say she's abused you.'

Molly swallowed hard and looked at Allison.

Allison shrugged.

Becoming suddenly conscious of the wig, Molly took it off and bundled it in her lap. She didn't want to tell that kind of lie, about anyone, because it was horrible, and even to think it made her feel all weird and sick inside. She wanted to ask what would happen if she didn't do it, but since she could guess the answer she decided it might be better to say nothing.

351

'That was awesome,' Donna declared, as she got up to change the music. 'It was one of the best seances we've had, don't you think?'

'It was wicked,' Allison agreed. 'Especially when we had to give the boys' names. Imagine, if they could have heard us. They would be like, so freaked out.'

Donna and Cecily were laughing, so Molly laughed too, though she was still all shaken up about the abuse thing, and miffed over what Cecily had said about her and Brad, though at least she'd got approval, so she was more prepared to forget about that.

'So, now we can smoke the joint,' Cecily stated, having decided earlier that they should wait until the ceremony was over or they'd go all giggly and silly.

Allison immediately grabbed the matches and went to retrieve the joint from the depths of her make-up bag, while everyone else checked their mobiles for messages.

Pleased to find one from Brad, Molly was about to start texting back when Allison passed her the joint.

Nervous, but eager to get in some practice before the party, she put the skinny end to her lips and sucked.

'Harder,' Allison insisted.

Molly pulled again, held the smoke in her mouth, then inhaled, swallowed and choked all at the same time.

'It's OK,' Allison assured her. 'Everyone does that the first time. Let Donna and Cecily have a go, then you can try again.'

With her throat and nose on fire, Molly watched the others to see how it was done, then taking the cigarette back tried again. Not so bad that time, just a little bit of coughing, and her head was already starting to feel all swimmy. She'd better send a text back to Brad before she got really stoned – and one to her mum to say goodnight, because she was staying over at Allison's tonight so Laurie Forbes could use her bed. That was just like so brilliant, because now her mum had let her stay here once, it should make it easy for her to stay on the night of the party. She'd say it was a sleepover then too, because no way in the world would her mum let her stay out for an all-night party, especially not at Allison's.

Chapter Sixteen

The storm had hardly let up all night, though it was starting to show some signs of exhaustion now as Katie and Michelle prepared breakfast, while Laurie spoke to Max on the phone.

'No, I haven't heard anything from Elliot yet today,' she was telling him, glancing at the clock and calculating that it was three a.m. in Washington. 'Is there something I can help with?'

'I'm not sure what any of us can to do about this,' Max responded, sounding unusually harried, 'but I've just got off the phone with Josh Shine's lawyer – someone's tipped him off that Shine's going to be charged with conspiracy to commit terrorism.'

Laurie felt a thud of unease and kept her back to Katie and Michelle.

'It's good news that someone on the inside's keeping us informed,' Max continued, 'but the bad news has got to be what this could mean for Tom, which is why I'm trying to get hold of him. We have to let him know that the stakes have been raised.'

'Of course,' Laurie murmured, her mind firing off in all kinds of directions. 'I'll keep trying their numbers, though Elliot warned me last night that his phone was going to be off for most of the day. I'm due to see him tonight though, he should be back in London by then.'

'OK. Anything new your end?'

'Not really. We spent part of last night going over the pages Nick sent and reviewing the section on Rebuilding America's Defences. To quote Katie, "it reads like a sweetheart note to the US armed forces", and with a $480 billion defence budget, I'd say that's putting it mildly.'

'And we all know who's lapping up the profits,' he commented. 'Look no further than the current administration and their campaign financiers.'

'And you don't care who hears it,' Laurie said wryly.

'You bet your ass I don't,' he responded.

She laughed, and mouthed a thanks to Katie as she passed her a coffee. 'Anyway, apart from the dizzying excitement of going over and over your government's intention to achieve global dominance,' she said, 'we're still trawling through the thousands of articles that have been written about the 21 Project, some of which are mightily entertaining, believe it or not, but I can't honestly say we're moving forward now. We need more of the original.'

'Nick's got most of it with him,' Max told her. 'He should be back there today. Now, I'm going to try to get some sleep before I meet with Josh's lawyer at noon. Call me if there's any news from Elliot or Tom. Or have them call me.'

As she rang off Katie passed with a plate of warm croissants. 'So what's the scoop?' Katie said, setting the plate on the table. 'It's got to be big for him to have called at this hour.'

Glancing anxiously at Michelle, Laurie speed-dialled Elliot's number and said, 'Apparently the charge against Josh Shine is conspiracy to commit terrorism.'

Michelle instantly paled. 'But that's preposterous!' she declared.

Laurie looked at Katie, as she said, 'What's it going to mean for Tom?'

'Too early to say,' Laurie answered, failing to make a connection.

Michelle was already using Katie's mobile to try Tom. 'He's not answering,' she said, almost angrily.

Seeing how upset she was, Laurie quickly tried the other numbers she had, but still no luck. 'They'll be in touch at some point,' she said gently. 'It's still quite early in the morning.'

Michelle nodded, and dashed a hand through her hair. 'Sorry, I'm overreacting,' she said. 'I didn't sleep too well.'

Though Katie was watching her closely, she made no comment as she pulled out a chair and sat down. A few minutes later she and Laurie were eating breakfast and discussing the results of their most recent research, while Michelle stood staring out of the window.

Though she was listening to Katie, Laurie couldn't help thinking that it wasn't only this morning that Michelle hadn't seemed her normal lively self. She'd been distracted last night, and slow to rise to the usual bantering with Katie, which had made Laurie wonder if something had happened between them that Katie was doing a better job of hiding. Or maybe it was the emotional wear and tear of going through this with her sister that was finally getting to Michelle, and now, with this new concern about Tom . . .

'Michelle, come and sit down,' Katie said softly.

Turning round, Michelle looked for a moment as though she'd forgotten they were there, then forcing a smile, she came over to the table. 'I hope you haven't scoffed the last of the marmalade, Katie,' she said, attempting a light-heartedness she was clearly far from feeling.

'I was too afraid to,' Katie responded, passing her the jar.

Michelle looked up, Katie winked, and as Michelle smiled, Laurie noticed her swallowing hard. She was obviously right on the edge, and Laurie was just wondering if she should tactfully suggest that she and Katie postpone their plans for the morning, when Michelle said, 'I was thinking I'd pop into Chippenham, or Bath, and leave you two to it this morning. I need to buy a car . . .'

'But you can have mine,' Katie protested.

'You need it,' Michelle responded, starting to clear the table.

'For now, yes, but . . .'

Knowing she wasn't in the mood to hear Katie's quips about her impending demise Michelle cut her short, saying, 'I'm just wasting money, keeping a rental outside, and I expect Laurie will welcome the opportunity to have you all to herself for once.'

Katie eyed Laurie sceptically.

'I can't think of anything I'd like more,' Laurie told her.

Chuckling, Katie said, 'If my life were only half as interesting as yours, I might believe you.'

Reminded of the evening she had planned with Elliot later, Laurie's insides twisted with nerves. 'Actually, my life is a mess,' she said lightly, 'but I'm not going to let you do a typical Katie and start steering the subject round to me, it's you I'm here to talk about.'

'Oh dear, how dreary,' Katie responded, and looked up as someone ran past the window. 'Was that Judy?' she said, turning to the door as it burst open.

'Bloody rain,' Judy grumbled, stamping her feet on the wire mat. 'And what a storm last night. Thought the roof was a goner at one point . . . Oh my goodness,' she cried, spotting Laurie, 'I forgot you were here, but don't worry, I'm not stopping. This is just madam's personal delivery service,' and she fished a small white bag out of her pocket and plonked it on the table.

'Have you met my supplier?' Katie asked Laurie.

Laughing, Laurie nodded. 'Hi Judy,' she said. 'Nice to see you again.'

'Stay and have some coffee,' Michelle prompted, taking down another mug.

'I wish I could,' Judy grimaced, 'but the boys have got football practice at nine, and I've still got a couple of errands to run before I go back to pick them up. Michelle, you haven't forgotten you're talking to us in the village hall later, have you? We're all really looking forward to it.'

Michelle looked at her blankly, then suddenly remembering said, 'Of course. I'll be there. Six o'clock, isn't it?'

'That's right,' Judy responded cheerily. 'We're expecting quite a crowd.' Then to Katie and Laurie, 'Have a nice shoot, if that's what you call it,' and a moment later she was bobbing past the window again.

Katie's eyes were ironical as she looked at Michelle. 'Nice recovery,' she told her. 'Slow, but I think you pulled it off.'

'I'd totally forgotten,' Michelle confessed. 'And I haven't even prepared anything.'

'So, I guess that's the car search off the agenda,' Katie remarked.

Michelle looked crestfallen.

'Unless,' Katie said, 'you restrict it to Chippenham for a couple of hours, then I'll help you put something together this afternoon on your life in the refugee camps.'

Michelle came to kiss her on the forehead, and tried to stifle the guilt she was feeling, but she had to be alone, if only for a short while, or she'd end up breaking down completely in front of Katie, and Katie just didn't need it.

By the time they were all showered and dressed, and Laurie had tactfully removed her things from Molly's room in case she came back early, it was almost ten o'clock, and at long last the rain had stopped. However, the debris the storm had left in its wake was strewn all over the garden. Michelle half-heartedly picked some of it up as she and Laurie went out to their cars.

'I'll tidy up later,' Michelle said, putting what she

359

had in a pile next to the front door. 'It'll come in handy for firewood when it dries out.'

Laurie went ahead through the gate, then stopping behind her car, she turned back to Michelle saying, 'I know this news about Josh Shine is worrying, but you seemed very low before. Is there anything I can do?'

Michelle sighed, and gazed off towards the overflowing pond where the ducks were squawking in alarm as a dog circled their domain. 'I'm just a bit tired,' she said.

Laurie waited for her eyes to come back to hers. 'None of this can be easy for you,' she said softly. 'I know how much you love her . . .'

Tears immediately welled in Michelle's eyes. 'Please don't say any more, or I'll start to cry,' she warned with a shaky smile.

Laurie put a hand on her arm, then realizing that might have the same effect, she turned to open the boot to take out the camera.

'I've spent the past ten years caring for the sick and dying in the most dreadful conditions,' Michelle said almost harshly.

When she didn't go on, Laurie said, 'But none of them was your sister.'

Michelle swallowed and shook her head. After a while her eyes came back up to Laurie's. 'Actually, it's not just Katie,' she confessed, 'it's Molly. I can't seem to get through to her, and I'm at my wits' end trying to think of a way.'

Wishing she could come up with a better answer, Laurie said, 'These things take time, and you haven't been here that long.'

Michelle nodded, but seemed lost in her own

thoughts until she said, 'Katie has to tell Molly the truth about what's going to happen, or Molly's just going to stay in denial, and go on hating me for being here.' She took a breath and looked off along the lane. 'The worst part of it,' she continued, 'is that by not making Molly face up to reality, Katie's denying herself what she needs most, which is to see Molly and me getting along.'

Almost able to feel the inner turmoil herself, Laurie said, 'Have you spoken to Katie about it?'

'We touch on it from time to time, but I don't want to force anything . . . I mean, would either of us want to be in her position?'

Knowing it was the very last position she'd ever want to be in, Laurie shook her head and said, 'Of course not. But I think you should tell her the way you're feeling.'

Michelle's expression reflected her dismay. 'You're probably right,' she responded, with a sigh, 'but not today. For some reason I don't seem to be coping very well . . . I keep thinking about Tom. I'm missing him so much, and now this news from Max . . .' Catching Katie watching them from the window, she gave her a wave, and said, 'I should go. I've got my phone with me, if you hear anything.'

'Likewise if you do,' Laurie responded, and lifted the camera from the car to take it inside.

The FBI's Acting Legal Attaché Stuart Fellowes was sitting at his desk in the suite of offices allocated to him and his staff at the US Embassy in Grosvenor Square. A cone of lamplight lit the keyboard in front of him, though for the moment his fingers were still as he read the message coming through on the screen, from the Counterterrorism Division in Washington DC.

Subject sighted in Italy. Be ready
to move re memo dated October 22nd.
Location to follow.

Fellowes waited in case there was more, then in accordance with the instructions laid down for all communication from this source for this case, he erased the message and eased his thickset frame out of the chair. If everything went according to plan, this particular assignment was going to afford him a great deal of personal satisfaction. Nailing the left-wing bastards who spouted their anti-government rhetoric in the papers every day, like they didn't seem to have a problem with what the fucking Arabs had done to one of the world's greatest cities and nearly three thousand of its people, and who seemed to get some kind of kick out of slamming their own president who actually had the balls to stand up and fight for freedom, unlike most of the rest of the chicken-shit world, had long been a dream.

'Nancy,' he said to his assistant through the intercom. 'Did you see the message?'

'Yes sir,' she answered. 'It's erased.'

'Good girl. Now get me Jack Wilding on the line, from the anti-terrorist branch. The flag should have gone up for him at the same time as us, so we need to find out how he's planning to play this.'

A few minutes later Jack Wilding's voice came

down the line saying, 'Russell's just turned up, back at his apartment.'

'Any sign of Chambers?'

'No. Someone's going round there to talk to Russell. We've been in touch with the Italians. I'll get back to you as soon as the location's confirmed.'

In her office in the next room to Fellowes, Nancy Goodman put down her own receiver and turned back to her computer to start typing a message.

Katie was watching Michelle drive away up the lane, as Laurie carried the camera in through the door. 'Is she all right?' she asked, turning to give Laurie a hand.

'She's worried about Tom,' Laurie replied, handing over the tripod.

'And probably getting sick to death of being stuck here with me,' Katie added, leading the way into the sitting room. 'I don't blame her. I'm sick to death of being stuck here with me, and this gloomy weather doesn't help. Talk about a fast track into autumn. There's hardly a leaf left on the trees, did you see? Though the forecast says it's supposed to brighten up a bit later.'

'Where are you going to be the most comfortable?' Laurie asked, looking around the cosy sitting room, with its large, downy sofa beneath the leaded window, non-matching armchairs either side of the hearth, and threadbare Persian rug, on which Trotty was currently having a snooze.

'I think we should get the fireplace in, don't you?' Katie suggested, squaring her hands to create a viewfinder around the big stone inglenook with its cast-iron burner, original bread oven and knotted oak lintel.

Amused by her mimicry, Laurie turned one of the armchairs to face out into the room, then set up the camera, a chair for herself and the few notes she'd made, while Katie tottered off to tart herself up a bit, as she so decorously put it.

'You look great,' Laurie told her when she came back sporting a fake tan down to her neckline, neat smudges of purplish-brown shadow to help the sunken effect of her eyes seem more moody and less ghoulish, and a delicate coral-coloured lipstick that blended quite beautifully with her chestnut wig. 'In fact, you look stunning,' she declared.

'Steady on, now,' Katie warned, though obviously pleased by the compliment. 'Now, is this where you want me?'

As she sank down in the armchair, Laurie adjusted the curtains to stop the sporadic blazes of sunlight beaming straight into her eyes, then after checking the camera, she discreetly pushed the record button, and sat down.

'OK?' she asked. 'Do you need anything? Water? Doughnuts?'

Katie chuckled. 'I'm fine,' she assured her, actually starting to feel a little nervous. 'It's weird,' she commented, 'I must have done a hundred or more TV appearances in my time, but now I've got to talk about myself, I'm like a jelly.'

Laurie waited for Trotty to snuggle down on Katie's lap, then giving Katie a gentle prompt to begin, she said, 'When you look back on your life now, what sort of things do you most regret?'

Katie grimaced, and tried not to think of the

camera as all her mistakes, missed opportunities and toe-curling embarrassments came strolling up for an airing. 'Oh, I could probably go on for days,' she responded lightly, 'but I suppose not being a better mother, or daughter, or sister rates pretty highly. And flunking it spectacularly as a wife . . .' She smiled, ironically. 'I've been an almost constant victim of the chattering in my own mind,' she confessed. 'I kept seeing the negative side to everything, when I could have bypassed all the self-destructive guff we feed ourselves by taking some time out to connect with my higher self and . . .'

'Can we have less of your spiritual counsellor, and more of you?' Laurie said, gently steering her back on course.

Katie's eyes narrowed. 'You're not hacking it as a Bodhisattva,' she told her.

Not entirely sure what that was, Laurie merely smiled and waited for her to continue.

'Well, OK,' Katie said, still much too conscious of the camera, and wondering if she really wanted the whole world to know what a sad old specimen she actually was, 'apart from regretting that I never made a few million, travelled the globe first class, and got blessed with Michelle's legs and Pamela Anderson's boobs, the thing I regret most is that, in my little box of life fireworks, God forgot to light the love and romance fuse. I mean, he tried a couple of times, but it kept going out, and then he just seemed to give up. And I'd hardly thank him if he got it all sparkling and fizzing up to the big explosion now, would I? Too bloody late, I'd tell him. Save it for Molly. She'll more than deserve it once she's through all this.'

Picking up on what might have been a note of bitterness, Laurie said, 'Are you saying you feel cheated?'

Katie's eyes dropped to Trotty, as though not wanting anyone to see what they might be giving away. 'How can I say that,' she finally answered, 'when I have so much? But yes, I suppose that is what I'm saying, because it's hard to come to terms with the fact that you've been excluded from life's biggest club; one that everyone else seems to find so easy getting membership to, while for you, every door is an exit.'

Laurie said, 'You've never been in love?'

Katie sighed and looked off towards the unused front door. 'Actually, yes I have,' she admitted, eventually. 'I loved Molly's father once, back in the early days, before I got wise. But then he managed to fleece me of everything, except, thank God, Molly, so, as regrets go, I'd say that marrying a man who didn't love me and staying with him as long as I did has to top the charts. And up there with it is the regret – or sadness, I suppose – that no-one's ever been in love with me. I would have liked to be adored and cherished, to feel as though I'm making someone's world a better place, just by being there and being me. If the ship was sinking, or the house was on fire, no-one would be thrashing about trying to find me. I'm excluding Molly, you understand, because she's a different kind of love altogether, and I know she'd be there for me, as I obviously would for her. What I'm saying is that if it weren't for Molly, I'm not sure there's really been any point to my life. The world, and everyone in it, would have trundled along just fine if I hadn't dropped in, and now I have to wonder why I bothered, if all I'm going to do is bail out on my daughter at the very time she needs me most. That's not a particularly admirable contribution to make to anyone's existence, is it, least of all someone you love.' She wrinkled her nose thoughtfully. 'I think that falls under the heading of regret, doesn't it?'

Laurie nodded.

'So, alas I have no heart-melting memories of romantic trysts in Paris or Rome. There were never any glittering little packages at Christmas or on birthdays for me, so no special trinkets to pass on to Molly. No flowers on Valentine's Day. Zippo from the Easter bunny; champagne and one glass on New Year's Eve.'

She paused as she thought of her and Molly's dream box and the crazy wishes they'd put in. They hadn't added anything to it for a while, and she realized sadly just how many unfulfilled dreams she had now.

'What are you thinking?' Laurie prompted.

Katie's eyes came to hers and slowly started to sparkle. 'Let's move on to something a bit cheerier now, shall we?' she said.

Laurie sighed. 'You're like someone who puts their toe in the water then runs off shrieking it's wet,' she told her.

Katie chuckled. 'Nicely put,' she responded. 'But I'm not a keen swimmer when it comes to self-pity, which is what regrets are all about really – well, mine are, and to tell the truth I am a keen swimmer, a bit too keen in fact, but I'll do my drowning in private, if you don't mind.'

'So that's it?' Laurie said. 'No more interview?'

'Oh yes, plenty, if you can stand it,' she answered, peering past Laurie towards the window. 'But I think we might have to take a break, because, unless I'm mistaken, we seem to have visitors.'

Laurie turned round, and seeing two men getting out of a white saloon car she frowned, for one of them seemed familiar. Then, realizing who it was, she immediately jumped up. 'It's Chris!' she cried, wondering what on earth he was doing here. 'Chris Gallagher,' she explained, and added darkly, 'the art dealer who represents Andraya Sorrantos, and who happens to be a great friend of mine and Elliot's.' If he was back from New York, she was thinking, did that mean Andraya was back too?

Katie was on her feet, staring past her in amazement. 'And with him,' she murmured, as the two men approached the gate, 'is Tom Chambers. Tell me I'm dreaming.'

'That's Tom?' Laurie cried, focusing on the handsome stranger who was moving ahead of Chris into the garden.

'That's Tom,' Katie confirmed, breaking into a grin. 'My God. This is going to cheer up Michelle,' and rushing out through the kitchen she threw open the door to greet him. 'What are you doing here?' she cried joyfully, as he scooped her up in an embrace.

'You have to ask?' he responded, a roguish twinkle in his eye that betrayed nothing of the shock he'd felt at how gaunt and wasted she looked.

368

'Michelle's going to get the surprise of her life,' she declared, stepping back to look at him.

Beside them Laurie was warmly embracing Chris. 'Is Elliot with you?' she asked.

'We dropped him at Biggin Hill,' he answered, 'then flew on to a private airfield a couple of miles down the road. I'm not stopping, I just offered to make sure our friend got here in one piece.'

Immediately Laurie said to Tom, 'Have you spoken to Max? Do you know about Josh Sh . . .'

'Yep, Elliot called him from a payphone right after we landed,' he told her, holding out a hand to shake. 'Tom Chambers. And I'm guessing you're Laurie Forbes.'

She smiled and shook. 'I feel I already know you,' she told him, meaning it, and turned to introduce Katie to Chris.

'It's a pleasure to meet you,' Katie said, shaking Chris's hand and somehow stopping herself from swooning, because though Tom might be a good-looking man, she wasn't sure she'd ever met anyone quite as handsome as Chris Gallagher. Inevitably a coquettish little bloom of hope began wondering if God was making one last attempt at the unlit romance fuse, but it quickly withered as Laurie said, 'Where's Rachel? I thought you two were still in New York.'

'We came back at the end of last week,' he told her. 'She's in Cornwall now, which is where I'm headed.'

'But you'll stay and have some tea,' Katie protested. 'Or champagne even. If I had some.'

Laughing, Tom slipped an arm round her shoulder and whispered, 'So where is she?'

'Out shopping for a car, but she should be back any time.'

'Let's ring her,' Laurie said, following Katie as she turned back inside.

'No. If she's due back any time, I'd kind of like to surprise her,' Tom said. Then to Katie, 'How is she? Or more to the point, how are you? You look damned wonderful.'

'Stage make up,' Katie informed him. 'But I'm fine. Now tell me about you, and how the heck you got here.'

As they talked, Laurie turned to Chris and with an uneasy feeling in her heart said, 'Did Andraya come back from New York with you?'

His expression showed his dismay. 'I'm afraid so,' he answered. 'She's in London.'

Feeling her tension increase, she said, 'Does Elliot know?'

'He didn't mention her when I saw him.'

She let her eyes fall away, still too easily able to picture the Brazilian bombshell in an intimate embrace with Elliot.

'It's over,' Chris told her quietly. 'He knows what a big mistake he made, so he's not about to do anything stupid again.'

Her eyes came back to his, but then becoming aware of what Tom was telling Katie, she turned to listen.

'. . . and by the time we spoke to Max,' he was saying, 'we'd already heard from Sajid that Farukh and three others have been arrested in Pakistan.'

'On what charges?' Laurie asked.

'Still vague,' he replied, 'but they'll be terrorist-related, and as trumped-up as Josh's, you can be certain of that.'

'Doesn't all this make it risky for you to be here?' Katie asked. 'I mean, if they're pulling the others in . . .'

'Probably,' he said, 'but by the time we knew what was happening we'd already landed, so I decided to take the chance. Let's just hope they don't have any long-range listening devices aimed in this direction. If they do, I guess we'll find out soon enough. Which,' he said, turning back to Laurie, 'is another reason I don't want you to call Michelle. The less said on the phone right now the better, because you can be certain they're all tapped, or sending signals to some spook satellite somewhere.'

Katie shuddered as she took a bottle of wine from the fridge. 'I don't care if it's barely midday,' she declared, 'I'm having a drink, and I hope you're all going to join me.'

'Sorry, but this is where I have to duck out,' Chris said with a grimace of apology. 'I'll take the car back to the airfield,' he told Tom. 'You know how to get hold of me if you need to,' and after embracing Laurie again, he left.

Katie tugged out the cork. 'So, your own personal . . .' but before she could say pilot Tom put a finger to her lips. 'Best not to discuss him,' he said in a whisper.

Katie looked at Laurie.

'I'll explain later,' Laurie told her, keeping her voice low. She was very well aware of the need for secrecy where Chris was concerned, since Elliot and Tom were almost certainly putting his contacts in the intelligence world to as much good use as his pilot skills.

A few minutes later, as they clinked glasses and started to drink, the door banged noisily open and Molly stumbled in saying, 'Mum! I have to have some new clothes. You've got . . .' Seeing the visitors she abruptly stopped. Then noticing her mother had make-up on, and that her eyes were all sparkly and gooey, she was on the point of backing out before anything got embarrassing, when Katie said, 'Where are your manners, Molly? Don't you remember Tom?'

Molly blinked. Oh yeah, he'd come here before, with Michelle. Years ago. Did that mean he was going to take her away again? 'Hello,' she said sweetly.

'And Laurie you know,' Katie said.

'Hello,' Molly mumbled. Then remembering what she'd been saying as she'd come in, she switched on the charm and sidled up to her mother.

'You're too transparent,' Katie told her, before she could begin. 'Now sit down and have a half-glass of wine if you like, or at least try to make civilized conversation before you start trying to wheedle anything out of me.'

'You're sure like your mother,' Tom said to Molly.

Katie's eyebrows shot up. 'I don't think she'll thank you for that,' she responded as she looked at Molly's pink cheeks. 'I'm not sure I do either. I mean, look at her.'

'Mum!' Molly responded. Then turning her eyes playfully on her, she said, 'Actually, I'm happy to be like you.'

Katie was immediately suspicious. 'Exactly how much do you want?' she demanded.

Molly threw out her hands as the others laughed. 'I *am*,' she insisted, and stealing a quick look at Tom, she slipped her arms round Katie's neck and said, 'You're the most beautiful person in the world.'

Katie looked at her askance. 'Have you been drinking?' she asked.

'I'll just go and clear in there,' Laurie said discreetly, and went off to dismantle the camera before Molly spotted it.

'So Molly,' Tom said, tilting back in his chair, 'tell me all about how life is with you these days. The last time we met I guess you weren't much more than ten, and you're obviously pretty grown-up now. What are you, fourteen?'

'Fifteen in January,' Molly told him.

'And do you have yourself a boyfriend?'

Molly coloured to the roots of her hair, but to Katie's amazement, she said, 'Well, there's kind of someone. It's not serious, or anything.'

'What's his name?'

'Oh, nothing. I mean, like, I don't want to tell you while she's here,' she said, poking a finger into her mother's waist.

'Then it must be something like Cedric, or Bartie,' Katie teased.

'It *so* is not!' Molly declared. 'If you must know, it's Brad.'

'As in Brad Pitt?' Katie said.

'Actually, he looks just like him.'

'So he's about thirty, is he?'

'Not even close. Forty-seven, actually.'

Tom chuckled. 'Even older than me.'

Aware of the way Katie was regarding her, Molly said, 'It was a joke, Mum. I know what you're thinking . . .'

'OK, OK,' Katie said, noticing Michelle's car pulling up outside. 'Just as long as it was,' and deciding not to say anything to Tom, she continued entertaining him with the silly banter with Molly, until Michelle opened the door saying, 'Someone's parked in my space. It must be hikers, but in this . . .'

Tom was grinning all over his face, and as he winked, her hands flew to her mouth.

'I don't believe it,' she gasped, as he came to take her in his arms. 'When did you get here? I mean . . . Oh God . . . Did you know he was coming?' she said to Katie, barely noticing how Molly's face had darkened the instant she came in.

Katie shook her head.

Michelle stood back to look at him, taking in all the craggy and badly shaven features of his beloved face. 'Are you OK?' she asked.

His eyes were alight with laughter. 'Don't I look it?'

'Of course, but . . . Do you know what's happened? Katie must have told you about Josh.'

'I'm ahead of you,' he responded, 'there's been more news since, but right now, I'd kind of like to focus on you.'

As they kissed, Katie watched Molly flounce off up the stairs, then deciding she too was extra to requirements she went to help Laurie.

'I should probably be heading back to London now,' Laurie said, as she pressed closed the steel camera case, while thinking of how different her reunion with Elliot was likely to be from the one going on in the kitchen.

'I'm sorry we didn't get much time this morning,' Katie told her. 'I guess I'm not going to be a terribly good subject after all.'

'You'll be excellent,' Laurie assured her, 'but if you'd prefer print . . .'

'I'll think it over.' She grimaced. 'I keep saying that, don't I?'

By the time Katie came back from seeing Laurie off, Michelle and Tom were sitting at the table, holding hands, and discussing everything that was happening. Katie listened for a few minutes, still feeling vaguely dizzied by the fact that he was actually here, so heaven only knew how Michelle must be feeling. Eventually, resisting the temptation to join in, she said, 'I was thinking about taking Molly to the cinema this afternoon. Or shopping. She obviously wants some new clothes. It'll give you two some time to yourselves . . .'

'Hey, no, we don't want to push you out of your own home,' Tom protested, 'and we've got a lot to talk about here, the three of us . . .'

Laughing, Katie said, 'You don't need me, and frankly, I'll be glad to get out for a while.'

'Then can we all have dinner tonight?' Tom asked. 'My treat.'

'Oh no,' Katie responded.

'Oh yes,' he corrected. 'Molly included. Then, if it's all right with you, I'd like to whisk your sister off to a hotel somewhere.'

Michelle's eyes were shining. 'Does the sister get any say in this?' she demanded.

'No,' he answered shortly.

'Oh my God!' Michelle suddenly gasped. 'The village hall. I have to give a talk at six,' she told Tom.

'I can make your excuses,' Katie offered. 'Maybe I'll treat them to one of my saucy little diatribes instead.'

'But I can't let them down,' Michelle said. 'That would be awful – if they really are looking forward to it. It just means I'll have to spend the afternoon preparing it.'

Tom frowned. 'I thought you'd have something like that sitting on a shelf,' he commented.

'I did, before my computer was taken.'

'Of course. Well, I'll tell you what, I'll help you put it together, and I'll even join in the talk, if you want me to, *then* I'll take you all for dinner. Does that work for you?' he said to Katie.

'I suppose so,' she replied, secretly delighted. 'I'm not sure about Molly though. She leads her own life these days.'

'Just you leave her to me,' Tom said. 'Hell, we could even invite Brad to join us.'

'Brad?' Michelle echoed.

'Molly's boyfriend,' he explained.

Michelle turned to Katie.

Katie nodded and grinned. 'He got it out of her, just like that,' she said with a click of her fingers. 'Now, if you'll excuse me, I'll leave you with the computer and go and make her day by taking her into Bath. Or maybe,' she said, narrowing her eyes at Tom, 'you've already managed to do that,' and leaving him chuckling after her, she walked off up the stairs.

Chapter Seventeen

Just thank God, Elliot was thinking, as he listened to the voice leaving a message on the machine, that he hadn't got to the phone in time, for the very last person he needed to talk to right now, or at any other time come to that, was Andraya Sorrantos.

'. . . so I was thinking,' Andraya was saying, in her dark, husky tones, 'it wasn't so much fun the way we said goodbye, so please call me. I am back in London now. Perhaps we could have dinner and talk a little, and later we can do the kind of things we like to do best.' She paused, allowing him time to conjure the memory, and to his dismay he could feel an automatic response stirring. 'Call me, *caro*,' she said, and the click of the phone going down was followed by the sounds of the machine resetting.

Immediately he erased the message, hardly able to credit the good fortune that had allowed him, rather than Laurie, to walk into the flat at that moment. He didn't even want to think about how that would have started things off for the evening, nor was he faring too well right now with the guilt of how he'd responded to Andraya's thinly veiled offer of sex. However, it had nothing to do with reality, for nothing, just *nothing*, would ever persuade him to go near her again. Not that he held her responsible for his weakness, the blame for that lay completely at his door. She was simply a reminder of how much he loathed himself for giving into it, and how bitter the price was that he was having to pay.

Deciding to dismiss her from his mind, as though the call had never happened, he was on the point of going round the bar into the kitchen when he realized there was every chance she'd call again, and if Laurie was here . . . Snatching up the phone he quickly pressed in Andraya's number.

'Elliot, darling,' she drawled in her rich, honeyed accent. 'I knew you would call. We can't resist each other, can we . . .'

'Andraya,' he cut in sharply. 'I don't want to see you, hear from you, or even speak to you . . .'

'But darling, I am lying here with no clothes on, thinking of you and all the wonderful things you do to me . . .'

The image of her exquisitely voluptuous body sprang before his eyes, large and tanned, sumptuous and unbelievably sexy. 'For Christ's sake, aren't you listening?' he cried. 'It's over, Andraya. *Finito* . . .'

'I don't think that is true,' she murmured. 'You sound so passionate already . . .'

'Jesus Christ,' he seethed, and not knowing how the hell else he could convince her, he slammed the phone down. This time, he noted with some relief, there had been no physical response to her, if he discounted the thundering beat of his heart.

Vowing to disconnect the phone if she called again, he scooped up the bags of shopping he'd brought in with him, and walked round to the kitchen to start packing it away. Laurie had called an hour ago to say she was on her way back, which was when he'd abandoned his computer to go downstairs to the exclusive shops of Shad Thames to pick up an expensive bottle of Montrachet, two fillet steaks and a lavish bouquet of autumnal flowers. It wasn't unusual for him to cook, he enjoyed it, though feeling as anxious as he did right now it was hard to imagine enjoying anything. He was too on edge, too liable to explode with the sheer frustration of not knowing how the hell to play this. Katie's advice was uppermost in his mind, to make sure Laurie knew she was loved, then to give her the space she needed to come to her own decisions, but would he be able to do that when it could mean she'd end up choosing Nick? For one wild moment earlier he'd considered calling Katie to ask for her advice again, but she had enough to contend with, and for God's sake, he was a grown man, he could work this out.

Or that was what he was telling himself as he went up to their mezzanine bedroom, not actually knowing if he would sleep there later, though she'd said, when she called, that she would be spending the night here. Whether that meant in the same bed as him, or one of them using the guest room, he'd doubtless find out when the time came, though right now he wasn't even sure himself which he'd prefer. All he knew was that he had no right to set any terms, that he couldn't even afford the luxury of losing his temper or threatening Nick, which was a big temptation. He simply had to do or say what he could to convince Laurie that it wasn't too late for them, that they could get through this, though for someone who found it so very difficult to express his feelings it was going to be hard.

After taking a quick shower and shaving, he returned to his study to carry on with some work, and was just opening the files that Katie and Michelle had attached to an email when someone pressed the buzzer downstairs. Surprised, he checked the time at the corner of his screen. It was still too soon for Laurie, and she'd surely use her own key. Then turning cold as he thought of Andraya, he quickly got up, and prayed to God he wasn't about to find out he was right.

'Elliot,' a male voice at the other end said, 'can I have a word?'

Though relieved it wasn't Andraya, he was no happier with who it actually was, for Jolyon Kember of the Special Intelligence Service was never someone he was eager to see. However, he should have been expecting the visit, and knowing there was no way to avoid it, he swore under his breath and pushed the button to release the downstairs door. He'd just better be out of here by the time Laurie turned up, or he'd damned well throw him out and to hell with the consequences.

A few minutes later a well-built, smartly dressed man in his late thirties, with a cheery pudding face that almost, but not quite, allowed the shark eyes to be missed, was standing in the middle of the sitting room, taking a good look round. 'Impressive place,' he commented.

'You're not here to discuss interior design,' Elliot responded coldly. 'So shall we get to the point?'

'Must have cost a fortune,' Kember continued, unruffled.

'And all paid for by Her Majesty's Government in exchange for my silence over their supply of arms to despotic African regimes, *and* the rebel forces who are trying to overthrow them,' Elliot retorted, feeling the need to spell it out. 'Keep up conflict levels, treble defence spending, and send Phraxos share prices through the roof. And who in our government is on the board of Phraxos?'

Kember's expression was bland. 'You did the right thing taking the money and keeping what you knew to yourself,' he told him, going to take a closer look at a photograph of Laurie. 'I don't imagine you're considering going back on your word,' he commented, almost to himself. 'No, that would be foolish, and that's not a category you fall into, so I'm going to reassure those who have concerns that you remain an honourable man, who stands by his agreements – one of which is to cease reporting for a year.'

Elliot would have liked nothing better than to thump him, for Kember knew very well how troubled he was by his decision to hold back on the Phraxos findings. He had finally made up his mind about this after weeks of the very kind of intimidation he sensed Kember was leading up to now.

'I would be correct to do that, I take it?' Kember prompted, turning to look at him.

Since Kember obviously knew he was already breaking the agreement, Elliot didn't bother to reply.

Kember continued to walk round the apartment. 'You need to let go of this thing with Tom Chambers,' he said, stopping to stare out at the view.

'Let go of what, exactly?' Elliot challenged.

'There are things you don't know, Elliot,' Kember said, turning round, 'so please take it from me, this isn't something you want to become involved in.'

Elliot's eyebrows went up. 'That wasn't an answer to my question,' he pointed out.

'I'm not here to answer questions. I'm here to try to stop you getting in this so deep that none of us will be able to get you out.'

Elliot feigned more surprise. 'Just what exactly do you think I'm getting into?' he asked, trying again to get Kember to spell it out.

'The information Tom Chambers obtained from a CIA asset by the name of Joshua Shine is not what you think it is,' Kember stated.

'Considering what I think it is, that could come as a relief,' Elliot responded.

Kember didn't even flinch. 'When were you last in touch with Chambers?' he asked. 'I'm not talking about recent days, I'm talking about regular contact?'

Trying to gauge where this might be going, Elliot said, 'I'd have to check, but it's been a while.'

Kember nodded. 'The truth is, Elliot, you don't know what's been going on with him these last few years, do you? You don't know who he's been mixing with over there in Pakistan, what he's been doing, how involved he's become with causes that are not aligned with our own.'

Knowing exactly what this was leading up to now, Elliot said, 'Then why don't you enlighten me?'

Kember's head went to one side. 'Ask him to tell you about the false passports found in his apartment, the terrorist training manuals, recruitment videos, arms and explosives . . .'

'Oh, come on, you're not that naive,' Elliot cut in. 'He's a known war correspondent based in Pakistan. Of course he'd have that kind of material in his apartment.'

'Admittedly, on its own it might not prove incriminating,' Kember replied, 'but when weighed with visits to a terrorist training camp, which no other Western journalist has ever managed, and his highly contentious writings that many including his own government would term rabidly anti-American, the case against him begins to strengthen.'

'For you, maybe, if you want to buy into all that bullshit. For me he's an exceptional journalist who made *one* visit to a training camp four years ago, and who's exercising his First Amendment right to free speech. If the current administration don't happen to like what he says, well I'd say that's just too bad.'

'There are plenty of journalists writing the way he does,' Kember countered, 'but none of them has in their possession details of a terrorist plot to attack a Western target.'

Finally, Elliot thought, we come to the point.

'And you're here to convince me that he's part of the group that's behind this plot?' he said.

Kember's eyes bored into his. 'Face it, Elliot, you don't know where that plot originated. You're trying to connect it to the US intelligence services, but you're not succeeding, and you won't, because that's not where it came from. Joshua Shine is a rogue agent, someone who's being used by the left to try and bring down the Republicans.'

Elliot was shaking his head. 'You can't have it both ways,' he told him. 'A minute ago you were branding Tom Chambers a terrorist, now you're trying to say he's part of some left-wing conspiracy to get the far right out of office. So which is it?'

'They're not mutually exclusive,' Kember responded.

Elliot thought about it and decided that maybe, in a far-fetched sort of way, they weren't. However, he was buying none of it, and Kember was a fool if he'd come here thinking he would. 'Do you actually know the details of that plot?' he challenged. 'Or are you just a messenger, someone who knows there's an envelope, but not what's inside.'

The skin around Kember's mouth paled.

Satisfied that Kember probably didn't have the full picture, Elliot said, 'Tell me what you know about the P2OG.'

Without any hesitation Kember said, 'It doesn't exist.'

Elliot allowed his scepticism to show. 'That's the official line?' he said.

'It's a fact.'

Elliot continued to regard him.

384

In the end, Kember said, 'Elliot, you know as well as I do that the Yanks don't mess about with this stuff. So take my advice and back off now, or you'll find yourself going the same way as your friend.'

Elliot blinked. 'What exactly does that mean?'

'The documents Chambers has are going to hang him,' Kember said darkly. 'Don't let them hang you too.'

'Are we talking literally, or professionally?'

Kember didn't answer, and Elliot felt a chill run through him. So here was the confirmation that if Tom pursued the story they would destroy his reputation and brand him a terrorist with all that that entailed – and a carefully managed campaign, with the full power of the American right behind it, stood a greater chance of success than anything Tom could put forward while they still lacked proof of the plot's origins.

'They'll never pull it off,' Elliot said. 'Too many of us are involved in this now, and you can't silence us all.'

Kember was staring at him hard, his face set like stone. 'I thought you were smarter than that,' he responded.

Elliot wondered if that was a reminder of just how powerful the forces behind all this were. If so, he hardly needed one, for he'd never been in any doubt. However, this might be a good time to underline what they must already know, that there was no way an aborted terrorist attack could be used in an election strategy now. So going right for it, he said, 'If you think I'm just going to stand back and watch this country pay with its peace of mind

385

for a neo-conservative victory at the polls, then you are mistaken.'

Kember's expression barely changed, making it impossible to know if he'd just learned something new. In the end he merely held out his hand, palm up, and said, 'Your passport.'

Elliot immediately baulked. 'On what grounds?' he demanded.

'On the grounds that you are considered a national security risk.'

Elliot was incredulous, though he should have seen this coming.

Kember said, 'We can do it the hard way, if you prefer.'

'You mean arrest me? On what charge?'

'Obstruction of justice would be a beginning.'

Knowing full well he could do it, and possibly even already had the officers outside to back him up, Elliot was almost tempted to force him to carry it through, for the sheer malicious pleasure of making them deal with the ensuing publicity. However, he wasn't going to be of much use to Tom if he did, nor would his plans for the evening with Laurie be helped by the divisive presence of a prison-cell door. So with no further protest he opened his briefcase and took out the passport.

After tucking it into an inside pocket Kember straightened his cuffs, then his tie, and said, 'You know our capabilities, Elliot, so don't be a fool. It's already too late for Chambers, but not for you. Let it go, man, and get on with your life.'

After he'd gone Elliot's first instinct was to drive down to Wiltshire to apprise Tom of the visit, and even arrange for him to slip back out of the country.

The problem was, the minute he left the flat there was every chance he'd be followed, and since they didn't appear to know where Tom was right now, he wasn't about to lead them straight to him. However, Tom needed to be alerted, and provided Elliot could pull it off, there should be a way of doing it that would also give Tom at least one night with Michelle.

In the hope that someone was monitoring his line, he picked up the phone and dialled Katie's number. 'Michelle,' he said, when she answered. 'It's Elliot. Still no news of Tom, I'm afraid. We parted company in Italy, and he hasn't been in touch again yet, but I've just been informed there's a chance he'll be joining Josh and Farukh on the other side of freedom in the not too distant future.'

There was a beat of silence before Michelle said, 'Do you know when exactly?'

'I got the impression not immediately, but if you hear from him before I do, please tell him what I've just told you.'

'Of course,' she promised. 'How did you hear this?'

'From a source that's pretty reliable – and who is now the guardian of my passport.'

Taking a moment to digest that, Michelle said, 'But how will you get to him now? They're making it impossible.'

Impressed by how smoothly she was handling this, and how expertly she'd just planted the suggestion that Tom was still abroad, Elliot said, 'I won't go into any more on the phone, but we'll find a way,' and after assuring her he'd be in touch again as soon as there was more news, he returned to his study to send a coded email to Chris Gallagher.

With all that done, he closed down the computer and went to pour himself a drink. Laurie should arrive any minute, and by the time she got there he wanted his thoughts focused entirely on her.

'Well, I guess as no-one's come calling yet,' Tom was saying, as he lay on Michelle's narrow bed looking up at her, 'then they really don't know where I am.'

Michelle's eyebrows went up. 'That, coming from the man who taught me information takes time to process, is cavalier in the extreme,' she responded, tightening the belt of her robe before going to peer out of the window. Apart from a couple of locals with pushchairs and toddlers, there was no-one around, nor had she really expected there to be. Katie and Molly had left half an hour ago, and to think she might spot a BT van parked where it shouldn't be, or a couple of birds in an uproar at finding some alien device in their tree, was just plain absurd. Dropping the curtain back into place, she untied the robe and let it slide to the floor.

'Mmm,' he moaned appreciatively as his eyes wandered lingeringly over her.

She sauntered towards him and sitting down on the edge of the bed, lifted one of his hands and held it to her. They'd just finished making love when Elliot called. Though she imagined they would again before Katie and Molly returned, for the moment Elliot's warning that an arrest warrant could be imminent was pushing all other thoughts aside. The warning, she thought, seemed to be bothering her a lot more than Tom, even though she'd half expected it.

Lifting his hand to her face, he gently stroked it. 'Look at me,' he said.

Moving her lovely green eyes to his, she nestled her cheek into his hand and smiled.

'I love you,' he told her softly.

Her heart tightened with emotion, and turning to kiss his palm, she said, 'I love you too.'

Sitting up, he drew her to him and covered her mouth with his own, letting the power of the words deepen the kiss, just as the feel of their bodies heightened the need to be close. 'It'll be all right,' he told her, pulling her down with him and gazing into her eyes.

'I want to believe you,' she whispered.

'Have I ever lied to you?'

She shook her head.

'Did I ever let you down?'

Again she shook her head.

His eyes turned playful as he said, 'Then that's more than I can say for you.'

She frowned.

'You forgot the necklace,' he reminded her.

With arched brows she said, 'Maybe because someone was in so much of a hurry to get up here, I didn't have a chance to put it on,' and responding warmly to the memory of their eagerness to be together as soon as Katie and Molly had left, she kissed him again.

'But you'll wear it tonight,' he told her. 'Where will we go? Any ideas?'

'There's a lovely manor house in the next village,

with an excellent restaurant, I'm told. *And* it's an exclusive hotel.'

'Sounds perfect,' and propping himself up on one elbow he continued to gaze into her eyes. 'Did you get more beautiful?' he asked, feeling certain she had.

'I'm sure only you would think so,' she replied, making them both smile.

He brushed the hair back from her forehead, and kissed her gently on the nose. 'So how's it working out here?' he asked. 'Any headway with Molly yet?'

Her eyes slanted away, as her heart sank with dismay. 'No,' she answered.

'But it's good with Katie? Better than you expected?'

'Yes.' She looked at him again, and feeling a quiet surge of relief that she had him here to confide in, she began pouring out everything she felt about coming back to England, trying to cope with the dread of losing Katie, Molly's recalcitrance, her own feelings of displacement, and how concerned she'd been lately that she just wasn't pulling it together. 'And then there's all that's happening to you,' she said. 'Can you imagine how frustrating it is not being able to get fully involved? We always used to go into battle together, and now I hate the fact that you're out there alone, without me . . .' Her frown softened as she saw the humour come into his eyes. 'I guess you're coping just fine, and I've been too used to being on the front line,' she said, reading his thoughts, 'so this is a bit of a lesson on how to keep the ego in check, and,' she smiled impishly, 'sitting here alone in this room staring at

390

all that sky out there gives me plenty of time to think about our last day together, and dream about it happening again – and again, like it did just now.'

Putting his mouth to hers, he kissed her for a long, leisurely time, stirring the deepest of their desires and seeming to seal the bond that held them together.

'I miss you so much,' she said when he pulled back to look at her.

'I miss you too,' he murmured. 'I don't know what took us so long to get here, but I do know I don't want to waste any more time. I want to spend the rest of my life with you. I want to marry you, if you'll have me.'

A lump immediately formed in her throat, as the joy of his words filled her. How many times over these last weeks had she allowed herself to imagine this moment and what she would say. How readily she'd seen herself melting into his arms and feeling happier and more loved than she ever had in her life. And she could do it. She could just blot out everything else and tell herself it would be all right, that somehow they would make it work . . .

'You're not about to turn me down, are you?' he prompted.

Smiling past the turmoil in her heart, she said, 'You have to know how much I love you, how much I've wanted to hear you say that, but . . . No listen,' she said, as he started to interrupt. 'I know how hard I'm finding it to be here, in this country, so how much harder is it going to be for you . . .'

Cutting her off more firmly this time, he said, 'I know where you're going with this, and I'm telling

391

you, it's possible to base myself here, or in London. OK, I might be away a lot . . .'

'But it's not only about where we live,' she said, 'it's about Molly and Robbie, and the fact . . .' she took a breath, 'the fact that I think I might be pregnant.' She looked at him, feeling almost as shaken by the admission as he clearly was, for this was the first time she'd actually allowed herself to speak the suspicion aloud.

'Can you see how complicated that would make everything?' she said. 'Not for us, but for Molly and Robbie . . .'

'Hang on, hang on,' he interrupted. 'You've just told me you could be carrying my child. Can I have a moment to deal with that first?'

Smiling, she lifted a hand to his face, and watched him as he absorbed the full impact of her news.

'You've got to know how happy this makes me,' he told her, finding himself very close to the edge, for he'd always wanted children, it had just never been the right time, or, until now, the right woman.

'Me too,' she assured him, 'but I'm so worried what it'll do to Molly, having to share me with a baby so soon after her mother . . . And to Robbie, who's already wondering why I'm here and not with him. How's he going to react to having two siblings in one go? And what if I make him and Molly feel left out, by focusing too much on the baby at the very time we're all trying to get used to each other?'

'Don't you know yourself at all?' he cut in. 'Haven't you learned anything this past ten years about how capable you are of making every child feel special, no matter who they are? Do you honestly think you'd be any different with Molly and two of your own? She's your niece. Your own flesh and blood. You won't let her down.'

'I wish I had your faith, but if these past weeks have taught me anything, it's that I seem to cope much better with strangers than I do my own family.'

'That's nonsense,' he told her, 'you've hardly given yourself a chance.'

'But what about you?' she protested. 'Why should I expect you to take on two children who aren't your own?'

'Robbie's my godson,' he reminded her. 'And if you marry me, Molly will be my niece too. Don't you think I haven't thought about this? I want you, Michelle, and everything that comes with you . . . No, keep listening,' he said as she tried to butt in. 'We love each other, we know neither of us is ever going to meet anyone more right for the other, and just what the hell else did you think you were going to do, except marry me? You love me, you want us to be together as much as I do, so are you seriously saying you're considering not letting it happen because you're *pregnant*?'

'Might be,' she corrected. 'I haven't taken a test yet.'

'Then can I suggest we go to a pharmacy right now to get one, because I, for one, would really like to know.'

Loving him so much she almost felt she could melt with it, she put her arms around him and said, 'If I am, don't let's tell anyone yet. I'll need some time to work out the best way to break the news.'

'Anything you say,' he responded, holding her tight, 'but before we go anywhere, I'd kind of like to hear a yes.'

She pulled back to look at him.

'I believe I asked you to marry me,' he reminded her.

Bubbling with laughter, she said, 'Yes. I will. I do. Forever. I love you, Tom Chambers. I love you. And to think, at our age, neither of us has ever been married before. How on earth will we manage?'

'I guess we're going to find out,' he responded, and giving her a gentle shove off the bed, he clicked his fingers for his clothes to be brought to him, and promptly had them tossed on his head.

Though Laurie had had the long motorway drive back to London, plus the entire time both Elliot and Nick were away, to think about this evening, she was afraid, as she pressed the lift button to take her up to their apartment, that she was even further from knowing what she wanted now than she'd been a week ago. Back then she'd felt almost certain it was Nick, but she only had to speak to Elliot to be thrown into turmoil, and now, since learning Andraya was in London, she was so full of doubt, about everything, that she hardly knew what she was thinking.

Knowing she had to pull herself together before she faced Elliot, she made a superhuman effort to force her mind past all her fears, because the last thing she needed was Andraya smuggling herself back into their lives via her paranoid imaginings. She must try to behave as though the woman was dead, or had simply never existed, and put a stop right now to all this jealousy and insecurity – the price *she* was having to pay for Elliot's betrayal, when in any fair world he would be the one suffering those ugly, destructive emotions. She had to concede that he probably was, for not even Andraya's return was going to convince her that he didn't care what she did with Nick, but Elliot was so much better at coping with his emotions, and such a master at disguising them, that at times she even wondered how deeply they ran.

As the lift doors opened, she was horribly aware that this was going to be the first time they had come face to face since the morning he'd caught her with Nick. She could hardly be dreading it more, and wished she could just push all the hurt aside and fall into his arms as though nothing had ever gone wrong in their lives. But there was no pretending the past didn't exist, and though it would be easy to tell herself that the score was even now, they'd both had affairs and one betrayal had cancelled out the other, she knew very well it didn't work that way. There was so much damage to repair, and with the trust between them still in pieces it was hard to know how they could even begin to put it back together.

She was on the point of slotting her key into the front door when hearing Elliot's voice inside, she paused to listen. What would she do, she wondered as her heart started a heavy thud, if he was speaking to Andraya? The very thought made her queasy, but she knew how unlikely it was, for she'd called from the garage to let him know she was on her way up, so he surely wouldn't be speaking to her now. But maybe Andraya had rung him . . . Or it could be a quick call to rearrange a plan they'd made earlier . . . With a horrible feeling coming over her, she wondered if this was how it was going to be from now on, her thinking everything he did was somehow connected to Andraya, and him wondering the same about her and Nick. If it was, then their relationship really was doomed.

Hearing the call end she quickly pushed in the key and opened the door. Turning to gather up the shopping she'd picked up at Waitrose, she stepped inside. She wasn't sure if a candle-lit dinner would be appropriate this evening, but she'd bought a fresh supply of candles anyway, and flowers, and wine and salmon steaks. After all, they had to eat, and though it was the very last thing she felt like doing right now, maybe she'd feel differently later.

He'd obviously heard her, because he came out of his study and seeing the shopping he immediately took it from her. 'Are you OK?' he asked, making no attempt to kiss her.

'Fine,' she answered, closing the door. 'Are you?'

He was already walking away. 'Seems we had the same thought,' he told her. 'I brought some supplies in too.'

She felt rebuffed. No kiss, no smile, not even a look to let her know how he was feeling, if he was glad she was here, or as anxious as she was about the evening ahead. 'Lovely flowers,' she said, going to sniff the arrangement he'd put on the dining table. 'They're beautiful. Did you get them downstairs?'

'The same place as you got these?' he asked, holding up the smaller bunch she'd brought in.

She looked at the artful arrangement and thought how oddly masculine they seemed for such delicate blooms. 'They're for you,' she told him, and immediately hoped he didn't think it was an inane attempt to buy off her conscience.

'I'll cherish them,' he responded, with an ironic lilt in his voice.

She smiled and watched him set them in a vase, which he slid to one side of the bar, next to the phone.

'Any messages?' she asked, taking off her jacket as he continued to pack away the groceries.

'A few,' he answered. 'They're still on the machine.'

Not wanting to listen to them now, she wandered over to the bar and fought the urge to ask if he knew Andraya was back. If he did, was he thinking about her now? Was he imagining that sumptuous body and the mesmerizing eyes? Or was he thinking about Nick, and trying to escape the painful images of her making love to him? She knew how hard that was, for barely an hour went by without her tormenting herself with visions of him and Andraya – sometimes they even came when she was with Nick. It was crazy, and she never liked to think of it afterwards, but in some horrible, warped part of her mind she would find herself imagining she was Andraya thrashing around under Elliot's powerful body, instead of her beneath Nick.

'So what did Jolyon Kember have to say?' she asked, cutting her mind free from the Brazilian whore.

'Quite a lot actually,' he answered.

As he brought her up to date he opened a bottle of wine and lifted two glasses from under the counter top. She watched as he poured and felt her heart tighten, for she loved his hands, and just wished she could stop herself imagining them on Andraya.

'Does Tom know about all this?' she asked, when he'd finished.

'He already suspected most of it, but yes, he knows I've had a visit.'

He passed her a drink, and as their eyes met she had a horrible feeling he had read her thoughts about Andraya. But that was impossible, and even if he had, they were hers, not his, and if she didn't stop doing this she was going to push him in the very direction she didn't want him to go.

'Cheers,' he said.

'Cheers,' she echoed.

They drank, then both started to speak at once.

'You first,' he said.

'No, you.'

'I was just saying I got some fillet steaks for dinner,' he told her.

'I bought some too, though mine are salmon.'

'We can have those if you prefer.'

'No. Yours will be better. We can have the salmon tomorrow. Or we can freeze it,' she added, remembering her arrangement to see Nick tomorrow.

His eyes stayed on her and she felt her heart twist. What was he thinking, she wondered. Did she really want to know? Not unless it was the same as her, that she wanted just to walk around the bar now and put her arms around him. And she might have, were she not sensing a resistance in him that made her afraid to attempt it.

'Are you hungry?' he asked, glancing at the clock. 'I could start preparing something now.'

'Then I'll go and take a shower,' she answered. 'Or I could help.'

'There's not much to do.'

As she walked up the spiral staircase to their master suite, he couldn't stop himself wondering if she had somehow managed to see Nick before coming here, and that was the real reason she was going for a shower now. He'd had the same thought when she'd walked in the door, that she'd just come from van Zant, which was why he'd made no attempt to kiss her – and the fact that van Zant's name hadn't been mentioned yet was almost seeming to confirm his suspicions. Maybe he should be the one to bring it up, but there wasn't much in him that actually wanted to acknowledge the man's existence, never mind the role he was playing in Laurie's life. He just hoped to God she wasn't going to tell him that the role was about to become permanent.

Taking a generous mouthful of wine, he began preparing some canapés. He had to stop thinking this way or he'd never get through the next hours with his temper in check, and losing it wasn't going to help either of them. Already he knew he wasn't handling things well, for the distance between them was almost palpable, but though he wanted nothing more than to close it, he just didn't know how. He thought of her upstairs now, in the shower, the water cascading over her, and the way he would normally join her after they'd been apart for a while, but the suspicion that it was van Zant's hands she wanted on her kept him where he was, for he could hardly think of anything worse than inciting her revulsion.

By the time she came down again he'd prepared a small plate of canapés, which he'd set on the bar, and was now chopping peppers and mushrooms to go with the steaks. He glanced up as he heard her on the stairs, and seeing her still brushing her damp hair, with no make-up on her face, and a casual T-shirt dress that showed she probably wore nothing underneath, he felt the fear of losing her tear through him so brutally he had to turn away. Just how the hell was he going to handle this, he was asking himself angrily. Someone please show him the way, because right now he could barely even think of his next move, never mind his next words.

As she came to the other side of the bar and helped herself to a canapé she began talking about Tom again. 'He's too high profile,' she said. 'If he disappears, or they put him in prison, questions will be asked, and we have the answers.'

'But not the proof,' he responded. 'Right now, those documents could have come from anywhere,' and keeping his eyes on what he was doing, he added, 'does Nick have any more of the '97 version yet?'

Only able to look at him because he wasn't looking at her, she said, 'Yes. He brought it back with him.'

'So when can we expect to see something?'

'Tomorrow.'

Still he kept his face averted. 'Is he bringing it here?'

'No. I'm going there.'

For several minutes he said nothing, only concentrated on dropping the vegetables into hot oil, and unwrapping the steaks. 'So you haven't been with him today?' he said finally, wiping his hands with a tea towel.

'No. You know where I was today.'

'You've spoken to him though.'

'Yes.'

He nodded, then turned to lower the gas. 'Would you prefer to be there now?'

'No, of course not.'

At last he looked at her, and though his expression was as harsh as his manner there was no mistaking the pain in his eyes. 'So just how serious is it between you?' he asked.

It was a question she'd dreaded, for she knew she wasn't going to give him the answer he wanted, and her face was pale, her voice horribly strained as she said, 'I – I don't know.'

He turned away, but she knew the doubt had hurt him deeply, and immediately she wished she could take the words back. But even if she could, what would she say in their place?

For a while neither of them spoke, until finally she said, 'I'm not doing it to punish you.'

His irony was bleak as he replied, 'Maybe it would be better if you were.'

She watched him pluck a garlic bulb from a hanging stem and break it apart. 'Do you want me to give him up?' she said.

His eyes came briefly to hers. 'If that's what you want to do,' he responded.

Though his answer annoyed her, she should have known better than to try and push him into making the decision for her, so after taking a sip of wine she stared down at her glass and tried asking herself what she really wanted. Of course it was him, being here now she wondered that she could ever have been in any doubt, but how the hell were they going to get past all the hurt there was between them? How was she ever going to be sure that he wouldn't be tempted by another Andraya, or indeed by the one who was only a few miles away right now?

Looking up, she found to her surprise that he was watching her, and as she looked back she couldn't help wondering what it would mean to him if she left. Would he be totally devastated, just as she had been when he'd gone? Would he feel as though his life couldn't go on, that nothing made any sense without her, or even mattered any more? It was hard to imagine someone like him falling victim to such debilitating feelings, or becoming so stuck in his pain that he couldn't move on.

'I wish I knew what you wanted,' she told him.

Seeming surprised, he said, 'You can be in any doubt?'

'If that means it's me, then you have a funny way of showing it.'

There was a note of impatience in his voice as he said, 'Did you consider that I might be finding it difficult to behave normally when I know you're sleeping with another man, and that you're not intending to give him up?'

'I didn't say that,' she retorted. 'I asked if you wanted me to . . .'

'I know what you asked and I gave you my answer.'

402

She took a breath, but he hadn't finished.

'I've wanted to think,' he said, 'that what you're doing is some kind of payback, but you seem to be telling me it goes much deeper than that.'

Her eyes went down as she said, 'All I know is that I love you and I don't want this to be happening, but when I'm with him it's as though it's something . . . something I need and . . .' She stopped, realizing how hard this had to be for him to hear.

It was how he'd felt about Andraya, he was thinking, at the mercy of a passion that he hadn't found the will to resist, and knowing how intense his feelings had been, and how much he had put at stake because of them, left him in no doubt of what he was facing now.

Needing to know what he was thinking, if she was right about his feelings, she said, 'Don't you feel angry? Doesn't it do anything to you to think of me with . . .?'

'Of course it does,' he cut in sharply. 'And yes, I'm angry. And jealous and frankly I'd like to kill him, but is that going to change anything? You'll do what you want to do, whatever you feel *compelled* to do, and it won't matter how I feel, because as you just told me, you can't make it stop.'

She was so close now to throwing Andraya in his face that she had to remind herself fiercely that if she went that route, she was the one who'd end up being hurt. 'Tell me,' she said, her voice edged in bitterness, 'when you talk to Nick on the phone, how does it feel? Can you put all this aside and pretend it's not happening?'

'If I have to,' he said shortly.

'You can compartmentalize me that easily?'

He didn't answer, but he didn't have to, because she knew he could. Detesting him for it, she got up to go and set the table. If they didn't stop this now they really would end up saying things they'd regret.

After laying out the cutlery and table mats, she unwrapped the candles and put them in the six oriental holders that formed a line down the centre of the table. She didn't imagine either of them was in the mood for romance right now, but she was eager to do something to defuse the tension and though it seemed naive to expect soft lights to do it, at least they were unlikely to make it any worse. In fact, by the time she'd lit the other candles around the room and turned down the lamps she was starting to feel a little more relaxed, and even slightly hungry thanks to the smells coming from the kitchen.

'What music would you like?' she asked, going to the CD player.

'You choose.'

As she went through their collection she couldn't help wondering what would happen if she selected *Die Fledermaus*, or *Tristan und Isolde,* or *Carmen,* for they almost never listened to opera without making love. She recalled the words he'd misquoted from *La Bohème*, when he'd asked her to take him back after Andraya: *Sappi per tuo governo, che darei perdono in sempiterno.* For your future guidance, I would be constantly forgiving you. What would he say if she reminded him of that now? But it wasn't his forgiveness she doubted, it was his fidelity, and there were never any guarantees about that.

She looked up as the phone rang, and felt slightly

breathless as she waited to find out who it was. If it turned out to be Andraya she was certain she'd walk out now and go straight to Nick, but when she realized it was her father, she relaxed again and chose a jazz diva medley to put on the CD.

'He sends his love,' Elliot said, putting the phone down a couple of minutes later.

'Didn't he want to speak to me?'

His eyes appeared droll as he said, 'Apparently not.'

She smiled and came back to the bar.

'He was just letting me know that he's received the cheque I sent.'

Realizing it must be to cover the expenses her father had incurred before the wedding was cancelled, she said, 'Is he going to cash it?'

'He's saying it's too much, so we need to discuss it.'

Deciding to leave that to them, she refilled their wine glasses and drank deeply as she wished it was three months ago, when her dress was being made, the church was already booked, and they'd just moved into this apartment and neither of them had even known either Nick or Andraya. Then remembering how stressed she'd been back then, she decided it wasn't such a perfect time after all. That had come later, when they were in Bali, a long, long way from reality. They'd been able to laugh then, in a way they weren't able to now, and talk without fear of hurting each other. She hadn't even worried about what he was thinking, the way she was now, though Andraya must have been in his mind, because she knew very well Nick had been in hers.

'Do you ever think about her?' she asked suddenly.

His eyebrows went up, then realizing who she meant his face immediately darkened. 'Not if I can help it,' he answered.

'But if something comes up on the radio, or in a newspaper, maybe about Brazil, or art, or when you speak to Chris . . . You must think about her then.'

'I told you, not if I can help it.'

'What about when we make love?'

His jaw tightened. 'Why are you doing this?'

She looked at him for a moment, then turned away and sighed. 'I don't know,' she replied.

His eyes were still hard as he regarded her, then in a tone that surprised and annoyed her, he said, 'Maybe you're trying to use my guilt to blot out your own.'

'Well maybe I am,' she retorted hotly, and drinking more wine, she got up and walked away.

It was only as she approached the window and saw her reflection that she realized she was feeling aroused. It shocked her to think she could be responding this way at such a time, but there was no doubt that her nipples were tight, and a gentle heat between her legs was making her wet. Just what the heck was going on inside her that she could actually want sex right now? And was it Elliot she wanted, or Nick? She didn't dare look back over her shoulder for she knew it was him. She imagined herself pressed up against the counter, or spread out on the sofa with him. Would he do it now if she took off her dress and asked him? Would seeing her naked arouse him as

406

intensely as the thought of him naked was arousing her? Or would the brazenness remind him of Andraya?

She took another gulp of wine, and almost as swiftly as it had come, the arousal subsided. She continued to gaze out at the night, and felt strangely sad, and even vaguely bereft. Her eyes moved to Elliot's reflection and she wondered about the gulf that seemed to keep opening and closing between them. Would they ever bridge it? At moments she felt sure they would, then at others she wasn't even certain she wanted to.

Finally the meal was ready and she carried their plates to the table, while Elliot brought in the wine. He wasn't sure who'd drunk the most from the previous bottle, but it had gone down quickly, and he guessed the next one might too.

As they started to eat he filled the silence by asking about Katie, how she was, how the interview had gone, and whether she'd committed to making the programme. Laurie answered, drank more wine, and watched him in the candlelight. For a while she felt oddly detached, as though she were dining in a dream, or with a stranger, then she looked at him across the table and felt such a surge of love that her appetite fled and her eyes filled with tears. Quickly she blinked them back and forced herself to go on eating.

'Tell me, is he expecting you to end it between us tonight?' he said abruptly.

Unable even to pretend she was hungry now, she put down her knife and fork and reached for her glass. 'No. I – I don't know,' she said.

'Did you tell him you would?'

'Not exactly, no. I – '

His face was turning pale as he said, 'Do you want to end it? If you do, let's finally get it out in the open and stop all this.'

'No, I don't want to end it. I told you, I love you and I don't want to lose you . . .'

'But you don't want to give him up. Then maybe you should spend some time with him, find out what it is you do want.'

She looked at him and beneath the angry reaction to his words she felt herself aching with the hurt it would cause him if she did that. Then she thought about Nick and being with him all the time, and felt so confused she just couldn't think any more.

'Where is he tonight?' he asked.

'He's at home I think. Elliot, please, let's stop doing this.'

He bit back the response that sprang to his lips and picked up his wine. She was right, they were hurting each other – or, more accurately, he was trying to hurt her, and what purpose would that serve when he wanted to keep her, not push her away?

Long minutes ticked by. They attempted to carry on eating, though without much success. In the end, she said, 'Can I come and sit with you?'

Surprised, and not entirely sure he understood, he watched as she left her place and came to sit on his lap.

'I love you so much,' she murmured, burying her face in his neck.

He kissed the top of her head and held her close. 'I love you too,' he said gruffly. Then tilting her chin up, he ran his thumb over her lips and gazed deeply into her eyes. 'Are you going to eat any more?' he asked.

'I don't think so.'

'Then let's go and sit down.'

Taking her hand he led her over to the sofa, where he pulled her back on to his lap and rested his head on hers. For a while they simply listened to the music, and felt their closeness as powerfully as they always had. In this moment it just didn't seem possible that he'd lose her, for he could feel her love as though it were flowing into him, and was certain she must be able to feel his too. This was how they had been in Bali, completely together, needing no-one else, and knowing they could get past their difficulties because they loved each other so much. It was sobering to realize how readily they had believed in their relationship then, yet how fragile it actually was now they could no longer deny that it lacked the vital element of trust.

With her thoughts travelling to the same part of the world, though connecting with a more light-hearted memory, Laurie started to smile as she said, 'Do you remember the monkeys in Bali? The one that wouldn't get off your head?'

He laughed. 'And the flaming creature's balls dropping in my eyes? How could I forget?'

She laughed too, remembering how she'd been so helpless at the time she couldn't even point the camera.

'And what about the spectacular entrance you made when we arrived?' he reminded her.

Closing her eyes she started to laugh again, for as they'd walked into the hotel she'd twisted her ankle, buckled to the floor, and rolled sideways down the steps into the lobby. Elliot hadn't stopped laughing for a week, and he was laughing again now.

There were other amusing incidents and people they'd come across during their trip, which led them on to other places they'd visited, or people they knew, until inevitably they found themselves talking about the time they'd spent at Max Erwin's place in Mexico. It was where they'd made love for the first time, in the candle-lit courtyard of Max's exquisite hideaway villa, where the vast tropical plants drooped over the pool like mystical guardians, while the gloriously triumphant arias of Puccini had urged them to even greater heights of shared bliss.

'I'd like to go there again, wouldn't you?' she murmured, turning to look at him.

His eyes rested on hers, then dropped to her mouth as she came forward to kiss him.

He didn't kiss her back, so she kissed him again, until finally she felt him starting to respond. Then he wrapped her deeply into his arms and kissed her for a long, long time, holding her close and feeling her desire pulling like a magnet at his own. Everything about her felt so right, and so profoundly his that he knew it would be the easiest thing in the world now to lift her in his arms and carry her up to bed. His hand moved to her legs and began to smooth the bare skin of her thighs. As he felt them part the temptation to move his hand higher was so intense that making it stop was one of the hardest things he'd ever done. He wanted her so badly, but tomorrow she was likely to be in the bed of another

410

man, and until that was resolved he wouldn't allow himself to make love to her again. So pulling away he gazed down into her eyes and said, 'I have some calls I need to make.'

For a moment she seemed dazed, as though she hadn't heard him, but as he eased her gently from his lap she moved aside and buried her face in her hands. 'I just don't understand you,' she said, as he got up.

He waited for her to look up at him, then in a voice heavy with meaning he said, 'I think you do.'

He started to walk away, heading for his study.

'Can we at least sleep together tonight?' she asked. 'Just sleep.'

'I've already made up the guest bed for myself,' he told her, and carried on walking.

Chapter Eighteen

'You fancy him, don't you?' Molly teased.

'Who?' Katie winced at the elbow in her side as Molly made herself more comfy in the bed beside her.

'You know who. I saw you last night, when we were having dinner, laughing at all his jokes and speaking in that funny voice . . .'

'What funny voice?'

'The one you always put on when you fancy someone. You should hear yourself, you go all like, posh and witty and blah . . .'

'I'm always like that,' Katie protested, laughing.

'Yeah, but you still fancy him.'

'Of course I don't.'

'Of course you *doooo*!'

Katie gasped as Molly started to tickle her. 'Stop it! Stop,' she cried, trying to push her away.

'Not until you admit it. Say, I fancy Tom Chambers.'

'Ssh, someone'll hear you.'

'Like who? It's not even eight o'clock and we're

412

the only ones here.' And feeling like, so released because Michelle wasn't there, and so able to breathe again, she wrapped her arms round her mother and hugged her hard.

'Ow! What was that for?' Katie grimaced, wishing she'd taken her morphine already, because the pain was quite bad this morning and she didn't want to get up yet.

'It was just for nothing,' Molly told her.

Turning on to her side so she could see her better, Katie said, 'So tell me about this Brad.'

'Oh no,' Molly protested, blushing. 'We're not changing the subject until *you* admit you fancy Tom.'

Assuming one of her best long-suffering looks, designed to tell someone of fourteen that they were right in what they'd picked up on, but wrong in the way they'd interpreted it, Katie said, 'He's a very attractive man, and I like him a lot, but even you must have noticed he's mad about Michelle and . . .'

'Do you reckon he'll take her with him when he goes?' Molly jumped in. 'It would be so cool if he did, wouldn't it? We'd be like, just you and me again, the way it used to be. It's better like that, isn't it? I mean, I know like, Michelle's your sister, and all that, and she's company for you, but this place isn't really big enough for all of us, is it?'

Katie's heart weighed heavily as she looked into Molly's pretty green eyes, that, ironically, were so like Michelle's and so unable to disguise all the inner turmoil she was trying to suppress. If ever there was a right time to tell her the truth it was probably now, she realized, while no-one else was around and wouldn't be for several hours, until

Tom and Michelle came back for lunch. So could she muster the words? Was she able to tell Molly right now why Michelle had to stay, and why nothing was going to be the same again?

Almost as though sensing what was coming, Molly started to draw back. At the same instant a giant fist of pain clenched Katie's insides. She gasped, and quickly turned it into a laugh as Molly paled. 'Come here,' she growled playfully, starting to tickle her. 'I haven't finished with you yet.'

'No! Stop! *Stop!*' Molly cried, laughing.

'Not unless you go and make some tea and bring up the paper.'

'All right! All right! Anything, just stop . . . tickling . . .'

Katie let her go, and grinned as she watched her catch her breath.

'You know what would be really cool,' Molly said, rolling on to her back and staring up at the ceiling, 'is if *Michelle* went and *Tom* stayed.'

'Molly! Will you get it out of your head that I fancy Tom. I told you . . .'

'I know, I know, but it would be cool, wouldn't it? I mean, we could be like a family, and then you might stop flirting with everyone and embarrassing me.'

Katie exploded with laughter. 'I do not flirt,' she protested.

'Oh, excuse me. What about that time with Elliot Russell? Oh my God, I wanted to die.'

Katie was still laughing. 'Actually, if anyone was flirting with Tom last night, I think it was you.'

Molly was totally grossed out. 'Oh puhleeze,' she snorted. 'He's old enough to be my grandfather.'

414

'I don't think so,' Katie responded. 'Not even close, in fact.'

'Well, he's definitely old.'

Though Katie was still smiling, the pain was forming such a grip on her now that she could hardly think past it. She closed her eyes and held herself rigid as she waited for it to peak, knowing she should breathe through it, but she couldn't with Molly there. At the top she thought she might scream it was so bad, but mercifully, after a moment or two, it started slowly to shrink back, and not long after that she was able to say, in a voice that was only slightly shredded, 'Where's that tea? I'm gasping.'

Springing out of bed, Molly charged off down the stairs, Trotty at her heels, while Katie forced herself up and into the bathroom. The fact that the pain was so bad this soon after the chemo top-up was scaring her badly, though she tried to take comfort from the fact that she was rarely this late with her drugs.

After swilling down the morphine, followed by the anti-emetics, then the megace, she stood over the sink waiting for the fiery swords inside to blunt, and finally fade. It was several minutes before she could lift her head, or even move a muscle, but finally as the morphine started to take effect she was able to inhale a deep, shuddering breath and look in the mirror. Thanks to the fake tan she'd used for her interview she didn't look as bad as she felt, though the yellowness of her eyes seemed much more noticeable this morning, and her lips were bloodless and cracked.

Improving that with water and a faint smear of

lipstick, she took another deep breath and started back to the bedroom. As she reached the landing she could hear Molly clattering about downstairs, while singing along to the radio, and chatting to Trotty. She paused for a moment to listen, and pictured her dancing about in her white lacy tank top and thin pyjama bottoms, thinking she was the coolest thing ever to hit fourteen. Was she really planning to decimate the poor child's rare good mood with the worst news imaginable? Tom was fairly certain he'd have to leave by tonight, tomorrow morning at the latest, so why spoil what little time he was here? It wasn't as if she was going to pop her clogs in the next twenty-four hours, or even the next week – perhaps even month . . . Aha, there was that old devil hope again, batting around in the positive court, and knocking back the horizons every time it took a swipe.

Going to snuggle back under the duvet she closed her eyes and let her thoughts drift as the pain continued to subside. Michelle's talk at the village hall had gone down well last night, and everyone had been delighted to have Tom join in. Molly, predictably, had muttered that Michelle was dead boring – though she'd looked fascinated enough – but it seemed Tom could do no wrong in her eyes, and for that, at least, Katie was thankful. Tom was going to play a big part in Molly's life, Katie was sure of it, because one look at Michelle's flushed and happy face last night was enough to tell her that something had been decided between them. Katie suspected, hoped, it was the commitment Michelle longed for, and that would give Molly the family and stability she needed.

416

After a while her thoughts moved on to Laurie and how things might have gone with Elliot last night. It was easy to imagine it all working out between them, for she didn't doubt that they still loved each other, but would that be enough in the end? She certainly hoped so, though if the past few months had taught her anything, it was that life had a peculiar way of changing the course just when you were least expecting it. Actually, she wouldn't mind it changing course for her right now, but since that was unlikely to happen, she'd pluck herself from the shallows of self-pity, and plump up the pillows a bit, because Molly was trudging up the stairs with breakfast. In fact, she was starting to feel a bit peckish, she realized, so the megace must be motoring home to the right address.

Putting the tray on the bed, Molly tucked one leg under her as she sat down next to it and began to pour out the tea. After passing a cup to her mother she sat chewing on the side of her thumbnail, while Katie spread out the paper.

'What's going on in that head of yours?' Katie asked, scanning the editorial page.

Molly shrugged. 'Nothing.'

'Yes it is, so come on, out with it. I expect it's Brad, so I want to hear all about him.'

'It's not Brad,' Molly protested. 'If you must know, I was thinking that it really would be cool if Tom could stay here, and Michelle could be the one to go.'

With a sinking heart Katie looked up and fixed her with implacable eyes. 'Michelle's staying,' she said gently.

417

Molly flushed and quickly picked up her toast. 'You're not eating yours,' she said, passing a slice to Katie.

Katie took it, and started to eat, wondering what was really cooking in those frontal lobes of her daughter's, for she surely wasn't telling herself that a relationship with Tom Chambers was possible. 'Are you going to help me with lunch?' she said after a while.

Molly sighed. 'OK, but do I have to stay?'

Katie looked at her in surprise.

Molly's expression was already moulding itself round a begging sort of protest. 'Oh Mum,' she cried, before Katie could even speak. '*Please!* You know I hate Sunday roast, and I said I'd go over to Allison's to watch *EastEnders*, because I haven't seen it all week, and she's got this new DVD with all these pop videos . . .'

'But Tom and Michelle are coming. I thought you'd want to see Tom . . .'

'I do, but he'll probably still be here when I get back so I can see him then. Oh, please, Mum, please.'

Katie was frowning suspiciously. 'Is this Brad going to be there?' she asked. 'Is that why you're so keen to go?'

'No! I swear. I just want to go over there. And you know what you're like, when you all get together. It'll be the same as last night, you'll just talk about politics and boring stuff like that, so you don't want me hanging around.'

Having to concede that it probably wouldn't be much fun for Molly when they became engrossed in all the research again, which they inevitably

418

would, she said, 'OK, just stay and say hello, and at least have a starter.'

'All right,' Molly agreed, and climbing back into bed next to Katie she rested her head on her shoulder and started flicking through the Review.

Stuart Fellowes was with DI Jack Wilding at Paddington Green police station. They were waiting for the arrest warrant to come through that would allow them to pick up Tom Chambers, who they now knew was holed up with his girlfriend in a Wiltshire hotel. Unofficially Fellowes was running the show, which wasn't sitting well with Wilding, but the man would just have to swallow it. Britain might be his territory, but this was predominantly America's war, and Chambers was one of theirs.

The instructions were to keep it low key. No SWAT teams, no sirens, and as few uniforms as possible. They already had a satellite positioning on both locations – the hotel and the girlfriend's home – knew how long it would take to get there, and had just primed the nearest safe facility to be ready for Chambers once they had him. An advance team of two was on its way down the M4 now to stake the place out and keep Fellowes and Wilding in touch with what was happening on the ground.

Slouched in his chair, Fellowes looked at the clock. Ten thirty-six. That would put it at five thirty-six a.m. in Washington. Someone had to be out of bed though, to have sent the email telling him a warrant was being prepared for Chambers's arrest, so he needed to get himself over to Paddington and be ready to move.

So he was here, and ready, and now Fellowes would like to know what the hell was taking them so long.

Not much more than a mile away, at SIS HQ in Vauxhall Cross, Michael Dalby, Sir Christopher Malton and Edmund Foxe-Randall, the Prime Minister's Chief of Staff, were engaged in a highly secure video-conference call to Washington. At the other end were Daniel Allbringer, Deborah Gough, and the deputy director of the FBI, Stanley Jacobs.

'I repeat,' Dalby was saying, 'to pick him up in this country is asking for trouble. The press will be straight on it, and if you're not ready to back up those charges . . .'

'He's carrying the evidence,' Allbringer interrupted, 'we just need to make sure he's in possession when they make the arrest. Or that it's in the vicinity.'

'And if it's not?'

'Our guys can deal with it. Once he's in custody, he won't be your problem.'

'Do you have a press statement ready?' Foxe-Randall enquired.

'It's being worked on now. It'll be finished by the time it's needed. Now, you're certain Russell, Forbes and van Zant are all in London?'

'That's right,' Dalby confirmed. 'But let me remind you again that if you want to do this out of sight of the press you're choosing the wrong location. Katie Kiernan, the girlfriend's sister, isn't only one of them, but in her time she was extremely influential, not least of all with the public. Add to that the fact that she's a single mother dying of cancer, then you tell me if you think that's the house to go storming into.'

'It won't be necessary if Chambers is still at the hotel,' Deborah Gough stated. 'And let's not forget, gentlemen, this man has a long track record of associating with terrorists, and since he's currently carrying evidence of a plot to attack one of your nuclear sites I don't see what the hell difference it makes where we pick him up.'

The three men in Dalby's office exchanged glances. The woman had obviously made up her mind about this. She wanted Chambers in custody, which none of them had a problem with, but for as long as he was on their territory they were going to be answerable to the House and the British public – and with Elliot Russell asking the questions, they had to be damned certain they could make this stand up.

'We need to see the press statement and the warrant,' Foxe-Randall stated. 'Until then, no-one moves.'

Laurie and Elliot were walking hand in hand along the river path, heading towards Tate Modern. It was a chilly, dull morning, so they both wore coats and scarves, and in Laurie's case dark glasses to mask her tired eyes. She hadn't slept well, and she didn't think Elliot had either, for the light in the guest room had been on when she'd gone downstairs to get a drink around three, and he'd been up before her this morning, because he'd brought her tea and croissants in bed.

He'd stayed to eat with her, and had linked his fingers through hers as they'd talked, but when she'd allowed the strap of her nightie to slide off her shoulder, almost revealing a breast, he'd merely lifted it up again, and after kissing her briefly on the mouth had picked up the tray and carried it back downstairs.

That his willpower was so unshakable was unsettling her badly, though for the moment they'd put their relationship problems on hold in order to discuss what Tom's next moves were going to be.

'Chris is already on standby to whisk him over to France,' Elliot was saying. 'He'll leave tonight, or in the morning, and I'll join him in a couple of days, down at Jean-Jacques' place in Burgundy.'

Remembering the long weekends they'd spent at the quaint little cottage at the edge of a tiny hamlet, Laurie said, 'Don't forget Jean-Jacques always expects the best wine to be left after he's loaned the place out.'

Elliot smiled. 'Considering the location, that's never a problem,' he responded. Then bringing them back to today, 'What time is Nick expecting you?'

'Around one,' she answered, managing to keep her voice as neutral as his.

'If the '97 version gives us the proof, or connection we're looking for,' he said, 'we could be ready for print by the end of the week.'

'Have you decided who you want to run it?'

'We think a simultaneous publishing event is probably the way to go – if we can pull it off,' he answered. 'It's what I was making calls about last night. One of them was to Nick. He's going to set up meetings with various European editors over the next few days to brief them on the way this is going, and get an idea of who's willing to run with it, and who's not. Pissing off the US isn't particularly recommended for the long-term health, so there might not be as many takers as we'd like. Max will have a bigger problem, because he's doing the same in the States.'

Thrown by the fact that he'd been speaking to Nick at the very time Nick was probably assuming she was ending the relationship, she found herself turning slightly hot with discomfort. 'Is there anything more I can do, besides help run a comparison of the documents?' she said, wondering what else he'd talked to Nick about. 'Any statements or interviews you need? Backgrounds?'

'Would you like some coffee?' he said, as they approached a café that was open.

'Not unless you would.'

'I'm fine. What I was thinking,' he continued, as they walked on, 'was that you might like to go with Nick when he leaves for Europe tomorrow. You're as informed on the details as he is, and it would probably help considerably to have a double presentation, plus it would give you the chance to spend some time together.'

Hardly able to believe what he'd said, or the matter-of-fact way in which he'd delivered it, she stopped and turned to face him. 'I take it you're not serious,' she said.

Experiencing relief that she'd responded that way, he said, 'On the contrary, I'm absolutely serious. I thought you would welcome it as a chance to find out if your relationship could work.'

423

Her eyes turned bright with anger. This wasn't making any sense, because no-one could just let someone they loved – *someone they were supposed to be rebuilding a relationship with* – take off with another man. If the roles were reversed and there was a chance of him going somewhere with Andraya she'd not only be beside herself, she'd be doing everything she could to stop him. So something wasn't right, and she had a horrible, sickening feeling she knew what it was.

'I want to know what's going on,' she demanded. 'Why are you doing this?'

'You told me last night that you don't know what you want,' he reminded her. 'I'm trying, for all our sakes, to help you find out, and I thought spending some time with him . . .'

She was shaking her head. 'No, there's more to it,' she insisted. 'You're trying to get me out of the way and I want to know why.'

He frowned in confusion. 'What on earth are you talking about? I'm not even going to be here myself. I'll be with Tom, in France. Jesus Christ, Laurie. You're the one having an affair here, not me, so don't . . .'

'Are you sure about that?' she cut in.

His jaw immediately tightened. 'Yes, I'm sure, but obviously you aren't.'

Fury was draining the blood from her face. 'I know she's in London,' she told him, her eyes blazing the challenge.

He didn't even flinch. 'This has got nothing to do with her,' he responded, 'so before we go any further with this, let me say it again, *you* are the one having an affair . . .'

'And you are the one who seems ecstatically happy about it. So I want to know why? Doesn't it bother you, to think of me with another man? You know what we'll be doing, so doesn't it mean anything to you?'

His face was turning pale, as his anger clearly deepened. 'If that's what you think, then we could be wasting our time,' he said darkly.

'I don't know what to think,' she shouted, 'but I do know that I'm finding your response to me and Nick very strange indeed.'

'Well I'm sorry if I can't oblige with the way you think I should respond,' he said bitingly, 'but this is it! This is the way I'm handling it, and if it doesn't work for you, then I'm afraid that's your problem, not mine.'

She was so angry now that it was right on the tip of her tongue to tell him that there was no point going on, they clearly weren't ever going to work things out, so they might just as well stop trying. Had an exuberant dog not suddenly bounded up to her out of the blue, knocking her back a few paces, nothing would have stopped her.

Immediately the dog's owners came rushing up to apologize, the dog was scolded, and as Laurie assured them there was no harm done, while ruffling the dog's head, the moment of intense anger passed.

As the couple walked on, Elliot turned back to Laurie. 'If you don't want to go to Europe with Nick, no-one's going to be happier than me,' he told her.

She turned sharply away to look off across the river.

'I can't help noticing that you aren't turning the opportunity down,' he commented.

Her eyes came back to his. 'Why should I, when you've made it perfectly clear you don't want me in your bed,' she snapped nastily.

'Not while you're sleeping with another man,' he told her. 'Now let's drop this, shall we? We're starting to become a sideshow, and I don't think that's what either of us wants.'

Realizing that they were indeed attracting attention, Laurie fell into step beside him as he turned back in the direction of Shad Thames, and though still furious, she slipped a hand into his pocket, and felt his fingers link around hers.

Neither of them spoke the entire way back, though she was acutely aware of the mounting tension. As they rode up in the lift, still silent, they stared harshly into each other's eyes, letting the air between them continue to simmer. Then quite suddenly, Elliot tilted her face to his and kissed her fully on the mouth. Almost buckling under the powerful surge of desire, she did nothing to resist. When the door opened he was still kissing her, and he didn't stop until one of their neighbours gave a polite little cough to let them know she was there.

Apologizing, they stepped out of the lift, but as they started towards the front door Laurie stopped dead in shock.

Elliot collided into her, then he too saw the woman standing outside their apartment.

'Elliot, darling,' Andraya purred, her big sultry eyes and pouting lips oozing more appeal than could ever be decent. 'I am sorry. Have I come too early?'

426

Laurie's heart twisted with horror. He'd invited her here?

'What the hell are you doing?' Elliot demanded. 'I told you . . .'

'I know, darling, you told me not to come while she was here, but I thought . . .'

'For God's sake! It's over, Andraya,' he shouted.

Andraya's lustrous eyes stayed on him as she let her raincoat fall open. Beneath was a skintight, snake-print cat suit that was open to the waist and revealed almost all of her enormous olive-toned breasts. 'I understand you are saying that for her benefit,' she purred, 'but she needs to know the truth, Elliot. I'm sure he's told you that it is over between us,' she said to Laurie, 'and it was . . . I thought I was bored, you see, but I was wrong . . . He is such a good lover, as you know.'

Laurie could hardly tear her eyes away. This was her nemesis. Her arch-rival. The source of all her misery and nightmares. She was like a snake shedding its skin in that cringingly tarty catsuit with its zip right down to her navel and all that garish black and silver lycra clinging to her limbs. Even so, there was no denying the power of her sexuality, nor the mesmerizing potency of her beauty, for it emanated from her in waves strong enough to stun any prey. Even Laurie couldn't claim to be immune, for next to a woman like Andraya it was hard to feel anything but drab.

Then she realized Elliot was saying nothing, and Andraya was smiling into his eyes.

'When you called yesterday,' Andraya was murmuring, her carefully manicured fingers stroking her cleavage, 'I know straight away that . . .'

427

Laurie looked at him. He'd called her!

Unable to bear another moment, she spun round and started to run. Elliot tried to grab her, but she was too fast, and tearing open the fire door she raced down the stairs to the car park.

It was only when she was halfway to Nick's that she realized Elliot had neither tried to call her mobile nor come after her.

The chicken was roasting away, the potatoes had just gone in and the rest of the vegetables were chilling out in cold water ready for the big steam-up. Now Katie had time to relax with the paper for ten minutes before Molly emerged from the shower, where she was currently blunting razors with her unhairy legs.

'Come on Trots,' she said to the dog, who was looking all downcast and fluffy after being plopped in the bath following her morning walk, 'time for coffee and a cuddle.'

As she led the way into the sitting room, her eye was caught by a small grey metal case that was poking out from under a cushion on the sofa. Recognizing it as Laurie's organizer, she felt surprised that Laurie hadn't missed it – or maybe she had, and hadn't realized it was here. 'Better call and let her know it's safe,' she told Trotty.

After dialling the Butler's Wharf apartment, she carried the phone back into the sitting room, and was just sinking into her sumptuous fireside chair when Elliot's voice came down the line.

'Hi, it's Katie,' she told him. 'Are you still in bed?'

'At midday?' he responded, 'that would be a treat. Is everything OK your end?'

'Yes, yes. We're all sizzling along. I'm calling to tell Laurie she left her life-support machine here yesterday, in case she's looking for it. By that, I mean her Palm Pilot thingy.'

'I don't think she's missed it,' he said. 'Or she hasn't mentioned it, but she's not here, I'm afraid.'

'OK, I'll try her mobile, but before I go, am I allowed to ask how things are between you?'

Elliot sighed. 'Probably about as bad as they can get,' he answered. 'Andraya turned up with no warning about twenty minutes ago and now Laurie's on her way to Nick's, or I presume she is. She has to go there anyway to pick up the pages he brought back from the States, and I'm trying to take your advice to give her some space.'

Katie's head drew back as she looked at the phone in amazement. 'I don't think now is the time to do that,' she told him. 'It's reassurance she needs, after coming face to face with your mistress.'

'She's *not* my mistress, and let's not forget, Katie, Laurie's the one having an affair here, not me.'

'No, what she's doing is fixating on another man because she's afraid of trusting you again, and if Andraya's going to start popping up all over the place . . . Where is she now?'

'God knows. I managed to get rid of her, but Laurie had already gone by then.'

Katie shook her head in dismay. 'Elliot, you have to get that woman off your back, or you really will be heading for trouble.'

'Believe me, I'm trying, but she's not someone who has a great understanding of no.'

429

'Then you'll have to be blisteringly brutal,' Katie told him, standing up as she heard a car arriving outside.

'Even more than I already have,' he said wryly. 'I didn't end it with much subtlety, I can tell you, but that's a story for another time.'

'I'm afraid it'll have to be, as my lunch guests have just bowled up early,' she said, giving Michelle a wave. 'But I will say this, there's giving someone space and then there's giving them so much space they end up thinking you don't care. So remember what I told you, make sure she knows she's loved, then let her take a look at what she's doing.'

Elliot groaned. 'This is too much for a mere male,' he complained. 'Tell me, was suggesting she should go to Europe with Nick next week the wrong thing to do?'

Once again Katie looked at the phone in amazement. 'What did she say?' she demanded.

'She wasn't very pleased.'

Katie chuckled. 'I'll bet she wasn't. I'll bet she doesn't go either. In fact, if it weren't for Andraya's bad timing, I'd say you'd be very much on course for relationship rescue right now. But all is not lost. You love each other, and in the end that's what really counts. Now I really must go.'

'I love you,' he told her. 'I'll call again later. And thanks.'

'Any time.'

Going to drop the phone back on its base, Katie beamed as Michelle came in the door with a bottle of champagne and a huge bunch of roses. 'Bottle from me, flowers from Tom,' Michelle declared.

Then frowning, 'Are you OK? You look a bit peaky.'

'Charming,' Katie retorted, and shoved her aside to get stuck into a good hearty hug with Tom. 'How was the hotel?' she asked.

'It was great,' he answered. 'Kind of old and charming and quintessentially English.'

'Much like the piece you were there with?' she said cheerily.

Michelle's eyes narrowed. 'I missed you,' she told her.

'I missed you too.' Walking into each other's arms, they embraced warmly. 'Can we open the bottle now?' Katie asked.

'I hope so,' Tom answered. 'We're celebrating.'

Katie's brows arched curiously, though one look at their faces was enough to confirm her earlier suspicions. 'Don't tell me, you're going to make an honest woman of her,' she declared.

Tom grinned. 'That's the plan. And we're going to base ourselves here, so you don't have to worry about a thing.'

Feeling her throat tighten, Katie wrapped Michelle in her arms again. 'I'm so happy for you,' she whispered. 'I knew it would happen, of course, though God knows you took your time, the two of you.'

'Which is why we're not going to waste any more,' Tom informed her, starting to open the champagne. 'Just as soon as we can arrange it, she's going to become Mrs Chambers.'

Michelle's eyes were so full of love as she looked up at him, that Katie might have imitated a violin had she not felt herself moving close to tears.

'I'm such a sentimental old thing,' she laughed, dabbing them away, and deciding that perhaps it wouldn't be a good idea to tell them that Molly already had designs on Tom as a father, since, for the moment at least, it was the wrong mother.

'We'd like Molly to be bridesmaid,' Michelle said, taking some glasses down from the cupboard.

'And you to be my best woman,' Tom added.

'Oh my, oh my,' Katie cried, as more tears began flowing down her cheeks. 'How wonderful. Of course, we'd love to, both of us. Wouldn't we, Molly?' she said, as Molly dropped down from the last stair into the kitchen. She was wearing, Katie noted immediately, not only the earrings and necklace Michelle had told her last night were actually from Tom, but a snazzy little top that concertinaed over her C-cups at full stretch. The sulky little smirk that she reserved for people she was happy to see, while not necessarily wanting them to know this, was also in evidence. In fact, Katie thought with a thud of alarm, she'd obviously decided to have a go at hooking Tom on her mother's behalf.

'Wouldn't we what?' Molly asked, blushing as Tom looked at her admiringly.

Bracing herself, and already praying the response wouldn't be too shudderingly horrible, Katie said, 'Tom and Michelle are getting married.'

Molly's face instantly drained.

'Have some champagne,' Katie coaxed, thrusting a glass at her.

'I don't want it!' Molly snapped.

'Hey, Molly,' Tom chided. 'I thought you'd be happy for us.'

'What's it got to do with me? I don't care what you do,' Molly said tightly, and shooting Michelle a scathing look she stalked out of the door.

'No, don't,' Tom said, as Katie started furiously after her.

'But she can't be allowed to get away with that,' Katie protested.

'Look, deep inside she's suffering,' he said gently, 'we know that, and we know why. So it's not something that can be dealt with by hauling her back here and making her apologize. We have to come at it another way, and I don't think today's the day to start trying. So let her go, she'll come back when she's ready, and if we feel it's appropriate to deal with it then, we will. If not, it *will* be dealt with, and hopefully in a way that's going to make her less hostile towards Michelle, and a little more receptive to what's actually happening.'

The lump was back in Katie's throat as she looked at him. 'You're going to make a wonderful father,' she told him hoarsely.

His eyes moved to Michelle. 'I hope so,' he said softly.

Michelle smiled and went to put her arms around him. 'You will,' she assured him, as he kissed her gently on the lips.

Katie watched, and as a new little suspicion began to take root she tried to decide whether it would be good for Molly if Michelle were pregnant. She wasn't sure it would, because Molly might start to feel left out, and if Robbie came to join them too then Michelle would have two of her own who'd inevitably come before Molly. Except

Michelle wasn't like that. She loved everyone, and knowing her she'd go out of her way to put Molly first, but the fear of Molly feeling lonely and left out was already descending. Knowing she wasn't going to be able to blank it out easily, Katie decided to give Michelle and Tom a few private minutes for their not-so-secret secret. So excusing herself, she trotted off upstairs for a quick slug of morphine and a hasty commune with her higher self, after which she should be able to come down again, all fresh and cheery and ready to put on the sprouts.

Fellowes's opaque brown eyes slid from the news-paper he was reading to the phone on Wilding's desk. The British double ring had always irritated him, and having waited so long for this one made no difference.

Wilding picked up the receiver, listened to the voice at the other end then passed it to Fellowes.

It was Nancy Goodman letting him know that the arrest warrant had come through. 'I'll bring it over right away,' she told him.

'We'll meet you out front,' Fellowes responded and put down the phone. 'OK,' he said to Wilding, 'let's move.'

Chapter Nineteen

Laurie was sitting on the sofa in Nick's spacious basement apartment, hugging her knees to her chest, while keeping her face buried in her arms. Her conscience was in shreds, her shame so complete that she just couldn't bring herself to look at him.

Next to her, Nick was staring at nothing, his face devoid of colour, his eyes livid with shock. Both of them were naked, still trapped in the nightmare of what had just happened, and the explosion of tempers that had followed.

They'd stopped shouting now, but it was only a temporary reprieve, for Nick's struggle to rein in his fury was fast turning into a losing battle. 'This wasn't the way to do it,' he finally growled. *'This wasn't the fucking way to do it.'*

'I know, and I'm sorry. I wish to God . . . I –'

'Just stop saying you're sorry. It doesn't make it any better,' and getting up he went to pull on the jeans that she'd virtually torn from him the instant she came in the door. 'I don't mind being used for sex,' he shouted, suddenly rounding on her again, 'that's fine, because who wouldn't want to fuck you, you're beautiful, and you give as good as you get, but I do mind being thrown off in the middle of it because I'm the wrong fucking man.'

'That's not how it was,' she cried, pushing a hand roughly through her hair. 'When I arrived I wasn't thinking straight. I was so angry with him . . .'

'That you couldn't wait to fuck me just to get back at him!' he snarled. 'Yes, you already told me, thank you very much, I don't need to hear it again.'

'You surely wouldn't have wanted me to carry on once I realized,' she said angrily.

'I would have preferred we never got started,' he spat. 'Jesus Christ, of all the fucking moments to choose to tell me that you can't go on . . .' Enraged, he spun away and slammed a fist hard into the wall.

Never having felt more wretched, she lowered her head again and fought back the tears. He was right, there hardly could have been a worse moment for her to realize she was only making love with him because she thought Elliot was doing the same with Andraya.

'You know what really sickens me,' he raged, turning back to her, 'is how I fucking fell for it all. You told me you were going to end it with him last night. You let me believe that you were going to be a part of my life, and I bought it all. I even told my daughter, do you know that? That's how big a deal it was for me, that you and I were going to be together, but why the hell should you care? All that matters to you is that you get your revenge on him for shagging some Brazilian piece and if the rest of

436

us get hurt while you do it, well what the hell does it matter?'

'That's not what it was about,' she shouted. 'I was with you because I care for you and because . . .'

'That's exactly what it was about. You wanted to show him he wasn't the only one who could be unfaithful, and that you had the power to hurt him the way he hurt you. Jesus Christ. I should have seen this coming . . . I should have known you couldn't give him up . . .'

'I'm not saying I can't give him up! And anyway it's immaterial now, he's with her, and I don't want to lie to you. That's why I made you stop. Not because of him, because of you. It's not what you deserve.'

'Spare me the sanctimonious bullshit,' he snarled bitterly. 'I don't need it, and I sure as hell don't need it from you.'

Flinching at his tone, she watched as he turned away and dashed a hand through his hair.

'Nick, you're the last person in the world I want to hurt,' she said, going to him, 'and if I could . . .'

'Don't touch me,' he said, raising an arm to block her. 'I don't want your pity any more than your lies.'

'It's not pity. I want to hold you because I think we both need to be held.'

'Get it from him,' he growled, swinging round. 'You know he wants you so . . .'

'He's with Andraya now,' she cried, 'and I don't want to be here because of that, I want to be here because of us.'

He was shaking his head. 'I don't want to hear any more,' he told her. 'It's over between us,

Laurie. I'm not waiting around while you sort out your mess, listening to your false promises and supplying you with sex when he crushes you again. We're through, so don't even think about coming here again.'

'Nick, please don't let's end it like this. You're angry now, and upset . . .'

'Angry and upset doesn't even begin to cover it,' he told her savagely. 'Now, if you don't mind putting your clothes on, I'll get what you came here for and you can be on your way.'

'I'm not going anywhere, or doing anything while you're like this,' she said.

'Don't you get it?' he shouted. 'It disgusts me to see you like that now, so for God's sake cover yourself up.'

Her face paled, and quickly turning to grab her clothes she was almost out of the room when the phone started to ring.

He kept his eyes averted as he lifted the receiver, nor did he look at her when he said, 'Elliot. No, it's OK. You're not interrupting.'

Her heart somersaulted, then started to slow as he listened to what Elliot was saying, until frowning deeply he said, 'Christ. Does he know?' He listened again, then said, 'Sure. I'll pass you over.' As he handed her the phone he said, 'A warrant's been issued for Tom's arrest. Apparently they're on their way to pick him up now.'

Her eyes immediately widened with alarm, and grabbing the phone she said, 'When did you hear?'

'About ten minutes ago,' Elliot responded.

'I take it Tom knows.'

'Of course.'

'So what's he going to do?'

'It's in hand. Do you still have the camera in the car?'

'Yes. Why?'

'I want you to drive down to Katie's now and get whatever you can on record. They've got a good head start, but they'll probably still be there by the time you arrive. Apparently they want to do this out of sight of the press, so let's make damned sure they don't.'

Attempting to drag on her clothes, she said, 'Where are you?'

'At the flat, about to leave. Tell Nick to carry on as planned with Europe – if you're going with him . . .'

'I'm not,' she cut in.

There was a pause before he said, 'It wasn't what you're thinking. Andraya. I didn't ask her to come.'

Realizing she probably already knew that, she said, 'Let's talk about it later.'

As the line went dead she dropped the phone on the sofa and continued to dress. Nick had disappeared, but as she zipped up her jeans he came back holding a large brown envelope.

'The full '97 version,' he told her, tossing it on to a chair next to her bag.

'Thanks,' was all she could think of to say. 'Elliot said to continue with Europe.'

He made no response.

When she was ready she scooped everything up and turned to look at him.

'Just go,' he said shortly.

She took a breath. 'Nick, I –'

'I said, just go.'

Realizing that he had to get over his anger before they could even think about becoming friends, she quickly went up on tiptoe to kiss his cheek, then without saying any more she left.

'Come on, come on,' Katie was muttering under her breath. 'Where the hell are you?'

She was standing at the kitchen window making a pretence of washing up as she watched two men in a wine-coloured Mondeo parked in front of the pond. That they'd made no attempt to come in yet, though were doing nothing to disguise their presence, was confirmation enough, according to Tom, that their orders didn't include making the actual arrest.

'They'll be the advance troops,' he'd said after Elliot's call had put a quick end to the delicious meal that was still sitting half-eaten on the table. 'It'll be their job to make sure I stay put until the big boys arrive.'

'So what are you going to do?' Michelle had asked, looking as unnerved as Katie had felt.

'Figure out fast how to refuse my invite to the party,' he'd responded with typical irony.

Since he knew neither the territory, nor anyone nearby, it was Katie who'd finally said, 'OK, here's what we're going to do.'

Now Tom and Michelle were standing at the far end of the sitting room, close to the front door, eyes fixed on Katie as they waited for her signal to go.

Katie swallowed hard and quickly cut off any thought of the consequences they might all have to pay for her sudden flash of inspiration, for they could be dire. Instead she just focused on her loathing for the power maniacs who were behind all this. They weren't going to win. They just bloody well weren't.

'Anything?' Tom said.

She shook her head, then Judy's grey Panda came nosing into view, and her heart went into free fall. 'OK, she's here,' she said in a loud whisper. 'Don't move yet,' she cautioned, sensing Michelle and Tom ready to burst out of the door.

The Panda was edging up behind the Mondeo which was face on to the pond. The Panda slewed slightly to the left, looking as though it was about to turn round, but instead came to a stop across the back of the Mondeo, totally blocking it in.

'Go!' she cried.

Immediately Tom and Michelle tore open the front door, raced to the fence, leapt over and dived into Michelle's hire car. As they went Katie had visions of all the adventures they'd faced together in the past, and wondered how high this one rated on the danger list. The tyres squealed madly as Tom made a swerving reverse, then threw the car into first and roared off up the lane almost before the two watchdogs had time to stumble from the Mondeo. Judy was still sitting behind her steering wheel, looking every bit the bemused Sunday tourist who'd lost her way and stalled her engine mid three-point turn.

Seconds later one of the watchdogs was yelling at her to move the car. Pumped up with indignation, Judy leapt out to give him a piece of her mind. Wasting no more time he shoved her aside, jumped into the driver's seat, and shot the Panda forward. Then, abandoning it with the door

441

open, he threw himself into the Mondeo as it screamed out of its trap, spun round and sped off up the lane in pursuit of the red Peugeot.

Catching Judy's eye Katie saluted her with a champagne glass, then downed what was left in it while thanking God again and again that Molly wasn't here to make things really exciting.

Outside, Judy slipped back into the Panda, turned it around and tootled off towards home. By the time she got there, if all had gone to plan, Michelle's Peugeot would be tucked away inside Dave and Judy's garage, Michelle would be watching for the Mondeo to go roaring out of the village, and Tom would be heading south to Cornwall in Dave's ancient Renault 4, possibly with Dave at the wheel, or possibly driving it himself, Katie would have to wait to find out about that. In the meantime, she hit the champagne again and prayed to God that Judy and Dave didn't end up paying a horrible price for helping a wanted man to avoid arrest.

Feeling far too hyped up to tackle any more dishes, she was engaging in another quick one-to-one with God, asking him to bring Michelle back in the next few minutes, when the telephone suddenly shrilled into the silence. Fearing the worst, which had plenty of potential, she hurriedly snatched it up.

'Katie. It's Laurie. Is Tom still with you?'

'No. Are you on your way?'

'Yes. I'm just passing Swindon. Who's with you?'

'No-one at the moment, but I'm expecting a houseful any time.'

'I'll be there as soon as I can. Is there anyone you

442

can ask to come over, so's you're not on your own when they turn up?'

'Michelle should be back any second. If not, I'll work something out. Just don't be long.'

As she rang off the kitchen door opened and she almost swayed with relief as Michelle came in, looking pale, breathless and disturbingly wild-eyed. 'It worked,' she announced softly. 'Dave's gone with him, Chris is meeting them halfway.'

Aware that she'd probably had too much champagne, Katie clasped her in a hug, saying, 'It'll be fine. He'll make it. I know he will.'

'He always has before,' Michelle responded, sounding slightly less certain.

'They're looking for a red Peugeot,' Katie reminded her. 'And by the time they realize they're not, he probably won't even be in the country any more.'

Michelle forced a smile, and tried to ignore the misgivings that seemed to be gathering on a close horizon. 'I wish I could have gone with him,' she said, picturing Tom beside Dave in the clapped-out Renault as they'd driven out of the village. She'd had a dreadful premonition come over her in those moments that, thank God, was no longer with her, but she'd been so convinced at the time that she was seeing him for the last time that she'd almost run after him. Of course she'd never have caught the car, and even if she had, what would she have done? She couldn't go with him, nor would she have tried to persuade him to stay. She understood as well as he did that the official warrant for his arrest meant that they'd now gathered, fabricated and doctored enough evidence against him to feel secure in their efforts to silence him.

'What's even worse,' she said to Katie, 'is that he's just turned himself into a fugitive, so maybe we've played straight into their hands, because there's nothing, not even the law, to stop them now. They could even kill him and claim he was resisting arrest.'

'They're not going to do that,' Katie protested. 'There are too many of us who know the truth. They'd never get away with it.'

'With a charge of conspiracy to terrorism hanging over him, they can do anything. They've rewritten the law books, remember, here and in the States, and if they think they can make it stick . . .'

'Let me remind you again who he is,' Katie said firmly. 'And frankly, they've got more to worry about, because they're the ones taking these desperate, insidious measures to stop us exposing what lengths they're prepared to go to to hang on to power and jackboot through the world. Trying to brand a reputable journalist a terrorist is going to be their downfall.'

As she finished Michelle's eyes came to hers. They continued to look at each other, the meaning of the last few words becoming more apparent with each passing second.

Still slightly stunned by what she'd inadvertently stumbled upon, Katie said, 'Are you thinking what I'm thinking?'

Michelle nodded. 'This could be our proof.' she said.

'It's been staring us in the face all along.'

Again Michelle nodded.

Needing to spell it out, Katie said, 'Why would they go after Tom like this, go to such extremes to silence him, if the P2OG doesn't exist and all our deductions are wrong? They wouldn't. So it has to exist, and all we have to do is report everything that's happened since he received those documents, then sit back and let them explain.'

'Because we're not presenting it to a court of law,' Michelle continued, 'but to the court of public opinion, so it's a question of who's most likely to be believed. Us or them. The media or the hawks.'

Katie got to her feet. 'Actually, it hasn't been staring us in the face,' she said, 'it's been building, coming into focus with each step of the process. Someone, our anonymous benefactor, knows what he's doing. He can't get the proof to us, so he's helping us create another kind of proof, and one that can't be traced back to him.' She spun round to look at Michelle. 'We need Elliot's opinion on this,' she said, 'but I'm convinced we're right, and if we are, the only issue we're facing now is one of credibility. We have to pull it together in a way to make it utterly believable and virtually irrefutable, which shouldn't be hard.'

'There has to be something in the '97 version that's going to seal it,' Michelle said. 'Why else would someone keep pointing us in that direction?'

'And Nick has that version now.'

Hearing a car approach, Michelle turned sharply to the window and immediately felt her blood run cold. 'OK, looks like they're here,' she murmured, as a dark grey saloon drove in alongside Katie's Fiesta, followed by two more similar vehicles that came up behind, totally blocking the lane.

'Remember, Elliot said their instructions are to keep it low key, so if they start threatening to arrest us, hold firm. It's unlikely they'll do it today.'

'Oh lovely,' Katie muttered, 'something to look forward to tomorrow.'

As the car doors opened Michelle's alarm began to grow. There wasn't a uniformed officer amongst them, only men in bulky sports gear and trainers, or plain grey suits. 'Eight,' she finished counting, as they came towards the house. 'Why so many? They're bound to know by now that he's not here.'

Downing the last of the champagne, Katie fought back her nerves and braced herself for combat. She was well used to taking on authority, had made quite a career of it in fact, but she had to confess she'd never faced it at this level before, or from the unfortunately shaky ground of having just helped a wanted man to escape arrest. Without question this gave them the upper hand, but it didn't *give them the right* to go trudging all over her garden, poking about without introduction or invitation as though Tom was secreted under a flower pot, or riding a bucket down the well.

'The bloody nerve of it,' she declared, as one of them began turfing her spades out of the shed, but as she started towards the door Michelle pulled her back.

'Don't antagonize them,' she warned. 'We can be fairly certain they've got the power to do pretty much as they please . . .'

'Not in my house they haven't.'

'Katie, please. If they want to arrest us they probably can.'

At that Katie deflated, and wishing she hadn't

446

had quite so much champagne, she tried to assimilate her thoughts as Michelle went to open the door.

'Good afternoon, gentlemen,' she said politely. 'Can we help you?'

Fellowes turned from where he was watching the search to face her. Seeing who it was, his left eyebrow arched. 'Michelle Rowe,' he stated, looking her up and down.

Since he'd almost certainly have been told she was with Tom in the getaway car, she understood his surprise. 'Legal Attaché Fellowes,' she responded. 'Can I ask what this is about?'

'You know why we're here,' he retorted, 'so don't let's waste each other's time. You've just assisted a suspected felon to escape arrest, now you tell me where he is, and I won't arrest you.'

'I don't know what you're talking about. Who's the suspected felon?'

His eyes seemed to cut right through her as taking two paces forward he came breath-smellingly close. 'We know you were tipped off, we even know who made the call, so I'll ask the question again, where is he?'

Her eyes stayed rooted to his. This man was full of hate, she could sense it as though it were crawling all over her. 'I don't know,' she answered.

He stared back and waited, but was the first to look away as DI Wilding joined them. 'Time to get them inside,' Fellowes said roughly. 'Make sure they give it a thorough going-over, and take the computers for forensics.'

After glancing at Michelle, though making no attempt to reintroduce himself, Wilding barked the order, and stood aside as the other officers came swarming towards them. Michelle went in ahead and shot Katie a warning look as they began filling up the kitchen.

Katie watched, then tensed with outrage as they began pulling out drawers, rifling the contents, then dumping them on the floor.

Michelle moved swiftly to her side. 'Just think of Molly,' she muttered. 'You want to be here when she gets back.'

Katie looked at her, then at Fellowes as he squeezed in behind the others.

'Mrs Kiernan,' he said. 'Let's hope you've got more sense than your sister.'

'If you want anything from me, you can tell these men to stop their vandalism right now!' she retorted fiercely.

'This house is known to have been used by a suspected terrorist,' he responded smoothly. 'It has to be searched.'

Michelle's heart was thudding. 'You know damned well he's no terrorist,' she said, unable to keep the contempt from her voice.

Fellowes's face was an unpleasant mask of distaste as he turned back to her. 'What I know,' he said, 'is that scum like him should never be allowed to call themselves an American.'

'What the hell?' Katie exclaimed, as something smashed in the sitting room, and charging in there, she saw one of her mother's vases in pieces on the hearth. 'What have you done?' she cried, glaring at the man who was turning a couple of pieces of paper over in his hand. 'Why did you do that? You could have just taken them out. They're my daughter's premium bonds, for God's sake.'

Seeing she was right, he tossed them on to a chair and continued his search.

Behind her, Fellowes said, 'Mrs Kiernan, if you tell us . . .'

She spun round.

'If you tell us where he is,' he continued, 'we can be out of here in a couple of minutes.'

'I don't know where he is,' she retorted. 'And I'd like to know what jurisdiction you have here in this country, and in my house.'

Ignoring the demand he said, 'The fact that he was here makes *you* a co-conspirator, Mrs Kiernan.'

Katie's eyes moved to Michelle. 'Tell him what happened,' she said. 'When you left here, tell him where you went, and what happened.'

Michelle turned calmly to Fellowes. 'We drove to the station,' she said. 'There were no trains due, so he took the car and I came back here. So neither of us knows where he is now, or where he's heading.'

Fellowes's mouth curved in disdain. 'You're not helping yourselves, ladies,' he told them. 'You've got to know what a bad position you're in, so why do this? You could be looking at as much as ten years for your part in all this.'

Overcome by a strong need to sit down, Katie started towards a chair. As she got there she heard the sound of heavy footsteps on the stairs, telling her that the bedrooms were now about to be ransacked too. She closed her eyes, took a breath, and gave a couple of little pants – a small effort to block the creeping exhaustion that was starting to claim her limbs.

Dragging her eyes from the window where she'd

spotted Laurie moving in behind one of the cars, Michelle looked at Katie and felt immediately concerned. She was horribly pale, and clearly had somehow to be released from this ordeal, so turning abruptly to Wilding and Fellowes, she said, 'Could I speak to you gentlemen outside please?'

As she closed the door behind them, she said coldly, 'I think you probably know how ill my sister is, so all you're achieving right now is considerable distress to a terminally sick woman whose only crime is to be related to me. She didn't know Tom was coming here, and when he arrived he certainly wasn't a wanted man. The minute we heard that he was he left, so she's provided no safe haven, nor was she in any way involved in his departure. Now, I've told you the part I played, you know he isn't here, you also know that not one of us, including Tom, is a terrorist, so can we please end this farce before my sister collapses under the strain.'

Fellowes's expression turned thunderous as his face closed in on hers. 'The evidence is stacked so high against your boyfriend, Ms Rowe, that none of you is going to escape the shadow. And you think she's the only one with cancer in there? Well, let me tell you, we've got a world full of cancer out here, thanks to the scumbags your boyfriend knocks about with. Oh yeah, we know all about him. We've got his every move tracked from Somalia, to Afghanistan, to Pakistan, and whose footsteps does that put him in? Eh? The most wanted man on the planet's, that's whose . . .'

'He's a journalist, for God's sake. Those are the kinds of stories . . .'

'. . . he covers,' he finished for her. 'And what a great cover, except we're seeing right through it. Sure, he might report the stories, but you know what he's really up to, you've known for years, because you're in on it too. You're Arab-lovers, the pair of you. Anarchists. Subversives. You've turned against your own to join their war and help them kill, maim and terrorize the innocent people of your own countries. That's who you are. You there in those refugee camps, stirring up hatred, recruiting for your boyfriend who hands them over to the madrasas where they get turned into the filthy, murdering bastards who spread out like a plague into the civilized world, waiting their time to tear it apart. Tell me, since when did either of you live in your own countries? Since a very long time. So it's all bullshit about your sister. You're only here, Michelle, to make contact with some sleeper cell to start . . .'

'Are you completely out of your mind?' she said tightly. 'If that's what you've been told, and you believe it . . .'

'He's been in those Afghan training camps,' Fellowes hissed. 'He hangs out in those hate-breeding Islamic schools and back-street cafés. His friends are all Arabs and Pakistanis and devout followers of the Prophet. He even dresses like them. Shit, he's even got himself an Arab name. And now he's got you here, doing his dirty work for him, connecting up with other operatives.'

Being quite clear now of the spin they were putting on Tom's life, and her own, Michelle turned to Wilding and said, 'This man who sounds very like a white supremacist, and certainly a racist, has

451

clearly been successfully brainwashed by the far right-wing elements of his own government into believing exactly what they tell him, so there's little point in me standing here trying to defend myself against such raging prejudice. But what would you say, Inspector Wilding, if I told you that the plans Legal Attaché Fellowes is referring to originate from a top secret task force known as the P2OG? That's Proactive Pre-emptive Operations Group, whose brief is to incite acts of terrorism in order to facilitate a swift military response in countries where the US has something to gain. And who's behind the P2OG? Who's giving the orders? For that we go straight to the highest corridors of power, where a small but select group of neo-conservatives is contriving by all means possible to keep the world's biggest power base under their control. Wreaking fear on their own people by constantly upping and dropping security alerts, cancelling flights, and sending sniffer dogs into crowded areas to search for non-existent dirty bombs is a part of it. As is subjecting anyone with a swarthy complexion to despicable human and civil rights abuses, and dispensing with due process of law if anyone, such as Tom Chambers, challenges their authority. The other part of it is to prove to the American people that the threat still exists – which it does, no-one's arguing with that – but that it still exists in a form that can reach them on their own soil, even in their own homes. To allow an attack on the American homeland would suggest they're not in control, but an attack on Britain, their staunchest ally, and partner in a special relationship, now that would be effective. Even an aborted attack, if its intent were

452

lethal enough, would get the American fear level soaring, just prior to a presidential election – and that's the date on this plot Legal Attaché Fellowes has told you about – and who's going to vote for a change of leadership when there's an emergency on?'

Fellowes started to applaud, a slow, sarcastic clap that earned him an unruffled smile from Michelle and an unreadable stare from Wilding. 'Congratulations,' Fellowes said scathingly, 'you just keep that up, because you're putting a big fat noose round your own neck with all that subversive bullshit.'

'I don't think so,' Michelle responded, watching Laurie as she came around the corner of the house with a camera on her shoulder. Fellowes and Wilding had their backs to her, so weren't immediately aware of her presence, though she'd been there the whole time, Michelle knew that. It was why she'd let Fellowes rant on just now, hoping Laurie was getting it all on tape, and had then gone into so much detail herself on their version of the story. What she didn't know was why Laurie was showing herself now.

Glancing in the direction Michelle was looking, Fellowes's eyes suddenly bulged with shock. 'What the fuck!' he spat when he saw Laurie, and grabbed the camera so fast she had no time even to tighten her grip.

'Who the fuck are you, and what the hell are you doing here?' Fellowes raged, tearing open the camera to check for tape.

'That's my property,' she said, 'and you've got no right . . .'

'Just get the hell out of here,' he hissed, snatching out the cassette and pocketing it.

'But I'm not trespassing, and this isn't a crime scene . . . Is it?'

Fellowes thrust the camera back at her. 'Disappear, or you're going to find yourself in a whole lot more trouble than you can handle.'

Laurie's smile remained pleasant. 'I think you know who I am,' she said, 'but just in case, my name is Laurie Forbes. I'm sure you've heard of me, so you'll be aware that one phone call from me is all it will take to fill this village up with press.'

Fellowes looked murderous. 'Are you threatening me?' he demanded.

'It probably sounds like it,' she conceded. 'Though it's really just a statement of fact.'

'You do realize I could arrest you right now for obstruction of justice?' he snarled.

Laurie nodded. 'I don't think you want the publicity though – do you?'

Fellowes looked at Wilding, as though expecting him to deal with this mess.

Wilding pulled him to one side. 'You've got the tape,' he muttered, 'the house has been searched. We're not going to achieve anything else here today.'

Fellowes was boiling with outrage, but Wilding was right. Chambers was long gone and what they were engaged in now was tantamount to intimidation, which wasn't going to read well with his superiors should it ever find its way to the airwaves. So biting back his temper, he fired a blistering look at Laurie, then throwing open the kitchen door he shouted, 'Time to go!'

Katie was still at the kitchen table, feeling slightly better now, but still tense enough to jump severely at the yell. She wondered what Michelle had been saying out there, and what damage had been done to her belongings.. She wasn't used to just sitting there while chaos erupted all around her, but the exhaustion that had suddenly taken her had been so debilitating that even now she was finding it hard to stand. However, she was in no pain, nor was she wholly dispossessed of her senses, so she was fully aware of the exodus as it happened, and the relief of seeing Laurie come in with her camera once they'd all gone.

'Are you OK?' Michelle said, going straight to her.

'Yes, I think so. It must have been all the champagne. I came over very peculiar for a while, but thank God you're here,' she said to Laurie. 'Look at the place. You have to shoot it. We have to get visual evidence of what they've done.'

Laurie was looking around in disgust. 'The bastards,' she muttered.

'So let's get to it,' Katie cried impatiently.

Coming to her senses, Laurie said, 'I need the tape I left here yesterday. There's plenty of space on it, and it's all I've got to shoot on.'

'Why on earth did you let them know you had a camera?' Michelle demanded. 'When I knew you were there . . . Did you get anything?'

'Come with me,' Laurie told her, and leading the way back outside, she raised the lid of the dustbin and extracted a videotape from under an empty carton of milk. 'He's taken a blank,' she said, 'which is really going to piss him off, so I can probably expect a bit of harassment from that direction now. The important thing is to get this to a safe place, because it's pretty powerful stuff – short on pictures, I'm afraid, but the sound should be perfect, and if we lay it over the shots of the mess inside . . .'

'They've taken the computers,' Michelle was saying, as they started back into the kitchen. 'And God knows what else. I guess we'll find out. Did you bring the document from Nick?'

'Three copies of it. They're in the car, which I left behind the pub. I didn't want to bring it any closer in case anyone saw me arrive.'

'Where's Katie?' Michelle said, frowning.

'Up here,' Katie called from the top of the stairs. 'Let's get Molly's room cleared up before she comes back. She'll go berserk about her computer, but thank God it doesn't look as though anything's been broken.'

As they joined her Laurie's phone started to ring. 'It's Elliot,' she told them, clicking on. 'Hi. Where are you?'

'Just coming into the village. How's it going there?'

'OK. They were still here when I arrived. I've got some excellent footage, and I'm about to get some more, because they've left the place in a dreadful mess.'

'Is Katie all right?'

'I think so. A bit shaken up.' Her eyes went to Katie. 'She'll probably enjoy a visit from you.'

'I'll be there any second,' he said.

'No news from Tom, I suppose?'

'There won't be. He can't risk it, and it's best if

none of us knows where he is. Have you got the stuff from Nick?'

'Yes. There are lots of copies now, so it won't do anyone any good to confiscate one.'

'OK. I'm just turning into the lane. Can you meet me outside?'

By the time she got downstairs he was pulling in next to Katie's car, so she walked across to the gate and waited for him to join her. 'Where have you been?' she asked, looking up into his eyes and thinking of those dreadful moments earlier with Andraya.

'I came via Portsmouth,' he said. 'I wanted to lead them to a channel port, so they'd think I was meeting Tom to make a dash for France.'

'Is that still the proposed destination?'

He nodded. 'But now I've made it look obvious, perhaps they won't focus on it quite so much.'

She was about to open the gate for him to come in when he said, 'About this morning – I know how it looked, and what she said, but I swear I had no idea she'd be there.'

She nodded. 'I think I know that,' she responded softly.

'She left straight away. I didn't let her into the flat.'

'Good.'

'I think she's got the message now.'

'Let's hope so.' Then because he needed to hear it, she said, 'It's over with Nick.'

She sensed the relief that went through him, and felt it too, for in spite of there still being a long way to go, it was just the two of them now, with no-one else to add to the complications or turmoil.

However, now wasn't the time to take it any further, so she stood aside for him to come in, saying, 'Who tipped you off?'

'Chris,' he answered. 'He had a call from a woman who didn't give her name, but was American apparently and, interestingly, knew he was the right person to get hold of.'

'Elliot,' Michelle said, pulling open the door. 'Judy just rang. She's had a visit from the police. They've obviously traced the Panda to her, and now they know that my car is in her garage.'

Not having been party to Tom's getaway, Elliot was confused. 'What does this mean?' he said.

'That they know Tom left in a Renault 4 with Judy's husband.'

His eyes closed in frustration. 'The traffic police will already have been alerted,' he said, quickly going through the ramifications. 'And if we call to warn him, we're going to lead them straight to him. Shit, they were fast!'

The trusty blue Renault 4 was roaring along the M5 at fifty miles an hour, swaying in the slipstream of mightier cars and shuddering in the wake of high-sided lorries. There was a blinding spray on the windscreen that the wipers were diligently smearing, and the sinister grating sound coming from somewhere up front seemed to be getting worse.

The journey so far had been uneventful, but that was about to change, for a fleet of three police cars was bearing down on the unassuming vehicle like hounds on a limping fox. Dave glanced in the rearview mirror, and blinked at the dazzling display of blue flashing lights. Resisting the urge to stick his foot down, mainly because it might go through the floor, he carried on zipping along, whistling tonelessly and scratching his unshaven face as he pondered his predicament.

The police cars were on him in seconds, forcing him on to the hard shoulder, and pulling up alongside, in front and behind.

'Tom, my friend,' he muttered as he wound the window down, 'you're a lucky man. And it looks as though I'm a popular one,' he added, as he watched his rusty old heap being surrounded by fluorescent jackets and chequer-band caps.

'David Penwright?' an important-looking flat cap demanded.

'That's me,' Dave responded. 'Is everything all right? I wasn't breaking the limit, was I?'

'Step out of the car please,' the flat cap responded, clearly not amused.

Obediently Dave struggled with the handle, then shouldered open the door and clambered out on to the tarmac. The noise was almost deafening as the traffic thundered by, though several motorists were slowing up now to catch a glimpse of what was going on. No gore and guts over here, Dave was thinking, or not yet anyway. 'What's the problem?' he asked, as two officers began inspecting the inside of his Renault, whilst another opened the back. 'I haven't got any drugs.'

'We've received information that you're assisting a suspected criminal in avoiding arrest,' the flat cap told him. He glanced down at his notes. 'Thomas Chambers. US citizen.' He looked at Dave, clearly waiting for an answer.

'If you're talking about my mate Tom, who I was

giving a lift to,' he said, 'then you're out of luck. I just dropped him off. But he's no criminal, not Tom . . .'

'Where did you drop him?'

Dave shrugged. 'Back there, at the services.'

Immediately another officer began speaking into his radio. 'Suspect thought to be at Exeter services,' he said, spreading the word.

'Where was he going from there?' the flat cap asked Dave.

Dave pulled a face. 'He didn't say. He just wanted a lift down that far, which I was happy to do, you know, give the old girl a bit of a run, she don't get out much . . .'

'Did anyone meet him? Did he hire a car? Take a taxi?'

'I think he just went in to have a cup of tea,' Dave answered.

'Or to wait for someone?'

'I don't know. All I know is he got out of the old girl here, and gave her a friendly slap on the roof as I drove off. I didn't want to stop the engine, see, in case I had trouble starting it again.' That much at least was true, but he didn't have to tell them the rest of it, that Tom's lift was already waiting when they got there, pulled up in front of Burger King, as arranged, or that it was a top-of-the-line S class Merc that had got his juices flowing, and the old girl's dander up, the way she'd coughed and spluttered as they'd lurched back down the slip road to start the journey home.

No, Tom was long gone by now, zooming off to only he knew where, with only he knew who, because Dave certainly didn't. Nor did he want to.

His part was over now. He'd just given a lift to a friend of a friend, and being the obliging fellow that he was, he hadn't even accepted any money for gas, as his mate Tom had called it.

Chapter Twenty

Two days had now passed since Tom's escape. There had been no word since he'd left Katie's, though Chris had confirmed he'd flown him into Brittany the next day with no mishap, so if all had gone to plan from there, Elliot was expecting to find him at Jean-Jacques' farmhouse, deep in the heart of Burgundy.

It was a dull, wet afternoon as Elliot drove his rental car through the vaguely familiar French countryside, heading towards the secluded hamlet that nestled cosily in the bowl of the valley, seeming as forgotten as the sprawling empty fields surrounding it. It was far from the beaten track and comprised no more than five eighteenth-century dwellings, each belonging to Parisians who only used them at weekends and for holidays. It was also virtually impossible to approach without being seen, for there was only this one road through, or the mountain pathways which, at this time of year, were almost totally exposed.

As Elliot began the gentle descent, passing

sodden, spiky hedgerows and golden trees, he was thinking about Katie and Michelle's certainty that the efforts to silence Tom were, in themselves, confirming the existence of the P2OG. And he wasn't arguing with that – however, it still wasn't providing that vital link between the P2OG and Tom's evidence of a Pakistan-based terrorist plot. Katie and Michelle were now examining both versions of the 21 Project in minute detail, while Laurie worked alongside them, making preliminary plans for a webcast in case they started running into problems about getting the story into print. Elliot foresaw several, for the reach of American power wasn't something he ever underestimated, and there wasn't much doubt, in this case, that they had all their guns loaded.

Slowing up to go over a cattle grid, he glanced in his rear-view mirror and saw the road stretching emptily behind. It had been like that virtually the entire way from Mâcon where he'd stopped to pick up a few supplies, so by now he was fairly confident he hadn't been followed. However, as he approached the tiny hamlet he was starting to become uneasy, for the place appeared as still and silent as a grave. Not a person, nor a creature in sight.

As he pulled into the driveway that ran along the side of Jean-Jacques' rambling stone farmhouse, he looked carefully over the creeper-covered frontage for any signs of life inside. Every one of the white-painted shutters was closed, and a handful of mail was jutting from the front door letter-box. This wasn't looking good. He edged the car further forward, then noticed the front end of another car, tucked away around the back of the house. Hoping it was Tom's rental, rather than a recent acquisition Jean-Jacques had forgotten to mention, he stopped the engine, and stepped out on to the drive just as the kitchen door swung open.

'At last,' Tom grinned, coming out to greet him. 'Thought you'd never get here.'

'I was beginning to think you hadn't made it,' Elliot commented, shaking his hand. 'You can open the shutters, you know.'

'I have at the back, I thought I'd leave the front the way it is. So tell me what's been happening. How did it go for Michelle and Katie after I left? Are they OK?'

'They're fine,' Elliot assured him, returning to his car to start unloading as he filled Tom in on all that had happened.

'So what's on this tape that Laurie has?' Tom asked, when he'd finished.

'I've got it with me, so I'll play it to you,' Elliot replied. As he stepped into the large, low-ceilinged kitchen, with its heavy oak beams and flagstone floor, he was mindful of the couple of occasions he and Laurie had spent here and hopeful they would be repeated. Sunlight suddenly streamed in through the French windows, and taking it as a good omen, he kicked the door closed and readily accepted Tom's offer of wine.

A few minutes later they were seated either side of the pine table, laptops, printouts, newspaper cuttings and various other documents to hand, as they ate and drank and listened to the sound recording Laurie had made of Fellowes's visit.

By the time it finished Tom's face was taut with

concern. 'We have to go to print before they catch up with me,' he said. 'If we don't, they're going to use this bullshit to try and nail me. While you might have the truth to set me free, with all the prejudice and fear they're stirring up over there, just the mention of me being in the training camps and dressing like a Pakistani, never mind all the stuff they found in my apartment, will be enough to make my stay in a federal prison a lot longer than I'd be comfortable with.'

'We should be able to pull it together by the end of the week,' Elliot told him. 'Katie and Michelle are taking those documents apart and Laurie's going to be feeding selected highlights of their findings through an email system we set up before I left. It means they'll be coming via several people we know we can trust, which won't make it the speediest contact, but it should work, at least for a few days.' As he finished he was carrying his laptop to the phone jack that was beside a big oak buffet, and after making sure a Web connection was under way, he turned back. 'The big deal now,' he said, 'is getting the right editors on board. Max and Nick are already on it, so we should have some news in the next couple of days. What progress are you making with story structure?'

Tom was looking at his own screen while sipping a glass of wine. 'Not bad,' he answered. 'I've copied what I've got so far on to a CD so you can upload and we can work it together. Obviously we'll lead with the plot itself – I think we should take the stand that it's a set-up, even though we don't know that for certain – then we need to follow up with how the information got to me, who it came from, who it implicates and what's been happening since. All the in-depth stuff on the 21 Project, P2OG, neo-conservatism and what it actually means, as well as backgrounds on the major players, their current positions, what policies they've influenced in the past, their goals for the future, etc., will come after.'

As he listened Elliot was waiting for Laurie's first emails to start downloading. There were several, but as nothing was flagged urgent, he knew they hadn't uncovered anything sensational yet. 'Why don't I take the in-depth,' he said, starting to tap out a message letting her know he'd arrived and that Tom was here too, 'while you focus on the upfront.'

Tom was distracted by the early changes he was already making.

'There's a message here for you, marked personal,' Elliot told him.

It was a moment before Tom fully registered, then realizing it had to be from Michelle, he went to join Elliot at his computer. As he opened the email, Elliot walked back to the table to pick up his wine.

Just to say I love you, we're all fine and remember, there's one more of us to think about now, so stay safe. M.

Tom's mouth curved into a lopsided smile as he recalled the moment they'd stood together in the bathroom, watching a little blue line appear inside a plastic wand. If ever he needed a reason to stay safe, that was it.

'Everything OK?' Elliot asked.

Tom nodded. 'No-one else from the press got hold of what happened on Sunday?' he asked, disconnecting and carrying the computer back to the table.

Elliot shook his head. 'So far it's still ours. Incidentally, did Chris tell you about the tip-off? Who it came from?'

Tom nodded. 'Yeah, and I agree with him, American she might be, but she's got to be at the British end, because whoever she is, she knew he was the person to contact and she managed it so fast.'

Elliot was looking thoughtful. 'So who's whispering in her ear?' he wondered aloud. 'Christopher Malton? Michael Dalby, or someone we don't even know about?'

'I don't reckon it's something we should pursue,' Tom responded. 'They obviously don't want their cover blown, and it's only important that the information bears out, which it did.'

Elliot nodded agreement. 'Though if it does all start turning nasty, let's hope at least one of them steps forward to save your tender skin, because any hospitality provided by the federal government could be an experience some might consider worse than death.'

Tom grimaced at the thought of what the inside of a prison would be like for someone branded a traitor and terrorist. 'I wouldn't count on an eleventh-hour rescue,' he said. 'So let's hope it doesn't come to that.'

'This is making horrible reading,' Michelle murmured as she scrolled slowly down the computer screen. 'All this abuse of power, and holding people without charge, is starting to make me very nervous about Tom's chances of being able to stand up against them.'

Laurie glanced up from where she was kneeling on the sitting-room floor, surrounded by the 21 Project printouts. 'Make sure you save the link so we can send it over,' she said, going back to the pages she was currently comparing.

After pasting the web-site address into the email they were compiling for Tom and Elliot, Michelle sat back and glanced at the clock. 'I think I'll pop up and check on Katie,' she said. 'Do you need to go online, or shall I disconnect?'

'Keep it going for the moment,' Laurie said. 'There are a few leads here I'd like to follow up. Is there anything from Elliot or Tom yet today?'

'Not yet,' Michelle answered, getting up and stretching out her limbs. 'They're probably still going through everything we sent yesterday,' and stifling a yawn she looked out at the dark, drizzly afternoon, and wondered what it was like in Burgundy now. Thinking of Tom brought a lightness to her heart, in spite of how worried she was, though it soon turned to impatience for this all to be over so that they could be together and start their new life.

Finding Katie's bedroom door slightly ajar, she popped her head round and saw that Katie was lying on her side, facing the other way, with one hand resting on Trotty and a foot poking free of the sheet. Since she was obviously still asleep Michelle crept quietly to the bed, and seeing how peaceful she looked, stooped to kiss her gently on the cheek before tiptoeing out again.

'Still out for the count,' she told Laurie, going back downstairs. 'I'll leave her for another half an hour, then take her some tea.'

Laurie looked up from the computer. 'Did she have another bad night?' she asked.

Michelle nodded and sighed. 'She's still worrying about Molly, and how withdrawn she's been these last few days. Well, you've seen her coming in from school and going straight to her room, hardly speaking to anyone. She doesn't have a computer now, so heaven only knows what she's doing up there, because we haven't heard much music either. We're not even sure what she's eating, because she's not having much here.' As she finished she looked up at the sound of Katie's footsteps on the stairs.

'Do I detect some slacking?' Katie demanded, as she reached the bottom. 'Honestly, the minute my back's turned . . .'

'You were fast asleep a minute ago,' Michelle told her.

'Ah yes, until someone clodhoppered in and gave me a bloody great snog on the cheek,' Katie retorted.

Michelle laughed. 'Must have been Prince Charming, having chopped his way through all those thorns of yours,' she told her. 'I'll put the kettle on. Do you want something to eat?'

'A loaf of toast and three dozen eggs should do it,' Katie responded, going to read over Laurie's shoulder. 'So, how many nails do we have for the neo-con coffin now?' she wanted to know.

'Still not enough,' Laurie responded. 'As we stand, they'll still be able to claw their way out, but it's definitely getting tighter. I've just finished compiling another email to send over, which is now on its way. Here, take a look, it'll bring you up to speed.'

As she started to get up, Katie pressed her gently back down. 'How about talking me through it,' she suggested. 'I'm starting to see double with all this reading.'

'Of course,' Laurie responded, and immediately began updating her on the findings of the past two hours, until she realized Katie wasn't really paying attention.

'Are you OK?' Michelle asked, watching Katie half-heartedly buttering some toast while gazing out of the window.

Katie looked round. 'Yes, of course,' she declared. 'Why shouldn't I be?'

'You just seem a little distracted.'

Katie looked down at what she was doing, then after a protracted sigh, she began shaking her head. 'I keep asking myself what difference all this makes,' she said. 'I mean, I know it's important, that we have to get to the truth, and I want to, but . . .' She stopped and stared blindly down at her toast. 'It matters, I'm not saying it doesn't,' she continued, 'but it's so huge and complex and my life here is so small and short now . . .' Again she trailed off.

Michelle said softly, 'I know you're thinking about Molly, and it's all right. No-one would expect anything else, so please don't start feeling guilty that you're not putting this first.'

Katie nodded and returned her eyes to the window. Whether she'd fully registered Michelle's words was hard to tell, but as she responded it was clear she was preoccupied with Molly. 'You know, I think I'd have preferred it if she'd gone ballistic over having her computer taken,' she said. 'It would have been more like her. Now, I just don't know what's got into her. Is it the boyfriend? Is it the way Tom took off so suddenly? Is it because he's marrying Michelle?' She looked at Laurie. 'Did Michelle tell you, I think she had her eye on Tom for me?'

Laurie shook her head.

Katie rolled her eyes in a show of exasperation, but Laurie could see how upset she was underneath. 'She's probably got all sorts of confusions roiling around in that head of hers,' Katie went on, 'who doesn't at that age – actually any age – but it's bothering me that she won't tell us anything about this boy.'

'Then maybe we should try other ways of finding out something about him,' Michelle suggested.

Katie's expression assumed some irony as she turned back to Laurie. 'More background checks,' she said wryly. 'Just what we need with all this lot to get through.' Then to Michelle, 'Have you mentioned anything to Laurie about what we discussed last night?'

'Not yet,' Michelle answered.

'We thought,' Katie said to Laurie, 'well, Michelle thought, that it might be a good idea for her to go away for a night or two, to give Molly and me a chance to talk.'

'I think they need some space,' Michelle added.

'Me being here is adding a pressure that Molly clearly isn't coping with, so I thought perhaps you and I could carry on with this in London.'

'Of course,' Laurie responded without a moment's hesitation.

Michelle looked at Katie.

Katie's eyes were still on Laurie. 'When were you thinking of leaving?' she asked.

'Tonight, or tomorrow,' Laurie answered. 'Actually, probably tonight, because the list of people I need to speak to is growing longer by the minute, and as far as I know we're still working to a Saturday deadline.'

'Which only gives you two days to get all the quotes and expert opinions you need,' Katie responded, 'so you're right, you should go tonight, it'll give you a fresh start in the morning. I'll plough on through my copy of the twenty-first century's version of *Mein Kampf* and if there's anything else I can help with, like making some calls, or tracking someone down, you just let me know.'

Michelle looked from one to the other. 'Well, I guess that's decided then.'

'Sounds like it,' Katie responded. 'In fact, if you left in the next half an hour you'd be gone before Molly gets home. Not that I'm throwing you out, you understand.' She smiled, and hoped her real feelings didn't show, because in truth, she was longing for Michelle to go. Not that she didn't want her to come back again soon, but at the moment she needed the space for herself as much as for Molly, because deep down inside she was bitterly angry with Michelle for getting pregnant now. They hadn't mentioned it, either of them, but Katie had seen the email to Tom so knew her earlier suspicions were correct, and she was finding it extremely hard to stop herself thinking of how often in the past Michelle had somehow contrived to stage an important event that overshadowed the one in which Katie was involved.

'Call me as soon as you get to London,' she said, hugging Michelle before she left, and already feeling guilty for the way she was thinking.

'Of course,' Michelle promised. 'And I've got my mobile, so if you need me before that, you'll be able to get hold of me.'

Katie nodded and hugged her again. It wasn't that she begrudged Michelle a second child, or her happiness with Tom – though God knew both were feeling like slaps in the face right now – it was the fear of Molly being neglected and lonely that was really upsetting her. Why on earth would Michelle and Tom want to put up with a problematical teenager who wasn't even theirs, when they had a brand new baby of their own to make a fuss of?

Molly's stomach was all in knots as she approached Judy's oak-panelled front door with its bottle-bottom window panes and shiny brass knocker. She was like, so freaked out and scared, she'd probably have run away if Judy hadn't popped her nets back at that moment and spotted her coming. Molly's heart turned over. She had to go through with it now, and anyway, it was OK, because she wanted to. It was all going to work out and end up being just like the DOLs said it would, because no-one would let Michelle stay in the house once they knew what she'd been doing, and then everything would be back like it was before, just her and her mum, and then it wouldn't even really matter that Brad hadn't called for three days. Anyway Toby had told Allison he was definitely going to be at the party on Saturday, so she'd see him then.

'Hello love,' Judy said, pulling open the front door. 'This is a surprise. Everything all right?'

Molly nodded, and felt herself colouring up as she stepped into Judy's plushly carpeted hallway, where the banister was all new and gleaming, and the wallpaper was green with white stripy patterns from Laura Ashley or somewhere like that. Sometimes she wished they lived in one of these new houses on the edge of the village, where everything was modern and always seemed to work, but really she wished they didn't live in Membury Hempton at all and were still in their lovely house back in London, where all her friends were, and before her mum had got ill.

'Would you like something to drink?' Judy offered, leading her through to the kitchen.

'Um, OK. Where are the boys?'

'Jason's up in bed with flu, and Lester's gone to his gran's for tea. Apple juice, all right?'

'Yeah, that's fine thanks.'

As Judy poured she glanced back over her shoulder and smiled. 'Sit down,' she said, nodding towards the round pine table with its matching rail-back chairs. 'Biscuit? Slice of cake?'

'No, nothing, thanks,' Molly answered, letting her school bag slide to the cushion-tiled floor as she sank down in a chair.

'So,' Judy said, bringing two glasses to the table

and sitting down too, 'how's everything with you? School OK?'

'Mm,' Molly answered, taking a sip.

Judy eyed her encouragingly, but it seemed she had no more to say, and was clearly going to look anywhere but at her. 'So everything's all right,' she stated finally, 'yet I'm getting the feeling it isn't really, and that's why you're here.'

Still Molly's eyes couldn't quite make it to hers.

'Whatever it is, you can tell me,' Judy said gently, though she suspected she already knew, and was wondering how the heck she was going to handle this, when Katie had remained adamant all along that she should be the one to tell Molly.

'Well, um, it's . . .' Molly said, looking down at her juice, 'it's Michelle.'

Not having expected that, Judy frowned. 'What about her?' she asked.

Molly took a breath, and shrugged as she turned to look out of the window. 'It's, like, well . . . She does things,' she said, feeling herself going all hot and prickly.

'What kind of things?'

'You know, those kind of things.'

Judy was quiet for a moment, hoping this wasn't going where she now suspected it was. 'I'm not sure I do,' she responded.

Molly's face was on fire, and she was starting to feel a bit sick. 'She like, you know, touches me,' she said, keeping her eyes fixed on her glass.

Judy watched her, and felt her heart aching, for she recognized this immediately for what it was – a desperate attempt to make everything go back to the way it had been before. 'I'm not sure I understand,' she said, needing to be certain that she really was reading this correctly. 'What do you mean, she touches you?'

Molly swallowed and felt sweat breaking out in her armpits. 'You know, in places where she shouldn't,' she said in a whisper.

Circling her hands round her glass, Judy took a deep breath. Knowing she had to tread very carefully now, she said, 'When did this happen?'

So much blood was rushing to Molly's head she could hardly think. 'Um, well, like it's happened a few times,' she mumbled. 'I can't really remember which days.'

'I see. And the reason you're here now is because you want me to tell your mum, is that right?'

Molly nodded and kept her head down.

Hardly daring to think about how Katie was going to take this, never mind Michelle, Judy said, 'Look at me, Molly.'

Molly's eyes almost came up.

'I know you understand what a very serious accusation this is,' Judy said, 'so are you sure you haven't misinterpreted something, or just got the wrong end of the stick?'

'No, I'm sure,' Molly told her, sounding quite firm, though the colour was draining from her cheeks now, leaving her looking horribly strained and afraid.

'OK. Then you sit here,' Judy said, 'and I'll go round to see your mum.' She waited for Molly to protest, but she only hung her head again and clung on to her juice.

Judy got up from the table, gave Molly's shoulder a comforting squeeze as she passed, then slipped on a fleece jacket. 'Listen out for Jason, will you?' she said. 'And help yourself to anything from the fridge.'

A few minutes later Judy was walking across Katie's garden, still trying to come up with the best way to break this. She really didn't have much of a plan at all, as rounding the corner of the house, she almost collided with Katie struggling in with a basket of logs.

'Judy!' Katie gasped, almost dropping the basket. 'You gave me the fright of my life.'

'Sorry. I didn't realize you were there,' Judy responded. 'Here, let me give you a hand,' and taking one of the handles she helped her across the kitchen to the sitting-room hearth where newspaper and kindling were already crackling away.

'It's turning chilly now,' Katie remarked, placing a couple of logs in the flames.

'Mm, yes,' Judy said, looking at the printed papers scattered about the floor. 'Seems like you've been busy.'

'We all have,' Katie told her. 'Though Laurie and Michelle more than me, and please don't ask what it's about, because I promise Tom will tell it much better when the time comes.' She sat back on her heels and used her wrist to push aside a stray strand of her wig. 'So what brings you here at this hour?' she said, already sensing that something wasn't quite right. 'I thought you might be Molly. I'm expecting her any minute.'

Judy took a breath, and going to perch on the edge of the sofa, she said, 'Molly's over at my house.'

Katie's surprise turned rapidly to concern. 'Is she all right?' she asked. 'Has something happened?'

477

'Not exactly,' Judy answered awkwardly, 'though Molly's saying it has.'

Katie was confused.

'You need to brace yourself a bit for this,' Judy cautioned. 'She's just told me that Michelle's been abusing her . . . Now I know it's not true,' she hastily added, as Katie's face paled with shock, 'so don't worry, it'll go no further than me, but she wanted me to tell you.'

Katie covered her face with her hands and began shaking her head in despair. 'I knew something was going on with her,' she said brokenly, 'but I never dreamt it was something like this. What did she say, exactly?'

Hating to repeat it, Judy said, 'That Michelle's been touching her in places she shouldn't.'

Katie's misery was complete. 'That she'd go this far,' she said almost to herself. 'To accuse Michelle of something so horrible . . . What on earth did she think it was going to prove?'

Knowing Katie already knew the answer to that, Judy said, 'You'll have to tell her the truth now.'

Katie's eyes closed. 'I was going to do it tonight,' she said, her voice trembling on the words. 'Michelle's gone to London with Laurie to give us . . .' She took a breath, then stared blindly down at the fire.

'Would you like to come and talk to her at my place?' Judy offered. 'I can go upstairs out of the way.'

Katie considered it for a moment, then shook her head. 'No,' she said. 'Tell her to come home. I think we need to be here.'

Judy got up. 'You know where I am,' she said.

'If you need to call, or if there's anything I can do . . .'

'Thanks.'

After Judy had gone Katie remained sitting on the floor, feeling the horror of it sliding through her again and again. She held her breath, as though somehow it would help her to centre and be strong, but when she let it go she was still sinking in a quagmire of self-blame and despair. How could she, who prided herself on getting it right for others, be getting it so badly wrong for herself and Molly?

She went into the kitchen and opened the small cupboard where she kept her herbal remedies. Though nothing she took would put this right now, she needed something to calm her and help her to find some inner strength, because this was no time to start falling apart. She had to hold it together for Molly, let her know that it would be all right in the end, it really would.

A few drops of hornbeam and several deep breaths later, she closed the cupboard door and started to pray. She honestly didn't know if there was a God up there, but right now she needed to believe, so she would. He had to help them through this, make sure she didn't break down as she told Molly what was going to happen, because she needed to make her understand that there was nothing they could do to alter it, especially not rejecting Michelle.

Hearing Molly's footsteps passing the kitchen window, she tightened the clasp of her hands and sent up one last prayer before the door opened. Fleetingly she wished she'd asked Judy to come

479

back with Molly, then she heard Judy's voice telling Molly it would be all right.

A moment later the door opened, but only Molly came in, and seeing her mother sitting, waiting, she looked for a moment as though she was going to bolt. But then she heaved her bag on to the counter top and closed the door.

Katie watched her trying to overcome her nerves – telling stories to Judy about Michelle was one thing, telling her mother was going to be another altogether. It was, of course, why she'd gone to Judy in the first place.

'Come and sit down,' Katie said gently.

Molly glanced over, and stayed where she was.

'It's all right,' Katie told her. 'We can sort this out.'

Molly looked away, her face pinched with defiance, her body taut as though ready to fight.

'It's not true, is it?' Katie said. 'What you told Judy about Michelle.'

Molly's eyes flashed. 'Yes it is!' she snapped. 'She's been touching me . . .'

'Molly.'

'*She has!*' Molly cried. 'Why don't you believe me? She's been putting her hands on me . . .'

'Stop,' Katie said firmly. 'I hear what you're saying, but now I want you to listen to me. Are you listening?'

Molly didn't answer.

'I want you to consider for a moment what this could do to Michelle,' Katie said. 'Her whole life has been about taking care of children. She wants to regain custody of Robbie, and she's going to be having another baby soon, so accusing her of something like this could totally ruin her life. And if it goes beyond these walls there will be no going back from it. She'll never recover her standing, or regain people's trust, because no-one ever does after a scandal like this. So now I want you to think very carefully about what you're saying, and what it could mean to someone who actually cares very much about you, and then you can tell me if you really want me to take it any further.'

Molly's eyes were full of tears, her voice mangled by fury as she said, 'Yes, I do. I want you to tell the police and make her go, because she's got no right being here. She doesn't belong with us. She belongs over there in those camps. She's just in the way here . . .'

Attempting to cut off the tirade, Katie said, 'Sweetheart, listen . . .'

'No! You listen,' Molly shouted. 'I hate her being here, and I hate you, because you always stick up for her. You don't care about me any more. You just care about her!'

'Molly that is not true. No-one matters more to me than you.'

'Well you've got a funny way of showing it. You're always talking to her and laughing and making fun of me. Well I'm sick of it! Do you hear me! I want her to go and if she doesn't, then I'll run away and you'll never see me again.'

Katie was on her feet, reaching for her. 'Hey, come on, come on,' she said, trying to hold her.

'Don't touch me! I'm not a baby . . .'

Grabbing her hands and holding on firmly, Katie said, 'Look at me. Come on now, I want to see your eyes . . .'

'I don't want to.'

'Yes you do. Now come on.'

It took a while, but finally, very reluctantly Molly began to lift her head. The instant their eyes met she looked away again.

'Sweetheart,' Katie said gently, 'I think, in your heart, you already know the real reason Michelle's here. So you know why she has to stay. She's going to be there for you . . .'

'*Noooo!*' Molly cried, wrenching her hands free and blocking her ears. 'I don't want her here. I want her to go. You hate her too . . .'

'That's not true, and you know it. Yes, we've had our issues, but she's my sister and I love her. More importantly, she loves you . . .'

'She does not!' Molly raged. 'And I don't want her to love me. I just want her to go away and never come back. I want it to be just us, the way it used to be . . .'

'Oh Molly,' Katie cried, 'I wish it could be that way too, my darling, but it can't happen now . . .'

'Yes it can! *It can!*'

'No, Molly, it can't, and we both know why it can't, so it's time for us both to start facing it . . . Not only you, but me too . . .'

'*Noooo!*' Molly screamed again, and dragging herself free she charged for the door.

'Molly, come back,' Katie pleaded, going after her. 'Running away isn't . . . Molly please,' she cried, as Molly dashed outside.

'Leave me alone!' Molly shouted. 'I don't need you. I don't need anyone.'

Katie was crying by now, unable to hold back any longer. 'Molly please don't run away,' she called after her. 'It won't solve anything, sweet-heart. Molly, please,' but Molly was already tearing down the lane, hands clamped to her ears, and unable to bear it, Katie broke down and sobbed.

'It's OK, it's OK,' Judy said, stepping out of the shadows. 'I've got you. Come on, in we go. She'll be all right. She'll come back.'

'Oh God, I'm making such a mess of it all,' Katie gasped. 'I tried to tell her, but she won't listen.'

'She will. Now you've opened it up, she won't be able to deny it much longer.'

Katie buried her face in her hands. 'I've been so busy trying to fill my life with Tom's story, and sur-rounding myself with people and things to blot it all out, that I haven't really been thinking about her.'

'Yes you have,' Judy assured her. 'She's always come first.'

Katie shook her head. 'No, I've been avoiding it every bit as much as she has,' she said, 'in fact that's why she's finding it so hard now, because she's taken a lead from me. Oh God, why didn't I see this before? How have I let this happen? She's so afraid and now she's gone off . . . She doesn't even have her phone.'

'She'll go to Allison's, you know that,' Judy said.

'I should go round there. She'll hate me for it, but we can't leave things like this.'

'Give her a bit of time,' Judy advised. 'Let her talk to her friend, then call the house and ask to speak to her. She'll probably be ready to come home by then.'

Sighing heavily, Katie blew her nose and looked down at Trotty who was eyeing her with deep concern. 'They worry me, those friends of hers,' she said, lifting the dog on to her lap. 'I wish I knew more about them. I should have insisted on meeting them, but I haven't because I'm afraid Molly's ashamed of the way I look.'

As Judy's face fell Katie raised a hand to stop her from replying.

'And then there's this new boyfriend,' Katie continued. 'He'll be one of that set, I'm sure, older than her, much more sophisticated . . . Oh God, Judy, how do I get this right?'

'Katie,' Judy said firmly, 'this is one of the hardest things in the world to get right, so please stop beating yourself up. You're trying, that's what matters. You're making sure that Molly has someone when you go, and you're doing what you can to forge that bond now.'

'It's not working though, is it?'

'You might be surprised. Often things have to come to a head before they get properly resolved, or before they can move on to the next phase, so perhaps you should look on tonight as a turning point.'

Katie's smile was wry. 'It feels more like a disaster,' she commented, glancing at the clock. 'I ought to call Allison's to make sure she's there.'

'Of course,' Judy said, and picked up the phone to pass it over.

A few minutes later Mrs Fortescue-Bond's voice slurred down the line. 'Oh yes, yes, Molly's just arrived,' she said, when Katie asked. 'Would you like to speak to her?'

'Yes please,' Katie responded, and put her hand over the mouthpiece as she said to Judy, 'I've never spoken to this woman when she's sober, which is another reason I'm not keen on Molly going over there. They're a dysfunctional family if ever there was one, and that's not what she needs right now.'

'No-one ever does,' Judy assured her, 'but we get them anyway.'

Katie couldn't help but laugh, for it was true. She, Molly and Michelle could hardly be described any other way with all that was going on between them, so maybe she shouldn't be so fast at slinging stones from her own dodgy greenhouse.

'What?' Molly's voice came abruptly down the line.

'Sweetheart, I want you to come home so we can talk,' Katie said.

'I don't want to.'

'Molly, don't be childish now . . .'

'Don't speak to me like that,' Molly raged. 'You're always treating me like a baby, and I'm not going to put up with it any more.'

'All right, but if you want to be treated like an adult, you have to behave like one, and running away isn't adult behaviour.'

'I wasn't running away. I just didn't want to listen to you going on and on . . .'

'We have to resolve this business about Michelle,' Katie said, hoping to lure her back with the easier option.

'I don't want to talk about it. You don't believe me, so what's the point?'

'But I do understand why you're doing it,' Katie told her. 'So please, sweetheart, stop hiding over there . . .'

'No way am I coming back if she's going to be there.'

'She's not here. She's gone to London.'

There was a moment's hesitation before Molly said, 'I'm not coming back unless you say you believe me.'

Katie closed her eyes and struggled desperately for the right words. 'All right,' she said eventually, 'I promise we won't talk about anything until you're ready to. Now will you come home?'

Molly's silence was mutinous.

'Molly?'

'You didn't say you believe me.'

Again Katie had to take a moment to think how to answer. In the end, wishing she didn't have to do this on the phone, she said, 'Do you swear on my life that it's true?'

The silence was deadly.

'Molly . . .'

Still no reply, but she knew Molly was there. Finally, unable to bear keeping her in such a terrible position, Katie said, 'Be home by nine. No later.'

'I'm not talking about anything, all right,' Molly snarled.

'All right. Just don't be late.'

Judy watched Katie click off the line. 'Doesn't sound as though it went too badly,' she said with a grimace.

Katie lifted her eyebrows and nodded. 'At least we know where she is, and she's agreeing to come home,' she responded. 'I suppose that's the best we can hope for tonight.' Her eyes went to Judy. 'You're a good friend,' she said. 'I really owe you for the way you've helped bail us all out these last few days.'

'If you're referring to Tom now, we enjoyed it,' Judy confessed. 'Most adventurous we ever are on a Sunday afternoon is a bit of rumpy-pumpy while the kids are at my mum's. So is he all right? Do you know where he is?'

'Yes, but it's better that I don't say. We've already put you in a difficult enough position, so I don't want to make it any worse. In fact, let's hope that someone out there has taken on board the fact that Michelle's not here any more, because frankly, I don't think I could deal with them *and* Molly right now.'

Chapter Twenty-One

Fellowes looked up as Nancy Goodman came into his office.

'Still nothing,' she told him, handing him the latest tracking report that had come in from GCHQ based in Cheltenham, who were attempting to locate Chambers and Russell.

Fellowes's face tightened with frustration. 'Well they've got to be somewhere,' he growled, 'and they've got to be using phones, emails, or some kind of communication, so it can't be that hard to find them.'

'Of course not, sir,' Goodman responded.

He glanced over the tracking report, then balled it in his fist. 'First we manage to screw up with the press . . . Anything broken on that yet?'

'Not yet, sir.'

'Now we don't know where the hell Chambers is. What the fuck is going on here?'

Goodman went to pour him a coffee. 'It'll work out, sir,' she assured him. 'The legal case against him is watertight now, and if he resists arrest the orders are clear.' She put the coffee down in front of him. 'Unless, of course, he manages to get the story to print before we find him,' she added.

'Well that's definitely not going to happen,' he told her roughly. 'Have we got those computers yet? The ones belonging to Forbes and Russell. The Executive wants a full picture by the end of today of how much they've got.'

'I believe the computers were brought in an hour ago, sir,' she responded, 'but I'll go and check.'

'If there's one thing I hate more than doorstepping politicians,' Laurie grumbled as she came into the flat, 'it's doorstepping the flaming police. What a day!'

'Did you get anything?' Michelle asked, looking up from her comfy cushion next to the coffee table, where the final pages of both projects were laid out.

'Plenty, actually, though most of it amounts to fudging or hedging, or deliberately misleading. I did manage a quick word with Detective Inspector Wilding though, who politely asked me to hand over the tape I shot on Sunday, and when I refused he informed me that my non-co-operation was putting me fully into the hands of the American authorities, who, I quote, "have their own way of dealing with terror-related cases".'

Michelle's eyes widened. 'What's that supposed to mean?'

'I guess I'll find out when our FBI attaché friend is ready to show his hand. I'm only surprised that no-one's contacted us already, if only to get heavy about the tape. Nothing while I was out?'

Michelle shook her head. 'Not from that quarter,'

she answered, 'but there is from this one. In fact, I think we've now got exactly what we're looking for.'

Immediately Laurie dropped her bag and sank down on the floor next to her.

'OK, I'll read the '97 version first,' Michelle said, handing her a single page. 'Then you can read the 2002, where it's highlighted.'

As she quickly scanned the words, Laurie's insides began knotting, for she'd spotted this paragraph before they'd had the '97 version, and even then it had rung alarm bells.

'So this is what the original 1997 version says,' Michelle began. '"The process of revolutionary change which would see the US as supreme global leader of a newly democratized world with systems set up by the US, is likely to be a long one. To speed up this process, and to galvanize public support behind our policies and our military, we would require a cataclysmic event such as Pearl Harbor."'

Laurie's eyes boggled as her ears almost refused to believe what they'd just heard. 'And that was written in '97,' she said incredulously, 'four years *before* the "cataclysmic event" that we now know rocketed forward the neo-conservative agenda and plunged us all into a global war on terror.'

'Now go to the revised version,' Michelle said, 'amended in 2002 *after* the event.'

Laurie read aloud. ' "The process of global transformation, even if it brings revolutionary change, is likely to be a long one, absent some catastrophic and catalyzing event – like a new Pearl Harbor." ' She looked up, eyes glittering with excitement.

'Almost the same, except the '97 version stipulates precisely what they need to happen to get their world-dominance agenda under way. Then lo and behold the "cataclysmic event" happens, and suddenly we have the totally watered-down 2002 version.'

'Precisely,' Michelle responded. 'So either someone very obligingly and coincidentally pulled off their cataclysmic event for them, or . . .' She deliberately left the sentence unfinished. Enquiries into the attacks of September 11th still abounded, but nothing as damning as this had come to light before.

Laurie was dumbfounded. 'Of course it's not proof of anything,' she said, 'nor does it give us an irrefutable connection to the P2OG, but it's got to be one of the most damning indictments against any political organisation in history. And if they're capable of something like this, no-one's going to have a problem believing they'd be behind the plot that's fallen into Tom's hands.'

'So what we have is not proof,' Michelle said, 'but total credibility, which is enough.'

Laurie was shaking her head in amazement. 'It's no wonder they're so keen to stop Tom. This is what they've been afraid he'd get hold of. It has to be. My God, once they know he's made this connection they are *not* going to be happy.'

Michelle shuddered. 'Don't let's go there,' she said. 'Let's just get it to him so he can go to print, because if this document proves anything at all, it's that we're up against an unstoppable machine here.'

Laurie was already on her feet. As she reached

491

her study she came to a sudden halt. 'My computer,' she said, blinking at her empty desk.

Confused, Michelle looked up.

Laurie's heart was starting to thud. 'It was here when I left. I used it. So where is it now?'

Mystified, Michelle came to look.

'What about Elliot's?' Laurie demanded, starting across the hall and throwing open his study door. 'His has gone too.'

'But it can't have,' Michelle protested. 'I was here the whole time – except when I went down to get a sandwich, which couldn't have been more than ten minutes.'

'Well it seems it was enough,' Laurie said, starting for the phone.

'Is the email routing system on either of them?' Michelle asked.

'No, thank God. Only the first stop. After that they'd still have a complete maze to get through before they could read any of the messages.'

'And anyway none of them matter as much as what we have here,' Michelle reminded her.

'Exactly.' After connecting with Gino, the only member of her team who was in London at the moment, and establishing that all was intact at the office, Laurie quickly helped Michelle gather up the documents, then grabbing their coats they dashed out to take the river bus along to Limehouse.

'All we need now,' Laurie said, starting to dial Nick's mobile, 'is confirmation that the editors are lined up.' Relieved when she merely got his voicemail she left him a message to call asap to update her on his progress, then left a similar message for Max.

492

By the time they reached the office on Narrow Street, there wasn't much doubt in either of their minds that they were being followed.

'They're not even trying to hide it,' Laurie said, as she unlocked the front door.

Michelle glanced back to where two casually dressed men in their mid-to-late thirties were idling in front of Bootles, the restaurant, only half-pretending to peruse the menu that was chalked on a board outside. 'We could find these computers snatched from under our very noses,' she said, cautiously.

'Just what I was thinking,' Laurie responded, as she pushed the door open, 'so stay by the window and keep an eye on them, while I send the email and erase everything, hopefully before they decide to strike – if indeed that's what they're intending.'

After taking up position by the window, Michelle stood quietly in the semi-darkness, listening to the tapping of the keyboard as Laurie typed in, word for word, what they'd found, while the two men kicked their heels, and one of them made a mobile phone call. Though this was by no means the first time she'd been in a situation where she was being watched, she was still gripped with unease, for no matter which language a stalker spoke, or which side of the law they were on, the encroaching sense of violation was still the same.

'I hope no-one's watching Katie like this,' she commented, thinking of how vulnerable she and Molly were down there, on the edge of the village. The only near neighbours ready to call on were Judy and Dave, who were out of shouting range, and woefully inexperienced when it came to dealing with authorities at this level.

'I don't see why they would,' Laurie responded, still typing. 'None of us is there now, and they know her situation, so there wouldn't be anything to gain. Besides, if there was a problem, she'd call.'

'Mm,' Michelle responded, experiencing a further stirring of unease as the two men strolled almost arrogantly across the road to lean against the park railings. 'I think, for her own sake, we need to keep Katie out of this altogether from now on,' she said. 'In fact, I got the impression yesterday that she wouldn't mind it going away, it's just that she doesn't want us to feel that she's bailing out.'

Laurie was checking her email for accuracy. 'Has she had the talk with Molly yet?' she asked.

'Not quite. Apparently she brought it up last night, but Molly blocked her. She's going to try again over the weekend, when Molly doesn't have school the next day, and after they've done a spot of retail therapy so Molly might feel less inclined to run out on her . . . How are you getting on there? They're starting to edge this way.'

'Oh hell,' Laurie murmured, quickly rearranging the pages. 'I've only got the '97 version in so far. Did you lock the door?'

'No, but I will,' and moving swiftly to it, she turned the key.

'Call Gino and ask him to come over,' Laurie said. 'We could do with some male back-up. He should be in the pub opposite. The number's written on the board there, do you see?'

After making the call Michelle returned to the window and felt a cold hand of fear close around

494

her heart. 'They've gone,' she murmured. 'I can't see them.' A moment later she started as someone came past the window, then realizing it must be Gino, she went quickly to the door.

'Is anyone around?' she called out.

'Can't see anyone,' he called back.

She turned to Laurie. 'Have you got both versions in yet?'

'Just about,' Laurie replied, her fingers moving like crazy.

'Hang on,' Michelle said to Gino.

Two minutes later, after making absolutely sure she had everything right, Laurie said, 'OK, it's done. I'm just typing in the address now, then it'll be ready to send.'

Michelle waited for the thumbs up to say the email had gone, then turned the key and gingerly pulled back the door.

'What's going on?' Gino said, stepping inside. 'Who's supposed . . .' The wind went from him as he was slammed out of the way and two men burst in behind him, brandishing badges and telling them all to move away from the computers, 'NOW!'

Quickly Laurie hit the keys, trying to erase evidence of the message.

'Laurie! No! No!' Michelle shouted. 'Leave it.'

Laurie looked up and to her horror saw a gun aiming straight at her.

'Move away now,' she was told.

Before she could respond, the other man grabbed her and hauled her out of the chair. 'Over by the wall,' he barked, shoving her forward. 'And stay back, all of you.'

Minutes later the computer was disconnected

and being transported out to the street. One of the men was on the phone, presumably calling for a vehicle, but that must already have been done, because almost immediately a police car was pulling up outside.

'What the hell?' Gino said, as the car drove away taking the computer and men with it.

'It's a long story,' Laurie told him, finding she was shaking. She turned to Michelle. 'At least I managed to send it,' she said.

'What about erase?' Michelle asked.

Laurie shook her head.

Michelle turned back to the window, where there was nothing to be seen now except a few commuters hurrying back from the station, and a teenage couple heading for the park. 'Then I guess,' she said, 'that all hell is about to break loose.'

'This is it!' Tom declared, staring excitedly at the screen. 'Shit!' he cried, thumping a hand on the table. 'Does it get any better? The neo-cons might just as well pack up now and join history. They're never going to survive this.'

Elliot was grinning widely. This truly was the breakthrough they needed, for there should be no credibility problems now. It all fitted. The remit was to employ all means necessary in order to hold on to power and further the aims of the 21 Project. Though they'd already known that, what they hadn't realized was how explicit the original was in its stunning recommendations on how to speed up the agenda's launch, increase defence spending, and export 'American-style democracy' to those parts of the world whose resources were vital to the

US. It was all unfolding perfectly. 'Talk about hoist by your own petard,' he commented, going to fetch two glasses. 'Definitely a cause to celebrate.'

Pushing back from the table, Tom reached for one of their better burgundies and started to open it. 'Based on this, I'm going to suggest two different articles,' he said, already going through it in his mind, 'one for Europe, Asia and the Arab world, with the focus on P2 and the use of a staged terrorist plot as part of an election strategy, the other for the States, leading with the "cataclysmic event" that advanced the neo-con cause beyond even their wildest dreams.'

Elliot was nodding and holding out glasses for Tom to fill. 'It'll make sense for you to handle the States,' he said. 'I'll take the rest of it.' He glanced at the clock. 'It's Thursday evening now, we've got no food, so I say we stick to our plan to go to Beaujeu for dinner, then make a start on everything first thing tomorrow. It'll give us time to discuss it tonight, then sleep on it before we get going. We should still be ready in plenty of time to submit edited highlights by Saturday.'

'Which is a reminder,' Tom said, 'that we still don't know which editors are up for it. Are there any other emails with that one?'

'It was the only one that came through,' Elliot replied. 'We'll check again when we get back, but Laurie will know how important it is to get that information to us, especially now, so she'll be on it, no doubt about that.' He raised his glass, and saluted Tom. 'To you, my friend,' he said, 'and the greatest story of your career. Of anyone's career.'

Tom grinned. 'We're in this together,' he

responded. 'I couldn't have come this far without you, so let's drink to going the rest of the distance and staying this side of freedom.'

'Not to mention the Styx,' Elliot added wryly, and laughing they clinked glasses and drank.

It was seven o'clock in the morning, Washington time, as the Special Operations Executive gathered in a secure office of the Eisenhower Building, close to the White House, to discuss the information that had come in overnight. Clearly seizing the British reporters' computers had paid off big time, for they confirmed that the worst-case scenario was on the brink of becoming a reality. Radical measures now needed to be agreed upon as to how to effect control of the situation.

'Is there anything yet on Chambers's location?' Deborah Gough asked, setting aside her copy of Laurie Forbes's email containing the damaging amendment.

'Nothing confirmed,' the CIA analyst told her. 'The Brits have been operating on the assumption he was still in the country, but we've just heard they're reassessing.'

'Based on what?'

'On the fact that the journalist, Elliot Russell, has close links with an ex-member of the SIS who could account for the tip-offs, and who apparently has a home in England's West Country, and a private plane. As Chambers was last known to be in that area, there's a good chance he's been flown out of the country, probably to France, though I'm told that the aircraft's capacity would allow for a much greater distance.'

Allbringer's expression was not pleasant as he said, 'So what you're telling us is, he could be anywhere in the damned world by now.'

'We have all possible resources on this, and the Brits are confident they'll have the net closed by the end of the day.'

Deborah Gough's patience was running thin. 'You're coming at this entirely the wrong way,' she told them bluntly. 'We're never going to find them in that time when we don't even know which country they're in, so we need to take a look at what we do have and how best to utilize it.'

All eyes were on her.

'First we need to get the Brits out of the picture,' she said. 'The leak's clearly at their end, and since our own resources are more sophisticated . . .'

'Not strictly true, not in all areas,' the analyst told her.

Her eyes flashed with anger. 'Well I'm not going to get into a pissing contest,' she snorted. 'We need to get our hands on Chambers and Russell, preferably within the next twenty-four hours, so now I suggest we agree on exactly how that should be achieved. I say we start with the women . . .'

'Actually,' the FBI chief came in, 'just prior to this meeting I was handed a recording of a telephone call between Laurie Forbes and Nick van Zant, the reporter who's soliciting European editors. I think you should hear it.'

Deborah Gough's fingers were tightening around a pen as she watched him go over to the bank of hi-tech equipment that covered one wall and slot a small cassette into a player.

'The call took place last night at eleven p.m.

499

British time,' he told them. 'The voices are clear, as are the implications.'

As the playback started, everyone was still. Laurie Forbes's voice was the first to come into the room.

'Nick! At last. Where are you?'

'Brussels. I got your message.'

'We've been waiting to hear. How's it going? Who's on board?'

His voice was tight as he said, 'Something came up, so I didn't get started until yesterday.'

'Are you kidding? Why on earth didn't you tell us you'd been held up? We could have sent someone else.'

'Laurie, I know this story means a lot to you and Elliot, but don't expect it to mean the same to me. I had contacts of my own to see, for a story of my own.'

There was a brief pause before her angry voice said, 'That's no excuse for not keeping us informed, and you know it. For God's sake, Nick, we have to get this off our hands and into print as soon as possible. It's getting really tight now, so what are the chances of having a decent line-up by the weekend?'

'At this stage, almost nil. You'll have to delay.'

'But I don't know that we can.'

'I don't know that you have a choice.'

'Nick, please tell me this isn't personal . . .'

'I'll treat that with the contempt it deserves,' he sneered. 'You'll have your editors and their private emails by Monday, Tuesday at the latest.'

'Well, clearly the important point here, gentlemen,' Deborah Gough stated, as the FBI chief removed the cassette, 'is that Mr van Zant has very obligingly bought us some time. So now I would return us to my earlier recommendation, made during our last meeting, that we hold him – and Max Erwin – until we've pinned down Chambers's location. Already too many editors have been informed of the impending story, and whilst a few can be persuaded into a change of mind, allowing the list to grow would be just plain foolish.'

'If we're talking about arrest, we'll need charges,' the FBI chief told her, 'and I wouldn't recommend the counter-terrorism route at this stage.'

'Of course not, and I'm not talking about arrest. I'm merely suggesting a little hospitality at a secure location, such as the farm for Max Erwin, and the München estate outside of Frankfurt for van Zant. Unless someone has a better idea.'

'Have you considered the kind of blowback we can expect if two prominent journalists just vanish off the scene?' Allbringer demanded bitterly.

'It should only be for a couple of days. Not long enough to cause any undue alarm.'

Allbringer was still far from happy. 'I think we're going down a very dangerous path here,' he said darkly. 'If we take out Chambers . . .'

'Nothing's been decided yet,' Gough cut in, 'the repercussions and ramifications of such an action are still being analysed and constantly updated. And don't let's forget, the evidence of his complicity in an act of terror is currently in his hands, so there should be no difficulty in connecting him with his own noose.'

Allbringer's face was paling with anger. 'And what about Russell?' he demanded. 'This email confirms he's actually with Chambers, so do we give the order for him to be taken out too?'

'If necessary,' Gough responded with no hesitation. 'Assisting a suspected terrorist to avoid arrest is a crime in itself, and carries its own penalty as does . . .'

'For Christ's sake!' Allbringer exploded. 'They're members of the press. US and British citizens . . .'

'. . . as does harbouring a fugitive,' Gough pressed on, 'and I'm sure there are several other more serious charges we could level his way too.'

'We'll never get away with this,' Allbringer told her. 'This isn't the way to go . . .'

'When you sit in this chair is when you get to call the shots,' Gough reminded him sharply. 'Until then, I'm accountable to my superiors, not this committee. If you have a problem with that, Mr Allbringer, may I suggest you step down now.'

Though he would have liked nothing better than to walk, Allbringer stayed right where he was, for he didn't want to add to the suspicion that he, with some help from the Brits, was behind the leak of information to Chambers.

Gough continued to speak. 'Our own press campaign is ready to go just as soon as I receive word. I've spoken personally to several editors, so they know it's coming, and the instant they receive anything from Chambers they'll forward it straight on to me. For the moment I'm recommending that we remain low key on the warrant for his arrest, because we certainly don't want the rest of the world's media helping us to find him. That should mean, when the explosion comes, we have everything well under our control.' She looked around.

'Is there anything else we need to discuss, gentlemen?'

There was a general negative grunting, so starting to pack away her pens, notebook and the email from Laurie Forbes to Elliot Russell, she said, 'OK. Let's reconvene at the same time tomorrow to assess progress, unless something happens to warrant an earlier meet. Until then our priorities are to move aside the Brits and assume full control – I will speak to Sir Christopher and Michael Dalby personally to inform them of this decision. Meantime, let's start finding ways to exploit the assets we have, namely the female contingent of this operation – not forgetting that Michelle Rowe is apparently pregnant. I'd consider that a sizable ace, wouldn't you, gentlemen?'

'So that's it, there's nothing more we can do now, except wait,' Laurie declared, as she stood aside for Michelle to go into the flat ahead of her.

'And pray,' Michelle added, as she shrugged off her coat and hooked it up in the small lobby where Laurie hung hers.

They'd just returned from Canary Wharf and the newspaper offices where Laurie used to work, before she'd become a producer. It was the safest place, she'd felt, to use a computer, for once inside the thirty-five-storey tower block and soaring away in a crowded lift, it would be extremely difficult for anyone following to know which floor they'd got off at, never mind which computer they'd used. So now Elliot and Tom had been warned that the Special Operations Executive was aware of how much they knew, and that Nick wouldn't be delivering a full list of editors until Monday or Tuesday.

'They're not going to be pleased,' Michelle commented, slumping down on the sofa. 'In fact, I wouldn't want to be in Nick's shoes when one of them comes to tackle him. What was he thinking?'

'I don't know,' Laurie replied. 'He said it was nothing to do with me, but I'm not sure I believe him. He was really angry last Sunday. He might have seen this as a way of getting back at Elliot.'

'If they're tracked down before Tuesday, he'll have managed to get back at Tom too,' Michelle remarked acidly.

Laurie shot her a look and sank down on the sofa.

Softening her tone a little, Michelle said, 'How do you feel about him now?'

'Absolutely furious,' Laurie answered, 'but awful for how much I've hurt him.' She smiled wryly. 'If only it were possible to have them both.'

'That sounds as though you're still not sure about Elliot.'

Laurie sighed heavily. 'There are moments when I'm so far from being sure I almost have to wonder what I'm doing here,' she said, wrapping her arms round a cushion.

Michelle's eyes twinkled. 'Could it possibly be because you love him, in spite of it all?'

'Yes, I think that would be it,' Laurie conceded. 'But I hate the person all this is turning me into – insecure, jealous, suspicious . . . And now, would you believe, the arch-bitch has apparently decided to set up residence in London, so she's going to be right here, in *my* city, on *my* territory. Ugh, it makes my skin crawl just to think of her being so close.

Let's change the subject. I don't want that woman in my life, and I certainly don't want her in my head. So shall I make some tea? Or would you prefer something stronger?'

Michelle sighed and kicked off her shoes. 'I'd love the second, but should probably stick with the first,' She answered, stifling a yawn. 'Oh God, this is making me so tired, but at least I'm not throwing up, so be thankful for small mercies. Any messages from Katie?'

Seeing a blinking light on the machine, Laurie pressed the button and carried on making the tea as they replayed. Nothing from Katie, but there was one from Chris, asking her to call him at his London gallery as soon as she got this message.

'Is that the Chris who helped Tom?' Michelle asked. 'The pilot?'

Laurie nodded and picked up the phone. 'I thought he was still in Cornwall,' she said, dialling his number. 'I wonder when he came back. Hi, it's Laurie,' she said when he answered. 'Everything OK?'

'Everything's fine,' he confirmed lightly. 'Rachel and I were wondering if you'd like to come round for a bite to eat this evening. Michelle too, if she's still with you.'

Surprised that he knew Michelle was there, she said, 'Sure, we'd love to.'

'Good. Bring a few things and stay the night. You won't have to worry about driving back then.'

Understanding there was probably more to it, Laurie merely said, 'OK. We'll be there around seven thirty?'

'Seven thirty it is.'

As she put down the phone Laurie related the conversation to Michelle, adding, 'My guess is, he's heard something and doesn't want us to be here alone.'

'Well, we are sitting targets,' Michelle remarked, 'and speaking as someone who's had experience of being leaned on heavily, I wouldn't care to repeat it.'

'Having been there myself, I couldn't agree more. So what do you say we abandon this tea and turn up at Chris and Rachel's early? I'm sure they won't mind, and as I've just announced seven thirty to the listening world, it could lessen the risk of us being waylaid somewhere en route.'

Michelle was reaching for the phone. 'Give me a moment to check on Katie, and I'll be right with you,' she said. 'Can I give her Chris's number? Or no, she has my mobile, she can use that if she needs to get hold of us . . . Hi, Katie. It's . . . I'm talking to a machine,' she said, and waited for the bleep. 'Hi, it's me. Hope you're OK. Call when you can, let me know how everything's going. My mobile's on. Love you,' and after waiting a few more seconds just in case Katie picked up, she rang off. 'I hope she's all right,' she murmured, as she put the phone back on its base. 'She's seemed quite distant the last few times we've spoken.'

'That's how we want it while all this comes to a head,' Laurie reminded her. 'She needs to be way out of the firing line now, because there's a very good chance it's starting to turn nasty, and God knows she's got enough on her plate without having to worry about the friendly Feds turning up to ransack her house again. Or worse, to take her

506

hostage as a means of forcing Tom to come out from where he is.'

Michelle smiled. 'Anyone who takes my sister hostage would be stupid indeed. A single mother, dying of cancer? They'd get hit so hard they'd regret any brain activity at all, never mind the idiocy that made snatching Katie Kiernan seem like a good idea. No, I'm not worried about them taking her hostage, because they really aren't that stupid, I'm more concerned about how low she's seemed since Sunday.'

Chapter Twenty-Two

It was a little after six on Saturday evening, almost dark outside, and starting to turn cold as Katie slid a scrumptious-looking lasagne into the oven, then set about clearing up the mess she'd made preparing it. It was a while since she'd gone to so much trouble over a meal, which wasn't doing much for her already beleaguered conscience since it reminded her of how neglectful she'd been of Molly these past months. Not that Molly had complained about the food she was served, but Katie wondered if she secretly missed the way they used to cook together on Saturday evenings, light candles, rent a video and snuggle up with a box of chocolates to laugh, or scream, or have a good sob at the latest film. There was a chance she'd out-grown it anyway, and felt relieved to be released from her mother's weekend rituals, but just in case, Katie had decided to resurrect this one in an attempt to recapture their closeness and show Molly that things didn't have to change yet. In fact, she'd started the ball rolling that morning, when she'd suggested they make one of their shopping trips into Bath, but Molly had immediately protested.

'I want to go shopping with my friends,' she'd cried. 'I'll feel stupid going with you, and anyway, you always make me buy things you like instead of what I like, and I'm fed up with it. I'm grown-up now, I can choose my own clothes.'

'All right, all right,' Katie had responded patiently. 'I just thought it would be nice to do something together, but I can see your point, so I'll give you the money and you can buy whatever you like.'

Molly had eyed her suspiciously.

'Go on, take the money before I change my mind,' Katie had insisted.

So off she'd rushed, presumably with Allison and those other two girls she was far too thick with, and had come back an hour ago with several bags, scarlet cheeks and an attitude that was every bit as wary as the one she'd gone out with. One wrong word from Katie and it was clear she'd go off like a rocket, so quite how Katie was going to get the subject round to what they needed to discuss, she was still struggling to work out. However, the lasagne – Molly's favourite – together with scented candles around the sitting room, a crackling log fire in the hearth and a couple of romantic comedies might make her a little less inclined to shoot off through the door the instant Katie attempted to talk.

Feeling nervous enough to shoot off herself at the moment, Katie took a quick slug of hornbeam then picked up the phone as it started to ring.

'Hi, it's me,' Judy told her. 'Just calling to let you know we'll be at the pub later, if you want to join us.'

'Thanks, but if all goes to plan, I imagine we'll be staying at home tonight.'

'Of course. I just wanted you to know where we were, should you need us for anything.'

'Bless you,' Katie responded. 'I'll keep you posted on how it goes, but hopefully not before tomorrow.'

As she rang off she was thinking of Michelle, and the similar conversation she'd had with her an hour ago, when Michelle had offered to jump on a train and come straight back if Katie needed her. Honestly, the way everyone seemed to be building this up into such a big deal, she was starting to wonder if she actually had a handle on its importance herself. But no, it was simply that they cared, for which she was deeply moved and grateful – and before she started riding the waves of self-pity towards her sad little beach, she decided to take her spiritual counsellor's advice and have a brief commune with her higher self to try and get in the mood.

Ommm . . .

Upstairs in her bedroom Molly was in a frenzy of indecision over what to wear to the party. She still hadn't told her mum she was going yet, or that she would be out all night, but this was like, the biggest, most important night of her life, so no way was anyone going to stop her. She just needed to choose the right top to go with the flared black mini she'd bought today, but then her mobile rang with a text and seeing who it was she started jumping up and down in joy and relief. It was from Brad! He'd got in touch last night, and now here he was again.

```
Hi Babe, C u
tonite. Lkng fwd
2 it. Wear smthng
spesh. Lv Bx
```

'He wants me to wear something special,' she cried down the phone to Allison. 'So which top? The red or the gold?'

'Bring both,' Allison told her, 'you can make up your mind when you get here. Or you can change halfway through. But definitely wear the black and white check shoes with the red bow and slingbacks, because they're like, sooo wicked. I wish I'd bought a pair too. Cecily nicked hers, did she tell you?'

Molly's heart gave a thud. 'No,' she answered, feeling queasy as she realized they could all have been arrested. 'Is she there yet?'

'No. Her and Donna are coming about eight. When will you be here?'

'I'm leaving in a minute. Oh God, I feel really nervous. What if he decides he doesn't like me?'

'No way. And I've got loads of Breezers here, so you can be like, really chilled out by the time the party starts, and Donna says she's bringing some weed.'

'Will any other girls be there?' Molly asked.

'Duh! It's a party!'

'How many are you expecting?'

'About forty, I think. My mother's already gone to spend a weekend in London with her husband who's supposed to be my father, but you'd never guess. They won't be back till tomorrow night, so we've got the entire place to ourselves. Toby's bagsed their bed for him and Cecily, but there's a guest room you and Brad can use which is like, OK, it just has two single beds instead of one big one, but that won't matter ... Anyway, listen, got to go. Just get here as soon as you can.'

As she rang off, Molly's nerves were churning up so badly that the smell coming from downstairs was making her want to hurl. Obviously her mum was cooking something, and she only hoped she wasn't expecting her to eat it, because just no way.

Her heart did a sudden lurch again as she thought about Brad and what they were supposed to do tonight. It made her hands all shaky, and her stomach like really blah.

'Shit!' she muttered, stuffing all her make-up back in a silver zip-top purse. She'd take it to Allison's and do it there. Perhaps once she'd had a couple of drinks she'd calm down a bit, because God knew, after the week she'd just had she needed to. What with the police taking away her computer, and Brad not calling, then that horrible business with Michelle that had *so* gone wrong it was turning her all hot and cold even now. Oh yeah, and there was the fact that Michelle was supposed to be marrying Tom, which had seriously pissed her off, because it had to be like, really upsetting for her mum, when she had no-one, and she didn't want her mum to be upset and on her own. Then Tom had disappeared, and – *thank God* – so had Michelle, but then her mum had started putting on the pressure for them to talk, which made her feel all panicky and weird, because like, didn't she have enough going on, without having to be lectured and preached to about something she wouldn't bother listening to anyway.

Still, none of it mattered now Brad had called. That was all that was important. She was going to see him tonight, and it would be like, bliss, and even though she still wasn't sure about going all the way, once she'd had some drinks and a few puffs of weed, she'd be like, really out there and up for it, just like the DOLs said. So, emptying out her school bag, she threw in her make-up, some clean undies, her trainers and jeans for tomorrow, and the gold halter-neck top – she'd keep the red one on for the moment, but make the final decision later. Now all she had to do was get past her mum. First though, she'd better put her check shoes in the bag and wear the trainers, because it was a bit of a walk to Allison's, and she didn't want to get her others muddy.

Katie was in the sitting room when Molly got downstairs, lighting candles and humming away. A stab of conscience immediately pierced Molly's chest, because this was what they always used to do on Saturdays, cook and light candles and watch videos, so maybe her mum thought they were going to do it tonight. Well, she was sorry, but she couldn't. And it wasn't her fault, was it, if her mum had gone to a lot of trouble. She hadn't said anything, so how was Molly supposed to know what she was planning? If she had, she'd have been able to tell her she was going out. God, it got right on her nerves, the way she was always made to feel as though everything was her fault, when it wasn't!

'Oh, there you are,' Katie said, coming into the kitchen. 'I was just going to check on . . .' Seeing Molly's best coat, trainers and school bag she stopped. 'What are you doing?'

'I'm going out.'

Katie frowned. 'But I've made a lasagne, and I thought . . . Well, I thought this was what you wanted, for us to spend a bit more time together.'

'Yeah, but not tonight. I'm going to a party. And before you start having a go, you never said anything about us staying in together, so how was I supposed to know you were cooking? I'm not a mind-reader.'

'You're not very polite either,' Katie retorted sharply. 'And I don't think I heard you ask if you could go to a party, so any more of that attitude and you won't be going.'

Molly's cheeks flamed. 'I'm just saying that it's not my fault you cooked,' she said sulkily.

Katie eyed her closely, keeping a strict face to cover her disappointment. 'Well, at least you can have something to eat before you go,' she said.

'No!' Molly cried. 'I don't want anything. I'm not hungry, and it'll just make me late.'

Wishing she could stop her, but knowing if she tried it would only turn into a row, Katie said, 'I suppose it's at Allison's.'

Molly's eyes slanted away. 'So what if it is?'

'Who else is going to be there?'

'*I don't know*. All her friends.'

'And Brad?'

'He might be.'

'I want to know more about this boy, so let's start with how old he is.'

514

Molly's mouth pursed. 'He's the same age as me, all right?'

Katie sighed. 'Molly, you're such a bad liar.'

'Well what difference does it make how old he is? If I was twenty-four and he was twenty-eight no-one would say anything.'

'But you're not twenty-four, you're fourteen, and if he's eighteen that is not acceptable. He's too old for you.'

'I never said he was eighteen. You did.'

Wondering how on earth she could reach across this horrible gulf, Katie inhaled deeply, then decided not to argue any further. 'OK, I want you back here by ten,' she said.

Molly's eyes flew open. 'Oh, no way!' she cried. 'It's a party, Mum! It'll just be getting going by ten, and then like, I'm supposed to leave? I don't think so.'

'Well, I do, and once again, let me remind you that your attitude is doing you no favours.'

Immediately Molly turned on the reasonable voice, saying, 'Look, I'm going to be fifteen in January, and loads of girls my age stay out late on Saturday nights. Some of them even go to discos and things, so they don't get home until gone two in the morning. I know you won't want me out wandering the streets at that time, so I've asked Allison if I can stay over . . .'

Katie was shaking her head. 'Oh no,' she said. 'You're not staying over if boys are going to be there. I'll come and pick you up . . .'

'No!' Molly raged. 'It would be like, so fucking embarrassing having my mother turn up to take me home. Everyone would think I was a right baby . . .'

'I'll wait at the end of the drive, no-one need know I'm there.'

Molly's expression was turning thunderous. 'I've told Allison I'm staying now, and I've got all my stuff packed . . .'

'Then you can just unpack it. And while you're at it, I'd like to see what you're wearing please, because this is hardly the weather for bare legs, so open your coat . . .'

'For God's sake,' Molly seethed, slamming down her bag and spinning away in disgust.

Katie moved over to the back door, to block an escape. 'Take your coat off,' she repeated.

Bristling with resentment Molly flung her coat open and let it fall down to her elbows. 'Satisfied?' she demanded, planting a hand on one hip and tapping her foot.

Katie took one look at the thigh-top mini and skimpy red bustier and said, 'You're not going out dressed like that.'

'What's the matter with it?' Molly shrieked. 'It's like, fashionable. I know you don't know what that is, but it's what girls my age are wearing.'

'You look like a cheap tart.'

Molly's eyes flashed. 'Well you should take a look at yourself, see what you look like,' she spat nastily. 'And at least I don't behave like a tart, the way you do when you're around men.'

'OK, that's it,' Katie said. 'You've gone too far, now. You're not leaving this house . . .'

'Just you try and stop me.'

Katie turned round to lock the door and found, to her annoyance, that the key wasn't there. 'I don't want to get into a fight over this,' she said, turning

516

back again. 'You know very well how difficult you've been this week, so I'm afraid parties and sleepovers are out of the question until you can mend your ways and learn some manners. Now go back upstairs, take off those trashy clothes, then we'll sit down and have something to eat.'

Molly's temper totally exploded. 'I've already told you, I don't want anything!' she shouted. 'And I'm going to that party, I don't care what you say. It's my life. I can do what I want . . .'

'I'm your mother and you'll do as I tell you. Now go upstairs . . .'

'Just try and make me!'

'Molly, please,' Katie implored, feeling the situation moving out of her grip. 'We need to talk, and you can't keep on finding excuses to avoid it.'

'I'm not finding excuses,' she yelled. 'I've been invited to a party, and I've got to be there.'

'Why?'

'I just have. You don't understand.'

'Try me.'

Molly's face was shaking with fury. 'Just shut up keeping on all the time!' she shouted. 'Now let me get past.'

'You know what we have to discuss, don't you?' Katie stated, her eyes blazing the challenge.

Molly almost recoiled.

'Yes you do,' Katie said, 'but you don't want to hear me say it. Well, Molly, it has to be said. We have to face it.'

'*Shut up*,' Molly seethed, blocking her ears. 'Just shut up.'

'It's not going to go away,' Katie cried. 'It's here, it's a part of me, and we have to deal with it.'

517

'No, no, no,' Molly gasped, shaking her head from side to side.

'Yes, Molly. Yes! I'm going to die. That's what we have to face, but Michelle will be here to take care of you . . .'

Molly lunged at her. 'I don't need anyone to take care of me,' she seethed, as she tried shoving her out of the way. 'I can take care of myself. Now let me get past.'

Katie grabbed her and started to shake. 'Stop running away,' she sobbed. 'This is hard enough, can't you see that?'

'Stop crying!' Molly shouted. 'I don't want you to cry.'

Not even realizing she was, Katie said, 'Then let's stop this now . . . Molly!' she gasped, as Molly's fists suddenly slammed into her, and as she fell back against the wall, banging her head on the corner of a cupboard, Molly tore open the door.

'I'm going out, and I won't be back till tomorrow,' she raged. 'And if you come anywhere near Allison's tonight, I'll never *ever* speak to you again.'

Still breathless from the blow, Katie stood where she was, listening to Molly running, the gate opening and closing, and the ducks squawking as she passed. She knew that those dreadful words had already been blocked from Molly's mind, cut out as though never spoken, but they'd be back, how could they not, and as the full horror of the last few minutes began closing in on her, Katie wondered if she'd ever handled anything more disastrously in her life. If she had, she was at a loss to know when or how, and with her head pounding and the rest of her turning so weak she feared she might actually pass out, she stumbled to a chair and sat down with her face in her hands.

After a moment she was able to start taking deep breaths – in, out, in, out. It worked to a degree, but she was still shaking badly, and was so torn about what to do next that even to try and think of it was making her faint.

Starting as the oven timer shrilled, she forced herself to her feet and went to turn it off. Suddenly she was sobbing, and tearing off a piece of kitchen roll she attempted to dry her eyes. More than anything she wanted to call Michelle now and ask her to come home, but she wouldn't. Nor would she go over to the pub later to join Judy. She simply couldn't bear anyone to know how dreadfully she'd just messed up with Molly, for the shame of it was already taking hold of her as though to try and drown her in its depths.

So no, she was going to see this through on her own, because really it only concerned her and Molly anyway. The best thing to do was sit here and wait for Molly to come back, because she would, eventually – she just hoped to God it would be tonight.

'If you drink any more of those now you'll puke,' Allison warned, grabbing a Breezer bottle from Molly before she could finish another.

'Let me have it! Let me have it!' Molly insisted, jigging up and down and already feeling drunk. 'I'm like, so nervous, and excited,' and throwing out her arms she started to spin. 'I'm going to see Brad and you're seeing Miles and we'll be a real foursome . . . And wheeee!'

519

Laughing as she spun her round, Allison cried, 'The DOLs are getting laid tonight!'

'Getting laid! Getting laid!' Molly echoed. Then, attempting to be serious, 'You know, I reckon after tonight we should start going down to see them at weekends. Oh God, yeah! We can like ride on their motorbikes and hold on to them, which will be soooo cool . . . Do you think they'll bring them tonight?'

'Probably,' Allison answered, going to change the CD.

'Oh my God! I am just so excited!' Molly squealed. 'Where's that bottle? I've got to have some more.'

'Save some for the rest of us,' Cecily drawled, as she and Donna came in the door.

'There are loads in the fridge,' Allison assured her. 'But better hurry up because she's going through them like they were lemonade.'

'This is going to be like, the best night of my life,' Molly bubbled.

Cecily shot a glance at Allison.

'I've got some weed,' Donna declared. 'Let's light up now, it'll really get us in the mood.'

'Oh yeah, definitely,' Molly enthused, turning to look at herself in the mirror, pouting and posing.

'What happened to the red top?' Cecily demanded, putting a match to Donna's joint. 'It's really sexy . . .'

'I thought it looked a bit tarty, so I decided on the gold one,' Molly told her.

'But it doesn't work as well as the red,' Cecily protested. 'You've got really great tits, so you should show them off. It'll really get him going.'

Donna sniggered and coughed on the joint.

Taking it from her, Cecily said, 'Where's Toby?'

'Getting ready in his room, I expect,' Allison answered. 'Or downstairs sorting out the music. Mother had some food sent in, by the way. It's in the kitchen, all set out on the table. Sometimes I could almost like her.'

'Do you think it's going to hurt?' Molly asked, lying back on the bed with Donna and taking a long drag of the joint.

'It might, at first,' Cecily told her, going to check on her make-up.

'It's going to be so cool,' Donna chanted. 'I want it now. Take me, take me.'

They were all laughing as Toby burst in the door to have a go at Allison about one of his CDs that was missing. Cecily sidled up to him, and slipping an arm round her he snogged her, then went on laying into Allison.

Molly giggled and hiccoughed and carried on lying on the bed with Donna. She didn't care if Toby could see all up her skirt, because she was in a great mood, and anyway he might tell Brad that she had fantastic legs and was wearing a thong. She took another puff on the joint, held it, blew it out, then drank. Next to her Donna started giggling, so she did too. Allison took the joint away and they laughed even harder. Then Allison told Toby to shut up and get lost while they finished getting ready.

By nine thirty the den downstairs was starting to fill up with people Molly had never seen before. They were all like, really cool though, and everyone seemed to know each other. They'd brought joints and more booze and stuff. Molly had switched to wine now, because it seemed a bit more sophisticated, but her legs were starting to feel all weird and rubbery, and her head was all fuzzy and thick. They were having a real laugh though, with the music throbbing off the walls and everyone dancing and chilling out, except she was starting to get a bit worried about where Brad was, because all his mates were here, so he should be too.

'Any sign of him yet?' she shouted above the music as Allison shimmied up to her with a samosa in one hand and an alcopop in the other.

'He'll be here, don't worry,' Allison assured her. 'Have something to eat.'

Molly pulled a face, and pushed the samosa away.

'The guy with the E's arrived,' Allison told her, biting into it herself. 'Are you going to try some?'

Molly started to answer, but a burp popped out instead, and they immediately dissolved into hysterical laughter. 'Where's Miles?' she asked, when they were finally able to stop giggling.

'Over there with Toby. You know what I did? Oh my God, this is going to totally freak you out, but I actually told him I want to go all the way tonight. Oh my God, you should have seen his face. He is like, so turned on now, and can't wait for it to happen, but I reminded him, I'm like, one of the hosts, so I can't just disappear straight away, I mean, can I?'

Molly shook her head. 'No, definitely not,' she agreed. 'Do you reckon I should tell Brad, as well?' she said, feeling a bit dizzy and like, so romantic at the thought of it.

'If you like,' Allison said, turning round as the music changed. 'Oh my God, I totally love this!' she declared, and putting down her drink and samosa, she grabbed Molly's hand and dragged her out to dance.

Molly gulped down the rest of her wine, parked the glass on a table as she passed and went happily into the middle of the room. This was one of her favourites too, and everyone said she was a brilliant dancer, so it would be like, so cool if Brad came in while she was really letting go. There were other people up dancing too, all rocking and jiving about, and the music was wicked, just kept going and going, so she could dance and dance. Her arms were in the air, her hips were jerking from side to side, then back to front and round and round. She knew people were watching her and she loved it, because she knew she looked really cool, and hip and like she should be a professional. The beat slowed in the middle of the record, so she slowed too, gyrating sexily, hands still linked above her head, knees slightly parted, then quickly knocking back someone else's drink, she launched herself vigorously into the last part of the song.

'Oh my God, that was like, just so brilliant,' she gasped to Allison, as they went back to the table. Then remembering she was still waiting for Brad, she started to feel all weird and irritable and began stamping her feet as she said, 'Where is he? He said he would be here. Do you think I should ring him?'

Allison was looking past her. 'If you turn round now,' she murmured, 'he's just walking in the door.'

Molly's heart stood still. 'Oh my God, oh my

God,' she muttered, keeping her back turned. 'Is he like really, drop dead? No, I know he is . . . Oh God, I can't bear it. What shall I say?'

Allison looked at her, but she wasn't exactly smiling. 'Up to you,' she responded.

Steeling herself Molly turned round, trying to look cool and laid back as she rested her weight on one leg, and picked up a glass. Immediately she saw him she virtually swooned. He was so tall and blond and unbelievably good-looking. 'Oh my God,' she gasped. 'He is a god. I can't believe he's been texting and calling me . . . I mean, he is just like so . . . He could get anyone. Do you think he knows where I am?'

'He hasn't looked over here yet,' Allison answered.

'I should go and say hello, shouldn't I? Give me a drink first,' and grabbing Allison's she downed it in one go. 'Is he looking this way?' she asked, breathlessly.

Allison shook her head. 'He's talking to someone.'

'OK. I'm going over there. Wish me luck,' and wobbling slightly as she turned round, she was about to start towards him when, to her confusion, he slipped an arm round a tall, blonde girl who was next to him, and was like so drop dead she had to be a model or an actress or something.

Molly couldn't make herself think. She was dreaming. She wasn't here at all, she was at home in her bed, but then she thought of her mum and everything turned really horrible, because she didn't want to be there.

The blonde was whispering in Brad's ear and he

was laughing. His eyes came briefly to Molly's, but he didn't seem to see her as he turned back to the blonde, said something, then pressed a kiss to her lips.

Molly's head was spinning. He'd said he was looking forward to seeing her, that she should wear something special . . .

He was coming towards her now, his arm still round the blonde. She watched him, then suddenly she was walking right up to him and saying hello.

Seeming startled, he glanced at the girl with him, then politely said, 'Hello.'

Molly turned to the blonde. 'Who are you?' she demanded.

The blonde blinked in surprise. 'I'm Jenny,' she said. 'Who are you?'

'Actually, I'm Brad's girlfriend.'

Brad couldn't have looked more astonished. 'I'm sorry,' he said. 'I don't think we've met . . .'

Molly's head was going round and round. She was aware of someone sniggering and laughing behind her. She turned to see Cecily and Donna . . . Allison was with them, Toby was turning away . . . Their faces started to swim . . .

'You fell for it!' Cecily shrieked. 'You really fell for it.'

'What exactly's going on?' Brad wanted to know.

Molly turned back, and felt herself swaying as huge racking sobs started to shudder their way up from inside her.

'Are you all right?' he asked.

She started to answer, but all that came out was a cascade of vomit which went all over him and the blonde and her and she just couldn't stop . . .

'Jesus Christ!' Brad cried, stepping back.

'Oh my God!' someone shouted.

'Oh puhleeze.'

'Someone get her out of here.'

The words, the room, the shame, the misery were spinning and spinning and everything was crowding in on her. She could hardly breathe, she was retching and sobbing so hard. Everyone was staring at her. She had to get out of here. She had to go somewhere a long, long way away and never come back.

Stumbling blindly from the room she dashed along the back hall, up the stairs and into Allison's room. As she started packing her bag her stomach heaved again and she raced into the bathroom. It just seemed to go on and on. Her throat was on fire, her stomach ached, and her body was so cold she couldn't stop shaking.

When she was able to stand she staggered back into the bedroom, continued stuffing her things in her bag, then grabbing her coat she ran down the back stairs and out into the night. She wasn't really thinking about which way to go home, she just wanted to get there. Tearing into the field she began running across the grass, but her heels kept sinking in the mud, so she had to take them off and put on her trainers. She was still sobbing and trembling, and feeling so horrified by what had happened she wanted to scream and scream and never see anyone again in the whole of her life. Why had Allison and Cecily and Donna done that to her? It was so mean. They'd made her look really stupid, in front of Brad, and everyone . . . But he'd been texting and calling her . . . They must have got someone else to do it, so they'd been laughing at her all the time, making a fool of her . . . She hated them so much now. She wanted to do something to really hurt them.

She'd got almost to their lane when she remembered what her mum had told her earlier.

'No, no, no,' she shouted. She couldn't go back there, she just couldn't. She didn't want it to be happening, so she wasn't going to let it. She'd find somewhere else to go. She wanted Tom to come back, because he'd make everything all right. He'd smash everyone up who'd been mean to her, and make them look even stupider than she had. Why had he gone away like that? Why did everyone always go away?

She turned round and started running back towards the woods. She couldn't see anything, it was too dark and her eyes were too clogged with tears and mascara. She didn't care though. She was never going home again, nor was she ever going to speak to anyone in the whole of her life. She was just going to find a computer somewhere and go on the suicide web site to find out how to kill herself. Yes, that was what she'd do. She'd kill herself, then they'd all be sorry, and feel terrible, and wish they could make it up to her, but it would be too bloody late then, and it would serve them all right . . .

Katie had waited up all night, torn between going to find Molly and giving her time to calm down. She'd barely slept, had paced and pleaded with Molly to call, or to respond to her texts, but so far there was no word. At eight o'clock on Sunday morning she tried calling the house, but a machine picked up. By nine thirty there was still no response to her message. Exhausted and unable to cope alone any more, she dialled Michelle's number, confessed what had happened and asked her to come.

Michelle didn't waste any time. It was just after midday as she and Laurie ran into the cottage to find Katie looking even worse than Michelle had feared.

'Any news?' Michelle asked, pulling her straight into her arms.

Katie shook her head. 'I keep trying her mobile, but it's either turned off, or the battery's run out.'

'Have you called the house?'

'Several times, but no-one's answering. It was a student party – much too old for Molly, but you remember what they were like . . . Drugs, sex . . .' Fear glittered in her eyes.

'We should go round there,' Laurie said to Michelle.

'Of course,' Michelle responded.

'I'm coming too,' Katie said.

'Katie, you can barely stand,' Michelle protested.

'She's my daughter. I can't just sit here!'

'You can and you will. Now listen to me . . . *Listen,*' she insisted, as Katie started objecting again. 'We'll find her, and we'll bring her home. So stop getting yourself all worked up and just remember, nothing's happened that can't be fixed.'

Katie attempted a wry sort of smile and clinging to the hope that they'd find Molly at Allison's, she said, 'Let's hope she's not too hung-over, or you could be bearing the scars of this mission for some time to come.'

Treating it to more of a laugh than it deserved,

Michelle kissed her, then followed Laurie out of the door.

An hour later they left the Fortescue-Bonds' house, feeling considerably more concerned than before they went in, for having spoken to everyone who was in a state to be spoken to, it was clear Molly wasn't there.

'There's something they're not telling us,' Michelle said as they walked to the car. 'Something about this Brad. OK, she was sick on him, and that's when she ran out, but where is he now? I'd like to hear what he has to say about it all.'

Looking through the notes she'd taken, Laurie said, 'I've got his number, let's give him a call.'

After five rings she was diverted to voicemail. 'Hello, if I've reached Brad Jenkins,' she said, 'I'd be very grateful if you could call me back. My name is Laurie Forbes, and I'm trying to find Molly Kiernan. Her mother is extremely worried, and if she doesn't turn up in an hour – it's twenty past one now – we will be notifying the police, so any help you can give us will be much appreciated.' After repeating her number twice, she rang off. 'Hopefully, if she is with him, the mention of the police will make her get in touch,' she said.

'If we don't hear from her,' Michelle said, 'we really will have to contact the police.'

'I'm sure it won't come to that,' Laurie responded. 'She has to be somewhere, and nine times out of ten in these situations, they turn out to be with friends.'

'I just hope Katie's going to take some comfort in that,' Michelle murmured, 'because right now, it's about all we have to offer.'

Chapter Twenty-Three

By four o'clock the fear of what might have happened to Molly was taking on so many terrifying dimensions that Katie could hardly bear to look at anyone in case she saw the same appalling thoughts reflected in their eyes too. There had been no call back from this Brad yet, though based on what she'd been told, it didn't seem likely they were together anyway. In fact, she almost wished they were, for there was more comfort in an abscondment with an eighteen-year-old boy than there was in Molly taking off alone while in such a disturbed and vulnerable state.

For the past two hours Michelle, Laurie and Judy had been contacting as many of Molly's schoolfriends as Judy and Katie could come up with, while Dave and a couple of other neighbours went out driving around Chippenham and the local villages to see if they could spot her. So far there had been no sign, nor had anyone from school either seen or been in touch with her by phone.

Now they were sitting in silence, Judy's words from the final call still seeming to hang in the air – a ghostly reminder that there was no-one left to ring. Gradually the same words were coming to each of them, yet no-one wanted to be the first to speak them, because no-one wanted to take that dreaded next step.

It was Michelle who finally plucked up the courage. 'I don't think we have any choice,' she said, 'we have to contact the police.'

Katie turned away, for the very idea of involving the police embraced every one of her worst nightmares to a point where she couldn't actually tell Michelle to do it. So she merely sat, mute and rigid, as Laurie, rather than call 999, looked up the local number, dialled it, then passed the phone to Michelle.

The next half an hour seemed to pass in a blur as two bobbies arrived, one male, one female, oozing friendliness, efficiency and calm. Katie wanted to scream at them to go away, because they shouldn't be here. They were giving it an air of reality, and it shouldn't be happening . . . It couldn't . . . Please God, it just couldn't!

Michelle did most of the talking, backed up by Laurie and Judy, while Katie sat and listened and ached for her daughter in ways she'd never known she could ache. The voices around her seemed distant, and strange, a persistent burble of noise that was happening beyond her awareness, yet was permeating it too, for she kept hearing them mention Molly, and wished they would stop. It was all an intrusion, a horrible misunderstanding. Molly wasn't missing. She'd just stayed out longer than she should have, which she'd done lots of times in the past, but she'd be home any minute. Katie could already see her, dawdling down the lane, texting someone on her mobile, hungry, moody, and – she could just hear her saying it: like, seriously embarrassed that her mother had gone and called the police.

'I'm sure there's absolutely no cause to worry,' the WPC was saying, looking at Katie.

Katie blinked as the words clattered like stones into the fog of her thoughts.

'We have so many cases of teenagers taking off like this, you just wouldn't believe, and they almost always turn out to be with friends, or other family members. It sounds as though that's what we're going to find here, based on what your sister's just told us. But is there anything else you'd like to add? Has anything unusual happened lately to make you suspicious or concerned in any way?'

Katie wasn't sure if she responded, but a moment later the WPC was talking again.

'I'm thinking of things such as anonymous phone calls, strangers hanging around, odd behaviour . . . Have you yourself been involved in something that has changed your own circumstances, such as a man, or a hobby, something that might have distracted you?'

Katie looked at Michelle. 'Didn't you tell her about me?' she said.

'Yes, I did,' Michelle said gently. 'She's talking about over and above that.'

Katie still looked bothered.

'They're just questions,' Michelle assured her. 'They don't necessarily mean anything, but they could prompt something in you that will help them to direct the search.'

The WPC assumed an even warmer tone as she said, 'Apart from this boy Brad, is there anyone else you think Molly could be with? Someone she might just have mentioned in passing?'

Katie shook her head.

'What about clubs or groups? I'm afraid computers have brought several more of those into the frame than we might like over recent years . . . Do you know if she's signed up for anything recently?'

Again Katie looked at Michelle. 'I don't know,' she answered. 'The police have her computer already.'

The WPC's eyebrows rose. 'We have? Why is that?' she asked.

Katie's heart was starting to thump as two totally disparate situations seemed to embark upon a bizarre and horrifying struggle to connect. 'I don't know,' she said, her head starting to spin with the craziness of it. 'I can't . . . It's got nothing to do with Molly . . . They took it last week.'

'But they must have given you a reason for taking it.'

Katie took a breath, found she had no words and looked at Michelle.

'What I think Mrs Kiernan is trying to say,' Laurie came in, 'is that if you want to see the computer at any stage, then it's already been impounded.'

'By us? In Chippenham?'

'Actually, by the FBI, which might go some way towards convincing you of Molly's lack of involvement.'

The WPC looked more baffled than ever and not a little dubious.

'Tell her,' Katie pressed. 'Tell her what's happening.'

Though clearly reluctant, Michelle explained as loosely as she could about the investigation they were involved in with Tom. 'This,' she concluded, 'is obviously in no way connected to Molly and what's happened this weekend.'

The WPC and her colleague both seemed to agree. 'Nevertheless,' she said, 'I'll get the chief to see if we can have the computer sent back so's our forensics can give it a going-over – if,' she added to Katie, 'it even gets that far, which I strongly doubt.'

'So what happens now?' Laurie asked, as the WPC stood up.

'We're going to speak to the friends you've already spoken to,' she answered. 'You'd be surprised what different answers seem to come up when someone in uniform is asking the questions. CID has already been informed, so I expect one of the detectives will be around to see you, but honestly, Mrs Kiernan, judging by everything that's been said, I'm pretty certain she'll turn up any minute.'

As Michelle saw them out Katie looked at Laurie. 'They always say that, don't they? Even when they're thinking the worst.'

'No,' Laurie replied. 'She said it because it's probably true. Molly was in shock last night, slightly traumatized even, she got drunk, maybe stoned, then had the dreadful humiliation of throwing up in front of everyone, even over this Brad – frankly, under those circumstances we'd all

534

want to crawl into a hole somewhere and never come out again. But we do, eventually, and so will she.'

Katie wanted to believe her, she wanted it so desperately that for several minutes she was able to, but then the demons were back, tearing at the delicate fabric of reason until she was almost beside herself with dread. 'What if,' she began shakily, 'what if this does have something to do with Tom?'

Michelle frowned. 'But how?' she asked.

Katie shook her head. 'I don't know. They could be holding her hostage . . . No, I know it doesn't make any sense, it's just with it all happening at the same time . . .' She put her hands to her head. 'I feel as though I'm going out of my mind, and if I weren't so worried and guilty I'd be furious with her for putting me through this.' She looked at Michelle again. 'We have to do something. We can't just sit here and wait. We should be out there looking for her.'

'The police are doing that, and you're not up to going out there yourself,' Michelle said gently.

Katie looked at the clock. It was twenty to five.

At a quarter to seven the police came back in the form of two detectives, who introduced themselves simply as Wendy Ford and Clive Painter.

'We've found something, Mrs Kiernan, that we'd like you to take a look at,' Wendy Ford told her. 'It could be nothing, but one of our constables stumbled upon it in a field next to the Fortescue-Bonds' house.' With a gloved hand she reached into a plastic bag and took out a black and white checked slingback shoe with a red bow on the toe.

Katie looked at it and felt the world rushing in on

her. In those horrifying fragments of seconds she saw her precious girl being raped, murdered, torn apart and screaming for her mother . . .

Immediately Michelle was behind her, hands on her shoulders, willing her to hang on.

'Is it Molly's?' Ford asked.

Katie nodded. 'Yes,' she whispered in a dry, cracked voice. 'Yes, it's hers.'

'Are they the shoes she was wearing when she went out last night?'

'No, she had her trainers on, but I expect those were in her bag.'

'Which means she could easily have dropped it without realizing,' Ford assured her. 'So let's not start jumping to conclusions yet.'

Katie looked at her in disbelief. 'It's a shoe,' she said croakily. 'It belongs to Molly and she isn't home, so what the hell do you expect me do?'

'I understand how you're feeling,' Ford responded calmly, 'and I assure you a thorough search of all the surrounding fields is already under way, and if you listen, you can hear the helicopters overhead.'

Yes, Katie could hear the clattering roar of the engines, but it did absolutely nothing to calm her. Instead it intensified her horror tenfold, for the reason they were up there was adding a terrible reality to the very worst nightmare of her life.

After reading the email from Laurie informing him of Molly's disappearance, Elliot pushed his computer across to Tom so he could read it too, and went to stand at the window, gazing out at the windswept hills where the leaves were being

536

tossed around like snow, and the sky glowered sinisterly overhead.

'What do you make of it?' he asked when Tom had finished.

'It's not connected,' Tom said decisively. 'It's just not their MO, the losses would too far outweigh the gains.'

Elliot turned back into the room. 'Laurie sent the email last night, so Molly could have turned up by now,' he said.

Tom was turning on his cellphone, knowing he had to be fast, for the signal alone would pinpoint their location. 'Any news on Molly?' he pressed into a text, and after sending it to Michelle he quickly shut down again. 'I'll check in a couple of hours,' he said, going back to the rest of Laurie's email. 'So still nothing from Nick and Max,' he murmured.

Rejoining him at the table Elliot said, 'They must have been pulled in for questioning, or they've been got at somehow.'

'Do we start contacting editors ourselves?' Tom wondered aloud.

Elliot pondered the question. 'If we haven't heard anything by tonight, I'm going to drive into town and call Chris,' he said. 'He should be able to find out what's going on. He might even know if there's any connection to this situation with Molly – though I'm with you, I just can't see it.'

Katie was standing in Molly's bedroom staring at all her treasured possessions – her glittery hair clips, beaded bracelets, the mauve bedspread and matching pillows rumpled from where she'd last

537

sat on them . . . It was so easy to picture her there, to hear her chattering away on her mobile, or yelling downstairs. 'Mum! *Mum!*'

Katie just couldn't bear it. Another night had now passed without that prized iron-framed bed being slept in, hours and hours of darkness, endless torment, too much fear. In the early hours she'd woken suddenly, drenched in sweat and certain she'd heard Molly calling her. She'd lain very still, waiting, praying to hear it again, but there was only silence, and the terrible emptiness coming from this room, next to her own.

It was now late on Monday morning. For a while it had been possible to hope that Molly might turn up for school today, but that had been dashed by a phone call from DS Wendy Ford at nine thirty. Registration was complete, and there was no sign of Molly. Now everyone in Molly's class was being questioned. If they got no joy there, they'd move on to the rest of the school. Meanwhile, the party-goers were still being interrogated, including Brad, whom they'd tracked down to his girlfriend's family home in Berkshire. Apparently he hadn't even known Molly's name until Saturday night, so he had no idea why she'd been telling people she was his girlfriend.

Katie now knew how Molly had been cruelly set up by her so-called friends to believe that Brad Jenkins was interested in her, when all the time it was a boy Cecily was paying who'd been making the calls and sending the messages. Hearing that had virtually broken Katie's heart. To think of her lovely little Molly being made the butt of those monstrous girls' jokes could turn her to violence.

538

They'd even formed some outrageous cult that involved all kinds of practices that the police were still trying to get to the bottom of, though so far there was nothing to say that some vile ritual, or evil hexing was behind Molly's disappearance. What couldn't be in any doubt, though, was the kind of mental state Molly must have been in when she'd run out of that party, and to think of it filled Katie with such anguish she just couldn't bear it.

As she walked towards the sitting-room window she felt herself stiffen with resistance to see the police cars parked in the lane. 'I should be out there, helping them to look,' she said to Laurie who was in the kitchen. 'I can't stand being cooped up here, doing nothing.'

'You're waiting for her to call,' Laurie reminded her.

Katie nodded, then struggled to subdue more impatience as she thought of Michelle, over there at the school, helping the police talk to the kids. Why the hell didn't she ring to let them know what was happening? She knew how terrified Katie was, how every minute that passed was like an hour of pure hell, so what in God's name was the matter with her?

Turning abruptly away from the window, she took a breath and forced back her frustration. Her control lasted only a moment before she suddenly erupted in a tirade that Laurie finally managed to stem by quickly dialling Michelle's mobile.

Michelle answered almost straight away.

'Where are you?' Laurie asked.

'On my way back. There are a couple of developments, though none of them good I'm afraid. How's Katie bearing up?'

'She's frustrated, obviously, and worried sick, but she's coping.' Laurie turned to Katie and smiled.

'Tell her we need to know what's happening,' Katie snapped, her temper on the rise again. 'I mean, does anyone at the school know anything?'

'Not exactly,' Michelle said, obviously having heard. 'DS Ford is with me, we'll explain everything when we get there.'

A few minutes later Michelle and DS Wendy Ford walked into the kitchen. Michelle knew immediately from Katie's white face that the only thing holding her together was anger, and that some of it was directed towards her. So refraining from embracing her, she merely suggested that they all sit down.

Finding it impossible not to read something horrendous into their apparent reluctance to begin, Katie shouted, 'What is it? Just tell me what it is.'

'It's OK,' DS Ford said soothingly. 'It's not what you're thinking.'

'How the hell do you know what I'm thinking? Are you a mother? Has this ever happened to you?'

DS Ford said, 'There's a boy in Molly's year called Rusty Phillips. Do you know him?'

Katie took a moment to think. 'Not very well,' she answered, feeling more reasonable now there appeared to be some kind of lead. 'I know he helps Molly with her homework sometimes. Why?'

'Well, he claims Molly called him late on Saturday night and asked him to meet her at the old railway bridge near his home. She told him something had happened, but apparently didn't go into any detail. He doesn't know where she was calling from . . .'

'But did he meet her? Does he know where she is now?'

'He says she didn't turn up. He waited for over an hour, and kept trying to ring her, but he never got an answer, so in the end he went home, presuming she'd just decided not to come.'

Katie's expression showed total horror as she looked from the detective to Michelle and back again. 'Do you believe him?' she said. 'Do you think he's telling the truth?'

'His phone log shows that she did call him on Saturday night,' Ford answered. 'Obviously we'll be talking to him again, and several officers are over at the railway bridge now, taking a look around.'

'Where is this bridge?' Katie demanded. 'I mean in relation to the Fortescue-Bonds'.'

'It's on the northern outskirts of Chippenham,' Ford answered, 'about two miles from the Fortescue-Bonds' . . .'

'Going in the opposite direction to here?'

Ford nodded. 'That's correct,' she said. 'The boy lives on the edge of a housing estate, actually in sight of the old railway line, so it would take him no time to get there. But without knowing where Molly was calling from we've no idea how close, or how far away she was when she asked him to meet her. What's baffling us at the moment is that her friend Allison confirmed that Molly was wearing the black and white shoes during the party, so the one we found must have been dropped in the field after she left. The field, as you know, is between here and the

541

Fortescue-Bonds', which could suggest that she was on her way home when she lost it.'

Katie rose abruptly to her feet, as though to avoid what was coming next.

'It's not necessarily what you're thinking,' Michelle quickly told her. 'Apparently there are no signs of a struggle in the field, so nothing to say that someone tried to stop her. It's highly possible that she just changed her mind, and decided to call Rusty instead.'

'Then where is she now? He says he doesn't know, that she didn't turn up . . .'

DS Ford flipped open her mobile as it started to ring. 'Yes?' she said into it. She listened for a few moments, then said, 'Is someone on their way here?' She listened again, and after telling the person at the other end to keep her posted, she rang off. 'Apparently one of the search officers has found something close to the railway bridge,' she told them. 'He should be here any minute.'

'What is it?' Katie demanded, almost wild-eyed with panic.

DS Ford's face showed her reluctance to answer. 'An item of clothing, I'm told,' she said softly. Her eyes came to Katie's. 'A red top.'

Katie immediately started to fight for air.

Michelle shot to her feet, and grabbed her. 'Breathe! Just breathe!' she urged. 'Come on, you can do it. In . . . out . . . In . . . out . . . It's OK. I've got you. Just breathe . . .'

Half an hour later Michelle came back down the stairs, leaving Katie lying down with Trotty. As she started to speak her voice caught on a sob, but she managed to push past it. 'Not what we need right now, me falling apart,' she chided herself.

'They'll find her. She'll be all right,' Laurie told her.

Michelle nodded. 'Yes, of course. I've just sent a message back to Tom. Has there been anything from Nick and Max yet?'

Laurie shook her head.

For several seconds they merely looked at one another, each knowing what the other was thinking, neither willing to voice it. In the end, Michelle shook her head and turned away.

'It doesn't make any sense,' she said. 'There can't be a connection.'

'No, of course not,' Laurie agreed.

'It's just not the way they operate, snatching innocent kids to force parents and relatives to meet their demands.'

'Particularly not when the press is bound to get involved,' Laurie added, 'and as we already are, they know very well that it would take one phone call from me, connecting the warrant for Tom's arrest to Molly's disappearance, for all hell to break loose.'

'Precisely, so it's all just a horrible coincidence. I know it in my heart, I feel it in my bones.' She looked at Laurie.

'I'm not arguing,' Laurie assured her.

'So how do I get that across to Katie, when I can sense the suspicion taking root in her mind, and when right now she's in no state to see anything through to a rational conclusion?'

'The only answer to that,' Laurie said, 'is that we have to find Molly.'

'Under no circumstances is anyone to go anywhere near that house until the child's been found,' Deborah Gough was saying into the phone. 'The last thing we need is to be mixed up in that.'

'There could be ways to use it to our advantage,' Allbringer suggested.

'I'm not even going there,' she snapped. 'The blowback, if it came out, would finish us all.'

Refraining from pointing out they were on the verge of it anyway, Allbringer said, 'What do you want to do about the two journalists we're holding? Questions are already being asked.'

'I'll get back to you on that,' Gough replied, making a rare admission that she wasn't actually calling the shots here. She turned aside to stare blankly out of her seventh-floor window. 'Damn!' she muttered furiously, 'this is slipping out of our control. Have Chambers or Russell made any personal contact with editors that we know about?'

'Nothing I'm aware of yet.'

'All right, I'm going to get authorization to launch our own initiative. One way or another Chambers has to be stopped, and if we have to do it through the media, so be it.'

The lack of response from the other end reminded her of Allbringer's views on the strategy to destroy Chambers's reputation in preparation for an arrest. She wasn't interested in hearing them again now, so before he could get started she said, 'Keep me up to date on that missing child. As soon as they've found her we can start leaning on Michelle Rowe.'

*

Molly couldn't stop shivering. She wasn't cold or anything, she was just scared and unhappy and she didn't want to be here any more. Rusty had promised to smuggle her into his house tonight, while his mum and dad went to their folk group, so she could go on the suicide web site and find out how to do it. She had to make sure she got it right, because she didn't want it to hurt or anything, or make a mess of anyone's house – even though this one was a mess anyway. It was about three doors down from Rusty. His mum was keeping an eye on it while the owners were on holiday in Spain. It had a really scruffy garden and rooms that smelled of cigarette smoke and something else that was horrible, she just didn't know what it was.

Earlier, from behind the yellowy nets, she'd watched the police going up the street towards the old railway bridge. They'd been up there for ages, then they'd gone over to Rusty's house, where his mum had let them in. Molly had been so on edge through all that, even though Rusty had sworn he wouldn't tell anyone where she was. He'd just say that she'd called him on Saturday night, then hadn't bothered to turn up. That way, if they checked his mobile phone he was covered.

He was a really good friend the way he was helping her. He'd even crept out a couple of times during the nights to make sure she was all right and not afraid. She was afraid, but she didn't tell him. What was the point? There was nothing he could do. He kept saying that she ought to go home, that her mum would be worried, but he didn't understand. Her mum wouldn't be there much longer, and then no-one would want her, so she might just as well die too. She'd still be with her mum then, and that was the only person she wanted to be with, because she was the only person who loved her. No-one else did. She didn't even have any friends any more, or a boyfriend. She didn't count Rusty because he was just Rusty, and after those horrible things she'd said about Michelle ... Anyway, she didn't want Michelle. She just wanted her mum ...

As tears welled up in her eyes, she got stiffly up from the bed and went to look in the mirror. She'd cried all her make-up off even before she'd got here, but she'd washed her face since anyway. She didn't really know why, because she was so ugly and rank who cared if her face was clean? She hated her face because it belonged to her, so she punched it. Then she punched it again, because it was what her nasty face deserved. It wasn't a good person's face, it belonged to a disgusting, horrible, wicked person, so it was no wonder everyone hated her. She expected her mum did now, after what she'd done, so why not just keep punching herself until she made herself bleed and bleed and all her teeth fell out?

By the time Rusty came home from school she was downstairs, watching from behind the nets. He went straight past the little caravan parked next to his house and disappeared round the back. He didn't come out again. He couldn't, because his mum was there, so he'd have to wait until it got dark and his mum went out. He couldn't ring either, because the battery had run out on her mobile, and anyway, it was too much of a risk. So she just stayed where she was, waiting for Rusty to come and telling herself not to think about anything any more, because if she did, she'd just have to start hitting herself again.

It was now Tuesday morning. Michelle was in the kitchen speaking on the phone to Laurie as Katie came down the stairs and stopped right next to her. Seeing her expression, Michelle immediately ended the call.

Before she could speak Katie said, 'You have to tell them.'

An uneasy beat in Michelle's heart belied her frown of confusion.

'You know what I'm talking about,' Katie said, her voice dangerously low, 'you've got to tell them where Tom is, because I can't go through another day of this.'

'But Katie, it's got nothing to do with Tom . . .'

'It has *everything* to do with him, and you know it!' Katie raged. 'They've got her somewhere, they're holding her to make him come forward, now you've got to tell them where he is, or so help me God, I will.'

Michelle put a hand to her head, trying to think how to handle this. 'Look, if Tom thought for one minute that they had her,' she said, 'he'd have done something about it the instant he knew she was missing.'

'No he wouldn't. The story always comes first for someone like him.'

'Katie, you don't mean that . . .'

'Stop stalling, Michelle, and make the call.'

As she handed her the receiver Michelle took it

547

and put it back again. 'Look, you know what Molly went through on Saturday night,' she said, 'what she's been going through for months . . .'

'I don't need you to remind me of my own responsibility in this,' Katie seethed, 'but you have one too, Michelle, so pick up that phone now and tell him he has to give himself up.'

'Even if I did, he won't do it,' Michelle responded, 'because he knows as well as I do – as well as *you* do – that they don't have her. Katie, this isn't the way they operate.'

'How can you say that?' Katie demanded. 'You of all people know what they're capable of, so you surely can't be standing there telling me that a fourteen-year-old girl means anything to them. They couldn't give a damn about her, or me, because little people like us don't count. Collateral damage, that's what we are . . .'

'Katie, you're not being rational. I understand how you're feeling, but . . .'

'Don't you dare say that!' Katie yelled, slamming an empty cup against the wall. 'You haven't got the first idea how I'm feeling, because you have it in you to give your child up. As a mother I could never do that. Molly means everything to me. *Everything*. And I want her back, God damn you.'

Michelle's face was ashen as she said, 'We'll find her.'

But Katie wasn't listening. Rage and grief were pouring out of her with an unstoppable might, tearing words from her that she barely knew she was saying. 'You make me sick, *sick*!' she yelled. 'I hate looking at you. I hate listening to you. You know they've got her, but all you care about is Tom, and the child you're carrying, and the future you're going to have together . . .'

'Katie . . .'

'You didn't tell me about that baby, did you? No, you kept it to yourself, because you didn't have the guts to tell me you've cheated me again. You said you were here for Molly . . .'

'I am!' Michelle shouted.

'*I want her back!* I want her in my house, and I want you and your baby to go. I'll find someone else for Molly, someone who'll care about her and not let her be used the way you are now.'

'How can you say I don't care about her, when I gave up everything to be here for her –'

'You gave up *nothing!* You're pregnant, you're marrying him . . .'

'I didn't know it was going to turn out that way . . .'

'But it always does for you! Everything works out in your world. It's only in mine that it all goes wrong . . .'

'Stop it! Just stop. You can't go on resenting me for things I have no control over . . .'

'But you have control over what's happening to Molly, and I want her back. Do this, Michelle, and I'll know that she means as much to you as she does to me. It's all I ask. I have to know you'll put her first.'

Michelle's eyes closed in despair. 'Katie, you can't ask me to prove it like this,' she said. 'It doesn't make any sense, and if you were able to think straight you'd know it. She's with a friend somewhere, or maybe she's gone off to London . . .

I don't know, but I do know she's not being held to force Tom out of hiding.'

'But *how* do you know?' Katie demanded. 'How can you be so damned sure, when the timing is perfect, the leverage could hardly . . .'

'Please, Katie . . .'

'*No!* I've had enough, Michelle. Do you honestly think she'd have stayed out there on her own all this time, just because she had a spat with her friends?'

'It was more than that . . .'

'But not enough to make her stay away from me all this time. I'm her mother, for God's sake, I'm the one she comes to when things go wrong, only this time, she can't, because *they've got her and they won't let her come back* . . .'

'Katie, stop! No!' Michelle cried, as Katie began smashing every dish in sight. 'This isn't going to help . . .'

'*Make that phone call!*' Katie yelled, rounding on her. 'Put someone else first for once!'

Michelle started to back off. 'I'm not going to continue with this,' she said, tears rolling down her cheeks. 'I know you're hurting, I understand that you're afraid, but I will not force Tom into doing something that . . .'

'Because he comes first!' Katie cried savagely. 'It's always him, or you, or someone else. Never us . . . Never me . . .'

'That is just not true!' Michelle yelled. 'You've got these things fixed in your head and they're based on nothing! You say the most horrible things to me, you're cruel and spiteful the way you throw Robbie in my face, and now you're trying to make

550

me choose between Tom and Molly to prove something that shouldn't even be in doubt. Well, I won't do it. For once I'm not going to give in to you, and not because he comes first, but because it won't give you what you want.'

Katie's eyes were wild. 'Get out!' she screamed, slamming a bowl to the floor. 'Just get out of my house. I don't ever want to see you again.'

Knowing there was no point trying to reason with her now, Michelle grabbed her bag and turned to the door. 'My phone will be on if you need . . .'

'I don't need you!' Katie sobbed. 'I don't need anyone, except my daughter.'

Closing the door behind her, Michelle paused for a moment, hating leaving her like this, but understanding that if she stayed she was only going to inflame her further.

Minutes later, Laurie drew up outside to drive them to the school.

'She knows in her heart that she's not making any sense,' Michelle said after recounting what had happened. 'It's fear that's unhinging her, and even in the state she's in she probably knows it. She just needed to release some of it, and it's usually the nearest and dearest that gets it . . . Or so I'm told.'

Laurie threw her a glance, and realized, in spite of the dryness, that she was a lot more hurt by Katie's attack than she was admitting. 'Do you think she'll make the call herself?' she asked.

Michelle shook her head. 'No. She just needed to shift the burden of guilt for a while, because she's absolutely racked with it, so blaming someone else, whether it's me, or Tom, or some invisible force in the United States was a way of easing some of the pressure. By now she's probably already starting to calm down, and wishing to God she hadn't said even half the things she did.'

However, at that very moment Katie was waiting to be connected to Stuart Fellowes's office at the US Embassy in Grosvenor Square.

It was just after four in the morning, Washington time, when the phone next to Deborah Gough's bed woke her. Blearily checking the clock, she turned on the light and grabbed the receiver on the second ring before it could wake her husband.

'We've just had word of Tom Chambers's location,' the voice at the other end told her. 'He's in France, the Burgundy region, holed up in a house belonging to a French reporter.'

Deborah Gough swung her legs off the bed and stood up. 'OK,' she said, thinking fast. 'Is a team on its way?'

'Even as we speak.'

'How long will it take them to get there?'

'They're being flown in from an RAF base in Suffolk. The French counter-terrorism people have been contacted to pick them up on the ground – I'd say we're looking at three hours max.'

'Good. Call Daniel Allbringer and give him the news. I'll be at my office within the hour.'

Chapter Twenty-Four

'I've just had a text from Elliot,' Laurie said, as Michelle came to join her at the school gates. 'He's on his way back to London.'

Michelle's face was pale. 'But Tom's staying put?' she said.

'I presume so. We'll know more once Elliot gets here. How's it going in there?'

'Still no joy,' Michelle responded, turning to look at the hundreds of students teeming around the school yard. 'I'd forgotten how monosyllabic kids can be at that age. It's like they're brain-dead, half of them.' Spotting Rusty Phillips lurking next to the iron grid fence about twenty yards away, she said, 'Ah, he's arrived. Apparently he's been at the orthodontist this morning, getting his braces tightened.'

'Well that should make him talk,' Laurie responded dryly, 'and he certainly seems to have something on his mind, the way he keeps looking over here. What do you say we help him along and go over there?'

But before either of them could move the boy suddenly lunged at a group of girls nearby and gave one of them such an almighty shove that it knocked her to the ground. Within seconds a major brawl had broken out with him at the centre, being kicked and thumped and berated so savagely that it took Michelle, Laurie and two teachers to pull the crowd off.

'Fucking raping bastard,' one of the girls spat, as she dusted herself down and started to walk away. Her progress was suddenly hastened as a teacher grabbed her ear and frogmarched her, howling, into the school building.

'You're mental. You ought to be locked up,' another girl snarled, as Rusty began picking himself up.

'Fucking look at you, you retard!' someone else hissed.

He was indeed a sorry sight, with blood trickling from his nose, his glasses skewed across his face and his shirt hanging out front and back. He glanced at Michelle, then ducked his head and started walking away.

'Rusty,' she called after him.

He flinched, but didn't stop.

'Rusty,' she repeated more firmly. 'I'd like a word with you.'

He spun round. 'I didn't rape her,' he cried. 'They're all making things up just because her top was found by my house, but I didn't do anything.'

Michelle moved quickly towards him. 'No-one's saying you did, or none of us,' she assured him. 'It's just girls – they can be pretty stupid sometimes, and say things they shouldn't.'

'They don't know what they're talking about,' he growled, glaring angrily at the crowd that was still trailing away, 'and the next person who says I cut her up in pieces is really going to get it.'

'Oh yeah?' a stroppy young blonde girl challenged. 'Like you and whose army?'

'Just you come here and say that!'

'All right, that's enough,' Michelle barked, as the girl began closing in on him. 'Just go away please, and you, Rusty, come with me.'

The girl wasn't easily put off, so Laurie stepped swiftly in front of her, while Michelle marched Rusty over to the gates.

'You know who I am, don't you?' Michelle said.

He nodded.

'You were on your way to tell me something just now.'

He looked away.

'Rusty, Molly's mother is in a dreadful state. She's very ill, so if you know where Molly is . . .'

'I said she had to go home,' he blurted defensively, 'but she says everyone hates her, because she's evil and nasty, so she doesn't have a home to go to.'

'Oh my God,' Michelle murmured, glancing at Laurie as she joined them. 'Where is she, Rusty?' she urged. 'Where was she when she said that to you?'

His head went down.

'Rusty!' she cried. 'You have to tell me.'

'She says you hate her,' he shouted.

'Oh Rusty, that isn't true. She's my niece. I love her very much, and I want to help her. Now please tell me where she is.'

He seemed to be withdrawing again, and flinched as she held onto him to prevent any attempt to take off. 'She said she'd kill me if I told anyone where she was,' he wailed.

'Rusty . . .'

'Come with me,' Laurie interrupted, firmly taking his arm. 'You can show us the way.'

'But I've got to be back in class,' he protested, trying to drag himself free, but Michelle was holding his other arm, helping to propel him towards the car.

'We'll make your excuses,' Laurie assured him. 'Or shall we call the police and let them know that you're withholding information? That's a serious offence and could land you in a lot of trouble.'

'I told Molly that,' he cried, 'but she wouldn't listen. Anyway, I don't care. I just wanted to help her, because she was all unhappy and afraid . . . And now her face is all bashed up, and I don't know how it got like that, because no-one's seen her except me.'

After stuffing him in the passenger seat, Laurie whisked round to the driver's side while Michelle leapt in the back.

'What do you mean her face is bashed up?' Michelle demanded, as they pulled away.

He kept his head down. 'I didn't do it,' he mumbled. 'I swear I didn't.'

'Which way?' Laurie barked as they reached the end of the road.

'Right, and up past the ambulance station.'

'Where is she?' Michelle asked. 'Where exactly are we going?'

'To my house. She was in our neighbour's house before, but she didn't like it there, so she's in our caravan now.'

'Is she all right?' Michelle demanded. 'What's this about her face?'

'I told you, I don't know,' he protested. 'It was just like it yesterday. She won't tell me how she got it, but I didn't do it. I swear on my mum's life, I never touched her, and it won't be my fault if something's happened to her now, because I was coming to tell you, before that stupid cow Kylie . . .'

'What were you going to tell me?' Michelle interrupted.

He hesitated a moment, seeming to think he'd said too much, but then he blundered on. 'She went on this suicide web site to find out how to kill herself,' he confessed. 'She wanted me to do it too, but I don't want to die. Anyway, I don't think she'll do it . . .'

Michelle's head was spinning as Laurie's foot went down. 'When did you last see her?' Michelle snapped.

'This morning, after breakfast, while my mum popped down to the butcher.'

'Oh my God, oh my God,' Michelle murmured.

'Where now?' Laurie barked, as they hared past the ambulance station.

'Go left after the pub, and then second right,' he answered.

The tyres squealed as Laurie took the corner sharply, straightened up and sped on to the second turning.

'I can't believe this is happening,' Michelle

muttered. 'Please God, we can't be too late. We just can't.'

Molly was slumped on the floor of the little caravan that filled up Rusty's driveway, tucked into the U of the two sofa bunks with the flowery blue and yellow curtains drawn. Her eyes were staring blankly at the shiny nylon carpet, her hands lay loosely on the floor, not quite touching the scissors and razor abandoned beside her. She'd cut her wrist a bit, but it had hurt and she hated the blood, and anyway, Mrs Phillips was really proud of her caravan so it would be really mean to mess it up. It might have been different if Rusty would have done it with her, but he wouldn't. She didn't know why he was so keen to go on living, when he was such a muppet. Anyone would think he'd be glad to get away from how horrible everyone was to him, with his stupid hair and braces and all those blobby freckles that splodged around his face like great big ginger pancakes. He'd twitched a bit and told her she was mean and cruel when she'd said all that to him last night, and then he'd really gone off on one, trying to make her go home, saying she was just being childish and selfish hiding away like she was a criminal or something. He was so stupid, he didn't realize she had nowhere to go, which had made her cry and straight away he'd said he was sorry. She was sorry too, because she didn't mean to be horrible to him, she was just like that, because she was evil and nasty and didn't deserve any friends anyway.

Her eyes strayed back to the razor and scissors. Maybe she ought to have another go, because her mind kept filling up with thoughts of her mum, and it was all horrible and she just couldn't stand it. She hadn't cried all morning, which was good, but she'd got really, really scared when she'd realized that even if she did go back now, the police would probably say her mum wasn't doing a good enough job looking after her, so they'd have to take her into care. If she hadn't been so mean and horrible to Michelle, then Michelle might try to stop them, but she wouldn't do it now. She'd just want to get rid of her, and who could blame her? She was ugly and evil and nasty and didn't deserve anyone to love her, even God thought that, because he was going to take her mum away.

Her fingers closed around the scissors. She sat staring at them, but wasn't really seeing them. She wasn't seeing anything any more, she was just feeling more and more miserable and wishing she could go home to her mum. She heard a car pulling up in the street, but didn't even care if it was the police. They could take her and stuff her in a home somewhere for all she cared. Everyone could laugh at her then, and be mean and nasty, the way Cecily and Allison had, and talk about how dumb she was for believing all their lies. They'd all be seriously horrible to her, and she wouldn't blame them, because why would anyone ever want to be nice to her, when she'd been so cruel to her mum and Michelle and Rusty and all the people who were kind to her?

She heard the caravan door open, but didn't look up. Someone came in and said her name really softly. She didn't mean to, but this really loud sob came out, and then another and another and then

Michelle was kneeling in front of her and pulling her into her arms.

Molly couldn't catch her breath. Her body was convulsing with sobs, her arms were clinging tight to Michelle, her face buried in her neck. She gasped and shuddered, choked and held on even tighter.

'It's all right,' Michelle whispered, tears falling on to her own cheeks, 'everything's all right. You're going to be fine.'

Molly tried to speak, but her voice came out all weird and in short, stammering sobs. 'I-I don't want-want her to die,' she choked. 'Please, Michelle, don't let her die.'

'Oh my love, my love,' Michelle wept. 'If there was anything I could do to stop it, I swear I would.'

Molly's sobs grew harder, and she moved in even closer, as though to absorb herself inside Michelle.

'We'll get through it,' Michelle told her gently. 'We'll get through it together. You and me.'

'It's not-not, going to hap-happen yet, is it?'

'I don't think so.'

'Please don't let it happen, Michelle. *Please*. Tell her I'm sorry . . .'

'Sssh, ssh,' Michelle murmured, kissing her hair. 'You've got nothing to be sorry for.'

'I didn't mean to hit her . . .'

'I know, and so does she.'

Molly continued to cry, letting all her grief and sadness pour out on to Michelle's shoulder. Finally she pulled back to look at Michelle, her face still quivering, her chest heaving as she said, 'I'm – I'm really sorry for what I said about you.'

Michelle smiled through her tears. 'Even if I

knew what it was, I'd still forgive you,' she said, stroking Molly's face and fearing that she knew what the bruising was about. 'Look at you,' she whispered, 'you're so beautiful and silly and we love you so much.' She ran her fingers through Molly's hair, then pressed a kiss to her forehead. 'I think we should give Mum a call, don't you? She'll want to know that you're all right.'

Molly nodded.

As Michelle put the number into her mobile, she shifted position slightly, to sit more comfortably, while still holding Molly in one arm. When she got through she half-expected Judy to answer, but it was Katie's voice that came tentatively down the line.

'Hello,' Michelle responded. 'I've . . .'

'Oh thank God, Michelle listen, I'm . . .'

'Katie,' Michelle said firmly, 'I've got someone here who'd like to talk to you,' and she passed the phone to Molly.

'Mum?' Molly said, brokenly.

'Oh my God,' Katie cried. 'Molly. Oh thank God, thank God. Where are you? Are you all right?'

'Yes, I'm fine. I'm with Michelle.'

'I've been so worried,' Katie said, starting to break down. 'Oh Molly . . . I'm sorry for what I said, the way I said it . . .'

'No, Mum, I'm sorry. It's all my fault.' She gulped and sobbed. 'Mum – Mum, I want to come home.'

'Oh Molly, please come home. I've missed you so much, yes, please come home.'

Michelle took the phone. 'We're not far away,' she told Katie. 'And she's fine. All in one piece.

Missing her mum, as you can tell, so we won't be long.'

Katie was standing at the gate as Laurie's car came down the lane, and almost before they came to a stop Molly was leaping out to get to her mother. Katie was already there, waiting to catch her.

'Oh Molly,' she sobbed, wrapping her in her arms. 'My baby. Thank God you're all right. Let me look at you,' and clasping Molly's tear-ravaged face between her hands she gazed searchingly down at her, wondering what all the bruising was, but not mentioning it now. 'I love you so much,' she said, her lips barely able to form the words, they were trembling so.

'I love you too,' Molly said, starting to cry again. 'And I'm really sorry . . . I just don't want you to . . . Please Mum, don't. Please, please don't . . .'

'Ssh,' Katie soothed, drawing her back into her arms. 'We'll talk about that later, let's just get you inside now, give you some food and a bath and you can tell me where you've been, what on earth you've been up to. They found your shoe and red top, you know . . .'

'I threw the top away,' Molly said, leaning against her as they started inside. 'I knew you didn't like it, so I didn't want it any more.'

Katie cried and laughed. 'Well you've got it back again now,' she told her. 'And don't worry, I know all about what happened at the party on Saturday, so I understand why you were so upset, I just wish you'd come home to me.'

'I was going to, but then I thought about what you said, and . . . I don't know, I just couldn't come.'

'OK, as long as you're here now, that's all that matters. We'll have a long chat later, just you and me, now what do you want to do first? Bath or food?'

'Is there any of that lasagne left?' Molly asked, as Trotty leapt up in her arms.

Katie chuckled. 'I'd forgotten all about that,' she said, 'so it must still be in the oven. Maybe it'll be all right to heat up. Let's have a look.'

Ten minutes later, having run Molly a luxuriously deep bubble bath, Katie left her immersed up to her chin, with Trotty keeping watch, and went back downstairs to find Michelle.

She was still outside with Laurie, who was speaking to someone on the phone.

'How is she?' Michelle asked as Katie joined them.

'She seems OK. What happened to her face?'

Michelle grimaced. 'I'm guessing, but I think it could have been self-inflicted,' she said. 'It's not that uncommon in kids who are highly distressed.'

'No,' Katie murmured, having already suspected it herself. She looked at Michelle again, and wanted so much to embrace her and thank her for bringing Molly home and not seeming to bear a grudge for the appalling scene earlier. It was just like Michelle to understand, forgive and let it go, but Katie knew already that wasn't going to happen when she confessed to what she'd done after Michelle had left. No-one, not even Michelle, was ever going to forgive that.

As she forced herself to utter the words, she watched the blood drain from Michelle's face.

'Oh my God,' Michelle murmured even before

she'd finished. 'How long ago did you make the call?'

'It was right after you left.'

Michelle's chest was tight, but her adrenalin was starting to surge. 'Almost three hours,' she said. 'We have to get word to Tom. Laurie!'

Laurie spun round, and seeing Michelle's face she immediately cut her call short. 'What is it?' she demanded, looking from Michelle to Katie and back again.

'They know where Tom is,' Michelle told her, returning to the car for her mobile. 'We have to warn him. Do you know the phone number for the house?'

Laurie was already pulling out her organizer. 'I don't think so,' she said anxiously. 'It's a number Elliot's always had.' She was scrolling rapidly through. 'No, it's not here. I'll have to try Elliot.'

Reaching Tom's voicemail, Michelle left a quick message telling him to leave the house immediately.

Laurie was trying all the numbers she had for Elliot, but only getting voicemails.

Katie said to Michelle, 'I don't know how to begin saying I'm sorry. I just . . . I don't know what came over me . . . If anything happens to him . . .'

'It won't,' Michelle said fiercely, wishing she felt as confident as she sounded. 'He's got himself out of tighter spots before, he'll do it again.'

'Oh Elliot!' Laurie raged, clicking off the last of the numbers. 'Not one of his phones is turned on. But I can call Jean-Jacques in Paris. He'll probably be at his office now – except it's France and the middle of the day.' She was already dialling the number.

'Jean-Jacques?' she demanded as someone answered.

'*Non. Il n'est pas là. Puis-je vous aider?*'

Laurie struggled for the French, then said, '*Est-ce que vous parlez anglais?*'

'*Oui. Bien sûr.* Who is calling please?'

She explained who she was, and that she needed to contact Jean-Jacques urgently.

'But I'm afraid 'e 'as departed *pour un rendezvous,*' the person at the other end told her. 'I can give you his mobile number, if you don't already 'ave it.'

'Yes, please,' she said, readying her organizer to scrawl it on. 'Thank you,' she said, when she'd finished. '*Merci beaucoup. Je vous dois,* big time,' and clicking off she quickly dialled the number.

'Oh no!' she protested, when she got the voicemail. 'I don't believe this. Jean-Jacques,' she cried after the tone, 'it's Laurie. This is life and death. You have to call your house in Bourgogne and warn the person there to get out fast. Please do it the instant you get this message, and call me back.' She reminded him of her mobile number, and rang off.

Michelle's and Katie's faces were bloodless. Katie put a hand on Michelle's arm, but Michelle started to walk away. 'I'm sorry,' she said. 'I can't talk to you about this now, I have to know he's all right.'

The road into the hamlet was blocked by French police cars. Each of the residences leading up to the farmhouse had been checked and declared empty, while the hillsides around swarmed with invisible agents, edging their way closer to the house, keeping all windows and doors in their sights, and all radio contact to a crucial minimum.

The wind was bitter, the sky an endless stretch of gloom. The only sounds were the whistling currents of air whipping around thickets and the occasional crackle of static on a hidden radio. Stuart Fellowes was watching the farmhouse from the passenger seat of an unmarked car. At the wheel was the senior French officer who'd driven him from the airfield, who seemed to speak no more English than Fellowes did French. Fortunately, there didn't appear to be any problem about who was in charge here, the Frenchie knew his place and apparently understood that they were here to apprehend a suspected terrorist who could be armed.

The special agent who'd flown in with Fellowes was already at the house. Fellowes tracked his progress, never taking his eyes off him as he rolled and crept around the exterior walls, gun clutched in both hands as he checked windows and doors, while keeping out of sight of anyone inside. A grey Renault was parked in the drive and a thin trail of smoke curled from the chimney, so someone was home, and enquiries had already confirmed that the vehicle was rented to one Thomas Chambers. Seemed the guy was intent on hanging himself, Fellowes was thinking maliciously, going about the place using his own name, like no-one was tracking him.

The agent at the house vanished around the back. Everyone waited.

The valley was quieter than a grave, just wind,

and the occasional bird. Beside him the French officer checked his watch. Fellowes ignored the man and stayed focused on the spot where he expected his agent to re-emerge. It wasn't happening though. The guy was taking too long. Chambers had lain in wait? Taken him hostage? Too many eyes on the hillside for that to have happened and not been reported. He was still taking too long. The tension crackled like static. The French officer heaved a little sigh. Fellowes bit down on his irritation. Across the street someone ran from behind a bush to the cover of a shed. Fellowes's radio came to a split second of life and cut.

'What the fuck's going on?' he murmured.

The Frenchman didn't reply.

'Come on. Come on. We know he's in there.'

A minute later his officer stepped out of the front door and waved his arms.

Fellowes grabbed his radio and started towards him. 'Give me some good news,' he growled into the device.

Before the officer could reply Fellowes was striding into the drive.

'There's no-one inside, sir,' the agent told him. 'The place is empty.'

Fellowes glared at him, then thrust him aside and stormed into the house.

'It seems they were through there, sir,' the agent said, coming into the gloomy hall behind him. 'The door at the end.'

Fellowes banged it open and found himself in a large, workmanlike kitchen, where a clutter of dishes lay abandoned on the table, and a small fire burned its last in the hearth.

'Have you checked all over?' Fellowes barked.

'Yes, sir. No-one upstairs either.'

'Do it again,' Fellowes ordered, and snatched up a mobile phone that had been left on the table. As he switched it on it immediately bleeped, signalling a message. After checking it he slammed the phone down in barely suppressed fury. The message was from Michelle Rowe warning Chambers to get out, but it had been sent a mere ten minutes ago, while Fellowes was sitting right outside in the car. 'So who the fuck tipped him off?' he muttered through his teeth. 'And who got him out of here?'

Hearing a small cough behind him, he swung round to find the Frenchman with a supercilious little smirk under his Hitler moustache as he studied the label on a wine bottle. Resisting the urge to deck the smarmy bastard, Fellowes began shouting to the other officers who were now pouring into the house, not knowing if they understood, but they soon would.

'I want the phone records for this place,' he roared. 'Every taxi and car-rental firm in the area. Contact all airfields and airports, set up roadblocks. Do whatever it takes. I want Tom Chambers in my custody by the end of the day.'

At that very moment Tom was walking with a small crowd into the arrivals hall at Nice airport, carrying a laptop and holdall. Having taken a domestic flight from Lyons no identity documents were required, so he merely breezed on through, heading for the taxi rank. He passed a couple of gendarmes hanging about the exit, who paid him no more attention than he did them.

Chris's call had come two hours ago, giving him plenty of time to organize a cab to pick him up at the house, and get him to Lyons for the twelve ten flight to Nice. The address Chris had given him was of an apartment in a block right on the Promenade des Anglais, though Chris had no idea who it belonged to, for it wasn't a safe house he knew of.

'It was the same woman who called me,' he'd told Tom on the phone. 'American accent, no name, no questions, just instructions. You're to get out of the house now, leaving your rental car and cellphone, but take everything else. Once you're at the apartment you just sit tight until she contacts me again to deliver further instructions.'

'So who the hell is she?' Tom murmured. 'And why's she doing this?'

'She's obviously right on top of what's going on,' Chris responded, 'so I'm going to guess she's inside the embassy.'

'Or even deeper than that,' Tom added, certain it was coming from the same source that had initially contacted Josh Shine. It had to be, who else was there?

Now, as he slid into the back of a Mercedes to travel the short distance into town, he was wondering if Chris had contacted Elliot yet, or if Elliot was even back in London. It was a long drive up to Amsterdam, plus a five-hour crossing on the ferry, so Tom didn't imagine he'd hit British soil yet, and even when he did there was no reason for him to contact Chris right off. His priority was going to be tracking down Nick and Max, while checking what deals might already be in place. And as far as Tom was concerned, provided Molly was safe, and everything was OK with Michelle, there was no other priority, for, frankly, he couldn't wait to get this damned story off his hands now so he could starting living something that at least resembled a normal life.

Deborah Gough's expression was far from pleasant as she regarded the other faces in the room, none of which was any less grim. 'Do we know who tipped him off?' she asked.

'Not yet,' Allbringer answered, having been the first recipient of the bad news. 'They're still working on it.'

Deborah Gough regarded him coldly. 'Where did our information come from?' she enquired.

'Apparently it was Michelle Rowe's sister, Katie Kiernan, who called the embassy.'

Gough was incredulous. 'And this was deemed a reliable source?' she said sarcastically.

Allbringer was bristling. 'She wanted to do a deal, her daughter for Chambers's location. We took the location, and told her we'd get back to her about the child. And might I remind you, her information bore out – Chambers had been there . . .'

'But was gone long before Fellowes arrived,' Gough came in with a cutting reminder. 'So did it occur to anyone that it was Katie Kiernan who tipped him off?'

Allbringer was becoming really pissed off now. 'She was waiting to hear back from us,' he retorted.

Gough slanted him a nasty look. 'So give me some other names,' she demanded.

'It's got to be someone inside the embassy.'

'I take it that's being investigated?'

'Naturally. The Brits are also looking into the possibility that the leak's theirs, considering how well informed their ex-agent seems to be.'

Gough got to her feet. 'This is a debacle,' she declared, walking to the window and staring down at the lushly landscaped gardens below. 'An utter debacle.' She wanted to spell out what it was going to mean for them all if that story ever made it to print, but they knew. The administration would never survive it. 'Where's Chambers now?' she snapped. 'No, don't tell me, they're still working on it.' She swung round, eyes dark with anger. 'Did I, or did I not say that we needed to utilize the female contingent?' she demanded. 'Has anything been done about that? Are our agents so inept that they haven't even managed to pull that off yet?'

'There was the issue of the missing child,' Allbringer reminded her. 'You yourself gave the instructions that no-one was to go there while . . .'

'But she's back now?'

He nodded.

'Then I shall contact Sir Christopher myself, to ask for his assistance in killing this story once and for all. Just please don't anyone tell me that Michelle Rowe has miscarried in the past few days.'

No-one did.

Chapter Twenty-Five

'How did it go?' Laurie asked as Elliot walked in the door.

'Not bad,' he answered, swinging his laptop on to the table, and throwing off his coat. 'I now know where Tom is, though I'm advised not to contact him; I've got the names and email addresses of at least six editors who were approached by Nick and Max, and four more whom we've pulled on board this afternoon. So once I've fixed myself a drink, I'm going to start transmitting the highlights Tom and I prepared. How's everything with Katie? Molly's OK, is she?'

'It's all fine, but I'll need to call Michelle and let her know Tom's safe.'

'Sure.' He was at the bar now, pouring a large shot of vodka into a tall glass. 'Are you going to have one?' he asked.

'Yep, same as you. What news on Nick and Max? Any idea where they are yet?'

'Ideas, yes, but no confirmation,' he responded, managing to keep his dislike of her concern for van

Zant out of it. 'Their abruptly aborted missions are forming part of the highlights.' He passed her a glass and drank deeply from his own as she made a quick call to Michelle.

'That should help repair relations between her and Katie,' she said, as she put the phone down. 'It's been a very stressful few days. Anyway,' she clinked her glass against his, 'it's good to see you.'

His eyes were penetrating as he watched her drink. Then tilting her chin he traced her mouth with his thumb. 'I've missed you,' he said gruffly.

'I've missed you too,' she responded, and her eyes fluttered closed as he stooped to kiss her. It was neither a passionate nor a demanding kiss, but one full of tenderness and promise.

'Has she gone for good now?' she whispered, when finally he pulled back to look at her again.

'I'm daring to hope so.'

'Even if she hasn't, she won't win,' she said.

'Of course not,' he murmured. This was the first time they'd been alone together since that disastrous scene out on the landing, and not wanting to spoil these moments of closeness with any more reminders of someone he'd rather forget, he kissed her gently again and said, 'Any messages?'

'A few,' she answered, 'they're still on the machine. Nothing that needs immediate attention.'

With relief, he said, 'I feel that we could benefit from some of that, don't you?'

'Immediate attention?' She smiled. 'I think you're right, but unfortunately only one of us has the time.'

He pulled a face.

'I'm not going anywhere,' she reminded him. 'I'll be right here, lending support, doing whatever you need me to, though with only one laptop between us right now . . .'

'You could end up cooking dinner,' he said, his mouth still almost touching hers.

Thankful for the calming effect a few days apart seemed to have had on them both, she pressed herself more closely to him, and felt the pleasure of his desire starting to spread through her.

'We'll pick this up later,' he murmured, when finally he let her go.

'I'll keep you to that,' she promised, and after making him laugh with a smouldering look, she took herself off round the bar to begin a raid on the fridge, stopping en route to answer the phone.

'Yes, he's here,' she said, in response to the voice at the other end. 'Can I tell him who's calling?' As she heard the name her eyes shot to Elliot. 'OK. Hold on please.' Covering the mouthpiece she whispered, 'Jolyon Kember.'

His exasperation was immediately evident.

'I'll top that up,' Laurie said, taking his glass as she passed him the phone.

Putting the receiver to his ear, Elliot said, 'If you're about to get on my case about leaving the country without a passport . . .'

'Please listen, Elliot,' Kember interrupted sharply. 'This isn't about your passport, your trip to France, or the personal consequences you could be facing for assisting a suspected terrorist . . .'

'Oh for God's sake,' Elliot snarled.

'Yes, I know he has you convinced,' Kember responded. 'He has most of the rest of your profession convinced and has for years, but that doesn't alter who he is, or what he was planning to do before the US authorities . . .'

'Jolyon,' Elliot cut in, 'save your spiel for the punters, it'll get a lot more play with them, because you know as well as I do that your propaganda machine's the biggest . . .'

'Elliot, once again, I ask you to listen,' Kember interrupted. 'I have a message for Tom Chambers that you need to relay. Do I have your full attention now?'

'Of course,' Elliot said, taking his glass back from Laurie.

'Good. You need to let him know that the net is about to be cast differently, and in a way that he won't be able to evade as effectively as he has recently. Make it clear to him that unless he hands himself over to the US authorities, all future access to the United Kingdom, either as a visitor or as a resident, will be denied. I stress the second category as we both know that he has plans to settle here, but he will render them impossible if he doesn't comply with law enforcement. He has twenty-four hours to respond.'

Elliot looked at the receiver as the line went dead. 'Jesus Christ,' he muttered, still assimilating.

'What did he say?' Laurie prompted.

He quickly repeated the message for Tom, watching her disgust match his own at the despicably low tactics they were now resorting to. 'It's an effective way to get him to come in,' he said, 'because even though he can hardly move any-where while there's a warrant out for his arrest, they're letting us know that if he runs the story and gains public support they'll have their revenge by tying him up in legal battles for years that will deny him access to this country. In other words, drop the story, or kiss goodbye to your loved ones.'

'We can't let this happen,' Laurie said. 'Michelle's pregnant, they want to get married, provide a home for Molly, and Robbie . . . We'll have to drop it.'

Elliot was shaking his head. 'No, what we're going to do is play them at their own game,' he said decisively. 'We've obviously already achieved our purpose in getting the terror threat removed from the election strategy – they can't go that route now, because we'd blow them clean out of the water. So what they want is assurance we won't run it anyway.'

'Then why not just ask for it?'

'Because then they'd be confirming it as a reality. No, they're not going to give us anything to back up our suspicions, they just want to make Tom aware that his life is going to be a misery if he continues to mess with them. They'll pull his IRS records, screw up his credit, lean on our own immigration to stop him coming and going, run this press campaign against him, and even try to nail him for terrorist activities. So what's holding them back? Why haven't they gone for it yet? Because they're not confident of winning. So what we need to do is prepare a story tonight.'

Laurie regarded him curiously.

'Not Tom's story,' he said. 'Our own – about how a US journalist is being persecuted by his own government and threatened by ours, to prevent him exposing something that the world – the UK in particular – needs to know about. Then we'll email it to them with a set of conditions of our own.'

Laurie could already feel the adrenalin buzz. 'The conditions being?' she prompted.

'That they cancel the arrest warrant for Tom, release all hostages including Josh Shine and Farukh Hassan, remove all listening devices and phone taps, rescind any instructions to interfere with immigration processes, and immediately return all computers.'

'In return for which we'll drop the story?'

He slanted her a look.

'So they win?'

'Possibly. Possibly not. Let's just deal with this first. We're going to need another laptop so you can write this with me. There are a couple of spares at my office, I'll call Murray and have him bring one over. Meanwhile, I'll make a start on a first draft, while you go out to a payphone to let Chris know what's happening so he can get word to Tom.'

'I'll pick up a Chinese while I'm out,' she told him, going for her coat and bag, 'and get Murray to meet me halfway.'

As she left he was already setting up his laptop, while assessing how he was going to approach this without impinging on the major scoop. That was wholly Tom's, but the more he thought about the action he was taking now, the more convinced he was becoming that it was absolutely the way to go. Set the scene, let everyone know how Britain was to be exploited in a US hard right election strategy, and these were the lengths the neo-cons were going to to prevent American journalist Tom Chambers from exposing it. He'd then detail everything that had happened from the time the damning documents had come into Tom's possession, to the raid on his apartment, the freezing of his bank accounts, the harassment of his girlfriend, right through to the warrant for his arrest and an FBI agent's tirade that more or less confirmed the campaign that was being planned against him. He'd add that even as he wrote Tom Chambers was in hiding, afraid for his freedom, if not his very life.

Should he actually go to print with all that – and he would if his conditions weren't met – there was no doubt that the entire House of Commons, along with the British public, would be on their feet demanding to know what the documents contained, and not one of them would sit down again until it had been revealed. At that point Tom could produce them, along with his theories and his conviction that a highly secret pre-emptive task force was at work in Pakistan, without having to prove anything, for the Special Operations Executive and their actions had more or less already done that for him.

By the time Laurie returned Elliot was reading through the overly long first draft he'd compiled, and barely looked up as she put the Chinese takeaway and laptop down on the table he was working at. He started to talk to her about what he'd written, asking her opinion, suggesting she read it herself, until finally he realized she wasn't responding. Looking up he saw, to his surprise, that she was extremely pale, almost angry.

'What is it?' he said, frowning. 'Did something happen?'

She took a breath, then dashed a hand through

her hair. 'I just saw Andraya, coming out of a restaurant downstairs,' she answered. Then in a voice tight with fury, 'Of all the restaurants in London she has to choose Le Pont de la Tour. What's the matter with the damned woman? Doesn't she know when to let go?'

Elliot was on his feet, coming round the table to pull her into his arms.

'If you'd seen the way she looked at me . . .' She shivered, still feeling the way those brazenly feline eyes had raked her with an expression of such malicious triumph that it was hard not to wonder if she knew something Laurie didn't.

'She's not going to win,' Elliot reminded her, tilting her face up so he could look into her eyes.

She stared at him, and felt her heart turn over. She loved him so much, but that woman, the memories, the images in her mind . . .

'Laurie, I love you, and I'm not going to lose you,' he told her firmly. 'She was the biggest mistake of my life, but she can only come between us if we allow it.'

'But what if she's stalking us . . .'

'Even if she is, it doesn't change the fact that she's nothing as far as I'm concerned. *Nothing*. Now you have to make her nothing to you, so that our relationship becomes only about us. We need to be together now, Laurie, no more running away from each other, or giving each other space, or hiding from truths, we have to start going through this. It's the only way we can put it behind us.'

She swallowed and nodded in agreement. 'I know,' she responded, and allowed him to enfold her in an embrace.

A few moments later she pulled back, and after slanting him a wry sort of smile, she said, 'I'll read the first draft.'

He let her go, and went to stand behind her as she slipped into his chair and started to read. After a while he put his hands on her shoulders, and she rested a cheek against one, letting him know she wanted him to keep it there. Gradually he sensed her being drawn back into the story, and as she sat forward, he began to set up the other computer.

'It's already quite powerful,' she told him when she'd finished reading.

'How long will you need to transcribe the Fellowes tape?' he asked.

'Probably no more than an hour. I just want to make a few changes here first, if you come and look at what I'm doing.'

After they'd completed a quick edit of his draft, she moved to the other laptop and set up the Fellowes tape, while he went to the phone and dialled Kember's number.

'We need your email address,' he told him, and after jotting it down he rang off without explaining why, and began dishing up the Chinese food.

An hour and a half later, with Laurie's input absorbed into the main body of the text, their conditions detailed at the end and Tom's hotmail address included in the distribution box, they were ready to transmit one of the most damning and sensational articles they'd ever compiled together.

'It needs a covering note,' Laurie said, starting to compose one.

The attached is self-explanatory,
and will be sent to press unless
the conditions detailed are met
within . . .

She glanced up at Elliot. 'Twenty-four hours?'
she said.

He shrugged. 'Why not? It's as long as they gave
us.'

Afer typing it in, she directed the cursor to send,
then reached up for his hand. 'OK?'

'OK,' he confirmed.

She clicked the mouse, waited for confirmation
to come up that it had gone, then let her head fall
back against him. 'So what do we do now?' she
asked.

'Wait,' he answered.

She closed her eyes, and as he pulled her up from
the chair to stand her in the circle of his arms she
felt nerves and anticipation in a way that reminded
her of their early days together.

'I think we have some unfinished business,' she
whispered, as he touched her face, and slid his
fingers into her hair.

'Yes, we have,' he murmured, and covering her
mouth with his he pushed his tongue gently inside
and drew her against him.

She could feel his desire growing with the same
intensity as her own, though his hands were
unhurried as he began to peel away her clothes. So
much emotion was filling her, bringing tears to her
eyes and such a powerful longing to her body that
she could hardly bear it. This was where she
wanted to be, where she belonged, in his arms,

with his breath on her face, his eyes on hers, and his body claiming her. Nothing could ever match the way they were together, it didn't even come close. She wanted him inside her so badly that she might have torn at his clothes, but she could tell that he wasn't going to let her lead the way. He knew her body even better than she knew it herself – for him it was an instrument that only he had the skill to tune.

When she was naked he moved his hands all over her, touching, yet not touching, watching her respond and playing her cruelly. Her nipples were hard and urgent, between her legs she was throbbing and alive. He touched her there and she drew in her breath. Moments later he was taking her so close to the edge that she almost fell against him. His fingers were expert and demanding, sensitive and knowing. He held her close, kissed her hard and took her from one climax straight into another. Only he had ever been able to do that to her, and only he knew how to do it again and again.

She was still breathless as he took her hand and led her upstairs, where he laid her down on the bed and undressed himself. As he lay down with her, her legs opened to take him. He didn't hold back and as he entered her, filling her slowly, pushing himself all the way into her, she looked up into his eyes and knew that whatever else they might have to face in the future, tonight their lovemaking was going to exceed anything they'd known before.

Deborah Gough raised her eyes from the email displayed on her computer screen, to the video image of Allbringer at the top right-hand corner.

'We have to presume they're serious,' he said.

She nodded thoughtfully. 'So what do you recommend, Mr Allbringer?' she asked.

With almost no hesitation, he said, 'That we accept the conditions and have legal documents drawn up right away to prevent any future publication of materials either directly, or indirectly related to this subject.'

She took a moment to consider it, though it was the conclusion she'd expected him to come to. 'I see no problem with that,' she said, 'provided the agreements are watertight.' She sat back in her chair and steepled her fingers. 'Have we managed to discover where Tom Chambers is yet?' she asked.

'Not that I'm aware of, but I'm told Nancy Goodman is on her way back to Washington.'

Gough's eyes narrowed as she pondered the information that had come in regarding one of the FBI's senior agents in London, believed by embassy investigators to be the most likely source of the leaks. 'Even if it does turn out to be her,' Gough said, 'someone had to be briefing her – so who would you put top of your list, Mr Allbringer?' As she asked the question her gaze returned to his image with all the directness of a pointing finger.

His discomfort was revealed by the smallest turn of his head. 'At this stage I would rather not speculate,' he responded.

Her smile was small. 'Very wise. We will need a full inquiry. Meanwhile, I suggest we interview Nancy Goodman together on her return. Would you be agreeable to that?'

'Naturally, though I should point out that

there are others more expert in the field of inter-rogation . . .'

'I'm aware of that, and they certainly won't be prevented from doing their job. I would simply like to meet Mrs Goodman in person. I imagine you would too, unless,' she added, 'you've already met.'

This time his discomfort was more pronounced. 'I knew Nancy some thirty-five years ago at college,' he said. 'We haven't had any contact since.'

Gough smiled pleasantly. 'Then you've nothing to worry about,' she said, and sitting forward she clicked off his image before picking up the phone.

As Tom presented his US passport to a British immigration officer at Heathrow his nerves were as on edge as at any other time during these last few weeks. No matter that Elliot's lawyers had extracted written assurances from the States that there would be no attempt to prevent his entry into the UK, he was still expecting someone to materialize any minute to escort him to a secure cell, or waiting car, possibly even to smack him face down on the ground and jam a gun to his head. However, the saturnine British official merely flicked through the passport's tatty pages, gave him a brief once-over to match the photo, then handed it back and switched his attention to the next traveller in line.

Tom moved on. So far at least, it appeared everyone was adhering to their word – in return for Elliot's and Tom's signatures on a contract agreeing not to act before a second, more comprehensive document could be drawn up (to block them completely), all computers had been returned, wire taps removed, captives released, warrants rescinded . . . Basically everything Elliot had requested was being granted, and if Tom weren't such a sceptic he might have been prepared to believe they'd won this round. In actual fact they had, because he was here, wasn't he? In London. And between them, Katie, Michelle and Laurie had already cooked up a plan on how to circumvent the agreement. Their scheme might be crazy, but right now, as he pressed on through the baggage hall where he had nothing to claim since he was carrying it all, he was so relieved to have the weight of a warrant lifted from his shoulders that anything felt possible.

Quickly winding his way through the passengers with carts and wheelchairs and slow-moving children, he emerged into the arrivals lounge and almost instantly spotted Michelle waving. Molly was with her, and as he hurried forward, Michelle caught her niece's hand to pull her to meet him. Flushed with shyness Molly tried to hold back, but he was having none of it. The instant he reached them his bags hit the floor as he swept them both into an enveloping embrace, kissing Michelle full on the mouth before pressing a long and noisy version of the same to Molly's forehead.

'What man could have two more beautiful women waiting to meet him?' he asked, hugging them again. 'How did I get to be so lucky?' And scooping them both up he swung them round.

Loving the attention Molly laughed and blushed and her eyes shone like jewels as he kissed her again, before turning back to Michelle. 'Everything

585

OK?' he murmured, his mouth very close to hers.

'We're both fine,' she told him softly.

Somehow restraining himself from shouting with joy, he said to Molly, 'How about you, Miss Cool Chick with the prettiest eyes I've ever seen? I want to hear everything you've been up to. And no skipping over anything. All cards on the table.'

Molly's shyness seemed magically to evaporate as she retorted, 'Including yours. Mum said no more secrets. I've got to know everything from now on.'

His eyes were dancing. 'Speaking of your gorgeously formidable mother,' he responded, 'where is she? I was expecting all my girls to be here.'

'She's at Laurie's preparing our little party,' Molly told him. 'Laurie has to work, but she's at the flat doing it – and Elliot's outside in Laurie's car, which isn't as cool as the Porsche, but it's bigger inside, so we can all get in.'

'Then what are we waiting for?' he demanded, and snatching up his luggage, he walked them both out to the short-term car park, where he presented them with several elegantly wrapped packages before dropping the rest of his bags in the boot.

As they travelled into London Tom and Elliot became engrossed in an urgent discussion of recent developments and how they were to proceed from here, while Michelle half-listened as she and Molly sat in the back unwrapping expensive perfumes, and pulling faces when Tom wasn't looking. The one he'd chosen for Michelle caused Molly to protest under her breath, 'Ugh, rank. It smells like Domestos.'

Michelle choked back a laugh and checked to make sure he hadn't heard. Then, wiping her wrist on her jeans, she turned to her next enticing package. She was just pulling it from the box when, realizing what it was, she immediately pushed it back in again, though not before Molly managed to catch a glimpse of the cream-coloured lacy undies.

Gross, she was thinking, as she tore the paper off her next gift. They were a bit old for all that, but anyway, it still didn't mean Tom wasn't like, really cool, because he'd actually bought her . . . 'A *Prada purse*! Oh my God!' Her eyes glittered with delight as she showed Michelle. Everyone was going to be like, so WOW and jealous when she showed them, because this was absolutely genuine, no fake, then her heart sank as she remembered she didn't have any friends to show – and she was really, really dreading going back to school on Monday, because of what everyone was going to say about how she'd run away, and about Brad. She still felt all hurt and upset about him, like as if their relationship had actually been real. *How sad was she!* Her mum and Michelle were really cool about that though, telling her stories of all the times they'd made chumps – *chumps!* – of themselves over boys, which usually turned out to be much worse than anything she'd done, and almost always ended up making her laugh.

As they reached Tower Bridge Michelle drew everyone's attention to the hotel on the river's north bank. 'You and I are staying there tonight,' she informed Tom. 'Katie and Molly have checked in on the South Bank, actually in that impressive red-brick building in front of you, where Laurie and Elliot have an apartment that's going to make you see stars, my love, both literally and metaphorically.'

Tom was grinning. 'Can't wait,' he responded, and reached behind for her hand. The way he squeezed it told her he was as eager for them to be alone as she was, but the party was planned and making everyone wait while they got reacquainted was hardly appropriate, when they'd have the rest of the night to themselves.

Laurie and Katie were poised ready to crack open the champagne as soon as the door opened, which delighted Tom as much as the 'welcome back' banners that were draped all over the place.

'I made that one,' Molly declared, pointing to a particularly colourful effort that was strung across the bar.

'The best of the lot,' he told her, as Katie put a glass into his hand and glowed with pleasure as he embraced her.

Toasts were made and several bawdy comments followed, mostly from Katie to Molly's dismay, though she was never far from her mother's side, which was how she'd been since Tuesday, even sleeping in Katie's bed each night and hovering around the bathroom while Katie was attending to business. Clearly she was afraid Katie might just vaporize, or get flushed away, if she didn't keep an eye on her, though thankfully she'd tanked off to the airport to meet Tom happily enough, giving Katie a welcome breather for a couple of hours.

Katie had wondered if Elliot hadn't been equally as ready for some space, for it hadn't escaped her notice that Laurie appeared almost as glued to him as Molly did to her. However, watching them now, she decided it could be he who was doing the sticking, because the minute he'd put some less groan-worthy music on – 'Yellow Ribbon' was her idea, she had to admit, but only as a cheesy joke, not as serious entertainment – he was back at Laurie's side and sliding an arm round her as she leaned against him.

Feeling pleased that they finally seemed to be finding the way back to each other, Katie readily accepted more champagne from the bottle Tom was offering, and even agreed to let Molly have a drop more too. Why not? It wasn't often they had this much fun, or even got out of Membury Hempton, and besides, it wasn't as if Molly had school in the morning, or she any work.

After returning the bottle to the ice bucket Tom produced more gifts from his holdall, this time for Laurie and Katie, which surprised and embarrassed Laurie, though she could hardly have been more thrilled with the perfume, since L'Eau d'Issey was her favourite, which meant he'd probably consulted Elliot before making the decision. For her part Katie gushed with delight at the elegant Gucci handbag with silver chain handles and G-logo clasp, then promptly sprayed herself all over with the same perfume he'd bought Michelle, before realizing just how bad it was.

Giggling, Molly and Michelle turned away and pretended to survey the scrumptious-looking food, while Elliot refilled everyone's glass and Katie smiled blandly on, hoping she didn't really smell like a toilet.

'So, the killer contract turns out to be a weapon of

only partial destruction,' Tom declared, when they all finally settled down on to the sofas and armchairs.

'Our lawyers are still going over it,' Laurie told him, 'but as far as publication is concerned it's looking watertight. There's just the one tiny airhole we've already discussed where TV production is concerned, so, provided they don't spot and plug it between now and when we sign the final agreement – which we can always stall anyway – we can start shooting as soon as you're ready.'

Tom raised an arm for Michelle to settle in more comfortably beside him. 'So let me get this straight,' he said, 'you're going to make a programme about everything that's happened since I was first approached by Josh Shine right up to now?'

'Everything,' she confirmed, 'with the main emphasis obviously being on the P2OG and suspect plot. So instead of writing it, you're going to be telling it.'

In truth it had taken Tom a while to get his head round this change of direction, for he'd never been a big fan of broadcast journalism, mainly because it rarely allowed enough time to present all the facts, and even if it did, no sooner was the information there on the screen than it was gone. And this certainly wasn't a sound-bite situation. However, faced with a legal contract that was allowing no way forward for print, he'd been persuaded in several phone calls from Michelle to set his ego and prejudice aside, so he was now more or less ready to accept that broadcast might have its merits.

'But we still have to look at our main objective

here,' he pointed out, 'which is to get the neo-conservatives out of the international policy-making picture. That means we have to break the story in the US, and believe me, persuading any of the networks, or the cable companies because most of them are owned by Republican backers too, to air a programme like that is going to be even more difficult than to get it in the press. Hell, you don't need me to tell you how many British-made programmes have been blocked over there since we went into Afghanistan.'

'That doesn't have to stop us making ours,' Laurie told him. 'And it's important that it shows here in Britain, because this country is every bit as affected by US pre-emption policy as Iraq or Pakistan, since we're being dragged into it too. We need to take a look at what the American inter-national agenda actually is, because most people don't know about the 21 Project. They need to understand who's really taking the decisions in Washington, and how we, in the UK, are being exploited to achieve political gain.'

'I'm not arguing with any of that,' Tom assured her, 'I'm just saying, getting it out there . . .'

'Will be impossible if we rely solely upon the mainstream media,' Laurie finished for him. 'Which is why we're setting up a simultaneous webcast which can be accessed in the States. It'll help the editors over there to get round the injunction, if they report on a Net-based story, rather than on information received direct from you.'

'And using those two mediums, TV and the Internet,' Katie came in, 'will make it an even bigger sensation than if you managed to run it in

591

five dozen papers on five different continents. Whether we print junkies like it or not, viewing audiences are a lot larger than readerships, and these days people come alive to moving pictures.'

Tom was laughing. 'It's OK, I'm convinced,' he assured them, 'but legally we're going to be running into a whole lot of trouble. Yeah, I know you realize that and you're prepared to take the risk, but once they know what we're up to, they'll shut you down faster than you can say cut.'

'That's still no reason not to give it a try,' Laurie said. 'And, as I outlined to you on the phone, we're going to disguise the shoot to make it look as though I'm continuing with a programme about Katie. It stands to reason you'd be a part of that, though there are other aspects we'll find slightly trickier to get around, it's true. However, we're coming up with circumventions all the time, and once we've got everything recorded, edited and ready for transmission, there'll be nothing they can do, because even if they slap an injunction on the broadcast company here in Britain, who by the way are determined to fight if that happens, there's still the Internet, and if they manage to block the site, we'll just flood the media with hard video copies and no-one will ever know how many have gone out, or where they've ended up.'

'So the all-encompassing contract they're planning to throw at us,' Michelle added, 'won't be worth the paper it's printed on by the time the public knows the full story. Besides, they'll be so tied up dealing with the fallout they won't have the time to sue.'

'Frankly, it's playing as dirty as they do,' Katie

said with no little glee, 'because they sure as heck don't have any regard for the law if it doesn't suit them. They just make up new ones where they need them and throw the book at the rest of the world when it comes to establishing an International Court of Justice, or ratifying the Kyoto Protocol, or tearing up an Anti-Ballistic Missile Treaty . . . OK, OK, too much . . . I know . . .'

'You can always bring those issues up when I interview you about the role you've played in all this,' Laurie told her.

'Am I going to be in the programme?' Molly asked.

'Probably,' Laurie answered, certain she'd manage to work out something.

Katie downed the last of her champagne and nudged Molly to fetch some more. 'So, I guess, that's my biography dumped on the back burner,' she grumbled. 'If you don't mind me saying so, Laurie, I think you've got a problem with your priorities.'

As they all laughed, Laurie said, 'Actually, your book is quite safe, and being expanded even as we speak, so no reason to feel overshadowed.'

'Not possible,' Michelle remarked. 'She wouldn't recognize the shade if it turned up in a black cape and gagged her.'

Katie's eyes widened with interest. 'I think I like the sound of him,' she responded.

'Muuu-uum,' Molly groaned.

Katie laughed and held out her glass to be filled. 'So, it seems as though we're all going to be pretty busy becoming stars of the small screen for the next . . . how long?' she asked Laurie, licking the over-fizz off her fingers and almost gagging at the whiff of bad perfume that wafted up with it.

'Two weeks, possibly three,' Laurie answered. 'I talked to my partner, Rose, last night and she agrees we should try to have it ready for the one-hour transmission slot we've got coming up in a month. It'll be well enough in advance of the presidential elections for this to play and play and get right into everyone's consciousness while they're taking the decision about who they want to run their country – and our world.'

Katie was rubbing her hands together. 'Oh the power,' she purred gleefully. 'And what Laurie hasn't told you yet, Tom, is that yours truly is going to present the programme.'

Tom looked at once impressed and delighted.

'Just topping and tailing,' Katie said modestly, 'but my name, my face, my input will all be there.' Consideration for Molly prevented her mentioning a swan song, but they all knew that was what she was saying, and Katie Kiernan just wouldn't be Katie Kiernan if she didn't go out on a controversial note.

'So when do we start?' Tom asked.

'Actually, tomorrow,' Laurie answered. 'I've drawn up a running order for you to look at, which entails you coming back here in the morning so we can start laying down the first part of your interview. We'll shoot a lot with you over the next couple of weeks, obviously, but where we can we should try to keep it in the general vicinity of Katie, and as she'll still be here tomorrow . . .'

'I was hoping to be in London for at least three days,' Tom said. 'I've got a lot to do here.'

'That's OK,' Laurie told him. 'Once Katie's gone you can stay here at the flat, then we should be able to shoot as much as we like without any problem.'

He looked at Michelle. 'Does that work for you?' he said.

Before Michelle's loyalties started tearing themselves asunder, Katie said, 'It's OK, consider yourself off the hook for a couple of days, because the three remaining boxes of photo albums that my daughter is insisting we trawl through can always wait. No, honestly, they can,' she insisted as Michelle started to laugh, 'and I'm sure Tom would enjoy taking a little jaunt down our memory lane too, so let's not deprive him.'

His eyes were shining with laughter as Michelle groaned and Molly grinned. 'I can't think of anywhere I'd rather go,' he responded. 'Katie in plaits and Michelle in hot pants, how could I not?'

'It's Mum in hot pants that does your head in,' Molly informed him, and yelped as Katie started to tickle her.

It was an hour or so later, afraid of putting too much of a strain on Katie who'd manage to stage a valiant performance for most of the evening, that Michelle and Tom finally left the apartment to walk back across Tower Bridge to the hotel.

'So are you really OK with this change of plan?' Michelle asked, as he drew her to him so they could walk closely together along the cobbled street of Shad Thames.

'It's growing on me all the time,' he admitted, 'and, frankly, it was never really going to work out the way we intended. The best-laid plans never do. And maybe I've got a better chance of persuading everyone I'm as patriotic as the next man if I present the case in person. I just wonder how far we'll get before an injunction's slapped on us.'

'We'll keep going until it is, and if it happens we'll deal with it then,' she replied.

He was quiet as they mounted the steps up to the bridge, then pulling her in tighter to him as the full strength of the wind caught them, he said, 'Meanwhile, we've got other things to think about, like when we're going to get married. I guess it can't be until this is over, but do you have any dates in mind?'

Loving the determination of his words and protective feeling of his arm, she closed her eyes for a moment and let him lead her on in the darkness. 'How would you feel,' she said finally, 'if instead of getting married when this is over, we do something special for Katie and Molly instead? I mean, we can tie the knot any time, but Katie's got a birthday coming up and it would be nice to mark it for her, don't you think?'

'Of course,' he responded. 'Do you have something in mind? Shall we take them away somewhere?'

'If things were different I'm sure Katie would love an exotic adventure, but even coming to London for the night was making her anxious. She's a lot weaker than appearances suggest now, so she likes to be near her own bed, in case she doesn't feel good. Which means if we do something, it has to be close to home, and Molly's come up with an idea that she wants to tell you about herself.'

Feeling pleased that Molly considered him

596

worthy of special attention, he said, 'She seemed on pretty good form today.'

'She's OK,' Michelle answered. 'She has her down times, obviously, and it could break your heart to see the state she gets into, but what can you expect? They're extremely close the two of them, and no matter how much we try to prepare Molly, nothing's ever going to make this easy.'

Hearing the emotion in her voice, he hugged her in tighter and pressed his lips to her hair. 'It won't be for you either,' he said gently. 'Actually, for any of us, considering the impact your sister makes, but Molly's the one who matters. I guess now's not a good time to talk to her about where she wants to live after, though we'll have to get something sorted.'

'Katie's fairly certain she'll want to come back to London. The cottage will always be hers, obviously, and everything in it, but if she does decide she wants to stay in the country, would that be OK with you?'

'We'd have to buy a bigger place,' he said, 'but I'm happy to be wherever you are, so a house in the country, a flat in London, or both, it all works for me. Though right now, I'm focusing on a riverside hotel which looks just the perfect setting for you to slip into some new underwear I think you got today – and me to check out how well I did on size.'

Chapter Twenty-Six

Going back to school didn't turn out to be as bad as Molly feared, though it was like, *really* embarrassing when the teacher made everyone clap and chorus, 'Welcome back, Molly,' when she walked in the class. She'd just wanted to curl herself up in her Prada purse and zip herself in when that happened. Still it was all right after, because amazingly no-one took the mickey out of her, or said anything nasty – in fact, they were all really friendly. She had a feeling Rusty had told them about her mum, so they were all like, feeling sorry for her now, but she didn't say anything, because she didn't want to talk about that to anyone – it was none of their business, and anyway she'd only end up crying.

Rusty was hanging around her all the time now, but she supposed that was OK. She was still horrible to him, but he never seemed to mind, he just blinked out through those jam-jar glasses like he didn't really get it, and then did a scary smile with his braces and teeth. Actually, only she was allowed to be mean to him. If anyone else was, she just got hold of his arm and walked him away, and now no-one was really being that bad to him any more. Her mum and Michelle kept saying she should invite him round for a meal, but no way was she going to do that – he might start thinking he was her boyfriend, or something, and like, no way. Brother maybe, because he'd be kind of cool to have on tap doing her homework, but boyfriend – *puhleeze*. Anyway, he couldn't be her brother either, because her cousin Robbie would sort of be that, if he came to live with them, but him and Rusty would probably get on, so Rusty wouldn't be left out. It was just a shame they were both boys, because she wouldn't mind having a sister, and even if Michelle's baby turned out to be a girl, she'd be like, much too young. So Molly was considering suggesting to Michelle that she and Tom could maybe like, adopt one of the Afghan girls from the camp where Michelle used to work. It seemed the kind of thing they'd do, and Tahira, who Molly had been emailing lately, who was thirteen and like dead pretty and didn't have any family and would really love to come to England, could come and live with them.

Anyway, Molly didn't really think very much about that, only now and again when her mind wandered off on its own, but then she'd remember her mum wouldn't be there when all that happened, and then everything came to a stop, because she didn't want to think about her mum going anywhere without her, even though she knew she had to.

Michelle was like, really cool now Molly was

getting to know her, and Tom was just awesome, though he'd gone off to Washington yesterday to see some senators or congressionals or something, and Molly wasn't sure when he'd be back. She understood some of the story he was working on, but it was quite complicated really and impossible to keep up with, because all the filming was happening while she was at school. Laurie had taken some shots of her too though, strolling in the woods with her mum and Trotty, having breakfast together, and even doing some homework together the other night. She was going to make a special copy of that for Molly to keep. It was all going on in their house at the moment, something always happening, or someone always there – Molly just hoped she and Michelle managed to get on the computer tonight, so they could carry on with their arrangements to make one of her mum's dreams come true in time for her birthday.

Now, she was just getting off the bus on her way home from school, when she heard someone calling out to her. She looked round, frowning against the sun, then her heart turned over as she saw Allison Fortescue-Bond standing on the other side of the road. Immediately Molly started to walk on.

'Molly, please can I talk to you?' Allison shouted. 'It won't take long.'

Molly was horribly torn. She really wanted to run away, but for some weird reason she was starting to feel sort of sorry for Allison. She must be feeling a bit stupid standing over there shouting and being ignored, which was no more than she deserved, but in the end Molly decided that maybe there wasn't any harm in at least finding out what she had to say. So, after waiting for a cyclist to whizz by, she crossed the street, keeping her expression set on hoity even though she could see that Allison wasn't about to pick a fight, and when she got to the other side she said, 'Well? What do you want?'

Allison turned a deep shade of red as she said, 'I just wanted to say I'm sorry for what we did. It was horrible and mean and like, I never really wanted to do it, but I know that's not a good enough excuse, and I shouldn't have laughed that night when Brad came in, I was just drunk and stupid and . . .' She took a breath. 'Anyway, my mum says I should have stopped Cecily and Donna coming to the house, because you're a nice girl and didn't deserve to be treated like that, while they're like, all screwed up and . . . Well anyway, I wanted to tell you I'm sorry, not just because my mum says I have to, and that I can't have my computer or DVD or anything back again until I do, but because I like . . .' She shrugged, 'Well like, I really miss you, and you were like, my best friend, and I don't have anything to do with Cecily and Donna any more, not even at school. So I was like, hoping that you like, might, you know . . . If you want to, that is. Anyway, even if you don't, I'm still sorry and wish we'd never done that horrible thing to you.'

As she finished Molly let her eyes drift off across the road to where Kylie and Greta were watching, then she was looking at kind of nowhere as she started to say, 'I'm not into hating my mum any more. I mean, I never really hated her anyway.'

'No, I know,' Allison said. 'I don't suppose I hate

mine either, I just wish she didn't always get so drunk.'

Molly's eyes came to hers. 'If you want us to be friends again then you'd better come to my house to make sure it's all right.'

Allison nodded. 'Can I come now?' she asked.

Molly shrugged. 'OK. I'd better just go and tell my other friends that I'll see them in school tomorrow.'

A few minutes later Katie stared in blank astonishment as Molly waltzed into the kitchen with Allison Fortescue-Bond behind her – but even more unexpected was the litany Allison immediately stumbled into.

'I've come to apologize, Mrs Kiernan,' she said, 'to you as well as to Molly. I'm really, really sorry for what happened. Molly's the best friend I ever had, and I know I don't deserve to have any friends after what I did, but if you'll let me have another chance, I promise I won't ever do anything like it again. I even promise to go away and never come back if that's what you say I have to do. I just would really like to have Molly as my friend again, even though I know I don't deserve to have any friends after what I did. She's like, really cool, and my mum says she always liked Molly best of everyone. And I do too.'

Katie had no chance to respond before Molly said, 'Allison doesn't see those girls any more, Mum, except in school, but she doesn't have anything to do with them there either, and it was all them really.'

Katie turned back to Allison, still blinking at the speed of the reconciliation, though touched by how much Allison seemed to value her friendship with Molly. 'I'm not going to pretend I wasn't angry about what you did to Molly,' she said carefully, 'you caused her a lot of hurt. However, it's not easy to say you're sorry, and you've just done a pretty good job of it, so if Molly's prepared to forgive you, I am too. Just no more secret cults or bogus boyfriends . . . All right, all right,' she protested, as Molly leapt on her and started to dance her round.

'Thank you, Mum. Thank you, thank you,' Molly cried. 'Where's Michelle? She's got to meet Allison properly now. You wait,' she told Allison, 'Michelle's like, really cool. Not a bit like I thought . . .'

'Spare my blushes out there,' Michelle shouted from the sitting room, where she and Laurie were viewing some of the rushes.

'Come on,' Molly demanded, grabbing Allison and dragging her across the kitchen. 'Oh, and me and Michelle have got like this surprise we're planning . . .' She glanced at Katie. 'I can't tell you what it is now, but it is like, so cool, isn't it Michelle?'

'The coolest,' Michelle confirmed, 'even Tom thinks so, and he wants you to call him later, because he has something to ask you.'

'Tom is just like, amazing,' Molly told Allison. 'You'll meet him when he comes back. He knows everything and everybody and Laurie's making a programme about him . . . Well, actually it's about Mum, but Tom's in it too. Anyway, this is Michelle, who's my auntie, but I just call her Michelle.'

As Katie watched from the kitchen she could feel a lump forming in her throat but she continued to

603

smile, for it was doing her heart so much good to see how everyone was closing in around Molly now, as though absorbing her into a protective realm of love and support and everything she needed to keep her going and carry her through. It was exactly what Katie had hoped and prayed for, and she felt especially moved by Allison's return, for everyone needed a best friend, and Katie had sensed how much Molly was missing hers, even though she hadn't wanted to admit it. So the time was almost right for Katie to let go now. She sensed that as clearly as if someone was telling her. She hadn't mentioned it to anyone, but she was becoming tired in a way she hadn't been before, and strangely peaceful, in spite of the pain. She just wanted to hang on for the grand surprise Molly was planning, and to share with Molly the very special gift she had for her too.

Had Tom been a more impressionable man, the number of senior officials who'd passed through the rather unassuming front door of his Adams Morgan apartment this past week might have dazzled him. The town was buzzing with rumours, largely fed by Max, though Tom had yet to confirm or deny any of them, but that wasn't stopping anyone wanting to get their own take on what they'd heard.

Elliot was in Washington too, helping keep track of what was being said and by whom. At the same time they were preparing a series of articles to run in *The New York Times* and *Los Angeles Times* to coincide with Laurie's programme, for they'd taken the decision not to sign the latest agreement that had turned up two days ago, that would stop them going to press.

'They've got to know they can't contain this now,' Tom had said after reading the contract through. 'It's gone too far, it's being talked about all over, so this here doesn't amount to any more than some last-ditch posturing.'

'Then we ignore the injunction and wait for their next move,' Elliot had responded.

There had been no word since, not even a call from the lawyers. So now they were pushing ahead, seeking as many quotes and opinions as they could get from experts in the fields of defence, military and intelligence, while still half-expecting someone to storm in through the door any minute and march them off in cuffs.

'Did you see this fax from Farukh?' Tom asked, glancing up from where he was slumped on a battered blue sofa surrounded by papers and half-eaten cartons of Nepalese food. 'He's hired himself a film crew in Karachi and he's already got interviews with a couple of the fundamentalists who are claiming to have been approached in this. They'll say anything to hurt America, we know that, but it's still going to make for some uncomfortable viewing in certain quarters here, and Laurie's going to have one helluva programme on her hands.'

'Then let's just hope the British government doesn't step in to block transmission,' Elliot remarked, looking at his mobile as it started to ring.

'Do you think that's likely?' Tom asked.

'Actually, no,' Elliot responded, and took the call.

A few minutes later, having said very little, he rang off and turned back to Tom. 'Well, that's just gone some way to endorsing one of my favourite theories,' he remarked.

Tom was intrigued.

Elliot's expression was ironical as he said, 'I think we're agreed that our mysterious source has to be way up there to have access to the kind of information he has?'

Tom nodded.

'So it's an inside job to break the neo-con stranglehold on the Republican party?'

Again Tom nodded.

'The call I just took came from someone at a very high level in Downing Street, and though it wasn't even close to a confirmation, my belief is that our own PM has been working behind the scenes with someone in Washington to help break that stranglehold.'

Tom's eyes widened, then narrowed. A moment later he started to grin. 'It's wild, but it makes sense,' he declared. 'The top man wants out from whatever agreements he's made with those guys.'

'Especially one that has the British people being exploited with a terrorist threat for American hard-right purposes,' Elliot added.

Tom was still weighing it up. 'I wouldn't mind betting he wasn't even consulted on that,' he stated, 'which is why he's got himself involved in a scheme to bring them down.' He was shaking his head in amazement. 'So who's he been colluding with over here?'

'It could be that even your top guy is finding it hard to stomach the neo-cons now.'

Tom thought about that. 'The ballast has turned into deadweight,' he said. 'Could be, because they've overplayed their hand badly this last couple of years, but he's their boy, so I'd be more inclined to put my money on someone at the top of the intelligence services. It would be great payback for the way they've been forced to take the rap for everything from bad policy-making, to prisoner abuse, to outright government lies this past eighteen months.'

Daniel Allbringer's pallor was pinched as he walked beside Deborah Gough in the gardens at Langley.

'. . . so, whereas on the one hand,' she was saying, 'we can claim to have done everything possible to contain and control this situation, I believe the time has now come to accept that the press injunction isn't worth the paper it's printed on, which means we can no longer avoid the battle being taken into the public domain. There are too many rumours, too much speculation and far too much pressure being put on us, as well as those we serve, to be able to rely on mere legal agreements to protect us from further media scrutiny.'

Allbringer swallowed. 'So what action are you proposing?' he asked, feeling certain he already knew the answer.

'Pre-emptive, of course,' she responded. 'It's what we're all about, so we shall instruct the *Washington Post* to run with their exclusive on Tom Chambers in the morning.'

It was exactly what Allbringer had expected, and the last thing he wanted to hear.

'I'd like you to take charge of that,' she told him, smiling at a colleague who was passing.

Allbringer's shock stiffened his gait. She was going to trust *him* to trigger the case against Chambers, when he knew very well she suspected him of being behind the leaks? What was she expecting? Him to hang himself completely?

She started to speed up. 'I've a meeting in ten minutes,' she told him, 'so I'll leave that with you. If there's anything you need, you know where to find me.'

As she walked on she was smiling blandly to herself, for she knew very well that it didn't matter what the hell the *Washington Post* printed now, Tom Chambers was going to win this, because there was simply no way he couldn't. The P2OG and its covert tactics were about to be royally exposed, careers and reputations would be left in ruins, and the neo-conservative chokehold on power would be blasted apart.

With a light spring in her step she trotted up to a side door of the building and pressed in a code to enter. The fact that she'd never met Tom Chambers appealed greatly to her sense of the sublime, though it was a pity, she was thinking, because in spite of their political differences she was certain they'd get along. Still, she had the great satisfaction of knowing she'd chosen well when she'd been approached by the Director of Intelligence, his British equivalent known only as M, and two prominent members of her own government to select a journalist to play this game with her, for Chambers had achieved everything she'd intended him to, and perhaps even more. Actually he'd surprised her a few times, and had impressed her a lot, but most of all he'd instilled in her a sense of how determined he, and reporters like him, were to expose the covert actions being taken by certain factions within their own governments in the name of profit, power and political gain.

So now all that remained was for her to disband the Special Operations Executive, rejoin Special Operations Command and set up a strategy for withdrawing the P2OG, while dealing with the blowback for their part in its existence. It was going to be a busy time, with more pressure on the US government than it could probably withstand, and not much opportunity to sit back and enjoy the neo-con disintegration. However, she'd be sure to make a space in her calendar for the transmission of Laurie Forbes's programme that should set it all in motion. The tech guys in Q-Tel would send a live feed from London through to her office, or maybe the Director was going to want it piped into his. Whichever, it was going to make extremely interesting viewing for all the invisible architects of its basis, including Nancy Goodman, who, in time-honoured CIA tradition, was about to receive a large financial settlement in exchange for her services, and her silence.

It was almost impossible, Katie was finding, not to be swept along in all the excitement of the programme, for everything was really hotting up now, especially over there in Washington, where, Tom had informed them, several high-level resignations had already been offered and accepted – and that was merely in anticipation of what was about to hit. Just imagine what the reaction was going to be when it finally did. In many ways Katie wished she could be over there, for she'd get such a kick out of watching the spectacular downfall at close quarters. However, this wasn't the kind of sensation that would fizzle out in a matter of days, or even weeks, it was going to take months for the full impact to be felt, and the ensuing hearings and commissions were likely to rumble on for years. So she'd have to content herself with the slightly lesser thrill of knowing she'd at least played a part in it all, which was enough. Despite all the excitement, she couldn't deny a certain relief that between them Tom, Elliot and Laurie were organizing everything so that she wouldn't have to deal with any of the immediate aftermath herself, for it was inevitably going to be huge.

It was always fascinating, she was thinking now, as she drove Michelle and Molly out of the village towards the main road, how perspectives changed with circumstance. What had seemed so vitally important to her a week ago, or even yesterday, wasn't ringing all the same bells now. Not that world issues ever ceased to matter, heavens, she'd be the last person ever to say that, but a sense of achievement on a global scale wasn't necessarily more satisfying than a little triumph on the personal front, even if it was only driving a car. Indeed, in their small world it meant a great deal for her to be at the wheel, since it was reassuring all three of them that she wasn't about to go floating off to paradise yet, though she had to admit the prospect of a world with no pain or exhaustion, no failures or fear, no earthly torments at all, was definitely starting to have an appeal.

Catching Michelle's eye in the rear-view mirror she winked, and pressed her foot down a little harder. Unlike Molly, Michelle was perfectly aware of where they were going, and though Katie knew she approved, it was also clear that she was finding it hard to cope with. Which was why Katie wanted to keep it all as upbeat as she could, because the last thing she wanted was for this to turn into a morbid memory for Molly, when it was supposed to be quite the reverse.

'So you two have finally finished whispering, have you?' she said, glancing in the mirror again. 'I feel like a chauffeur who can't keep secrets up in front here.'

'Yeah, but we've got a lot to talk about,' Molly told her, 'because it's only two weeks to your birthday and there's still a lot to organize – and don't start going off trying to guess what we're doing again, because you just show yourself up saying really dumb things.'

Katie chuckled.

'Did you speak to Tom last night?' Michelle asked Molly.

'Yeah, and he's totally cool about, you know, but it was his idea so he'd be a bit weird if he wasn't.'

Michelle had to laugh, while loving Tom for being so attentive to Molly and her plans when he had so much else going on. 'Laurie's sending down a rough cut of the programme at the weekend, did she tell you?' she asked Katie.

'I can hardly wait. Are we allowed to give notes?'

'You can always try,' Michelle laughed.

Inside her waxen skin Katie was twinkling. 'As Tom's getting a copy too, I guess we'll leave the editorial input to him,' she said. 'When's Elliot coming back, do you know?'

'I'm told in time for transmission, so Laurie's not left on her own in London dealing with the fallout here.'

Katie frowned. 'So it'll be just us three watching it in Membury Hempton?' she said. 'Seems a bit damp-squibbish. Maybe we should whoop it up and invite Judy and Dave round?'

'Oh yeah, like really, out there,' Molly declared.

'Rusty can come too,' Katie offered.

'Very funny. Anyway, where are we going, because we're like, heading in the direction of nowhere.'

'I think we're like, here,' Katie said, indicating to pull into a layby.

Molly looked around. 'I know you're not serious,' she said, 'because I mean, like, there's nothing here.'

'Yes there is,' Katie assured her. 'Can't you see the trees? Come on, get out, I've got something to show you.'

'You go on ahead,' Michelle said. 'I'll catch you up.'

As she watched them trudge into the little woodland, she remained in the back of the car, trying not to see the starkly naked branches against the backdrop of a colourless sky, for their symbolism was simply too harsh an indicator of what she already knew they were about to face. The time was drawing close for Katie to leave now, and though she was trying hard to keep cheerful and strong, Michelle understood very well that bringing Molly here today was probably one of the last trips out she would make.

Inside the barren little copse the air was perfectly still. The ground was covered in sodden leaves, the brush netted in silvery cobwebs. Branches dripped randomly into the gloom. As Katie looked around at the skeletal trees whose limbs twisted sharply, yet somehow comfortingly around each other, she wondered if, without its glorious summer or autumn foliage, she'd recognize her own. However, once she saw it there was no doubt in her mind, for though it was as naked and enmeshed as the others, to her it appeared as a gleaming white beacon on the darkest night.

'Do you see it?' she said to Molly.

Molly screwed up her nose. 'What?' she asked.

Katie smiled, and linking her arm tighter took her right up to the tree. 'It's a hornbeam,' she told her. 'It has all kinds of healing qualities that I'll tell you about later, but it's a very special kind of tree, and this one here is ours, because we pay two pounds fifty every month to keep it alive.'

Molly's green eyes moved up over the bark to the spiky grey limbs above.

'I could have asked Michelle to do this,' Katie said softly after a while, 'but it's you I need to tell really, because you're growing up now, and because you're my daughter, and because no-one else in the world matters more to me than you.' She swallowed and forced a smile. 'When the time comes, Molly, I'd like you to bring my ashes here.'

Molly's eyes immediately came to hers and flooded with tears. 'No, Mum, no,' she gasped.

Katie smiled again, and pulled her into her arms.

'I don't want you to go, Mum,' Molly said, clinging to her.

'I know,' Katie whispered, 'but I'll never really leave you, my love, not completely. We'll always be a part of each other, and nothing's ever going to change that, but we both have to face the fact that it's coming time for me to let you go on with your life now, which is why I've brought you here. I'd like this to be our special place, Molly, somewhere just for us, where you can come if you need to talk to me, or simply to feel me close. I'll always be with you anyway, but sometimes life gets all fraught and crowded, and you might need to feel a bit more private. This hornbeam will let you do that. You just have to put your hands on it, or your cheek, and . . . Come on, try . . . You'll see what I mean.'

From where she was standing Michelle could see them beside the tree, arms around each other, cheeks resting on the bark, and she doubted anything would ever touch her more deeply. She remained where she was, watching as they talked and even laughed once or twice, and when finally she sensed the time was right she began walking across the clearing to join them.

'Come and listen to Molly's poem,' Katie said, as she reached them.

Michelle turned to Molly and was surprised by the humour shining through her teary eyes.

'We came here, my mum and I,' Molly began, 'and through the trees we could see the sky, she said to me this will be our very special place, and I said, couldn't you pick somewhere a bit warmer?'

Michelle laughed and then cried and held them

both tight. 'That's the worst poem I ever heard,' she declared.

'She has a gift,' Katie said proudly.

As their laughter eventually faded they placed their cheeks on the bark again and held onto each other. Katie wasn't sure if they were feeling the same stirring of energy that she was, but all that really mattered was that they'd claimed this big old hornbeam as theirs now. Any time they felt like it they could come here and know that somehow, in its own special way, it would link them. She smiled privately to herself, for, just as she'd hoped, this one last fix on the tree was giving her the strength to stay long enough to let Molly make one last dream come true.

Chapter Twenty-Seven

It was four o'clock on the day of transmission. After working flat out for a full three weeks, with virtually no time to eat, sleep, or even think about anything else, Laurie finally delivered the edited master tape to the transmission centre in person, then called Elliot to let him know she was on her way home. By the time the taxi reached Butler's Wharf the driver had to come and prod her awake, before helping to pick up everything that had spilled from her bag at a sudden stop.

Elliot was waiting with a drink, food and the strong arms she needed to carry her up to bed, where he left her until an hour before the programme was due to air, by which time several friends and colleagues were already starting to arrive.

Laurie showered quickly, threw on a pair of black trousers and white lacy top, called Michelle and Katie from the bedside phone, then feeling strangely remote from the building excitement, as though it were happening on some other kind of plain that she ought to be on, but couldn't quite get to, she tripped downstairs to mingle with their guests. There were many more than she'd expected, so it took a while to work her way over to Elliot who was in the kitchen making cocktails.

'Still tired?' he murmured, as she slipped her arms around him and rested her cheek on his back.

'Mm,' she responded, loving the smell of him and tightening her arms. 'But you did right to wake me, I don't want to miss the show, even though I know how it ends. Katie and Michelle are having a little party too, they just told me. It's a shame Tom's not with us. Have you spoken to him?'

Turning to kiss her, he said, 'Yep. He's got a live transmission feed set up at the St Regis in Washington with a stellar guest list, apparently, ranging from three actual secretaries of state, to senators and congressmen from both sides of the House, to editors, broadcasters, political commentators . . . Frankly, if you haven't made that list, you just haven't made it.'

Laurie chuckled. 'Then let's hope he found good caterers,' she quipped, 'because there's a lot to digest.'

Smiling and kissing her again, he shook the cocktail and began filling the glasses.

Wishing they were alone so she could kiss him the way she really wanted to, she settled for a drink and was about to start mingling again when Elliot said, 'Nick's here, have you seen him?'

Her heart immediately jumped, but her expression remained neutral as she looked across the bar.

'Over by the window,' he directed her, while handing a couple of glasses to the closest guests.

617

Finally spotting him, Laurie felt her insides tightening, and wondered how difficult she was going to find it to come face to face with him with all these people around, many of whom knew they'd been involved, even if they didn't have all the details. She had to admire Elliot for inviting him, though he'd been right to, not only because Nick had played an integral part in the story, but because they moved in the same world, so needed to get used to running into each other.

'Do you recognize the woman he's with?' Elliot asked, slipping an arm round her.

'I feel as though I should,' she responded, looking curiously at the strikingly attractive blonde who seemed, even without the silicone and collagen enhancements, to be oozing a similarly brazen appeal as spilled from Andraya. 'Who is she?'

'Her name's Sandy Paull. Theatrical agent?'

'Oh yes, I recognize her now,' Laurie murmured. 'Did they come together?'

'Yes. Apparently she's an old friend of Tom and Michelle's.'

'Really?' Laurie commented, making a mental note to ask Michelle about her, but then on second thoughts, maybe she wouldn't, because she really wasn't that interested in Sandy Paull, in spite of Nick's apparent fascination with her. In fact, she just felt happy for him that he'd met someone else already, and more certain than ever that she was exactly where she wanted to be.

When finally it came time for the programme to start, she sat down on the floor in front of Elliot, with a third Cosmopolitan and slightly blurred vision that allowed her to see only the flaws that lack of time had made inevitable. However, the message seemed to come across loud and clear that the US power merchants were out of control, for everyone gave her a rousing ovation when the final credits rolled, and almost instantly the phone started to ring.

The next few hours were crazy, just as they'd known they would be, as were the next days, right through to the weekend and into the following week. They'd already worked out how to handle it, with Laurie taking on the endless round of TV interviews, while Elliot handled radio and print, for he preferred to keep a much lower profile. Nick, Rose and several other members of the team did their share of live links, panel discussions and phone-ins too, as did Michelle, though in her case it was all by phone.

They spoke to Tom daily in Washington, whose schedule was even crazier than theirs. Immediately after the airing of the programme in Britain, two American papers had run his and Elliot's full accounts of the story, complete with copies of the documents that had set it all in motion. However, nothing, but nothing, was going to prevent Tom from jetting over at the weekend to take part in Katie's grand birthday surprise. His ticket was booked, the schedule had been kept clear, so, right on time, he flew into Heathrow early on Friday afternoon where Laurie was waiting to pick him up and drive him down to Wiltshire.

'Elliot's already there,' she told him, as they drove out of the car park heading towards the M4. 'He's checked you into the same hotel as us, where you stayed with Michelle, she tells me.'

'I know and love it,' he confirmed. 'So how are all my girls?'

'Under the firm command of Molly, I believe, who's absolutely thrilled to bits that she's got all us adults dancing to her tune, which is Michelle's way of putting it. Katie's is to say that Molly's sprouting a tufty little black moustache that she'd better wax off before the big event, because it's not very becoming.'

Grinning, Tom said, 'I take it Katie still doesn't know what it's all about?'

'At the moment she thinks Molly's got her a glittery little thong and a shiny pole to gyrate around.'

Tom turned to look at her.

'One of Katie's more bizarre dreams, to be a pole dancer,' Laurie explained.

Giving a shout of mirth, Tom said, 'Then she is in for a surprise. Tell me, did Molly opt for the live music, or recorded?'

'Recorded, I think, but we'll find out when we get there. Elliot says the van's already parked outside, and Katie's going berserk trying to work out whether MI5 have flipped and forgotten to disguise themselves, or if she's about to be carted off in a coat without sleeves.'

'I can just hear her,' Tom laughed. 'And what about the catering?'

'All taken care of, mostly by Judy and Michelle in Judy's kitchen. They had some professional help too, apparently.'

'So,' he declared, releasing his seat to give his legs more room, 'sounds like we're all set. I've brought my tux . . .'

'Tux! That reminds me,' Laurie gulped, and jabbed the speed dial on her mobile. 'Elliot!' she cried when his voice came over the speaker. 'Where are you, can you talk?'

'I'm in the car,' he told her, 'and I've just picked up the dresses . . .'

'Oh thank God, that's why I'm calling.'

'That's why you called last time,' he reminded her.

She laughed. 'Really? And you've got your DJ?'

'Yes. Did you remember my shoes?'

'They're in with mine. How's Katie today?'

'Aquiver, she tells me. Though Michelle's making her lie down at the moment, because she's getting out of hand.'

Laurie and Tom laughed.

'I'm just pulling up at Judy's now,' Elliot informed them, 'she's keeping the dresses, while I go to pick Molly up from school. Apparently she's spotted a tiara that's totally wicked, and I just have to see it.'

'I'm sure it'll suit you,' Tom informed him.

Elliot laughed. 'Good flight?' he asked.

'Fine. A lot to talk about . . .'

'But not this weekend,' Laurie reminded them.

'Ah, if you can keep Katie off the subject, you'll be doing well,' Elliot told her. 'Anyway, I'll see you when you get here. Katie and Michelle won't be joining us for dinner – Michelle's insisting Katie conserves her energy for tomorrow night, and Katie's expending a great deal of it anyway informing Michelle of what a tyrant she is.'

'I have to call them,' Tom said, laughing, as Laurie rang off. 'Do you mind?'

Laurie pressed the speed dial for him and continued to drive.

'Hi honey,' he said as Michelle's voice came over the speaker. 'I'm with Laurie, we're on our way. How are you?'

'We're all fine, looking forward to seeing you.'

'You're not doing any of the heavy stuff?'

'No, Elliot's been taking care of that, and the guys from the rental company, though most of it's still outside in the van.'

'Did they bring everything?'

'They forgot the floor, but it's here now, and we added a couple of outdoor heaters, otherwise everything's more or less ready. By the way, Molly's totally flipped out over her new micro-system, which makes you the coolest person ever. She'll be thanking you in person, I'm sure. We're using it tomorrow night.'

'What about the CDs?' Laurie suddenly cried. 'Has someone got the CDs? Please don't tell me we've forgotten them . . .'

'Elliot brought them with him,' Michelle told her, 'so it's all taken care of, and Katie still doesn't have the faintest idea what we're planning, which is driving her nuts. She's just threatened me with a stick if I don't tell her, so I've had to send her up to bed again.'

'How is she really?' Tom asked.

Michelle's tone was slightly more sober as she said, 'She's not doing badly. They've given her a syringe driver now to help with the pain, and if she were being honest I think most of the time she'd rather be in bed than on her feet. But you know Katie, come what may she'll pull it together for

622

tomorrow night. It matters too much to Molly for her not to. And actually it matters that much to her too.'

Forty-three today and Katie couldn't remember ever feeling so happy. She lay quietly on her bed, listening to all the banging and shouting downstairs, the heavy footsteps, strange voices, drilling, sawing . . . Heaven only knew what they were all up to, she could hardly even begin to guess. She just knew that Molly was delighted by the way it was all proceeding, and kept popping upstairs to make sure her annoying mother wasn't peeping out of her bedroom door like a kid trying to spot Santa. She could hear her giving orders to Elliot and Tom, or squealing with laughter, or yelling for Michelle. It was obviously all go down there, and though it exhausted Katie to imagine it, it cheered her too, because whatever it was, it was apparently going to be 'like the best birthday ever', Molly assured her.

Lifting Trotty in a little closer, Katie glanced at the bedside clock and snuggled deeper into the pillows. Four fifteen. Still enough time for a nap before it all began, and even as her eyes closed she was aware of how the sounds downstairs were starting to drift, moving out into the trees with the birds, across the fields and on to places beyond imagining. She heard Molly, then Tom. A tractor in the lane, a siren way in the distance. She thought of people she'd known and loved and would maybe soon see again. There was so much peace inside her and tiredness and love.

Trotty snuffled and put her head on the pillow.

Katie's eyes blinked open to look at her, then closed again as she sank deeper and deeper into a welcome oblivion.

The next thing she knew, Molly and Michelle were tiptoeing into the room to see if she was awake.

'Are you ready to get up now?' Molly whispered, coming to sit next to her.

Still bleary, Katie looked at the clock.

'Six fifteen,' Michelle told her, putting down a cup of tea.

Katie struggled to sit up. 'I must have drifted off,' she said, then smiled as she noticed Molly's anxious little face. Catching it between her bony hands, she said, 'What are you up to down there, Molly Kiernan? What terrible fate awaits me?'

Molly instantly started to twinkle. 'You are so going to love it,' she assured her. 'It's like, so cool and everything's here, and you should see . . . Well, you will when you come down.'

'We just have to get you ready,' Michelle told her. 'So drink your tea while I go and run you a bath.'

'And I'll do your wig,' Molly said. 'Oh, Elliot and Tom have got birthday presents for you, but we'll bring them up when you're ready, because you'll want to wear them.'

Katie's smile was widening. 'What on earth . . . ?' she said, shaking her head.

A while later, after she'd managed to get in and out of the bath unassisted, she was back in her bedroom, wearing undies that were too loose and a petticoat that Michelle had just flourished from a box and that fitted slightly better.

'Are you ready?' Molly said from outside the door.

'Ready,' Michelle told her.

Katie looked round as Molly came in, and her mouth opened in surprise when she saw her holding up the most exquisite white floaty dress that looked as though it belonged to Napoleon's Josephine.

'We had it made specially,' Molly told her. 'It's real silk and chiffon, nothing fake.'

Katie turned to Michelle. 'Don't tell me you've found me a husband?' she said, actually starting to fear it.

Michelle laughed. 'Come on,' she said, unzipping the dress and sliding it off the hanger, 'in you go.'

With one hand on Michelle's shoulder Katie stepped into the beautiful silk folds, first one foot, then the other. She managed to stand quite still as Michelle and Molly drew the most elegant gown she'd ever worn up over her frail, yellowing body, holding out the small puff sleeves for her to put her arms through, then taking it on up to her shoulders where it settled in a deep scoop neck with a tiny ribbon running beneath her meagre bustline.

'Now madam's shoes,' Molly said, and opening a plain blue box she produced a pair of white silk pumps.

Dazed and delighted, Katie lifted the hem of her dress and allowed Molly to put them on her.

'I don't know what to say,' she laughed, as she started to sway in front of the mirror. 'I feel like Cinderella getting ready for the ball.'

Michelle and Molly exchanged looks. 'Hair?' Michelle said.

Immediately Molly turned to lift the chestnut wig from its stand. She'd styled it into a faultless chignon with a diamanté hairpin holding it in place.

As they put it on her Katie couldn't help thinking how lovely she might look were it not for her sallow and blotched complexion, but then Michelle and Molly were whipping out the make-up to smooth over the blemishes, define her eyes and frost her dry cracked lips.

'Beautiful,' Michelle murmured, looking at her reflection. 'Absolutely beautiful.'

Molly was beaming. 'You have to stay here now,' she told her, 'while we do a couple of other things, then we'll be back to get you.'

Letting Molly go, Michelle hung back to ask about the syringe driver. 'Shall I help you to put it on?' she asked.

Katie shook her head. 'I'll do without it for tonight – or at least for as long as I can,' she answered. 'We don't want to spoil the effect.'

After Michelle had gone Katie sat down on the edge of the bed and gently scrunched the glistening silk in her hands. To think that they'd had this marvellous dress made especially for her . . . It had obviously cost someone a fortune, and she could only presume that someone was Tom. She wondered what they were all up to now, for she could hear voices downstairs, the sound of footsteps, the odd blast of music then none. It was all mightily mysterious, and she was enjoying every minute, for she'd guessed what was coming and could hardly have loved everyone more for indulging Molly in such a ludicrously nonsensical affair.

The door opened and Laurie came in, dressed in a lovely white evening gown.

'Oh Katie,' Laurie murmured. 'You look wonderful.'

'So do you,' Katie told her. 'Are we having a double wedding?'

Laurie laughed. 'Not quite,' she responded. 'The others are waiting downstairs, but I have something for you.' She held out a flat, square box and watched as Katie looked at her, then at it and finally took off the lid.

'Oh my goodness,' Katie gasped when she saw the diamond teardrop necklace.

'It's from Elliot,' Laurie told her, lifting it out and putting it on her. 'And this,' she added, producing another smaller box from the same jeweller, 'is from Tom.'

Katie couldn't raise her eyes from the box, because she knew if she did Laurie would see her silly tears, so she kept them lowered and carefully eased off the lid. Instantly another lump formed in her throat, for nestling on a cushion of black silk were two little diamond studs – the earrings that matched the necklace. She took a breath, tried to speak, then had to take another. 'You'll have to give me a moment,' she said. 'I've never had . . . never had any diamonds before.'

'Here, let me put them on for you,' Laurie said, taking out one of the earrings.

As she fixed it into place neither of them mentioned how Katie had confessed to regretting that she had no special jewellery to pass on to Molly, but both were thinking it. Katie couldn't even begin to express how very special these diamonds were, for not only had they come from Elliot and Tom, they were also Laurie's way of making another dream come true.

After Laurie had gone Katie turned to look at herself in the mirror and wasn't sure whether she wanted to laugh or cry, for in truth she looked like the bride of Dracula, yet the dress, the diamonds, the hair . . . It was all so exquisitely beautiful, and even though she couldn't really do them any justice, they were making her feel lovely anyway.

A few minutes later, after checking her make-up wasn't too smudged and dabbing herself with a perfume not from Tom, she opened her bedroom door and stepped out on to the landing. To her surprise everything seemed quiet in the house, no chatter, or music, not even a footstep. As she reached the top of the stairs she saw Laurie standing at the bottom, waiting. There were other people in the kitchen too, because she could see their feet, black trousers, white gowns . . .

Slowly she started to descend, lifting the front of her dress with one hand, while holding the rail with the other. Her jewels glinted like stars as she moved, and the wispy sound of her breath was soft in her ears. She was almost at the bottom when Laurie nodded towards someone she couldn't see, and a moment later the house began to fill with the impossibly romantic music of Johann Strauss the younger.

Laurie guided her into the kitchen, where everyone was dressed for a Viennese ball, even beautiful, darling little Molly, who'd taken this long-forgotten dream and was now, in her way, making it come true.

'Happy birthday, Mum,' Molly said, as Katie embraced her. 'This is what you meant, isn't it?'

'It's exactly what I meant,' Katie assured her.

'Well, we couldn't like, go to Vienna, so I thought we'd make it come here.'

'It's wonderful,' Katie told her. 'Absolutely perfect,' and looking round she felt herself filling up with emotion, because corny as it might seem to some, for as long as she could remember she'd adored this music, and had always yearned to go to a Viennese ball – and now, here she was, guest of honour at one of her very own.

'We were going to have like, live music,' Molly went on, 'with a band outside under the heaters, but then we thought the neighbours might come and stare.'

'It's better like this,' Katie said. 'Just us,' and still slightly dazed she looked at Judy and Dave, Laurie, Michelle, Tom, peculiar little Rusty . . . Then someone was beside her, saying, 'May I have the pleasure of this first dance?'

It was Elliot. As though in a dream she put her hand on his arm and walked with him into the sitting room where the carpet had transformed itself into a dance floor and all the furniture had been magicked away. Later she'd find out it was all stored in the truck outside, but right now she really didn't care, for Elliot was starting to whirl her gently round in time to the music, and then the others floated in to join them, the ladies in their exquisite white gowns and the men in their

629

dashing tuxedos. This had to be a dream. How could it be anything else? And then she was laughing as she heard Molly saying to Rusty, 'This does *not* mean you're my boyfriend, right? Have you got that? This does not mean . . .'

'Ow, you just trod on me,' Rusty complained.

'Well that's your fault, you can't dance.'

Elliot was laughing too, and, tightening his grip on her waist, he twirled her on, expertly leading her through a dance she loved above all others. Then Tom came to take over and she melded into his arms, revelling in the way he spun her round and round, so handsome and romantic, so attentive and dear. The music swept her up into its euphoric peaks, then set her down in its tantalizing lows, while her heart seemed to fill and fill with so much joy and love it was bound to overflow. Laurie brought her champagne, which she drank, then Judy brought her Viennese cakes and delicacies which she ate sparingly. She danced again with Dave and Rusty, then with Laurie and Michelle, before going back to Elliot and Tom again.

It wasn't long before the pain was making it hard to keep smiling, but then her favourite, *Tales from the Vienna Woods*, swelled through their little ballroom, and reaching for Molly she took the lead. The floor cleared and everyone watched as they glided and twirled, gazed into each other's eyes and became royal princesses at the grandest of all the Viennese balls.

Michelle pointed the video camera and captured it all. Tom stood beside her, his hand on the back of her neck, until easing the camera from her, he motioned for her to go and dance with them.

Seeing her coming Katie reached for her hand and pulled her into the circle. As they swayed and twirled and the music embraced them as though to enclose them in a world of their own, Katie's eyes moved between their precious faces, and she knew that this was the real dream coming true. Molly was going to be happy with Michelle, and Michelle would love Molly as her own. It was everything she had prayed for, all that had ever really mattered. So there was nothing left for her to do now, it was all right to let go, and feeling more love than she could ever express, she put their hands together and slipped gently away to watch them carrying on the dance alone.

Order further Susan Lewis titles
from your local bookshop, or have them delivered direct to your door by Bookpost

☐ Intimate Strangers	0 09 945329 0	£6.99
☐ Silent Truths	0 09 941458 9	£6.99
☐ Wicked Beauty	0 09 941459 7	£6.99
☐ Strange Allure	0 09 941457 0	£6.99
☐ Obsession	0 09 941715 4	£6.99
☐ Vengeance	0 09 943509 8	£6.99
☐ Cruel Venus	0 09 944143 8	£6.99
☐ A Class Apart	0 09 943615 9	£6.99
☐ Chasing Dreams	0 09 942635 8	£6.99
☐ Summer Madness	0 74 932055 9	£6.99
☐ Dance While You Can	0 09 942174 7	£6.99

Free post and packing
Overseas customers allow £2 per paperback

Phone: 01624 677237

Post: Random House Books
c/o Bookpost, PO Box 29, Douglas, Isle of Man IM99 1BQ

Fax: 01624 670923

email: bookshop@enterprise.net

Cheques (payable to Bookpost) and credit cards accepted

Prices and availability subject to change without notice.
Allow 28 days for delivery.
When placing your order, please state if you do not wish to receive any
additional information.

www.randomhouse.co.uk/arrowbooks

arrow books